CUPID GRANTS A SECOND CHANCE

THE BOYS IN THE BAND
BOOK ONE

CARISSA HARPER

CHAPTER 1

"I walked into a job interview last week and who was there waiting to interview me? The guy always working on his laptop at my favorite coffee shop that I've been crushing on for the past few months. How was I supposed to sound professional when I was talking to *Cappuccino Hottie*?"

-Elise, Guest
Duquan's Downlow on Dating and Love
Podcast episode #14

Three years earlier...

Lexy wasn't taking any chances.

She checked her watch, nerves churning in her stomach. Her interview was in forty-five minutes, and Google Maps told her Manor House Productions was a two-minute walk away. She'd allowed for plenty of time in case she got lost, the trolly derailed, the lions escaped from

Woodland Park Zoo, or any other disaster that might cause her to be late.

Interviews made her nervous at the best of times, but this wasn't any old interview. This was a face-to-face with Merelda Sterling, founder and owner of Manor House Productions. Legendary in the television industry, and rumored to be terrifying.

Shaky hands smoothed back her blonde ponytail, ensuring no stray tendrils had escaped in the Seattle springtime breeze. Landing a position as Assistant Producer at the distinguished boutique production company would be the next step in her five-year career plan.

A chalkboard sign outside The Coffee Pod invited customers to "Come in and try the worst coffee that one woman on TripAdvisor ever had." Chuckling, she pushed open the door. What the heck? She had time. If today went well, this might become her regular stop on her way to work.

The sharp tang of ground coffee beans filled the warm air inside, and the shrill whistle of the espresso machine steaming milk drowned out the chatter of conversation around her. Waiting for her order, she studied the mural of whales painted on the wall, a clever play on the name of the coffee shop.

"Medium latte," The barista called out.

She grabbed the drink and took a cautious sip, mostly foam.

"For Nate," the barista continued.

She froze mid-swallow. She had taken someone else's beverage? How mortifying!

"I'm so sorry," she said to the guy with tousled brown hair who stepped up to the counter, looking for his drink. "I took yours. I have an interview down the street, and I'm nervous."

"Ah, you need it more than me then," he said. His green eyes crinkled with laughter.

"Plus, I already drank from it."

"Consider it yours." He adjusted the motorcycle helmet in his grip. "Is your interview at Manor House Productions?"

"Yes. Do you work there?" Inside info would be a good thing.

"Mostly in their studio location across town. Nate." He offered his hand. "Sound tech."

"Lexy. Assistant Producer hopeful." His hand clasped hers in a reassuring shake.

"Medium latte for Lexy," the barista said.

Nate released her and reached for the coffee, flashing a grin as he covered her name with a paper sleeve. "If the guys see your name on my cup, they'll never call me anything else."

"I really am sorry."

"No problem. A word of advice regarding Merelda?"

"Happily."

"Don't let her intimidate you. That way, she'll respect you."

"Easier said than done."

"If you start to feel intimidated, picture her in those high heels she totters around on, trying to ride the S.L.U.T."

"Excuse me?"

"The Seattle Lake Union Trolley. The S.L.U.T. Are you new to the city?"

"No," she laughed. "You just caught me off guard."

"See? You're already less nervous."

She nodded. "I am. Thanks, Nate. If I get this job, I'll owe you a coffee."

"I'll hold you to that."

It wasn't until they'd parted ways that she realized Nate, 'sound tech', was also Nate Douglas, lead guitarist in the up-and-coming local band, The Rainy Day Astronauts. If she landed this job, not only was she one step closer to her goal, she'd be working with a celebrity.

Present day...

LEXY'S blue MINI gave a cheerful chirp as she locked it and followed the sidewalk to the front of the elegant character home that had been converted into the business front of Manor House Productions, a Victorian-era building with jaunty navy-blue paint and burgundy trim. She walked confidently up the steps, completely at home between the columns that gave the porch an impression of grandeur, paused to tap the discreet sign with the company name for luck, and pushed open the turquoise door. Merelda described the door as a statement piece. Her boss was big on statements.

"This is it," she muttered under her breath, anticipating today's meeting and how best to pitch her latest show idea. The song she'd been listening to as she'd arrived at work, Macklemore's *Glorious* with a line about being born for this, still echoed in her head.

For two years she'd paid her dues, taking on every thankless, boring, grunt task that was asked of her. A year ago, she was ready for more. Ready to produce her own show. Unfortunately, Merelda had rejected every idea pitched her way, which only strengthened Lexy's determination.

This idea was the one.

"Morning, Lexy." Sarah from payroll walked out of the kitchen. "Nice day out today."

"Yes." She crossed her fingers. Destined to be her lucky day. She'd even brought her car today instead of taking transit as she often did.

The ground floor of the manor held the old kitchen, now a staff break room, on one side of the entrance. The parlor where Merelda entertained clients and industry bigwigs occupied the other side. Along the back were washrooms and offices for accounting and payroll.

The main staircase took her to the work area known affectionately as 'the hive'. Merelda insisted the writers, directors, producers—employees directly involved with productions—were in close proximity. Most of the walls had been removed to create an open space filled with desks, including hers. Down the hall toward the back was a conference room and the staircase leading to the third floor. Though it had a smaller footprint than the rest of the house, the top floor boasted the best views and was occupied almost entirely by Merelda's office. A small reception area and her assistant's desk sat at the top of the stairs.

The hive was already humming with the sound of Merelda's busy worker bees as she hung up her lightweight jacket, put her purse in the bottom drawer of her desk, and booted up her computer.

"Lexy. She's asking about the budgets." Joey, Merelda's assistant, stood in front of her desk, tablet in hand. Not much older than Lexy, he was always impeccably dressed, accessorized with an air of self-importance. Today was no exception.

"No problem." She flashed a helpful smile. "I have the revised budgets for the next episodes of *Call for Backup* and *Vamping Out*. I'll send them immediately." The Seattle-set cop drama and teen vampire series respectively, were two of the biggest MHP productions.

Joey nodded curtly and made a note on his tablet.

"Also, the next grant proposal will get finishing touches and be sent off today." She'd long ago given up trying to befriend her boss's second-in-command. "I'm still on her calendar for later?"

He rolled his eyes as if piqued he was forced to keep track of her appointment. "Apparently."

Behind his back, Lexy couldn't contain her grin. By 2:15 she'd be the proud producer of her own show.

"You look like the kitten who stole the cream." From three desks over, Enrico, Merelda's star director, studied her with amusement. "What's put that smile on your face, Bella?" His sexy Italian accent crested over her, those dark, smoldering eyes hinting that he wanted nothing more than to delve into her deepest, darkest secrets and desires.

Heat bloomed on her cheeks. "I—I look like what? I didn't steal..."

"Isn't that the expression?"

When Enrico joined the MPH team a year ago, every female in the place had done an instant swoon. From his wavy dark hair and bedroom eyes, to a body created solely to honor the designer suits he wore as casually as if they were jeans, he projected a certain savoir faire not found in the average American male. Not only that, he was the best director on the team, a fact which earned him the respect of the entire staff.

Once upon a time, one look from the man had several synapses in her brain misfire, disabling her powers of speech. These days, she retained the mental faculties to speak, banter, and even make him laugh sometimes. Most of the time.

"Oh, you mean the cat that *got* the cream."

"I think my version describes your expression better."

She gave him a conspiratorial smile "I'm *stealing* some of Merelda's time later. Making a new pitch."

"Good luck. Maybe we will get to team up on this project of yours."

Flashing him a smile, she crossed the fingers on both hands, touched when he returned the gesture.

AT NOON, Lexy bounced down the stairs to the staff break room for lunch, walking on clouds anticipating this afternoon's meeting and how great it would feel to finally be a producer. Even this morning's grant proposal, which had required more rewrites than planned and had a frustratingly inefficient online submission form, hadn't dimmed her spirits.

"Your day is obviously going well." Her friend Jules looked up as Lexy entered the room. The vibrant MHP wardrobe designer's love of fashion inspired outfit choices as bold as her personality. She swallowed a pang of envy at Jules's colorful floral print blouse tucked into a cream and mustard yellow patterned pencil skirt. Tall and slim with a striking main of long, wavy red hair, Jules pulled the look off beautifully. Average height and blonde, Lexy tried hard to shed her life-long label as 'cute' by wearing classic business outfits in muted tones, her bid to look 'professional'.

"Oh yay. I love when our lunch breaks coincide. And no one is around to eavesdrop. Especially Sonia. My day is going great, thanks. Isn't yours?" Lexy took her salad to the end of one of two large farmhouse tables and plopped next to Jules and Renata, her other best friend. The savvy social media manager for all of MHP productions and Jules's polar opposite in fashion taste, Ren was dressed in all black as usual. The dark tone matched her perfect fall of glossy black hair, yet she managed to look chic instead of goth.

Ren looked up from her phone where she was rapidly typing and widened almond-shaped eyes enhanced by meticulously applied makeup. "Great? Not with the backlash we're getting from comments on TikTok about this promo clip for *Vamping Out*. I'm trying to put out the fire now."

"Oh dear. That's not good. We've just lined up new advertisers for that series. If anyone can put out that fire, you can."

"My day is at least as bad as Ren's." Jules twisted her riotous red curls into a loose bun before leaning over to take a bite of sandwich. "One of our lead actresses refused to wear the dress I selected for this morning's scene, because it was too 'shamrock' green and she will only wear 'jade' green." Her fingers made air quotes to emphasize the shades of green. "It's basically the same color. So I had to find her a new dress. Then one of our day-player cast members, who insisted she was a size zero when I spoke to her last week, did not fit her size zero outfit. So I was running around finding two new wardrobe items. Now everyone's grumpy and it looks like I'm the reason shooting got delayed."

"That's sucks. Especially because it's not your fault." Lexy dipped a carrot stick in hummus. "In other news, did you find a side hustle?"

Ren looked up from her phone. "Why are you looking for a side hustle, Jules?"

"I want to bring my parents out to visit from Ireland. They'll never be able to afford the trip, with all my younger siblings at home. So yes, Lex, I am going to be a personal shopper on the side, and I've already landed two clients."

"That's amazing. It's the perfect gig for you."

"Thanks. I think it will be fun. Now that Ren and I have both complained about our days, tell us why yours is going so well."

"I'm pitching to Merelda this afternoon. My renovation show. This is the one ladies. The show I'm going to produce, that is going to change peoples' lives."

"What's your tagline again?" Ren asked. "It was so clever."

"Fixer Upper, hosted by the Simon Cowell of renovations."

"If Merelda doesn't like this one, I don't know what to say. She shares Simon's talent for blunt critique," Ren said.

"I'll let you know how it goes."

"Hey, Ren." Jules paused with a fork full of coleslaw half way to her mouth. "Didn't you have a date last night? How did it go?"

"Another dud? Obviously you would have told us by now if he showed promise," Lexy said.

"What's wrong with this one?"

"This is so embarrassing," said Ren. "More so for him."

Lexy and Jules waited expectantly.

"We met on Bumble. Dating apps are the only way to meet anyone these days."

"Even though they suck," Jules said.

"Even though they suck." Ren agreed. "We'd been messaging each other for a week and I agreed to go out with him. He's a film buff, he's working on creating an app with a friend, which of course I am interested in."

"Sounds like a good fit. I'm not hearing the embarrassing part yet," Jules said.

Ren took a breath. "His name is Keanu."

"Keanu? Really?"

"You can't really hold that against him," Lexy said. "Our parents pick our names."

"Just wait. Over our first drink, I asked him about it, because it is unusual and the only other Keanu I've ever heard of is Reeves. He told me he saw *The Matrix* when he was thirteen years old and loved the character Neo so much, he made his family and friends and everyone start calling him Keanu. He only responded to them if they called him that."

"Are you serious?" Jules giggled.

"Dead serious. I thought he was joking, so I laughed. I mean, at thirteen I can kind of see it. But the dude is thirty-three years old now and still calls himself Keanu."

"What's his real name?" asked Lexy.

"It took a while, but I finally got it out of him. Brad."

All three girls burst out laughing.

"At this rate I might have to give in and let my parents set me up with a "nice Chinese boy" like they keep wanting to."

"I'm so glad I'm with Jameson and all this nonsense is behind me," Lexy said.

THE BACK of Lexy's neck prickled, and she looked up from her computer screen to scan the hive. Was she imagining someone's eyes burning a hole in the top of her head? Nope. Across the room, Smug Sonia gave her a calculating look, not appearing the least bit uncomfortable being busted.

Lexy sighed. She and Sonia had started work here around the same time, and although Lexy didn't feel they were in competition with each other, Sonia made it clear she did. The subtle digs and passive-aggressive comments. 'Helpful' critiques of her wardrobe, and 'concern' Lexy couldn't handle her workload. Lexy did her best not to engage in Sonia's tactics. 'You catch more flies with honey', her Gran always said.

As Sonia smirked and shifted her sharp gaze back to her computer, Lexy glanced at her watch before smoothing the sides of her hair which she'd pulled back into a pony tail this morning, hoping to portray a polished, no-nonsense, professional look. After all, it had worked for her interview. Scant minutes remained before her audience in the Throne Room, the staff's nickname for their boss's office.

If The Queen liked her latest proposal, she'd be Producer of her own reality show. Enough with writing grant proposals and chasing leads, while everyone around her achieved their dreams.

Staring down her upcoming big Three-o birthday, she'd expected to have achieved a lot more by the age of thirty. Including showing that condescending prof at film school that he'd been wrong about her. She was not some entitled airhead with an unrealistic view of the film industry, but someone with the drive and determination to make it in her chosen field.

As she rose she took a deep breath, smoothed the front of her knee-length grey pencil skirt, and straightened the lapels of its matching jacket. She wasn't the only one who found facing Merelda intimidating. If Meryl Streep had a redheaded sister in *The Devil Wears Prada*, it would have been Merelda. Even the sound of her walking down the hall, the tapping of those red-soled designer stilettos, her signature piece of every outfit, sent shivers down Lexy's spine. When she joked with her friends that they were blood-red from the other poor souls whose dreams Merelda had already trampled on that day, she was only partly joking. As she climbed the stairs, old doubts began to creep in.

You won't be taken seriously in this industry looking like that. And your final project failed to demonstrate any other reason to take you seriously. You have nothing to offer. I think you're in the wrong program, Ms. Smith.

She shook her head in an effort to clear her old film prof's voice out of it. Now was not the time. Mr. Snyder's attitude was one of the reasons she had been so determined to work for a female-run company.

Joey didn't look up as she passed his desk. Reaching Merelda's door she blew out a breath and straightened her shoulders as she struck her 'power pose'. The one recommended by the many professionals sharing their success stories in a fifteen-minute *Ted Talk*.

I'll be fine. I'm a professional. I've worked hard and I deserve this opportunity. Viewers everywhere were sure to love her proposed home renovation show, *Bulldoze or Overhaul*.

She knocked and entered on Merelda's command, struck anew by the impressive view of Lake Washington. From a brightly colored, ergonomically-designed chair behind her desk, Merelda eyed Lexy overtop of a pair of cat's-eye designer frames. Years earlier, Merelda's chair had been dubbed 'the throne' by an unknown staff member. Rumor has it he didn't last long after that.

Never one for pleasantries, Merelda said, "I read your latest proposal."

She leaned forward. "And?"

"And the last thing the networks need is another renovation show." Merelda clasped her hands on the desk in front of her, multi-diamond rings reflecting the late summer sunlight that spilled through the window to her right. "Please stop wasting my time."

Lexy swallowed her disappointment. "I'm an assistant producer. I'm here because I want to produce my own show one day."

"Right now, the only thing you need to produce are the grants and incentives offered by various government bodies to help offset the cost of what we do. You're good at it. Stick to what you do best." Merelda reached for a stack of papers. "That's all. Shoo! Back to work."

Lexy stood, shock eclipsing her disappointment. Had she really just been shooed? Was that even a thing that could happen to a twenty-first century working professional? Eyes downcast, she returned to the hive and walked past Enrico's corner desk.

"Everything all right in your world, Bella?" Even his sexy accent failed to raise her spirits. "You look like you're about to face the firing squad." He inclined his head toward the stairs to the Throne Room. "Or maybe you already did."

"She shot down my latest proposal. Be warned, she's in full Queen of Hearts mode. I kept waiting for her to point her imperious finger at me and shout 'Off with her head!'"

"I'll be sure to let her win at croquet." Enrico rose lazily, tossing her a smile and a wink.

"While you're at it, you should probably stay away from small bottles labeled 'Drink Me'."

His laughter trailed behind him as he strode down the hall and up the stairs to Merelda's office. Though in his case it was more of a swagger. The man couldn't help it. It was just the way he moved.

She sighed and picked up her phone to text Jameson about her latest crash-and-burn pitch to her boss. Her wonderful boyfriend would know just the thing to cheer her up. A fuzzy warmth spread through her when she saw he'd messaged her first. Probably checking in about her meeting.

JAMESON

Hey babe, I know we were going to meet up
tonight, but I have to work late. Deadline
coming up. Boss is freaking out.

She swallowed the sharp sword of disappointment. He hadn't remembered today was a big deal for her after all. He wouldn't be at her house later suggesting a round of Trivia Touchdown, a game they'd made up that had them laughing so hard it was now their go-to whenever one of them had a bad day.

Hardly motivated to return to budgets and spreadsheets, the only thing Merelda thought she was good for, she stared at her phone screen. Checking their socials would be a suitable distraction, and still counted as 'working'. As assistant producer, she tried to stay in the loop on the shows she was involved in.

She opened Instagram but before she could click on @VampingOut, something in her story bar caught her attention. A local restaurant she followed had re-posted a story by @TiffLovesLife. The guy in the photo looked familiar.

It couldn't be.

Her finger shook as she clicked on it. Her stomach plummeted, her throat tightened, a buzzing started in her ears and grew louder as she stared at a picture of Jameson and some girl sharing a bowl of ramen. There were heart GIPHYs all over the image.

What. The. Hell. She stared in disbelief for several seconds before tapping on the tag for Tiff's account. More pictures of Tiff and Jameson. Lexy's body flashed hot then cold. She grabbed screenshots of several of the most incriminating photos and texted them to him.

LEXY

Is this what you mean by working late?

We're over. Obviously. If you can manage to tear yourself away from Tiff, your stuff will be outside my house. No guarantees it will still be there in the morning

CHAPTER 2

"It's happened to me. It's happened to some of my friends. You know my wish for all those cheating bastards out there? That liars' pants really *did* catch on fire."

-Mia, Guest
Duquan's Downlow on Dating and Love
Podcast episode #91

She survived the commute home alternately hoping nothing else bad decided to pile on her day, and plotting revenge fantasies about Jameson. Even through her fury, her little turquoise houseboat, bobbing gently at the dock on Lake Union, was a welcome sight. Thank God she'd listened to her gut last month, ignoring Jameson's less than subtle hints about moving in.

Although she had been about to give him his own key.

Because I thought he was the one.

Inside, she pulled out a black garbage bag, growling as it

got caught coming out of the box. Starting upstairs in her bedroom, she made the rounds, gathering up his things. There wasn't much, a toothbrush, some jeans and sweats, a couple of shirts, a sweater, some worn out Van's, a filthy baseball cap and a rickety skateboard.

She bundled everything into the bag, tied a knot and tossed it onto the edge of the dock like the trash that it was. At least there'd be no more unfortunate gifts like last Valentine's 'Love Fern'. He'd thought it was cute to copy the idea from a rom-com they'd seen, but the fat pink pig in a tutu containing the straggling fern was the world's ugliest plant pot. Perfect to weight down the bag full of his stuff.

"Love Fern? More like Fraud Fern." She dropped the planter on top of everything else.

A firm believer that avoidant coping was still coping, she slid her paddleboard into the water and took off along the lakeshore. She wasn't ready to talk to Jameson, hear the excuses and pleas she knew were coming. As each stroke put more distance between her and the garbage bag on the dock, her shoulders relaxed another fraction and her breath came easier.

Paddleboarding was good, but surfing was her true love. Maybe the Oregon coast would see a little swell when she went home next Friday for the long weekend, which couldn't come soon enough. She frowned. When had the familiar small town she'd longed to escape become a place of comfort and refuge?

Probably around the time being single and bingeing too many Hallmark movies over the holidays resulted in an ill-advised relationship that blew up in my face on the same day my boss stomped out yet another idea, squashing my confidence along with it.

This was not how she'd pictured the lead-up to her thirtieth birthday; single again, Merelda's gofer, and no closer to producing her own show. Basically, a personal and professional flop. Had she got it all wrong? What if she hadn't left everyone and everything behind to follow her dreams?

As if watching a home movie, the lake's surface reflected watery scenes from a parallel life. Where she stayed in Cannon Beach and married her high school sweetheart, Tyler. A beach wedding followed by a surfing honeymoon someplace tropical. After which she'd work with her parents at their gallery. Fast forward to a big backyard bash with family and friends when her parents retired and she took over the gallery, while Tyler ran his father's hardware store. Both of them doting on their two adorable children, a boy and a girl. Right now, 'Door number one' looked a whole lot better than reality.

She slapped the surface of the lake with her paddle, sending a spray of water through the air and erasing the image. *This* was the life she wanted. Here in Seattle. Wasn't it?

Resolutely she turned and paddled for home, relieved to see the garbage bag no longer there when she pulled up to the dock. If only she could avoid her boss's dismissive attitude and Smug Sonia'a knowing looks as successfully.

~

JULES

How was coffee with L-ameson?

LEXY

Your best nickname yet, J

REN

I'm only calling him Lameson from now on fyi

LEXY

Terrible thanks. Turns out meeting your cheating ex for coffee only days after breaking up with him in a text is miserable. Who would've thought?

REN

But it's over. You did it. Closure

JULES

It was more than he deserved. Rat-bastard

Hey, you got anything left of his at your place? I can put an Irish curse on him

LEXY

Not a trace. Not even a strand of hair

JULES

Shame ;-)

REN

I stashed a pint of ice cream in the freezer at work with your name on it. Seriously. It says: Do not eat me. I belong to Lexy

LEXY

Thanks for the ice cream and the curse offer. I'm feeling better already

SHE WASN'T, but her friends had put in a solid effort to cheer her up, and she appreciated it. The one-two punch of Merelda's latest rejection and Jameson's betrayal had her reeling. Off-balance. The idea of moving back home was starting to sound better and better. She hadn't been able to get the vision of her alternate life out of her head since the post-breakup paddle. Her cozy coastal surf town; a place where she belonged. Where people knew her and actually wanted her to succeed. A place where she'd be immune to men like Jameson with their cute dimples and flashing eyes.

"Please, Lex." Nate's eyes twinkled with merriment as he placed his palms together in a pleading gesture. "Bribery and begging are not beneath me. You would be doing me a huge favor." He smiled wide enough for his hint of a dimple to appear.

Shit. Her resolution wasn't even going to last a week.

"Shopping? Aren't guys allergic?" Honestly though, this could be exactly the distraction she needed. She'd been spending her time since the break-up avoiding her friends and eating Baskin-Robbins from the carton, cursing Jameson for his infidelity, cursing herself for falling for him. On top of being shooed by Merelda, trying to keep up the pretense at work that everything was fine was exhausting.

"We are," Nate said. "But we push through for a few crucial occasions. Kid sister's birthday makes the list."

"What else is on the list?"

"Top secret. Guy Code. No one can find out I even admitted there's a list."

Narrowing her eyes, she tapped the tips of her fingers together in a distinctly evil-movie-villain gesture. "Oh, I'll get more out of you, Nate. We women have our ways. Girl Code. But first, how old will your sister be?"

She watched him do the math in his head. "Twenty-seven, I guess. I'm five years older."

"Did she give you any hints?"

"Hint? Hah!" Nate said. "She wants a waterproof raincoat. Nothing ugly. Long enough to really keep her dry. Plus, it needs to be warm enough, but not too hot. She wants to be able to add layers underneath. There might have been more. I hope I got the main points."

Lexy nodded sagely. "I see why you need help." Retail

therapy sounded good right now. Even if the retail was for someone else.

"I might take a stab at 'nothing ugly'. But the rest? No clue."

"Fortunately, I know what constitutes the perfect length and 'warm enough'. But my expertise will cost you."

"Name your price," Nate said over his shoulder as he walked toward his boss, who had motioned him over. "We'll go tonight after work. You came by transit, right? I'll drop you at home after."

Her phone vibrated on her desk with an incoming text in her girls group chat. Jules and Ren were keeping close tabs on her right now, and she appreciated it.

REN

Hey ladies. Food Truck Festival is on all this week and we talked about going. It's getting a ton of buzz. Does tonight work?

LEXY

I can't tonight. Thursday?

JULES

What do you have going on tonight that's more important?

LEXY

Nate asked me to help him pick his sister's bday gift

REN

For that you would miss out on the Food Fighters truck, and trying their Big Me Burger or Thymes Like These Bowl???

jk, thursday works

JULES

More on this Nate thing then too

HER RESCUE from cramming onto sweaty public transit on a sweltering summer day came in the form of a helmet Nate handed her as they left work. "Brought an extra. I hoped you'd take pity on a desperate coworker in his hour of need." He grinned. "It's even your color."

What was it about the appeal of a guy who rode a motorbike? As she strapped on the midnight blue helmet and hopped up behind him, wrapping her arms around his waist, she noticed Enrico slowly get into his car and watch them leave. Was that jealousy she saw in Enrico's smoldering gaze?

Things like this didn't normally happen to her. Cozy'd up on the back of a bike with one man, while another looked on enviously. Even if she was imagining the envy in Enrico's eyes. Jameson who? It was too fun not to enjoy her rom-com-esque moment to the fullest. She waved to Enrico as she and Nate took off.

Meg Ryan, eat your heart out!

After striking out in the first two boutiques, she was starting to feel disheartened. Raincoat offerings thus far were not exactly cute. But Lexy Smith was no quitter, even in the face of ugliness. Hangers rasped as she slid them one by one along the rack until— She stopped and turned to Nate. "Does your sister have green eyes like yours?"

"I guess. Not in the habit of staring into my sister's eyes."

"But does she wear a lot of green, because—"

She pulled out the most adorable mint green number with a flourish, making it dance on the hanger for Nate. "Look at the cute lining. Flannel. So Seattle."

He didn't look convinced. "Are you sure?"

She slipped it from the hanger, shrugged into it and tied the belt. With her best 'serious model' face, she strutted away from Nate, pivoted sharply before her catwalk improv took her back to stop directly in front of him. Smiling, she held out her arms. "This is it. The one. It fits all the criteria and is seriously cute."

"It's perfect." He slung an arm around her shoulders. "Best Raincoat Model Ever."

"Are you trying to win the Best Big Brother award?"

He gave her a smug smile. "I've owned that badge since the day Marcie was born."

"Don't expect me to take your word for it. Verification required. If I ever meet your sister, we'll have a lot to talk about."

His smile widened. "I can't risk you blowing my cover. Marcie thinks her big brother is the best." He leaned in closer, lowering his voice as if sharing a secret. "It's important I keep up the myth. It helps set high standards for the guys she dates." After a beat he added, "which keeps me from bashing their heads in with my guitar."

"Can I blame my current dating woes on the fact that I have no big brother to set that bar? Failure would be easier to swallow if it was my non-existent brother's fault instead of mine."

"Yeah, I heard things didn't work out between you and what's-his-name."

"Feel free to bash him with your guitar if you ever see him," she said, only half-joking, as she slid her arms from the sleeves and handed him the coat.

"Noted." He took the coat and handed it to the cashier. "How about grabbing a bite? Part of my payment for your expertise."

"I'll accept the first instalment of my fee in the form of

food now," she said. After living on ice cream all week, she was suddenly famished.

"Great, I know a good place." Bag in hand, he held the door open for her.

"You realize," she said as they stood in the hostess line at a popular waterfront eatery "that you took our friendship to the next level today, right?"

"Next level?"

"You know. Level one is work friends. Level two is work friends who go for after work drinks in a group. Now you invited me to do something just the two of us. *And* you asked for my help. I think that constitutes two levels at once."

"Any hidden traps in this next level of friendship that I should know about?"

"At this level, you get added to the list of people I can call in emergencies: my car has a flat tire, my water tank explodes, there's a zombie apocalypse..."

He shrugged. "I guess I can share my apocalypse bunker. How good are you at fighting zombies?"

"I've seen *Pride and Prejudice and Zombies*," she said. "And watched every episode of *The Walking Dead*."

"Uh-huh. Not good then," he said with a smile, as they followed the hostess.

The restaurant gods were smiling down on them, because despite the fact that getting a patio table on a sunny August evening was about as likely as getting a parking spot in downtown Seattle on Black Friday, by some miracle they got one of the coveted outdoor tables.

"For the record," Nate said, once they were seated and staring at the menus, "if your non-existent brother was real, he definitely would have done something about that guy you were seeing."

She glanced up at him. "Aww, that's sweet."

"'Cause he wasn't that into you." He reached for the drink list.

She put down her menu. "What are you talking about?"

"You and what's-his-name. I saw you together a couple of times. I could tell, you know, like he didn't give you his full attention or something, that he wasn't that into you."

He's just not that into me? Like the movie?

"And you're only telling me this now?"

He shrugged. "It didn't come up before."

"Ren and Jules didn't think Jameson was right for me, either. Why does everyone wait until the relationship is over to tell you they knew all along you shouldn't have been with the person?"

"*You* ever try telling a friend you don't like her boyfriend?"

"Good point." She looked over in time to catch his understanding look.

"No one wants to come under the firing squad. Or hurt a friend."

"The girls know if they ever see me dating someone so totally wrong for me again, they have my permission to tell me and I won't get upset." She picked up her menu. "They're never going to tell me, are they?"

"Sorry, but no."

"It's a moot point anyway, since I have sworn off men for the foreseeable future."

Nate looked around as if worried, then leaned in. "What if they see us?" he said in a mock whisper.

"Who?" She looked around at the other diners.

"Whoever it is you've sworn off men to." He aimed his thumbs at his torso. "Can't have them see you sitting with a man, talking and enjoying a meal."

She giggled. "You know what I mean. I'm off *dating* men.

I can still hang out with *you*." She glanced back at her menu. Her mom said her chronic indecision came from being a Libra, which made deciding what to order from a restaurant menu one of her hardest choices.

"That's a relief." He slid his menu to the side. "Do you know what you want? Oh, I forgot. I'm with Lexy. The girl who can never make up her mind."

"Very funny!"

He started to laugh, then caught himself. "Sorry. Didn't mean to laugh at your—ahem—difficulties. How about we pick a couple of things to share?"

"Would you?" Jameson hated sharing food.

"Sure. You order one thing, I'll get something different and we'll split," he said, just as their server walked up.

"I thought that was you, Nate." The wanna-be Kim Kardashian, with her slicked-back hair and contour-heavy makeup, eyed Nate hungrily. "I haven't seen you in ages," she added, with what Lexy assumed was her attempt at a sexy pout.

"Hey, Vi," Nate said with a noticeable lack of enthusiasm. "This is Lexy. We work together."

Vi was a gusher. She gushed over Nate. She gushed over his band. Never mind the proprietary hand she laid on Nate's shoulder. Or the way she inched closer to him with each sentence. "Nate's just the best, isn't he?" Closer. "Have you seen him play? He's so amazing on stage." Closer. "I just love The Rainy Day Astronauts—I was wearing my band T-shirt just the other day. It looks snatched on me, if I do say so myself."

She's practically in his lap!

"Oh, Natey."

Natey???

"Um, we should probably order," Nate mumbled.

Vi didn't react to the brush-off, but continued to flirt as she took their order for fish tacos from Lexy and Szechuan bowl for Nate. "I'll have to check, Nate, but I think there might be a little something on the house for you." She sent him a broad wink as she walked away.

Lexy didn't try to hide her smile. "So, that was Vi—?" She left it as a question hanging in the air.

He sighed. "She's one of those girls who loves a guy in a band. I met her after one of our shows. She said she wanted to start an all-female rock band, and asked for my advice."

"Let me guess. The band never happened."

"Nope. Why did it take me several bad dates to figure out she only wanted to date a musician? Want to pretend to be my girlfriend?" he asked.

"I'd rather watch you squirm. Much more entertaining. Speaking of entertaining, how did the Rainy Day Astronauts come into being?"

"Connor and I, Seattle grunge-loving boys to the core, started off in high school playing pitiful but ardent covers of our favorite Pearl Jam, Nirvana, and Soundgarden songs. Eventually we hooked up with Adam and Griffin and discovered our own style."

She propped her chin in her hand. "I would think it's hard to write songs."

"My mom says it satisfies my 'creative side'. Sometimes it's intentional. Other times we're jamming and messing around. Joking about the lyrics, making up hilarious lines and trying to one-up each other."

"You make it sound so easy. I wish it worked that way when I'm pitching show ideas to Merelda."

"How are things going with Her Royal Highness? You come up with the right pitch yet?"

"I thought I had," she said. "I think that every time, but

this time I *really* thought it. At film school they told us to do 'the same only different'."

"Yeah, I've heard that. Take something successful, then give it a twist to make it your own."

"Right. So I thought what if it was a renovation show where—"

"You pitched a renovation show?"

"Yeah, and the premise was—"

"Are you interested in home renovations?"

"Um, not really," she said slowly. "But the viewers like—"

"How can you be excited to pitch a show about something you're not even into? Plus, you know there's already a billion renovation shows, right?"

"Yes, but I'm following Merelda's lead. To pitch something that she'll go for. Look at the line-up coming out of Manor House Productions. Every last one of them has a built-in audience, stable advertisers, and a guaranteed profit."

"I'll let you in on a little-known secret about Merelda. That woman wants to be noticed. She keeps the steady shows like you're talking about for a financial safety net. But she wants to flip the industry on its head, to do truly innovative projects and dazzle the world. Not to mention, stack more shiny awards on her trophy shelf."

She tucked back some strands of hair that the breeze had blown in her face. "How do you have the inside track to what Merelda wants?"

"I'm one of the 'noise boys'. You'd be surprised what we hear when no one thinks we're listening."

"Better watch what I say if I'm in the studio."

"For example, just the other day I heard Sonia bragging to one of her cohorts that she found out Merelda has budget for a new show. She sounded pretty determined to move up from AP to Producer."

Smug Sonia?

Sonia reminded her of a handful of cutthroat classmates in film school. The ones who'd do anything, step on anyone, to get ahead. The same ones who'd smirked every time Mr. Snyder used her as an example of what not to do.

"I'd better up my game pitching a new show to Merelda." The idea of Sonia heading up an original concept while she sat on the sidelines made the fish tacos she'd eaten turn sour. "Can't think about it now. Distract me. What's the best concert you've ever been to?"

"No contest. Pearl Jam. Hands down. I wanted to *be* Eddie Vedder when I was a teen."

"I'll bet you did."

"I saw them for the first time when I was nineteen years old, at what used to be the KeyArena. I was saving for school that fall, but I still considered the ticket a justifiable expense. Necessary even. And when they ended their second encore with "Yellow Ledbetter"." He put his hand to his heart. "There are no words."

"Wow, yeah. That's a good one."

"What about you? Anyone good pass through Cannon Beach when you were growing up?" he joked.

"Funny guy. Since I can't top Pearl Jam, I'll tell you my best 'brush with music fame' story instead. Which happened to take place in Cannon Beach, so there. Have you heard of Daisy Jordan?"

"Sure. Bad-ass, blues-rock singer from New Orleans."

"Exactly. When I was a senior, she filmed a music video on Cannon Beach for "Beach Dreams" and some friends and I were extras."

"No way, really?"

"She was awesome. It was the same song over and over, but at the end of the shoot she played a couple other songs to thank the extras. And if you watch the music video, and pause it in just the right spot, you can see my ponytail."

"Your claim to fame." He gave her ponytail a gentle tug.

"So far that's it," she said with a laugh.

"But listening to you share that story, music gets you excited. I'm not saying you should do a show about music. But if you can think outside the box and come up with a show idea you're actually excited about, you might really have something."

"Think the rest of the world would watch a show about pro surfers and famous musicians, and how they decide what to order off a restaurant menu?"

He laughed. "Sorry, but I think you'd be an audience of one for that."

THE AIR WAS NOTICEABLY COOLER as he slowed the bike to a stop at the marina. "Wow, Lex. You're really roughing it aren't you?" The picturesque rows of colorful houseboats tied to the docks barely moved on the lake's glassy surface.

She hopped off and handed him back the helmet. "It's a tough life, but someone's got to live here." She smoothed a hand over her hair, stopping to pull out the elastic and give her head a shake. "And thanks to my Gran's generosity in her will, I inherited enough for a downpayment."

"For the record, in a zombie apocalypse, I'm coming here. We can stock up and just push off into the lake."

"Is it true zombies can't swim?"

"We'll hope so. Which one's yours?"

"The turquoise one, third one down."

"Nice. It suits you." He adjusted his stance. "Thanks again for helping me pick Marcie's gift. You're a lifesaver."

"My pleasure. Thanks for dinner. And for sharing your insider knowledge about Merelda."

He watched her pick her way down the gangplank to the dock that led to her home. He'd never seen her hair loose like that. She looked younger and more carefree. When she reached the bottom of the gangplank she turned and called back to him.

"What about 'Dine Out Like A Pro'?"

"For your menu-deciding TV show? Keep thinking." He chuckled as he started his bike. He could just imagine Merelda's reaction to a show pitch for that.

As he wove his way through light evening traffic from Lake Union to his loft in Belltown, his mind drifted to next weekend's show. Outdoor venues had their own unique brand of energy he always looked forward to. Unexpectedly, his stomach clenched, nothing to do with pre-show jitters. It had been years since *she* had caused a public scene at a gig of theirs, but the memory of that night had a habit of sneaking up on him.

He shook his head to clear unwanted images as he parked and went upstairs. He and the guys were happy playing local venues around Seattle. It had never been their dream for The Rainy Day Astronauts to hit it big.

Or is that just what you convinced yourself, after what happened?

CHAPTER 3

"Sexiest thing God ever invented? A guy with a guitar.
Placing that guy on a stage is the icing on the cake."

-Lucy, Guest
Duquan's Downlow on Dating and Love
Podcast episode #55

Friday before Labor Day took forever to roll around. Finally, it was noon; in a rare show of humanity, Merelda had decided to close the office early. As Lexy raced for her car, she ran head first into Nate. He clasped her shoulders to steady her.

"Making your escape before Merelda changes her mind?"

"Something like that," she said. "What are you doing here? Shouldn't you be in the studio?" Half a dozen studios in an industrial park where they shot all of their in-house shows, and confusingly referred to as *the studio*, was where Nate spent most of his time.

"I'm Ian's errand boy before I'm off the hook. Delivering this to Merelda." He held up a package he was holding. "But I'm glad you ran into me—"

"Sorry about that, I was rushing to my car and—"

"It's okay, didn't you hear me say I'm glad? The guys and I are playing an outdoor concert this weekend. You should gather up your posse and come out. We could use a few adoring groupies in the front row," he added, with a joking wiggle of his eyebrows.

She half-smiled. Nate took his music as seriously as his work at the studio. Groupies were not on his wish list.

"As you well know, I've caught your act before," she said. "All four of you Rainy Day Astronauts leave a trail of hopeful hearts in your wake as you exit the stage, Nate Douglas. You'll be just fine."

"See? We play better with you there."

"I'm about to hit the road for Cannon Beach, I always spend Labor Day weekend with my parents. Rain-check on seeing you guys play?"

"Sure thing. Drive safe." He put on his helmet. "Hope you've got a good playlist queued up."

"You know it. And road trip snacks." She pointed to her passenger seat where Smartfood popcorn, Swedish Berries and M&Ms awaited her.

"Salty, sweet, and chocolate. Bases covered for the chronically indecisive. There'd better be a Rainy Day Astronaut song on your playlist or you'll break my heart," he said, before starting his motorbike and driving out of the lot.

She smiled after him. There was. She slid into the driver's seat of her MINI, anticipating her parents' surprise when she arrived early. Across the lot, Enrico waved as he slid into his Porsche Boxter, the vehicle only adding to his GQ image. She wondered what he was doing for the long weekend.

A few miles later, her stereo muted for an incoming call on her Bluetooth.

"Hey Jules."

"Lex. Can't you go home a different weekend? I just found out Casey is going to be at Owen's party on Saturday. You remember, the cute one I wanted to introduce you to?"

"Jules, I only *just* broke up with Jameson. I'm not ready to meet anyone new."

"I know. I just hate how he treated you. I thought a little attention from Casey could take your mind off things."

"I don't think a kayak guide who forages for his own food is the right person to take my mind off things."

Although maybe Tyler is, a little voice whispered.

She shook her head. She was not hoping to run into her high school sweetheart this weekend. Unless...

Maybe it was time to give up on the TV industry and her life in Seattle. While she was loathe to give her arrogant film prof, Mr. Snyder, the satisfaction of knowing he was right, she could always move home. Take over her parents' gallery like they'd always hoped she would, surf regularly, and rekindle things with the thoughtful and reliable man who was at the heart of her best Cannon Beach memories.

DID life get any better than this? Nate looked out over the crowd gathered in the park, listening to him and the guys play. From the dancers in the front rows, to the swayers, then the head-nodders, the lawn was packed. Beyond the concert area was a further sea of people just hanging out enjoying the day.

Nothing beat the feeling of playing a show where it just felt on the rails, everyone was playing their best and connecting with the audience. This may not be Climate Pledge Arena, but he loved a good outdoor concert and Mother Nature had pulled out all the stops for Labor Day, gifting Seattleites with a stellar mid-70's day beneath a cloudless blue sky.

Griffin chucked his drumsticks into the audience to signal the end of their set. Dozens of arms flew up in the air, followed by a flurry of scrambling and scuffling as fans vied for ownership. Nate chuckled.

Every time.

He unplugged his guitar and handed it to one of the stagehands before he followed Connor, Adam, and Griffin to the far side of the stage and down the steps.

"I'll catch up with you guys in a bit. I gotta go see the fam."

"Bring me one of your mom's chocolate brownies," Connor called.

"If you're lucky." He started through the crowd to where his mom and Marcie were seated on a colorful blanket. Partway there, his attention was caught by a sudden wail from a toddler in her mother's arms. The little girl was reaching both arms in Nate's direction, with the dad trying to shush her as the parents continued through the crowd, seeming embarrassed by her outburst.

When Nate narrowly missed stepping on a stuffed pink bear, he realized the toy must be the cause of the toddler's distress. He picked it up and jogged lightly toward the family.

"I think you dropped this," he said, placing the bear into

the little girl's outstretched arms. She stopped crying imme-diately. Both parents smiled in gratitude.

"Thank you. You're a lifesaver," the mother said. "I didn't realize she'd dropped Pinkie, but bedtime would have been a nightmare without her!"

"No problem. I think Pinkie was sad without you too," he said, with a wink for the little girl.

"My big brother the hero," said Marcie when he reached their blanket.

"Just doing my civic duty. I can remember a time when someone else I know lost a favorite teddy bear." He dropped down next to her.

"I forgot about that," Marcie said. "I was inconsolable at bedtime because I couldn't find Waffles. Mom was searching the house frantically for the millionth time when you walked in holding her."

"Trust you to name a teddy after your favorite breakfast food."

"She was golden brown, exactly the color of mom's waffles."

"I remembered you had been playing under the tree in the neighbors' yard earlier, and had a feeling someone might have got left behind."

"Well lucky for you, I'm old enough not to need looking out for any more."

"I doubt that's true, brat." He ruffled the top of her head. "The duties of a big brother never end. I've been looking out for you since you were old enough to crawl and I always will. Now hand over the fried chicken."

"Wait for Mom."

Nate glanced over where their mom stood chatting with someone near them and felt a surge of pride. A superhero in disguise. The female version of an unassuming Clark Kent. Not only had she finished putting herself through nursing school after his dad left, she made it to all his basketball games and Marcie's dance recitals, never mind baking cookies for the school bake sales and making the best fried chicken and potato salad on this coast. She couldn't have accomplished all that without super powers.

"Too hungry. Can't wait," he said, poking Marcie in the ribs. He hit her most vulnerable spot with the skill and precision that only a brother can develop after years of practice. She giggled and fell sideways. He dove at the cooler.

"Just for that, I'm not telling you all the nice things I was going to say about your act." She was still laughing as she sat up and straightened her top.

Crafty. She knows my vulnerable spot too.

"I'll share if you tell." He held out the container of chicken, not quite within her reach.

Her smile widened. "You guys were lit!" She took a thigh and waited a beat. "Especially Connor."

As I said, crafty. Gotta admire that.

"I tried to get Mom to come up front with me, but she wouldn't leave our spot. Oooooh, now I see why."

He followed Marcie's gaze to a man he'd never seen before. One who was obviously no stranger, judging by the way his mom's face lit up as she gave him a hug. A pretty long hug for a casual acquaintance.

"Who's that?" he asked Marcie quietly, out of the side of his mouth.

His mom turned their way. "Nate," she said. "Great show. I'd like you to meet Walter," she added, indicating the man at her side. "Walter, my son Nate. Marcie you've already met."

Marcie waved as Nate got to his feet, wiping his greasy hands on a napkin. "Nice to meet you." He shook the other man's hand, sizing him up the way Patrick Mahomes might assess Tom Brady on the football field. Despite Walter's solid grip and kind-looking eyes, he wasn't crazy about the way the older man looked at his mom, or cinched his left arm around her waist.

"Terrific performance," Walter said. "You guys really know what you're doing up there."

"Thanks. It helps when the audience is into it." Nate cast a longing glance at his barely-touched plate of food.

"Walter and I met when he came over to fix the back fence," his mom said.

Shit! "Sorry Mom, I was going to do that for you." And he had meant to. Truly.

"Selfishly, I'm glad you didn't get to it," Walter said with a fond look at his companion. "Or Linda and I might not have met."

"Let me know if there's anything else on her list you want me to procrastinate on," he muttered.

"Nathan Everet." His mom swatted his arm playfully. "My list is not that long and for the record, I do most of it myself."

Only because Nate tried to take care of repairs and stuff around the house and yard before they even made it on his mom's list. Admittedly, things had been sliding lately. Guilt niggled between his shoulder blades.

"You're an amazing woman." Walter smiled down at her. "Now if you two have no objections," he clasped Linda's hand in his, "I'd like to steal this lady for a little walk along the water's edge."

"Have fun," Marcie said.

"Water's edge," Nate said with a roll of his eyes after they were out of earshot. "He knows it's just a pond, right?" He turned to Marcie. "You didn't tell me mom was seeing someone."

"He was fixing the fence," Marcie said pointedly, turning the guilt blade. "Anyway, he seems nice. Treats mom well. Makes her happy." Marcie took a bite of her brownie. "She's been singing around the house lately."

"Our mom? Singing?"

Huh.

Nate had a distant memory of their mom singing when he was little, but didn't recall it happening once their dad walked out.

"Is it serious, do you think? Have you asked her?"

"Are you crazy? And open the door to her prying into *my* love life?"

"Fair point."

"*You* ask her if you want." Marcie popped her last bite of brownie in her mouth.

He opened his eyes as wide as possible, shaking his head slowly at her. Not in this lifetime.

Just then, Marcie jumped to her feet, waving madly at someone Nate couldn't see from where he sat. She grabbed her purse and dropped a kiss on the top of his head. "There's Olivia. See you later."

So much for time with my family.

Just then the band onstage started playing a cover of "Lonely Boy" by The Black Keys. Someone up above had a sense of humor.

His phone pinged.

ADAM

James got some great shots of us playing today. Here's a few. He's sending me the rest later. I'll edit our website and update our feeds.

Nate scrolled through. They were excellent pics, and the group could use some new ones. He fired one off in a text to Lexy.

NATE

Not a single good ponytail in the crowd.
Hope you're having fun.

He showed his mom the photos when she returned with Walter, but soon began to feel like a third wheel. His mom flushed prettily every time Walter paid her a compliment, which was often.

Nate's phone pinged again.

CONNOR

Where are those brownies at, yo?

Thank God!

"Sorry mom. Gotta go." Eager to escape, Nate grabbed a couple brownies. "For Connor," he said as he kissed her cheek. "Love you, Mom."

"Love you too, honey. I always enjoy watching you play. I'm so proud of you."

"Nice to meet you, Walter." He shook the man's hand.

"Likewise. I look forward to seeing more of you."

Nate headed off to find the guys. So that's the way it was? Walter staking his claim. And while Nate was the first to agree his mom deserved a great man in her life, he wasn't sure about this sudden shift in his family dynamics.

Weaving his way to the outdoor backstage area set up for

the bands, Nate spotted a woman wearing a familiar polka dot dress, her distinct caramel-colored hair dancing in the sunlight. He stopped, paralyzed. All the air left his lungs. Was Adele back in Seattle? He broke out in a cold sweat. Last he'd heard she was living back home in Chillicothe. If she'd moved back here and saw him playing with the Rainy Day Astronauts...

Would his ex-girlfriend be vindictive enough to destroy his band a second time?

CHAPTER 4

"Do you think it's possible for Mercury to be constantly in retrograde where my love life is concerned?"

-Celeste, Guest
Duquan's Downlow on Dating and Love
Podcast episode #83

The sight of her colorful sticky notes and organized file folders waiting on her desk at work had never been so welcome, proof of what a weird weekend it had been. Going home had always been her comfort retreat, but this time things felt different. Nothing she could put her finger on, but kind of like a favorite outfit that always made you feel good when you wore it, and suddenly no longer fits.

"You're glaring at your computer the way I was glaring at the letter I got from my landlords this morning." Jules propped a hip on the corner of Lexy's desk.

"Oh no, what now?" Jules had had to move twice in the last two years.

"I have the worst renter's luck. Maybe it's a renter's curse. They're selling too. I have to move *again*."

"Jules, I'm so sorry." She placed a comforting hand on her friend's shoulder. "I know when you moved here from Ireland, you were so excited to find your place and settle in. It's really unfair you keep getting kicked out."

"Just when I thought it was safe to get rid of my moving boxes." Jules shook her head mournfully, then glanced up and forced a smile on her face. "Here's hoping my next building doesn't smell like cabbage rolls in the hallway."

"That's the spirit. You know I'll happily captain Jules's Moving Squad again. We've practically got this packing thing down to an art by now."

"You're a logistical genius when it comes to packing. And nobody organizes a new kitchen the way you do."

"True story. Plus, my offer from the last two times stands. If you don't find the right place, you can move into the houseboat with me. Stay as long as you need."

"You're the best, Lex. Hopefully it doesn't come to that, but I appreciate it." Jules stood. "Drinks after work? Help me drown my sorrows so I can face the onerous task of apartment hunting again?"

"Of course. I take my moving squad duties seriously."

"Besides, I'm dying to hear more about your weekend in Oregon. You haven't said much, but something's up." Jules tapped the side of her head with her finger. "Irish intuition."

THE SHIP and Anchor was packed as usual but Jules, with

her internal radar, bee-lined for a table in the far corner, arriving just as the group stood up to leave.

"Guard the table," Jules said. "I'll get drinks. Don't say anything important until I get back."

"Nothing important. Yes boss," Ren said, setting aside her phone.

"Poor Jules, having to move again," said Lexy.

"I know. I offered to help, and a couch to crash on if needed."

"Me too."

"Jules's Moving Squad reunites again. If she's stuck for a place, I'd totally pick the boathouse over my one-bedroom if I were her."

"I think she's counting on her Irish luck to find her somewhere even better than the place she's leaving." Lexy glanced at the bar to see Jules toss her red mane, flirting with the bartender.

"We missed you at our Friday Pizza and Movie Night last weekend."

"By next month I will have forgiven you for re-watching *Letters to Juliette* without me. How was Owen's party on Saturday?"

"Pretty fun. But since you weren't there, Jules tried to set *me* up with the foraging kayak guide."

"Why is she obsessed with one of us dating this guy?"

"No idea. He's not my type, but I got to see some incredible wildlife photos he took."

"We all like gin, right?" Jules asked as she returned. "Greyhound cocktails are on special." She passed them around without spilling a drop. "To my next great apartment, may I never have to move again!" They all clinked glasses.

"To not having to forage for these cocktails," said Lexy, taking another sip. She and Ren burst out laughing.

"You two are laughing at me," said Jules, "but I don't know why. And I feel like I *did* have to forage for these. It's crazy up at the bar. Anyway, Lexy, time to dish."

Lexy picked a hole in her cocktail napkin with her thumb nail. "I don't know where to begin."

"Play the magazine headline game," Jules said.

"The what?"

"You know. When you're bored standing in line at the grocery store and catch up on your celeb goss by scanning the headlines on the magazines."

"Yeah..."

"So do that. Give us the headlines, like: The Secret Life of Lexy Smith! Family and friends share untold stories of her wild teenage years."

Lexy laughed. "What wild teenage years?"

"You get the point. Give us three headlines that sum up your trip home."

"Let me think a minute." She took a sip of her drink. Working up the nerve to relive her run-in with Tyler, Lexy chose an easier one to start. "Messages from the Afterlife. Lexy's dearly departed gran left a letter for her to read on her thirtieth birthday."

"Wow," Ren said. "Your parents gave it to you when you were home? That'll be emotional to read."

"I know. It's so like her to think of other people and know I would be missing her. She was such a special lady."

"Well you've definitely got the hang of the game," Jules said. "That was a very dramatic headline. What's next?"

"Okay." Lexy took a breath. "Too Late for Love. On the verge of moving home to win back her ex, Lexy runs into him and his charming new girlfriend. Has he become 'the one that got away'?"

"You ran into Tyler? But you've been avoiding him every time you went home," Jules said.

"Yeah well, this time I saw a nice woman I'd said hi to earlier smooching her hunky firefighter on the beach. Then I realized who she was with."

Did he see you?"

Lexy nodded.

"Noooooo."

"Oh, yes. Before I could make my escape."

"And?"

"He introduced us. We made polite small talk. And for my third headline: True Love for Tyler? His new GF is a sweetheart even his ex couldn't hate."

"Oh Lex," Ren sighed sympathetically. "That's tough. It's always hard to see your ex smitten with someone new, 'specially when your recent relationship just went up in flames."

"Let's go back to the part where you were thinking of moving home without telling your two closest friends," Jules said.

"Jameson cheating on me and Merelda's latest rejection had me questioning all the life decisions I've made up till now. Maybe I'm not cut out for this industry. Maybe I never should have left home."

"And Tyler?"

Lexy propped her chin on her hand. "Contemplating moving home made me think about him. Wondering what if we *were* right for each other, only the timing had been wrong before?"

"I think we're all guilty of that," said Jules. "Wondering about an ex, or a guy from our past we wish we'd had the opportunity to date. *Breakup-itis* I call it. The symptoms are worse after a new breakup."

"So this is normal? What I was thinking about Tyler?"

"Perfectly normal," Ren said. "Why do you think so many people rebound after a breakup? Same diagnosis, different symptom." Jules and Ren high-fived their clever analogy.

Lexy was nearly blinded by a flash of inspiration. She'd been thinking small, focused on her own experience. Ren and Jules said she wasn't alone. If there were others in the same boat, wondering about someone from their past— maybe *that's* what her show should be about?

Jules's gaze narrowed on Lexy. "What is that look? Like you just got comped the chocolate trio dessert."

"Even better." She leaned forward and lowered her voice. "I think I might have an idea for a show." She could hardly speak for excitement so settled on whispering. "A show where people get a second chance with someone from their past!"

"And are reunited in front of an audience on television?" Ren kept her voice low, like Lexy's. "I love it."

"We could have a host, get different people to tell their stories about the one that got away and why they're hoping for a second chance." Lexy began thinking out loud as the ideas came to her.

"Genius! I knew you'd think of something brilliant," Jules said, checking her watch. "Sorry Chica, have to run. I don't want to be late for Zumba." She tossed a handbag the size of an overnight bag over her shoulder.

"Atta girl. Don't let a little thing like having to pack up your life cramp your style."

Jules shrugged. "I'm enjoying my denial phase. Panic is

for later. I'm excited for your show idea, though. I'll have Pat send another drink your way to celebrate."

"You're on a first name basis with the bartender?"

"I am now," Jules said with a smirk. "And once you've figured out who will be on your show, I'm your girl for wardrobe. I'll make them all stars."

"I've gotta go too, Lex. Sorry. I've got a Skype call with my brother. The time difference between here and Beijing is brutal."

"But—"

"Don't worry." She leaned over to hug Lexy. "I'm already planning how to use Social for your show. Like a campaign to get people to send in videos telling their stories."

"You are the best, Ren!"

"See you tomorrow."

And then there was one.

With a fresh Greyhound delivered courtesy of Pat, she wasn't about to leave just yet, even if newcomers were hungrily eyeing her table. Buzzing from her new show concept, she pulled over a cocktail napkin and started to jot down ideas and questions. Hopefully, she had learned something from her failed pitches.

She wrote down a potential title, then narrowed her eyes as she studied it. Was her first idea for the show's name the best? Or the first to be discarded?"

Who made bar napkins so small anyway? It was common knowledge some of the best novels and rap songs started out on napkins. She'd seen *8 Mile*. Wait, Eminem had carried a notebook in that movie. She added 'get notebook' to her napkin list.

CHAPTER 5

"I was getting over a break-up when I walked past this pub with a sign outside that said 'We have beer as cold as your ex-girlfriend's heart'. I went in, obviously. Best beer of my life."

-Marcus, Guest
Duquan's Downlow on Dating and Love
Podcast episode #6

Nate knew exactly how he'd gotten sucked into this. He'd been so rattled seeing Adele's lookalike at the Labor Day concert he hadn't protested when Connor nominated him to do recon for the band's gig at the Ship and Anchor this weekend. No reason he'd never been here before, except the sports bar a couple blocks from his place had become his 'local'.

The place was packed, but it didn't take long to find the manager and scope out the stage setup and sound equipment. As he turned to leave, he spotted Lexy all by herself in the back corner. A quick scan showed no sign of her usual sidekicks. Something on the table had her complete attention. Which was strange, because The Ship didn't seem like the type of place Lexy would hunker down and do some work. She was scribbling something on a napkin and didn't look up until he spoke.

"'Of all the gin joints in all the towns in all the world'."

She looked up with a smile. "'And he walked into mine.' Though I'm surprised to hear you quoting *Casablanca*."

"I was outnumbered by women growing up. Is it?" At her blank look, he clarified. "Your gin joint?"

"On occasion. I happen to be drinking gin tonight." She lifted her glass and gave it a little wiggle. "Isn't this technically more your gin joint? Your neighborhood?"

"It is my 'hood, but this is my first time in. We've got a gig here this weekend and I came to check out the set up. What about you?" he said as he sat down. "Are you meeting someone? You're looking very studious for being in a pub."

"Jules and Ren wanted to come out tonight, then they ditched me after one drink."

"So they left and you decided to set up office? What's going on with the napkins?" He glanced over and tried to read the notes she had scrawled on them. Did that say Eminem?

"Nothing," she said quickly as she gathered them up, hiding her scribbles from his sight. "How did Marcie like her gift?"

Hiding her notes and changing the topic only piqued his curiosity more. "She loved it."

"Best Big Brother Award in the bag yet again?"

"Thanks to you." He leaned back in his seat, at ease. "Since we're both here, want to grab a bite? Maybe I've got some expertise you could use," he said, with a pointed look at the napkins she was still trying to hide.

"Sure. I didn't realize how late it was getting."

They scanned the plastic-covered menus, standard bar fare with a few additions like roasted cauliflower wings and deep-fried pickles. When their server stopped by, they both ordered burgers along with a beer for him.

He gave her a teasing look. "Menu decision, just like that? No consulting the server?"

"You might have noticed I got half fries and half salad."

He laughed. "Another technique for the indecisive." After a beat he asked "What's up with your napkin notes? Are you writing a secret novel or something?"

"I don't want to say," she said. "I don't want to jinx it."

"You think telling me will jinx it?"

"Can't chance it."

"Did you tell Jules and Ren?"

"Had to. They were here when I got the idea."

"So, you've either already jinxed it, and telling me won't matter. Or telling them didn't jinx it, so it's safe to tell me." He could see she was weighing this logic as their burgers arrived.

"I promise not to steal your idea, no matter how good it is," he said, as they both nibbled on a fry. "And I won't tell anyone about it either. Pinkie swear."

"Pinkie swear? What are you, five?"

He propped his elbow on the table, pinkie finger aimed in her direction. "I will have you know that a pinkie swear is a solemn oath, and I haven't broken a single one since childhood."

She looked across at him with skepticism, then relented, grinning as she reached over their burgers to hook her pinkie to his.

Grinning back, he gave her finger a playful tug before he released it and reached for his burger. "Okay, hit me with it."

She cut her burger, picked up half and leaned toward him. "I've thought a lot since you told me the kind of show Merelda is looking for."

He nodded, pleased that he could help.

"When I went home last weekend, something happened to spark this idea which has been rolling around in the back of my brain ever since." They ate. She talked. He listened.

After she was done, he pushed his empty plate to the side. "You sold me. I'm in."

"You're in what?"

"Your idea. I want to help."

"I appreciate the offer, but how could you help? And why would you?"

"I like championing an underdog." He shrugged. "It will be fun."

"Who says I'm an underdog?" She sounded mildly offended.

"Sorry sweetheart, but you against Merelda? You're the definite underdog."

"Hmph." She forked salad around on her plate. "I guess I'll have to rise up and triumph."

"Exactly. And for that, you need my help." He reached for one of her fries, grinning when she slapped his hand.

REN

How's it going with your show pitch, Lex?
Any progress?

LEXY

Not really. How's the apartment hunting Jules?

JULES

No progress there either. What's your roadblock Lex?

LEXY

Either of you worked on live TV?

REN

No

JULES

Nope. I hear HRH finds it too unpredictable.

REN

Which is what an audience loves

LEXY

Anything can happen. And does

REN

You've got a great concept. They say you never forget your 1st love

JULES

Who says it's a 1st love for all of them?

REN

Either way I think viewers will tune in to find out what happens to the couples

JULES

I second that. You need a kick-ass host

LEXY

I know. Any ideas???

REN

I can put feelers out

LEXY

Thx

REN

I'm thinking on how we can use our platforms to hype your show once it's running

LEXY

You're the best xx

btw I'm not telling anyone else at work. No jinxing. No idea thieves

Except Nate knows

JULES

How?

LEXY

He came by The Ship after you left

CHAPTER 6

"I'm an outdoor gal. Hiking, mountain biking, kayaking, skiing, rock climbing. I find dating hard because honestly, most guys can't keep up with me. Is The Rock single?"

-Holly, Guest
Duquan's Downlow on Dating and Love
Podcast episode #142

Even the host of the cooking show seemed to be mocking her decision to stay indoors, tightly-closed blinds doing their part to shield her from the temptation of a sun-filled Saturday.

To make matters worse, she was missing this month's 'Clean & Cruise', a beach clean-up followed by a social paddle put on by the Surfrider Foundation. A longtime member in Oregon, she'd joined the Seattle chapter when she moved, regularly participating in the clean-up events, joining other paddleboarders and kayakers on the water after.

She sighed. Hopefully a worthwhile sacrifice. Prioritizing her show. Absently she twisted the ring on her pinkie finger. It had belonged to her Gran and she'd put it on for luck, hoping Gran could help from beyond.

She'd take any help she could get because right now she was over her head trying to solve the mystery of what, exactly, pulled an audience in and kept them hooked.

She twisted the ring again. Gran had had it sized smaller as she got older, and Lexy's pinkie was the only finger it fit. Wearing it usually made Gran feel closer, but today, the weight of it on her pinkie reminded her of someone else entirely.

Who still pinkie swears as an adult? Ridiculous!

Ridiculous. At the same time adorable. And more than a little distracting, if she was being honest. Which she wasn't. Because *if* she was honest, she would have to acknowledge the zing of electricity when she linked fingers with Nate. Something which did not happen. She'd imagined it. Or it was static electricity. No chance it was a—a *thing* between her and Nate.

I'm off men. And even if I wasn't, I'd never date Nate. I vowed, after Tyler, to never date a friend. It hurts too much. Losing the friendship and the relationship when things don't work out.

She'd made so many memories with Tyler, memories they'd never laugh over or reminisce about again. Memories which left a sad, empty hole.

Enrico, now, there's someone she could date. He'd take her mind off Tyler, Jameson and everyone else not worthy of her attention.

She straightened her shoulders and focused on the TV.

She needed to figure this out so her show could help other people with their love lives. What qualities made people obsess over *Survivor*, *The Bachelor*, and *Real Housewives*? Viewers not only talked about the contestants as if they were close personal friends, they were heavily invested in the outcome.

Can you believe Tara didn't get a rose from Noah last night? I'm so upset, I soooooo wanted them to get together.

Why were viewers invested? What was it about these shows that touched people to the core? The longer she stared at the screen, the more the X factor that would make her show a hit eluded her. She was deep in thought when she heard a loud knock at the door.

Oh, for the love—!

Whoever it was had better have a good reason for interrupting. Jules and Ren were in Woodinville for a wine tasting. They'd been shocked when she turned them down in favor of research. So help her, if it was Jameson, he was going in the lake.

She opened the door to see Nate holding a large pizza box.

"Nate, hey. What are you doing here?"

"Didn't you get my texts? I'm here for the great show plan-a-thon. And I brought sustenance." He hefted the pizza box as he stepped inside.

"My phone is on silent. To avoid distractions," she added pointedly.

Ignoring her, he moved inside where the blinds were drawn to keep the glare off the TV. "Nice cave. You against sunshine?"

"I was researching," she said defensively, pointing to a muted Gordon Ramsay on the screen. "Trying to figure out the recipe for success with a show like mine."

"How's that going for you?"

"It's not."

He gave her a sympathetic look. "What say we try it my way. Including fresh air." He headed for the doors to the deck. "And the best pepperoni pizza you've ever eaten. They add fresh basil and a drizzle of honey. It's—I'll let you taste for yourself."

Since he obviously wasn't going away, and the smell from the pizza box was making her stomach growl, she grabbed napkins and followed him to the bistro set outside.

He sat back and linked his hands across his chest. "What have you got so far?"

She blew out a frustrated breath. "Not much. It's a show about love and relationships, so obviously a happy ending. But I don't know where to start. I recognize the hooks the other shows use, but not how to transfer them to mine."

"You know your finish line, but how you get there is key. At the risk of sounding corny, it's the old 'journey not the destination' cliché."

She laughed. "Did you really just use the most clichéd cliché of all time?"

"Think about it. Your happy ending isn't going to be nearly as satisfying for the viewers if they don't really get to know the contestants." He rested his forearms on the table and leaned toward her. "They need a reason to care."

"You're right. It's not just the stories. The viewers need to connect with the people telling them. Maybe even feel it could have happened to them."

"Exactly. If you simply reunite a group of star-crossed lovers in front of an audience, that's nice, but so what? Your audience needs to feel emotionally involved. You have to make it personal, give them a good reason to root for the people they're meeting on screen. *That's* what will keep bringing them back."

"Nate, that's brilliant. Where were you four hours ago?"

"Sitting at home, waiting for you to invite me over to brainstorm." He grinned as he lifted the lid of the pizza box. "I got tired of waiting."

"I'm glad." The now-open box emitted a mouth-watering smell, and she carefully lifted out a slice. "Emotional investment. That's why so many of us love watching rom-coms, and Hallmark movies. Or shows like *The Bachelorette*. We want to see the story unfold, sure. But we also live to vicariously feel the emotions of the people on screen."

"Love to watch rom-coms? Speak for yourself."

She made a face at him "Fine. The target audience watches them. And creates or escapes their own drama by watching someone else's."

"One hundred percent it's about the drama. Look at the rose ceremony on *The Bachelor*. It doesn't get much more dramatic than that. Not without a car chase and several explosions."

"For a guy who claims not to watch rom-coms or dating shows, you seem to know a lot about them," she teased.

He balled up a napkin off the table and tossed it at her in mock retaliation. "You want my help, or what?"

"Or what. Definitely 'or what'," she said as she took a first bite of her pizza. "Kidding...kidding," she said as Nate made a move to close the pizza box. "You've been very helpful. Plus, this pizza," she groaned with pleasure as she took another bite, "is absolutely incredible."

"I know my pizza."

"I'll give you that." She took another bite, thinking while she chewed. "So if not everyone on the show gets reunited with their 'one', people would watch to see who did, hoping their favorite is the one who gets a second chance.

"That's good."

"And we need our own suspenseful ceremony."

"Heighten the drama before revealing the lucky winner."

She gazed thoughtfully out over the water. "Do you think anyone learns stuff from watching these kinds of shows? It would be even more impactful if they could from ours." She bit off her words. She'd meant to say 'mine', not 'ours', but he didn't seem to notice. "Some love lessons are universal, right?"

"So I've heard." He leaned close. Her breath caught. He really did understand. "You need the right host. Someone who could share with the audience and make them feel it's all about them. Make it personal."

Personal. She blew out a breath. "I know."

He reached for another slice. "Any ideas?"

"The host needs to be charismatic. Someone with a psychology or counselling background."

"Tricky, because you're looking for an unknown. Merelda won't bankroll the budget to hire a household name. But you're right, a host's background and personality can pretty much make-or-break a show's success."

She gave a shaky laugh, "No pressure, just don't screw up picking the mystery host."

He sat back, biceps on full display. "What happened to kickstart this whole idea?"

"Just, you know, ran into an old flame and it got me thinking." She hoped she sounded casual. "It's easy to romanticize the past."

"Yeah, some people tend to romanticize past relationships. On the flip side, they can let the bad things that happened take on epic proportions."

He sounded like he spoke from experience. "Very insightful." She studied him closer. "Which one is you?"

"Me?"

"In your past? A romanticized fairytale? Or an epic nightmare?"

A pained look crossed his face. Uh, oh. Wrong question to ask. "I only ask because I'm wondering, do you think guys will come on the show too? I'd like a variety, not just women participants."

Nate was silent, looking out over the water. Then he turned back to her. "I've definitely got the nightmare. So, you won't find me on your show looking for a second chance. But yeah, do it right and I think guys will come on your show." He took a sip of the soda he'd picked up with the pizza. "You really never heard?"

"Heard what?"

"I thought it might be standard MHP orientation. Here, sign your contract, do this education module on workplace code of conduct, and watch this YouTube video of Nate's former girlfriend losing her shit about their relationship in front of the entire audience at one of his shows."

She covered her mouth with her hand in shock and sympathy. "Nate, no! Really? I'm so sorry. I had no idea. I can't imagine someone filming one of my worst moments and posting it for the world to see."

"Yeah well, it's in the past." His casual response sounded as forced as hers when she mentioned running into Tyler.

"I've got the romanticized memory, and you've got the nightmare. Either way, it's hard to move forward in love if you're worried about a repeat of everything that went wrong before. That's where a show like mine could really help." Isn't that what she wanted? To help people as well as build her career.

"Which gives me an idea. Do you want to really knock Merelda's socks off?"

"You mean her Louboutins?"

"Whatever. They say a picture's worth a thousand words."

"Another Nate cliché."

He pulled a face that was actually pretty cute. "Instead of pitching a written proposal, what if you made a video? A mock-up of what the show could look like. Hook her the way you want to hook your audience. Then back that up with your stats, your comps and projections."

"Interesting idea," she said, turning the concept over in her mind. "I bet I can convince Jules and Ren to be part of it."

"We have a set up in Connor's garage. Sometimes we film our rehearsals. You could record there. I'll even man the camera."

"Awesome. I bet Ren has some helpful tips, from all her social media videos."

"I love it when a plan comes together." He rubbed his hands together gleefully. "Admit it. My brainstorming technique is far superior to yours."

Superior? No way she was admitting that. "Your technique was tolerable."

He laughed. "Liar."

CHAPTER 7

"Some people go all crazy-like over an ex. My old roommate set up a fake Instagram account so she could befriend the new woman her ex was seeing, and keep tabs on him that way."

-Eva, Guest
Duquan's Downlow on Dating and Love
Podcast episode #38

"Don't judge me," Lexy instructed her computer as she opened YouTube to search for the video of Nate's ex freaking out. Except her fingers refused to move, frozen with guilt. The way Nate had talked about the video, it was obvious the memory still upset him. He didn't need someone else witnessing his humiliation.

She closed her browser and checked her phone instead, scrolling through the wine tasting photos from Jules and Ren. Along with the message, *Lub you Lex*

Oh dear, drunk misspellings were occurring already.

LEXY

Lub you both too

She cleared the bistro table, ignoring the lure of YouTube. And a wheedling inner voice telling her that imagining what Nate's ex had said was worse than knowing.

She picked up a pen. She needed to keep working on the show proposal. Minutes later she threw the pen down. Who was she kidding? She was no saint. And she was *dying* of curiosity.

"Please forgive me, Nate," she whispered.

Thirty minutes later, a search of YouTube and her subsequent deep dive on the Internet came up empty. She tried every variation of 'woman losing her shit at a Rainy Day Astronauts show' she could think of. Nothing. All she got was the RDA website, a list of upcoming shows, and a handful of favorable reviews. In fact, there was no mention of RDA prior to six years ago. Odd. They'd been playing together for longer than that.

Normally Ren would be her go-to Internet Detective, but she didn't want to betray Nate's trust by telling anyone else. Her phone rang, interrupting her online sleuthing. Did Nate have a sixth sense she was creeping him? She breathed a sigh of relief when her screen showed it was her friend Duquan on the line.

"Duke. It's been ages. How's the surf back home?"

They'd met in the water when she was seventeen and still relatively new to surfing. Duke had become her hero that day, giving her pointers. From there, she'd adopted him as a sort of surrogate big brother.

"I wouldn't know, Lexycakes. I fell in love and moved to

Seattle," he said, the familiar Caribbean lilt tingeing his deep voice.

"I'm thrilled you're here, but what happened to me getting to vet your next boyfriend before you commit?" When Duke's last partner broke his heart, Lexy had taken on the role of protector even though he had over half a foot and a good fifty pounds on her.

His roar of laughter boomed through the phone. "No time like the present," he said. "Come join us for a drink. Meet the love of my life. Second only to you, of course."

An hour later, Lexy found herself atop the Space Needle in a revolving bar she never frequented. Tourists loved the place and she tried to look apologetic as she passed the long line waiting to get in, following the booming sound of Duke's laughter.

"How is it that you picked the most touristy spot in the entire city?" she teased as she reached their window table.

"Here's my girl!"

Both men stood, and Duquan swooped her up into a giant bear hug that nearly squeezed the breath from her lungs. "And this is Paul." Duke indicated the slim, attractive blond man who had been sitting across from him. "Blame him for the location," he said, affection lacing his voice.

Talk about opposites attracting.

Paul gave her a quick, far gentler hug. "So, this is the famous 'Lexycakes' I keep hearing about."

She chuckled. "It's been thirteen years and he still insists on calling me that."

"It's because you're so sweet, girl." He turned to Paul. "I'm out in the water one day and I watch this wide-eyed young thing paddle out. She's too nervous to come and sit at the peak where she needs to be to catch anything."

She picked up the story. "Duke whistled to get my attention and waved me over in the water. It was pretty intimi-dating over there in the pack, all guys, everyone more experienced than me. But no one messes with Duke, so when he started yelling for me to paddle, the other guys backed off and let me have the wave." She smiled fondly, lost in the memory of simpler times.

"No way was that thirteen years ago."

"It was." She leaned in and stage-whispered, "I'm turning thirty this year."

Just then a server delivered a tall, icy pink drink. Duke pointed to it. "I hope that's still your favorite."

"The first legal cocktail you bought me? Of course," she said, touched that he remembered. "We don't talk about all the post-surf drinks consumed in the parking lot *before* I was twenty-one," she said in an aside to Paul.

Duke winked at her. "I plead the fifth."

She took a sip of her Blueberry Cocktail. "I can't believe you're here!"

"Me neither." He squeezed Paul's hand where it lay on the table between them.

She sighed. *They are too cute. And if I had to guess, I'd say Paul knows just how lucky he is.*

"It's a point in your favor that you convinced Duke to move here." She gave Paul a teasing grin. "But time to make sure you're good enough for my surrogate big bro. Prepare to be grilled."

By the end of several rounds, Lexy's stomach hurt from laughing and she was completely won over.

"I approve," she said quietly into Duquan's ear as they parted ways on the street. Duke grinned at her as he held her hand in his firm grip. "You'll call me soon?"

She nodded. "I have a work project I could use your help with. Top Secret."

"Work secrets. Intriguing. I got you. Always. P.S.," he added. "After what I heard about your last relationship, I'm vetting the next guy you date!"

She laughed. "I deserve that."

Duquan cast a glance over at Paul. "Maybe you'll be as lucky as me with the next one."

If only.

~

HE SHOULD HAVE EXPECTED IT, but somehow the transformation that occurred when Lexy, Jules, and Ren descended on Connor's garage took him by surprise. Connor, coward that he was, had made himself scarce, and the place felt different full of girls instead of guys. It barely looked like their jam space anymore. Instead of an open bag of chips on the coffee table, snacks were arranged on plates and in bowls alongside paper napkins and cans of sparkling water.

"I made my famous Lemon Coconut Bars." Lexy peeled the lid off of container and placed it in the center of the table. Nate caught a whiff of tangy lemon scent and his mouth watered.

"Ren, I brought some for your parents too." She handed a matching container to Ren. "I know they love these. Every time I stop by, your dad asks if I brought any with me."

Lexy smiled as she turned to Jules. "You're a peach for helping. I know you're crazy busy getting ready to move."

"Well, you've been a peach helping me sort through stuff and start packing. Seriously," Jules said, "I only moved last year. How can I have acquired so much stuff again?" She pulled a giant piece of fabric from her massive handbag. "Help me with this? It'll make a great backdrop."

Nate watched Ren and Lexy hold up the blue and white swirled fabric while Jules tacked it to the garage wall. He grabbed the box of sound gear he'd borrowed from the studio. "I didn't know you were moving, Jules."

"The joys of renting," Jules said around the tack she held in her mouth, as she straightened the fabric and stabbed another tack into the wall. "But I lucked out. A friend of mine who works for Capitol Couture knows someone who was looking for a tenant. She gave a glowing reference and the place is mine without competing with a hundred other prospective tenants."

He set the camera tripod up facing the backdrop. "Lucky you."

"If that's what you call having to move three times in three years." Jules laughed and stepped back to assess her handiwork. "That looks perfect. It's giving off 'summer sky' vibes with a touch of whimsy."

He set the camera on the tripod, then turned to check the batteries in the pack for the lapel mic.

""What's the rush with getting this filming done so soon, Lex?" Jules rummaged in her bag, pulling out a dog-eared book, various clothing items, and a bag of almonds in her search for some elusive item.

"I work better with a deadline," Lexy said. "Being a glutton for punishment, I picked my birthday as the absolute latest date to have this ready and pitch it to Merelda."

"September 26th," Ren said. "That's coming up soon!"

"I know. Hence the rush. And the glutton bit."

Nate made a mental note of Lexy's birthday. He was scheduled in studio that day, but maybe he could swing by Manor House and bring her a birthday latte.

"Well, my friend," Jules said cheerfully, "you are setting

yourself up to have either the best birthday ever, or you'll want to drown yourself in a tub full of Guinness."

"I don't like Guinness."

"I think that's her point." Ren chuckled.

After several practice runs, lots of laughter and the all-important snack break, they began making real progress on the mock videos.

"Ren's doing great," he said quietly to Lexy, who stood watching the camera screen over his shoulder. "All her hours on TikTok are paying off. Her delivery is spot on."

"I know. She's killing it," whispered Lexy as they listened to Ren give an animated account of the man she met while backpacking in Europe. How they fell in love exploring the cobblestone streets of Paris and the ancient ruins in Rome, before their heart-wrenching separation at the end of her trip.

"It's a side of her I've never seen before. I hope I can do half as well when it's my turn."

"I'll make you look good. Promise," he added with a grin, confident it would be hard to make any of the trio look bad.

"I'll hold you to it," she said, as Ren finished her story on camera.

"That's a wrap," Nate said, to make it official. He'd gotten some good stuff out of both of the girls. All it would take now was a little editing.

"You two were brilliant," Lexy said. "I know the stories are made up, but I still got emotional listening to you."

"Nice job ladies." He gave them each a high-five.

"Ren, you're a natural," Lexy said. "And Jules, I loved the bit about how you got dumped the week before your sister's wedding, so grabbed the next cute guy who walked into the coffee shop and asked him to be your wedding date. So adorable."

In the time it took him to put away the equipment, the backdrop was down and any signs of a female invasion were gone. As were Jules and Ren.

"I think that went really well."

He could tell Lexy was excited and still a little wound up. "Me too. Want a beer to celebrate?" When Lexy made a face, he said, "There might be a canned vodka drink kicking around."

"I'd take one of those."

He opened the fridge and pushed aside bottles and cans, hunting for the lone non-beer drink he thought he'd seen. "Success!" He handed Lexy her can as he joined her on the couch. "I'll edit those videos over the next couple of days and get them to you as soon as I can."

"That would be amazing. Cheers!" They popped their drinks and tapped them together before taking a sip. "After this, filming the show will be a piece of cake, right?"

"Oh sure, a multi-cam, live studio shoot is pretty much the same as filming your friends in a garage."

"Exactly." She gave a wry smile. "And if I keep telling myself that, I won't panic."

"No panicking. You've got this pitch in the bag."

"Thanks. For everything. You've been a big help," she said. "I know this has taken up a lot of your time."

He shrugged off her words. "I had the time. And it's been fun."

"You said the Astronauts film rehearsals sometimes. Ever made a music video?"

"No." His eyes shuttered. Cold washed over his entire body.

"Really? You totally should. That would be so fun..."

Lexy was still speaking, but she sounded far away and

like she was underwater. His vision blurred around the edges.

"I can see it now," she said enthusiastically, spreading her hands in the air as if revealing a headline. "The Rainy Day Astronauts Present—"

"No!" he said, louder this time. "We don't do music videos."

She looked startled by his sharp tone. Great. Now he felt like he'd kicked a puppy. "I'm sorry," he said. He thumb-picked the label on his beer bottle, avoiding her eyes. "I didn't mean—"

"It's okay. Forget I mentioned it." She stood. "I should get going anyway."

"Don't go yet." He grabbed her hand and tugged gently so she sat back down on the couch. "I'm an ass. Forgive me?"

She looked at him for a long moment. He should explain his outburst. But didn't want to bring his dark past into their bright friendship. Hopefully, she'd read between the lines, remember what he'd told her before.

When she smiled softly, his body sagged in relief.

"I can forgive a little artistic temperament from the man who is filming and editing these clips for me for free."

"Speaking of artistic temperament, did anyone tell you the story about Pierre? His sudden exit from MHP was legend. I wish I'd been there to witness it myself, but I did hear about it from a reliable source."

Her ponytail bounced as she shook her head. "What happened?"

"He'd been a producer there for several years," he said, warming to his tale. "There were rumors he was more than just eye candy for Merelda. He got first pick of the shows."

"Sounds like someone else we know." Could there be

more than met the eye between Enrico and Merelda? She'd never seen evidence of it.

"Then one day, out of the blue, he threw the biggest tantrum. He stormed around the office ranting at Merelda. Didn't care who heard him. Said he can't work under these conditions."

"What conditions? Merelda dropped him for another guy?"

"No!" He leaned in, building the suspense. "Merelda had taken advantage of the writer's strike when everyone was off work to have the office repainted. When we came back, Pierre lost it. Said the new colors stifled his creativity. He demanded Merelda change the wall color back. She refused."

"What?" Lexy leaned back, slack-jawed. "No..."

"Yes."

"No one leaves their job because of the color of the walls."

"Except Pierre."

She tipped her head, studying him. "You made that up."

"Scout's honor." He held up his right hand, pinkie and ring finger tucked under his thumb.

"You are full of it, Nate Douglas. So full of it your eyes are brown, as my grandpa used to say."

"Nuh-uh." He pointed to his eyes. "These babies are pure green."

"Then what's that brown speck I see right there..." She leaned in close, pretending to examine his eyes, a teasing grin tugging at her full, rosy lips.

Hard to say which of them moved first. Maybe they moved at the same time, but suddenly their lips met. Gently at first, testing. Her lips were soft against his. She tasted sweet as honey. After a few seconds, her arms slid around his neck.

He deepened the kiss, angled his head for better access. His arms circled her waist to draw her closer. A fevered jolt blazed through him as he lifted the hem of her shirt, teasing the bare skin of her back just above her jeans. She let out a soft moan—which had the effect of a bucket of cold water dumped on him. She stiffened at the same moment. They slowly drew back from each other. Both catching their breath.

"Shit. Sorry, that was—"

"No, I'm sorry. I shouldn't have..." she trailed off, as though uncertain what to say.

He ran an unsteady hand through his hair. Hell, he didn't know what to say either. "I like you Lex, but I'm not looking for..."

"I know. Me neither." She stood. "Let's chalk it up to an over-enthusiastic celebration of a good video shoot."

He stood as well, making sure to leave adequate space between them, tucking his hands in his back pockets. "Works for me. It was a one-time thing. Not to be repeated."

"Agree." She eyed him a moment longer. "Friends?"

"Of course. Friends."

"Good. Now I really should go." After she gathered her things, he walked her to the door of the garage.

"See you at work," she said with a little wave from the driveway.

"See ya." He returned her wave, closed the door, leaned back against it and shut his eyes. What the hell? Lex might be cute and fun. And they'd been spending lots of time together. But that shouldn't have happened. She wasn't even his type. And yet. There'd been something behind that kiss.

He sat on the couch, picked up his beer bottle, disappointed to see it was empty, and set it back down. Lexy had rattled him when she asked about the band filming a video. His defenses kicked into gear. Was that why he'd kissed her? Something to prove?

CHAPTER 8

"My garage is a *Man-Cave*. 'No women allowed' is implied in the name. Not that my wife pays any attention…"

-Jacob, Guest
Duquan's Downlow on Dating and Love
Podcast episode #70

"Hey, Loverboy! Focus!"

Nate looked over at Adam and scowled. He *was* focused. For the most part. Except when his mind wandered a little. Which wasn't like him during rehearsal, even if it was a sunny Saturday and the garage door was wide open.

"Focus on this." Nate winged a guitar pick at Adam's head, then pulled a spare out of his pocket. He'd be spending a lot of time in Connor's garage today. After rehearsal, Lexy, Jules, and Ren were coming over to film Lexy's scenes as host for her proposal.

"Let's try the new one," Adam said.

Nate switched guitars for the next song, picking up his beloved Fender Telecaster and sliding the strap over his shoulder. In a practiced move, he situated the guitar just so before he adjusted his vintage pedals. He heard Griffin tap his drumsticks together as he counted them in.

"One, two, one, two, three, four!"

Total focus.

"It sounded good that time," he said once the song ended. "What do you guys think about cutting the bridge in half and going straight back into the chorus without the breakdown?"

"Sure, let's give it a try." With a sly glance at Nate, Connor added, "When's your girlfriend coming by?"

"She's not my girlfriend." He rolled his eyes. He'd expected a certain amount of ribbing when he asked about using the space to help Lexy film something for work.

"That's right. Lexy can't be his girlfriend, since Nate decided he can only date other musicians." Griffin punctuated his statement with a little drum roll.

"Right," said Adam, "Nate wants to be the next Kurt Cobain and Courtney Love."

"Too much drugs and drama, plus a sad ending." Connor plucked his bass strings thoughtfully. "The next Gavin Rossdale and Gwen Stefani?"

"That didn't work out either," said Griffin. "Now she's married to that country singer."

"Sonny and Cher?"

"Divorced."

"Jack and Meg White split before The White Stripes were even famous."

"How sure are you about this 'musicians only' rule, Nate?" Adam improvised a few jazzy sounding notes on the keyboard. "Doesn't seem like it works out as well as you think it does."

"Shut up," Nate said with mock irritation.

"Besides," Connor chimed in, "all I hear is Lexy this, Lexy—Oh hey, Lexy."

He thought Connor was messing with him, but one look at his friend's face told him otherwise.

Oh, shit!

Slowly Nate turned to the doorway where Lexy stood wearing a blue sundress and framed by the sunshine streaming in behind her.

"Hey. Sorry. I'm early."

"No problem. Have a seat. We're just going to try this song one more time. Then the guys will clear out."

"Thanks." She moved several of their discarded hoodies before she sat on the sofa.

It was probably too much to hope for that she hadn't overheard Connor. The guy would get him into trouble every time. Without even trying. When Griffin tapped his drumsticks together, Nate tuned out everything but the music.

SHE COULD DO THIS. She could totally do this.

I can't do this!

She'd been practicing her mock role as show host at home, and with Duke, who'd had a lot of good pointers. But now, sitting in the jam space as the guys finished their rehearsal, she was positive she was going to screw it up. She was nervous enough about being on camera. Never mind the guy filming her was the same guy she had kissed a few days ago.

She hadn't exactly been avoiding him at work since 'the kiss'. If they hadn't seen each other much at the Manor, if she had sent him fewer texts the past couple of days, it was purely coincidence.

What happened was partly her fault. Okay, mostly her fault. Which left her with no idea how to act around him.

I've got about five minutes to figure it out.

Just because they were here, the same place where they'd kissed, didn't mean they couldn't behave perfectly friendly and normal while filming. To test her theory, she looked directly at him while he played.

Together, the four guys made quite the picture. Her heart kicked. So what if she happened to notice Nate made a plain white T-shirt and jeans look outrageously good? It didn't have to mean anything.

At that moment, he looked up, caught her eye, and shot her a grin. Same familiar grin as always. Same old Nate. Lexy's apprehension dissolved. Except for saying her lines on camera.

She felt almost silly for having built in a safety plan so she and Nate would not be tempted to 'celebrate' the same way as last time. The girls were coming to do her hair and makeup. Jules had an outfit for her she declared to be 'so boss'. When she'd made them promise not to leave without her, she'd gotten a puzzled look before they'd agreed.

Feeling more at ease, she studied the other members of the band. Connor, on bass guitar, fit the classic 'tall, dark and handsome' description of old romance novels.

"Who's that on the keyboard again? I just love a guy with sexy stubble like that."

Lexy hadn't noticed Jules and Ren till they joined her on the couch.

"Adam," she answered in a low voice. "He and Nate met playing basketball in college."

"The drummer, Griffin, is giving me serious Duke Simon vibes from *Bridgerton*," Ren said. "Only less 'proper' and more 'funky' with his hairstyle of all those little spiky twists." She gave a little hum of appreciation. "I had a major crush all through Season One"

Lexy and Jules nodded. The actor was very crush-worthy.

Once practice wrapped, Jules kicked the other guys out, declaring them all far too good-looking not to be a distraction. Then began the 'Lexy Transformation'.

Ren was a genius with hair and makeup.

"How was your Skype call with your brother the other night?" Lexy tried not to move as Ren coaxed her pin-straight hair into holding a sleek, stylish curl.

"Good." Ren passed the curling iron through another section of Lexy's blond locks. "You know Bay. I love him, but he has turned 'dutiful eldest son' into an art form. I wish he would tone it down just a smidge so I don't feel so shabby by comparison."

"Shabby? The social media wizard who has boosted viewer engagement of all MHP productions by a minimum of twenty percent, promotes her dad's business on the side, helps look after her grandparents, and teaches Mandarin in her spare time is most definitely not shabby."

"Thanks, Lex." Ren patted her shoulder. "You're all done."

"My turn." Jules handed Lexy a garment bag.

She looked in the bag and gasped. "I can't wear this."

"Just put it on," said Jules. "You told me you didn't want to look like yourself and that is a very un-Lexy outfit. And by the way, it is fab-u-lous."

She emerged from the makeshift dressing room they had rigged in one corner, self-conscious in a bold, floral print blouse in shades of fuchsia, orange, and teal. The blouse's deep V-neck was far more revealing than anything she ever wore. Behind the camera, Nate appeared frozen, as if he couldn't rip his gaze from her and her discomfort quadrupled.

"Here, let me help." Jules partly tucked the front of the blouse into the slim, high-waisted, black cigarette pants. "It's called a French tuck, and I've been doing this since before Tan France made it all the rage on *Queer Eye*."

Fuchsia heels, ridiculously high, and a long gold pendant that hung far too low into the V of the blouse completed the outfit. "Are you sure?" she asked Jules.

Just then Ren let out an appreciative whistle. "Lex, you look amazing!"

"I'll second that." Nate approached to fix the mic to her blouse. "Here," he said, his fingers gently brushing the skin of her collar bone. "I just have to get this...there. It's on." He backed away so fast he nearly tripped.

Forty-five minutes later, Lexy swore she'd sweated through the fancy floral blouse several times over. She kept screwing up. The harder she concentrated, the more she flubbed her words.

"Take a deep breath and try again," Ren said encouragingly. "You'll get it."

"I swear, I was doing really well when I practiced with Duke. He gave me pointers on body language, and how to look into the camera without feeling awkward. He said I was doing a great job connecting with my fake audience."

She was babbling, but she couldn't help it. She gave her head a shake, worked to center herself the way Duke had taught her, and started again.

"You'll know someone really loves you when they're willing to move mountains on you— I mean *for* you. Dammit!"

"Okay, let's take five," Nate said.

Lexy wanted to crawl into a hole. This whole video idea had been stupid. Merelda would never go for anything she did. Smug Sonia would become MHP's next producer, and Lexy would never hear the end of it.

"You're overthinking. Don't worry about Merelda or anyone else," Nate said as he reached her side.

She stared into his eyes. How did he know exactly what she was thinking?

He placed his hands gently on her shoulders in a calming gesture. "Remember when you were an extra in that music video?"

She nodded.

"Close your eyes, and imagine yourself back there. You had a lot of fun. It was exciting. Hold on to those feelings. Then open your eyes and say your bit. You've got this." He clapped her on the shoulder before he stepped away.

Ren and Jules couldn't miss the interplay between her and Nate, and judging by the look that passed between them, she'd have explaining to do later. For now, she took Nate's suggestion to heart, and by some miracle got through her prepared script, even having fun by the end.

She looked around in relief as she finished. Connor stood leaning against the door frame.

"Wow, Lexy. I dig the look." He sauntered over and draped his arm around her. "What are you doing tonight after this?" he asked with a flirtatious smile.

"Well, big guy, I've got a date."

"Break my heart," Connor said. "Any way I can get you to ditch him for me?"

She laughed. Connor was such a flirt. "My date is with my computer, editing video and reviewing my proposal. It promises to be a late one."

"You're wearing that number to go home and sit in front of your computer on a Saturday night?" He shook his head sadly. "Such a waste."

"Will you feel better if I tell you I'm planning to take these clothes off?" she said, tongue-in-cheek.

Connor clutched at his heart in jest. "What are you trying to do to me, woman?"

"If it helps, I put a case of beer from Sound Brew Co. in the fridge as thanks to you and the guys for letting me use this space."

"Thanks Lex, that takes some of the sting out of your rejection," Connor teased.

"Actually, I have thank you gifts for all of you. Your help really means a lot." She carefully took three presents out of her bag, and handed a thick envelope with a purple bow to Jules.

"The last thing you need is something else to move, but I thought a meal delivery gift card would be helpful. Since you're going to be so busy and we already started packing your kitchen stuff."

Jules opened the card. "Northwest Nourish? They're my favorite. Healthy and delicious. Thanks, Lex. You didn't have to, but this will come in really handy."

Lexy handed a flat, wrapped package to Nate, and a yellow gift bag with lime green tissue paper to Ren.

First to emerge from the layers of tissue was a candle in a glass jar. "'Smells like Movie Night'," Ren read off the label. She laughed, lifted the lid, and gave a sniff. "Mmmm, it smells like buttery popcorn and..." She gave another sniff. "Licorice. Lexy where did you find this?"

"Etsy has everything." Lexy smiled. "There's something else in the bag."

Ren pulled out a pair of earrings on a cardboard backing. "They're teeny movie posters for *Gravity*. They're adorable, I love them!"

"You've chosen more than a few 'against all odds' films set in space on our movie nights and I know this is a fave."

Ren slid her earrings out to trade them for her new pair.

Lexy turned to Nate, who was reading the back of the book he'd just unwrapped. "You don't have that one already, do you?"

"No, I don't." He held up the book with the cover facing her. *Entertain Us: The Rise of Nirvana.* "This is so cool, Lex."

"I know lots of authors have written about Nirvana's fame, but I like that this one tells the story of their early days."

His smile told her she'd nailed it. "You know Nirvana's music runs through my veins."

"I do."

"If I don't show up for work tomorrow, it'll be because I got too caught up reading this."

Lexy gave each of them a hug, then slung her bulging Tides and Vibes canvas tote bag over her shoulder and picked up her purse. She waited for Ren and Jules, and they all moved toward the door.

"Hey Lex," Nate said as he wound up an extension cord. "Do you have a name for your show?"

"I have the perfect name, but I'm not telling."

"Lexy always thinks she's going to jinx herself," Jules teased.

"I was thinking, if you called it *Renovate My Relationship* then you'd still get that renovation show you wanted to pitch."

"Very funny. Good thing I already have the best title."

"Think about it." He placed the wound extension cord in a bin. "Or maybe *Level Up My Love Life*?"

"Goodbye Nate. Goodbye Connor," Lexy called with exaggerated cheerfulness before walking down the driveway between Jules and Ren, swallowing a smile.

She turned when Connor called after them. "Hey ladies, come watch us rehearse again sometime." He blew them a kiss. "I'd be happy to give you a guitar lesson, Lexy. Get you playing with us."

Connor laughed as if he'd said something hilarious. Nate punched him on the arm.

NATE

I guess you can't call the show I Screwed Up the First Time. But you could use Second Time's the Charm

LEXY

Haha. I told you, I already have the perfect title

NATE

It doesn't hurt to have a back-up. You know that reality show they made, trying to find love for that 90s rapper Flavor Flav?

LEXY

Flavor of Love?

NATE

That's the one! What if you got a former celebrity looking for a comeback and got them to be the host?

LEXY

I'm guessing you have one in mind

NATE

How about this…Two Scoops of Love with Vanilla Ice

LEXY

Bahahahahaha

Or I could set it on a cruise ship instead of in-studio, and call it Cruise Into Love. Or Cruise In2 Love. Because it's about a second chance

NATE

Genius! If I'd known about this idea, we could have converted Connor's garage into a cruise ship for the filming

LEXY

Probably for the best. Ok I'm going radio silence while I finish my pitch. Wish me luck

NATE

You don't need it, but good luck

One last thing. Check your email

STILL SMILING, she clicked on the message in her inbox to see the meme of a guy staring intently at his computer with the caption, 'When you're behind at work, but you need to finish your BuzzFeed quiz to know what kind of garlic bread you are,' was accompanied by the message—don't fall victim to the BuzzFeed quizzes!

More appropriate would be, *Don't fall victim to another rejection from Merelda.*

CHAPTER 9

"For me, birthdays are all about self-love. But don't let that stop you from buying me a gift, honey."

-Scarlett, Guest
Duquan's Downlow on Dating and Love
Podcast episode #133

This was it. The day of reckoning. Officially thirty years old, and psyching herself up to beard the lion in his den. Make that The Queen on her throne. She might rather the lion.

So far, her birthday had started off pretty much as expected. Emotional moment reading Gran's letter this morning? Check. Lovely birthday phone call from her parents? Affirmative. Mother-daughter birthday spa weekend planned? Confirmed. Wearing her lucky outfit, her favorite royal blue suit, and Gran's sapphire ring, for today's pitch to Merelda? Absolutely.

Presentation saved on her laptop, with a backup on an external hard drive, another on a USB, and an emergency copy sent to Nate just in case? Definitely.

Nauseous at the idea of Merelda's reaction, while simultaneously fearing the earthquake experts predicted to be 'the big one', or some other calamity occurring before she could meet with her boss? Unfortunately.

Happy birthday to me!

Her phone pinged as she was heading out the door.

JULES

Hurry up and get your cute butt to work birthday girl. We want cupcake breakfast.

She sent back a gif of a girl running down the street. Sugar was always good for breakfast.

AT THE MANOR HOUSE, her desk and surrounding area had been blitzed by some industrious birthday elves, and she had a pretty good idea who. A bright bouquet of balloons was tied to the arm of her chair, blue streamers were festooned around, and there was a surf-themed banner taped to the wall behind her desk that read 'Happy Birthday Lexy Slater!'. While she was nowhere near as good a surfer as eleven-time world champion Kelly Slater, she appreciated the comparison.

Before she could move enough streamers to sit at her desk, Enrico appeared at her side, his espresso-dark eyes and warm smile enough to turn her knees to water.

"Happy birthday, Bella." He leaned in, giving her a whiff of sexy male, underscored with a hint of spice and the outdoors, so faint she wondered if it came from a bottle or was just his essence. His lips brushed her cheek and her heart leapt into her throat beating a million beats a minute. Wow! That never happened before.

Before she could react, he sauntered across the hive and down the stairs. She turned to sit down, just as the tap-tap of Merelda's stilettos came her way and stopped. She froze, then straightened, head high. This was it. Her chance to request a meeting.

"What are we celebrating?" Merelda asked in deceptively mild tones.

Lexy eyed the decorations behind her, then offered up a meek, "My birthday."

Merelda eyed the tell-tale posters. "At least no one divulged your age. *They* will use it as a weapon against you."

They?

"They." Merelda waved her hand dramatically. "Anyone. Especially men."

I could have sworn I only asked that in my head.

"They will say you are too young to know anything, then too old to know what is current." Lexy swallowed and nodded. She had no idea what to say to that. Merelda started to walk away.

Come on Lexy. Before she's gone.

"Um, Merelda?" Her boss paused and slowly turned, giving her a withering look. "Could I—Could I see you sometime today? It won't take long."

"I'll try to find a few minutes later."

She blew out a breath as Merelda walked away. She'd done it. Now she just had to get through the actual pitch.

She was booting up her computer when Nate stopped by her desk.

"Happy birthday, Lex." He handed her a to-go cup. "Latte for the birthday girl."

"Thank you. Wait. Are you sure this is mine?" She smiled as she pointed to his name on the cup.

His eyes lit with amusement. "Promise I didn't take a sip." He gestured to her desk area. "I love what your decorator has done with the place."

"Thanks. You know, I was getting bored of the old motif."

"Ready for your pitch?"

"I'd better be. I think Her Royal Highness is going to grant me an audience later."

"I'm sure she'll go for *Two Scoops of Love with Vanilla Ice*."

She chuckled. "Unfortunately, Vanilla never replied to my DM so I couldn't confirm him for the show. Guess I'll have to pitch her my original title."

"Which is...?"

"Still a secret."

"Well, I'm headed to the studio where I'll be for the rest of the day. Let me know how it goes."

"Thanks. You'll be the first to know."

"See you tonight at your party," he said as he strolled away. "I'll buy you a drink no matter what the verdict."

"Deal."

Her inbox had no sympathy for the fact that today was her birthday and she had celebrating to do. By the time she was able to head to the break room, not only had she missed cupcakes for breakfast, it was well past lunch.

"Surprise!" said Jules and Ren as she walked in. Lexy put her hand on her thundering heart. They'd caught her totally off guard.

Ren passed her a cupcake with a sparkler.

"Red velvet? My favorite. You guys are the best." Lexy gave her friends a three-way hug. "Also, kudos on the decorations." She licked at some of the frosting. "How did you know I was coming here now?"

"We pay our spies well," said Jules.

"I'll say." Just as Lexy took a bite of her cupcake Stan poked his head in the door. "Her Highness wants to meet with you now Lexy. You might want to hurry."

Lexy widened her eyes at Jules and Ren as she hastily swallowed. "Showtime," she said, trying for confidence over terror.

"Wait!" Jules grabbed her, swung her around and wiped her mouth with a napkin. "Icing on your face. Not the impression you want to make."

"Thanks. Close one. Anything else? Toilet paper stuck to my shoe?"

"Nope, you're good."

She figured things were off to a good start when she made it to Merelda's office without tripping, dropping her laptop, or bringing her cupcake up for another look.

Joey must be at lunch. She took a deep breath and knocked on Merelda's open door.

"Come in."

Lexy brushed a fingertip across her gran's ring – Constance Smith would not have been intimidated by Merelda – and strode into the room. "Thank you for making time to see me."

"Yes, yes. Make it quick." Merelda barely looked up.

"I have something I'd like to show you," Lexy said, the quiver in her voice barely noticeable. "An idea I've been working on. But I thought rather than tell you, this would give you a better picture."

She walked around Merelda's desk, placing her laptop where they could both see the screen. Merelda raised her brows over Lexy's bold act, but said nothing as the video started.

"I see that's you on here. Not angling for a job in front of the camera, I hope."

Lexy shook her head, then held her breath. She was torn between watching the video, mentally willing it to be as good as she hoped, and gauging Merelda's reaction. Though the scarier of the two choices, she kept a stealthy eye on her boss.

Merelda was not easy to read. Her eyes narrowed in concentration as she studied the screen. Was that a glimmer of interest? Was it possible Merelda leaned a smidge closer? That would be a good sign. Unless it was an eyesight issue.

"Well," Merelda said, as the video finished, unfortunately frozen on an unflattering image of Lexy's face. "What do you expect me to do with this?"

Make it an award-winning TV show? No, don't say that to the boss.

"I have information here." She passed Merelda the portfolio she had painstakingly put together. "Research and statistics on relationships, marriage and divorce rates, and a raft of other information that supports a show of this nature drawing the interest of a sizeable viewing audience."

Unblinking, Merelda's eyes met hers, her expression inscrutable. As an intimidation tactic, it was extremely effective. A look that usually sent Lexy scurrying. But not today.

"Online dating sites and apps have continued to see a rise in users. People don't just marry their high school sweetheart any more. They have multiple relationships in their quest to find true love. And the search for their 'one' consumes a lot of time, energy and thought for those still looking." Since she hadn't been shoo-ed or shushed, she continued.

"I bet there isn't a person alive who doesn't have at least one niggle of 'what if' about someone from their past.

Which is why I think the format of this show will appeal to viewers. Watching a contestant get a second chance at love. The way they fantasize they might."

"And the ones who have already found love? Why would they tune in to a show like this?"

"Everyone loves a happy ending. Well, that coupled with drama and anticipation."

After a lengthy silence during which Lexy waited for a sudden beheading, Merelda said, "Is anyone out there doing anything remotely similar?"

She shook her head. "No. I've done a thorough search nationally and internationally."

"How many episodes do you envision?"

"As per my budget sheet you have there, I was planning for seven. An opening, five individual contestant episodes, and a finale."

"And what are we calling this piece of brilliance?" Merelda said.

She took a breath, praying Merelda loved the show's title as much as she did. "I'm calling it *The One That Got Away*," she said in a rush.

"*The One that Got Away*," Merelda said with a sniff. "It sounds like a fishing show."

"It's a well-known dating expression, too," Lexy said, defending her idea. "Like the expression, 'plenty more fish in the sea.'"

"It won't work. Don't you have anything else?"

Panicked, all Lexy's brain could think of was joking with Nate about calling it *Cruise Into Love*. She couldn't suggest that. Reluctantly she shook her head, seeing her dream evaporating like morning mist on the Sound.

Merelda drummed the desk with her nails. "What's the name of that little fat cherub with the bow and arrow?"

"Cupid?"

"Right. We need Cupid in the show's title. That way we can use him on the logo."

"But won't people think the show's about Valentine's Day?"

Merelda shot her a look. "Better that than fish. Besides, why would they?"

Lexy shrank. Cupid it was. "I'll work that into a new title." She held her breath. Did this mean the show was going ahead? And she just needed a new title? She was afraid to ask, in case by questioning it she jinxed everything.

"See that you do. I want a clever, catchy, Cupid name on my desk by tomorrow. Now, who, other than Renata and Jules O'Shay, knows about this idea of yours?"

"Nate Douglas has been a big help, including the filming."

"Hmph. I don't know what a sound tech who, last I heard is single, knows about a relationship show," Merelda said. "But he does know sound. Play it again."

After that, everything passed in a blur. A really lovely blur. The type usually reserved for Disney Princesses toward the end of the movie.

Following the second viewing, before she had time to grasp that Merelda had approved her idea, pending a new title, The Queen was issuing rapid-fire instructions.

As she struggled to process this was really happening, she caught snippets of her boss's commands. "....Enrico will be your director...", "If we have seven episodes we can fit it in...It's the end of September and I want the first episode to air in November..."

Wait, November? Not this November! There was too much to do first.

Merelda was still making pronouncements. "We'll have

the grand finale of Season One just before Christmas. Everyone starts watching Hallmark movies after that anyway. With a Special Bonus episode on Valentine's Day. Cash in on that Cupid hype." Lexy also caught something about 'awards season' and 'launching a dark horse'.

Merelda's words ran together. Finally, she was going to produce her own show. Best birthday ever! No tub full of Guinness required.

"You wanted to see me, Merelda?" Enrico filled the doorway looking tall, dark, and impossibly handsome. She closed her eyes, recalling his earlier kiss.

"I'm at your service. Both of you." He flashed her a smile and her insides turned to molten honey. Her heart sped up.

Merelda sniffed, ice-blue gaze behind her glasses like a dash of cold water. "I hope you're up to this latest challenge. Both of you. Until now, MHP has made a point of steering clear of live TV. Too many things can go wrong." Her eyes skewered Lexy. "Don't make me regret that policy lapse."

She looked at Enrico, her new director. She couldn't wait to see Smug Sonia's face.

CHAPTER 10

"Why y'all gotta ghost me after two dates? Why can't you just say 'Hazel, I'm intimidated by your fierce combination of intelligence and hotness.' Or whatever."

-Hazel, Guest
Duquan's Downlow on Dating and Love
Podcast episode #67

Nate finished wrangling the cords, one of the less glamorous aspects of his job, and made sure all the microphone batteries were charging for the next production. He glanced at his phone. Still no word from Lexy.

Oh man, if Her Royal Highness rejected this latest proposal, the birthday girl was going to be in no mood for celebrating. Which was too bad, because Ren and Jules had gone all out planning her party.

Nate sat down at one of the computers in the sound

booth to check his email, surprised to see one from Enrico in his inbox.

From: enrico.rossi@MHproductions.com
To: nate.douglas@MHproductions.com
Subject: Looking for a Senior Sound Tech

Hey, man,
Lexy said you helped with her proposal, so I hope you don't object if I drag you over to work with us. Nothing but the best, I always say. Plus, you already know the premise. We're keeping things tightly under wraps. Chat more soon, E

What the—? A grin split Nate's face.
She did it!
And Merelda must be pumped if she's already got a director on board. Nate's excitement for Lexy was only slightly dampened by not hearing about it from her first. But she'd let him know when she could. It looked like filming sample clips in the garage had paid off, and they could drink to their success together at her party.

His smile faded as he re-read the email and Enrico's tone got his back up. The director sounded like he was already calling the shots. Nate had seen Merelda's 'Golden Boy' in action before; Enrico was used to getting his own way and dominating the operation. Nate didn't want Lexy pushed aside on her own show.

"Congratulations, champ." His boss Ian, cut into his thoughts. "Pretty big deal; a personal request to be involved in this top-secret new show."

"Thanks, I just saw the email."

"Smith's first swing in the big leagues as producer.

Merelda must really think it's something, to keep it so hush hush."

"It's a fresh idea, for sure."

"Lucky birthday girl. Her wish was granted before she even blew out her candles. Producing her own show with Enrico directing."

Nate hesitated. "You think he's a good director for her to work with?"

"Are you kidding?" Ian propped a shoulder against the doorframe and crossed his arms. "He's got the Midas touch. Bet she'll be ready to celebrate. See you at the restaurant tonight?"

"I'll be there. Now I guess I'll be getting her two celebratory drinks."

"I'll figure out who should take over for you here, then let you know so you can transition them."

Nate nodded. "Sounds good."

By the time he finished the day's sound edits and accompanying notes, he still hadn't heard from Lexy.

She was probably caught up in a million details. Judging by Enrico's email, they were hitting the ground running. But still. How long did it take to send a text? Maybe she wanted to tell him in person.

He checked his watch. Still a little time before the party, but not enough to bother going home. What he didn't want was to show up early and get roped into setting up. Marcie always said he had a knack for getting out of those kinds of things. Speaking of Marcie, maybe his sister had time to meet up. He sent a quick text.

NATE

Hey sis, you free for an after-work drink?

MARCIE

Only if after work is at 7 AM. I'm pulling a
double at the hospital :(

Since Marcie was out, he'd see if Adam was still working on that job site nearby.

THE FAMILIAR SMELL of beer and nachos greeted Nate and Adam at their favorite little hole-in-the-wall. They snagged a table and ordered a couple of pale ales. As soon as they sat down, Adam started tapping his thigh with his fingers, like it was an imaginary keyboard. A habit Adam didn't even notice he was doing half the time.

"I heard Black Pistol Fire are coming to town," Adam said. "Playing the Paramount. We should get tickets."

"Definitely. They make their gritty garage rock sound so slick. And Kevin's vocals are something else."

"Did you know he and Eric have known each other even longer than you and Connor? They've been friends since kindergarten."

Nate smiled. "Trust you to know random facts about the band."

"Steel trap for music facts," Adam grinned and tapped the side of his head. "Any word on Lexy's show thing? The one you were filming in the garage?"

"Yeah. She got her birthday wish. HRH approved Lexy's pitch and already has a director lined up."

"Go Lexy." Adam took a sip of his draught and wiped leftover foam off his lip. "She must be stoked."

"I guess. I haven't talked to her yet."

Adam raised his brow and resumed tapping his fingers

to the music. "I figured, with how much you helped her, you would have been one of her first calls."

Nate shrugged.

Adam rested his forearms on the table, hands around his pint glass, a serious expression on his face. "Anything going on between you two?"

"What? Me and Lexy? No."

"Just asking."

"We're just friends."

"Hmph." Adam didn't sound convinced.

Nate straightened. "I liked helping her. I'm glad her idea worked out. But friends is the extent of it."

Adam looked at him for a long time before saying quietly, "I know Adele did a number on you, but you've got to let that shit go, brother."

"Let it go?" Nate began shredding the cardboard coaster. "Adele didn't just do a number on *me*. That 'shit' impacted all of us."

"Lexy doesn't strike me as the jealous type."

Nate shook his head and stared into his beer. "Neither did Adele. And look how that turned out."

"She might not have come across that way, but there was something about her..."

"What do you mean?"

"When you were with Adele, it's like instead of living your life, instead of defeating King Koopa and beating the level, you were off rescuing Princess Peach."

"What's with the Super Mario Brothers reference? Does anyone even still play that?"

"It seemed the most appropriate. There are no princesses in Call of Duty. And to answer your question, they do, though they mostly play Mario Kart. But that's beside the point." Adam took a sip of his beer. "Let's liken

Adele to Princess Leia then, if you prefer that analogy. Except *she* chained herself to Jabba the Hutt so you had to play Han Solo and rescue her."

"Adam, I'm not even one beer in, and I'm struggling to decipher your video game and movie references."

"My references are totally on point. Look man, what Adele did sucked—"

"Sucked?" Nate struggled to keep his voice down. "It was way worse than 'sucked'. We had to go on hiatus, re-brand ourselves with a new name, and start over from scratch. All because my girlfriend couldn't handle the amount of time I spent rehearsing. Or the girls in the audience who came out to watch us play." Nate angrily pushed away the pile of shredded coaster pieces. "At least if I date a musician—"

"I know, I know," Adam sighed. "We've heard it before. Someone in the industry will understand the time you need to dedicate to the Astronauts. She'll get that the female fans are just that. Fans."

"How did we even get on this topic?"

"You keeping Lexy in the 'friend zone' because she's not a musician." Adam shot him a grin, cutting the tension. "I guess our list of failed musician couples the other day didn't convince you?"

"What about Jay-Z and Beyonce?" Nate sipped his beer with a smug grin. No way could Adam refute that legendary power couple of the music world.

Adam barked out a laugh. "Dude, and I say this with love, you will never be the next Jay-Z."

Nate laughed too. "Let's just keep the fact that I compared myself to one of the best hip-hop artists of all time between us. Otherwise, I'll never live it down."

"I make no promises." Adam drained the last of his pint

and smirked at Nate. "Hey Jay-Z, don't you have a party to get to?"

Nate checked his watch. "You're right. Want to come? I know Lexy'd be happy to see you."

"You know that, do you?"

"Same as I know you're a dick," he said affectionately. "So do I tell her I'm disappointed she didn't share her good news?"

"Not on her birthday, asshole."

Right.

ARRIVING AFTER THE 'TEPID TWENTY', once people had warmed up, and leaving before things got sloppy was a party strategy that had never let him down.

Inside the doorway, Adam let out a whistle. "It looks like someone bought out the entire blue section at the party store."

"It's her favorite color," Nate said, looking around for familiar faces. The restaurant's private function room was packed, and guests spilled out onto the patio. "Jules and Ren sure know how to throw a party."

"Decent tunes too," Adam said, as "Bust A Move" by Young MC gave way to Journey's "Don't Stop Believin'".

Nate agreed. "Nothing kills a good party faster—"

"Than a lousy playlist" Nate and Adam finished in unison.

"Hey, there's Danielle," Adam nodded in the direction of a stunning brunette in a sleek black dress. "We met at music trivia a few months ago." He clapped Nate on the shoulder. "I'll catch up with you in a bit."

Nate fingered the surf-themed birthday card tucked in

his jacket pocket as he scanned the room for the guest of honor. Marcie had told him not to ruin the perfect card with a generic message, so he'd pulled up the Daisy Jordan music video Lexy was in and caught a screen grab with Lexy's bright blonde ponytail clearly visible. He'd printed the image and glued it inside her card. Then he'd circled her hair and drawn an arrow to where he'd written, 'Move over ponytail, Lexy's got a new claim to fame when her show hits the air'.

He hadn't given her the card when he saw her this morning. Lexy wasn't the only one worried about things getting jinxed.

"You look like you need a beer." Ian appeared at his side. "I'm getting a round for the noise boys. Come on." Nate followed Ian, passing a table laden with cards, gifts, and bouquets of flowers. He'd rather give his card to her in person.

"Lexy's new show is the big buzz," Ian said as they waited at the bar. "Everyone is trying to get it out of the tipsy birthday girl what the show is about, but mum's the word. It's still under wraps." Ian handed him a beer.

"Don't think you can bribe the secret out of me with only one beer," Nate said with a laugh. "Any news on a time-frame for production?"

"I heard Merelda wants it to hit the air in November, with several episodes in the can."

Nate almost choked. "That's not possible. No one launches a show in only six weeks."

"And no one says 'no' to The Queen."

"This exciting new show I was brought over for just got a lot more stressful."

"Which reminds me, Simon's taking over for you. I'll leave you guys to work out a transition plan."

"Sounds good. Thanks for the drink." Nate lifted his bottle in a salute. "I'd better go congratulate the new producer."

He glanced around the room for Lexy. Ren was off to one side with a guy he'd never seen before. They were standing close together, not a moment he wanted to interrupt.

Jules was holding court on the other side of the room, in one of her colorful outfits that only she could pull off. When he asked if she'd seen Lexy, she paused long enough to point him in the direction of the patio.

He stepped outside. Lexy stood leaning against the railing in a photo worthy moment with the sky joining the celebration and creating a backdrop of red and purple streaks above the golden glow from the last of the autumn sunset. He started toward her, then stopped. She wasn't alone. A man's dark head was bent toward hers in what appeared to be an intimate conversation.

Enrico.

Whatever he said made her laugh. Nate's eyes narrowed at Enrico's answering chuckle. Was this how the director got his way? Flirting and charming the producers into agreeing with him. Nate's hands started to clench before he shook his head. Lexy deserved more credit than that.

He started to back away. He'd find her later to congratulate her. But before he'd taken two steps his foot connected with an iron umbrella stand, the clatter overloud in the still evening air.

Shit! So much for a stealth getaway.

The pair turned his way.

"Nate." Lexy hurried toward him. "Can you believe it?"

To cover his blunder, he walked forward to meet them. "I never had any doubt," he said as he gave her a hug. She gave him an extra tight squeeze back.

"And you didn't even jinx it by telling me," he added with a teasing grin.

She laughed. "Must've been the pinky swear."

"Pinky swear?" said Enrico.

Lexy just smiled and shook her head.

Enrico extended a hand in his direction "Lexy said you played a big role helping her with the proposal. Well done. Glad to have you on board."

"Thanks." He shook Enrico's hand. "I'm happy to be part of Lexy's team." He emphasized 'Lexy's team' so Enrico knew whose side he was on. As a director, Enrico had a rep for shifting the spotlight to himself and his vision, often overriding the voice of a show's creator. So subtly, they didn't see it until it was too late. Enrico might outrank him, but he figured his moral support would help Lexy stick to her guns if push came to shove.

Enrico nodded. "I'll see you two inside." He gave Lexy's shoulder a squeeze before walking away.

"Congratulations!" Nate clinked his beer bottle against her champagne flute. "It's a double celebration now."

"Thanks. I was so nervous when I went in to meet with Merelda today." He listened as she described how her pitch went, words pouring out of her quickly, matched by wide, expressive hand gestures. He barely managed to save his beer from getting knocked out of his hand.

"And then she hit me with one of her signature withering looks, which would normally send me scurrying away, but not today. Instead, I—"

Nate smiled. He might have been upset she hadn't shared her good news with him first, but as she regaled him with her story of matching wits with The Queen, it was hard to stay that way.

"Then Enrico told me we're getting you—" she pointed

at him, "—for our sound tech. I'm so glad. There wouldn't *be* a show without you!"

"Aw shucks," he said with mock bashfulness.

"It's just been the best day," she continued. "And now all these people are here to celebrate my birthday."

"Speaking of." He pulled her card from his pocket and handed it to her. "Happy birthday."

"You got me a surfing card? I love it!" She laughed out loud as her eyes scanned the message inside. "Did you just throw shade at my ponytail?"

"I would never," he said as she came at him for another hug.

Just then someone called Lexy's name from the doorway.

She turned. "Duke?"

"Happy birthday, Lexycakes." The newcomer reached them in three long strides and engulfed her in a bear hug. This must be the guy Lexy had talked about that day they were filming.

"Is Paul with you?" Lexy peered behind him.

"No. He had something else on. He sends his best wishes and a birthday hug."

"That's sweet." She patted the other guy's arm. "Duke, I want you to meet Nate, a friend from work. Nate, Duke is a friend of mine from Oregon."

"Nice to meet you." Nate's hand was gripped in a firm, friendly handshake.

"And this," Duke handed Lexy a small wrapped gift the size and shape of a hockey puck, "is for you, even though neither of us is getting in the water for your birthday this year. Can't break tradition."

"My birthday surf wax." She clasped the package in both hands and turned to Nate. "Duke and I met surfing. I couldn't believe it when he called and told me he had moved to the city. I never thought he would leave the Oregon coast. Except he fell in love, and when I met Paul I could totally see why."

"I'm glad I made the move," Duke said. "It means I get to be with you for your birthday. Didn't you have some elaborate plan you were trying to pull off today?"

"My pitch to my boss. Nate's the one who helped with the whole idea," she said, one hand fluttering in his direction. "This morning, I thought I must be crazy for making my deadline today, of all days. But it worked out. The Queen said yes. You are now looking at Manor House's newest producer." She executed a dramatic curtsy.

Duke chuckled. "I am suitably impressed, Lexycakes. Congratulations."

Nate had been trying to place Duke's accent. Jamaican? Some other island in the Caribbean? He'd love to record that voice.

"Your tips for filming were really helpful," Lexy said to Duke, snugging an arm around his waist affectionately.

Nate nodded. "Lexy mentioned you during her shoot. You're a counsellor of some sort?"

"That's right." Duke's deep voice reverberated through the night air.

"If you ever want to change careers, the radio would love you."

"Doesn't Duke have the greatest voice? I told him once he could read me the history of calculus, and I wouldn't be bored listening to him."

"Let's hope my podcast listeners agree."

"Duke's relationship podcast is super popular." Pride rang through her voice. "I thought he should name it *Everything I Need to Know About Love I Learned from Surfing*, but

Duke told me that was too long." As Lexy laughed, Duke smiled down at her. Clearly, lots of history between these two.

"I'll have to check out your podcast."

"It's called *Duquan's Downlow on Dating and Love.*"

"Good name. I'll remember."

"Speaking of names, what's your show going to be called, Lexy?" Duke asked.

She heaved a sigh. "I had the best show title picked out. But I was keeping it secret, because, you know."

"You didn't want to jinx it," Nate and Duke said in unison.

She nodded. "But it doesn't matter anymore, because Merelda hated it."

"What was it?" Duke asked.

"*The One That Got Away.*"

"Great title," Nate said. "She didn't like it?"

"Too much like a fishing show." She rolled her eyes. "Now she wants a new title on her desk by tomorrow."

"I told you. You should have gone with *Level Up My Love Life,*" Nate said with a wink.

She turned to Duke. "Nate has been providing me an ever-expanding list of awful titles."

"*Dating Do-Over,*" Nate suggested.

"*Try Again for True Love,*" Duke said.

"You two are terrible. The thing is," she turned serious, "I love the way that title pops."

"It's clear you need our help." Nate exchanged a sly grin with Duke.

"True." Duke nodded, a serious expression on his face. "Given your suggestion for my podcast name, we know you like long titles." He stroked his chin as if thinking. "What about *Lexy Grants a Second Chance at Love....*?"

"*...to People Who Missed it the First Time,*" Nate added.

"*...and Now Have Regrets,*" Duke finished.

"It's got a real ring to it," Nate said.

"Your boss might love it."

She burst into laughter and raised her champagne glass. "A toast. To *Lexy Grants a Second Chance at Love to People who Missed it the First Time and Now Have Regrets.*" Duke and Nate clinked their beer bottles to her glass, then each took a sip.

"Now *that's* a catchy title." They all started laughing.

From the corner of his eye, Nate spotted a figure sticking to the shadows, inching their way to the door and the boisterous party inside. Sonia! How much had she overheard? He wouldn't put it past Lexy's ambitious co-worker to try and steal the show out from under her.

Over his dead body.

CHAPTER 11

"Nothing good ever comes from texting your ex at 3 a.m. Trust me."

-Savannah, Guest
Duquan's Downlow on Dating and Love
Podcast episode #18

Lexy woke up extra early the next morning. To think she'd been dreading turning thirty. She executed her version of a victory dance while lying in bed, replaying the moment Merelda had approved her show.

With a gasp she bolted upright, remembering what had woken her up out of a deep sleep at 3 a.m. Merelda had demanded a new show title by today. While she slept, her brain had been working away on the problem. It woke her in the middle of the night with the idea of combining the Cupid Merelda demanded, with part of Nate and Duke's joking show title.

Cupid Grants a Second Chance. It was perfect. It conjured romance, it rhymed, it was catchy. Maybe even a better title than her original one.

"Merelda *has* to like this one. And Smug Sonia can slink back to her cubicle."

Thanks to Nate's warning, she knew to be on guard. As if she wasn't already around that woman. This new title would cement her role as MHP's newest producer. The icing on the cake of yesterday's success.

She smiled as she flopped back onto her pillow. Her birthday party had been so much fun; all the happy faces and congratulations, the laughter, the champagne. The impromptu dance party later in the evening.

To top things off, Enrico had not only come to her party, he had driven her home. She smiled at the bouquet on her bedside table. From Enrico. Maybe this was his subtle way of signaling his interest, having watched her from afar, waiting until she was no longer involved with Jameson.

So why no kiss when he dropped her off? She'd been too caught off guard to react to his kiss in the morning. Maybe he'd taken her surprise as disinterest.

Argh! She was doing it again. Overthinking things that weren't worth her time and energy, instead of focusing on the positives. When she went to work today, it would be as producer on her own show. Alongside Enrico. No reason to think good things can't come to those who wait.

Including the relationship of her dreams.

Since it was still early, she extended her birthday joy with coffee in bed while she opened her cards. Re-reading Nate's made her laugh out loud. She couldn't believe he'd actually printed her photo from the music video. And when she'd told him Merelda approved the show...hmmm. Why couldn't she remember his reaction? She'd shared every minute detail at the party. But before that—

She'd promised to tell him first. Why did she have no memory of their conversation?

She grabbed her phone. Her heart pounded. No outgoing call to Nate yesterday. A heavy weight squashed her chest as she pulled up her text history. She could barely swallow as she read their last text; his encouraging, *you got this.*

Ooooooooooooooh shiiiiiiiiiiiiiiit.

He'd congratulated her right away when she saw him at the party. Which meant he'd heard it from someone else.

How could she forget to tell Nate?

Worst. Friend. Ever!

She flung back the covers and swung her legs over the side. Her feet landed with a thud. Friday he was usually in meetings before he left for the studio. Hopefully she could get to work early, find him and apologize.

FINDING NATE WOULD HAVE to wait. As she passed the boardroom she heard a knock on the window. Seeing Enrico gesturing her to join him, her heart gave a little flutter. Her insides sighed in anticipation.

The room was dwarfed by a conference table that seated a dozen or more. This focal point, crafted from a huge northwest-grown tree was typical Merelda. Rather than buy something already made, she'd hired a wood artist to turn the slab into a functional work of art, complete with knot holes and a bark-roughened edge. Balanced on curving driftwood legs, the whole ensemble had been finished with a shiny, clear lacquer.

Lexy, Jules, and Ren secretly called it The Round Table, because only her chosen ones were invited to sit at it. Whenever Merelda held department meetings in here, Lexy and the other lower-class denizens of Manor House crowded around the edges of the room.

Enrico had removed his jacket and rolled his shirt sleeves up past his elbows. "Grab your laptop and whatever else you need. This is us until we move into the studio."

"Ummm, sure." She needed to find Nate, but the significance of working at the Round Table was not lost as she grabbed her stuff and hurried back.

Enrico didn't look up. "I've sent you a short list of potential hosts. Look over their CV's and get back to me."

"Right." She hoped she sounded focused while she tried to keep an eye out for passers-by.

"Merelda has given us the green light to cherry pick our crew. I took the liberty of emailing Nate and Ian yesterday first off, letting them know we want Nate for sound."

"First off." Lexy's stomach dropped.

Please don't let that be how Nate found out.

Enrico glanced up. "I told you I talked to him yesterday. I assumed you'd want Nate on this, since he's already involved."

Yesterday she hadn't realized an impersonal email to him and his boss qualified as 'talking to', or that that was the first he heard of her show getting approved. She pasted on a cheerful smile. "You're right. I was going to suggest him."

"See? We are on the same page already." Enrico gave her his winning smile and her heart smiled back. She liked being on Enrico's page.

Just then, Nate passed by. His meeting must be over early. She jumped to her feet. "I'll just grab a coffee first."

From the door she turned to catch Enrico's frown. "Can I get you one?"

"I'm all set." He lifted his full mug, the frown still creasing his handsome features.

She hesitated. She didn't want Enrico to think she wasn't fully invested. But she had to talk to Nate. She hurried down the hall just as the roar of a motorcycle sounded outside. She was too late. She'd missed him.

She'd barely settled in at the conference table and sent Merelda a hurried email with the new show title, when Ren joined them. Lexy's inbox already overflowed with emails from Enrico; ideas on which of Manor House's studios to use, which cameramen, and a myriad of other details that she'd learned about in film school.

No worries. I've got this. It's just like riding a bike...I hope.

Except getting back on a bike was much easier than building the bike when she wasn't sure she had all the parts.

She frantically scribbled notes as Enrico and Ren tossed around names and expressions, trying to keep track of the conversation and important details.

"Who's scripting?" Ren asked.

"I've asked Johnson and Riley."

Ren nodded. "Those two are good."

"We'll need plants in the studio audience."

"Plants?" Lexy looked up, puzzled. Surely, he didn't mean house plants?

Ren nodded again and typed herself a note. "For social, with such a short lead up time, I suggest a three-pronged approach." Ren began outlining her ideas, starting with a 'whisper campaign', whatever that was, and quickly blowing things up to a 'feeding frenzy'.

Lexy glanced down at her list. Some of the expressions were familiar, but the rest seemed to be MHP in-house shorthand. Shorthand she hadn't been privy to in the grant proposal writing dungeon.

Ren scrolled through her tablet. "To have the most impact, I need to know what's more important. The contestants or the audience?"

Lexy and Enrico spoke at the same time.

"The contestants," Lexy said.

"The viewers," Enrico said.

They exchanged a look.

"It's all about the ratings," Enrico said. "Without satisfied viewers, we don't have the ratings. Without good ratings, we don't have a show."

Lexy's throat tightened and her mouth went dry. Enrico wasn't wrong, but the contestants and their stories were what would bring the audience back episode after episode, making *them* more important. Yet she couldn't get the words out.

"In order for the show to succeed, the viewers are the priority."

For the first time, Lexy saw another side to Enrico. Gone was the charming man who called her Bella and bantered with her. This was the Enrico other people at Manor House talked about. The firm, opinionated, self-assured Enrico. Who expected things done his way.

Ren gave her a look, waiting for her to defend her position. The words wouldn't come. She felt like she was back in grade school when the teacher called on her in class and she didn't know the answer.

She straightened her shoulders and lifted her head. If she didn't speak up now, it would get even harder. "You make a valid point, Enrico."

"I'm glad we are in agreement."

Ren watched her closely.

"But the contestants are also extremely important," Lexy added.

"Of course they are," Enrico said smoothly. "Go ahead and focus on the audience with your campaign, Renata."

Lexy sagged, disappointed with herself for not saying more. Then forced herself to listen and learn as Enrico and Ren ironed out additional details with an audience focus. This was her show! The others might know more than she did, but she'd learn.

No sooner did Ren leave than Merelda swept into the conference room. "How are things going in here?"

"I'd say we're off to a good start," Enrico said.

She felt the heat of Merelda's gaze. "Coming up with an idea is one thing, Smith. Executing it is a whole other process." Merelda moved to stand at the window looking at the view, her back to Lexy. "I've got a lot riding on this. Important people will be watching to see how the show does and I need it to be a success. I'm trusting your inexperience won't be a problem." Merelda turned to face her. "If you think it will, let me know now and I'll put someone else on *Cupid Grants a Second Chance*. Sonia approached me this morning with some title suggestions of her own. She's keen to take the helm."

Merelda likes the title!

Lexy silently cheered, then sobered. How dare Sonia try to hijack her hard work and claim the glory for herself? Sonia didn't even know what the show was about, yet she was pitching titles? The nerve. "I'm absolutely ready to take this on."

"Enrico?"

"If Lexy says she can do it, then she can."

"Remember, it's your neck on the line, too. I hope you've got this in hand." With that, she exited the boardroom, the tapping of her high heels loudly ominous in the silence following her departure.

Lexy avoided Enrico's gaze. How naïve to think all she had to do was come up with the brilliant idea and the other details would magically fall into place.

That Merelda would mentor her.

Sure, and if I sing to them, cute forest animals will come to help with my chores, too.

"Perfect timing. Our sushi is here," Enrico said, checking an alert on his phone. "I hope you don't mind that I ordered for us. It's a working lunch today."

So much for phoning Nate at lunch.

"Don't make any evening plans for the next while either," Enrico said as he unpacked the delivery bag. "Working late is the only way to meet Merelda's deadline." He didn't sound bothered in the least about giving up his evenings. Did that mean he had no one needing his attention in the evenings?

He waved a hand toward the food. "Ladies first."

She scooped a piece of spicy dynamite roll as well as some green papaya salad and sashimi, watching Enrico from the corner of her eye. Not only did they like the same kinds of sushi, she didn't have to make a decision. She could have one of everything. And spend her evenings with the sexiest director, make that the sexiest man, in her orbit. Not bad for her first day as a thirty-year-old.

She waited for him to fill his plate, still mentally kicking herself for not speaking out more assertively earlier. Enrico may have more experience, but her opinion mattered.

"Hey, Bella" Enrico said gently. "Don't let what Merelda said get you down."He smiled at her over his food.

A jolt like an electric current traveled straight through her heart and down to her toes, warming her all over.

"She's just being Merelda." He reached across the table and captured one of her hands in his. "It's your first time at the helm and you have much to learn, but you've got me."

She melted at the warmth in his eyes and the kindness in his voice. So supportive. She truly was living her dream.

"Look how we've been in agreement over everything so far today. We are simpatico, you and I. The start of a beautiful partnership."

Did he mean partnership or *partnership?* It felt so natural, her hand captured in his, the two of them sharing a meal. Like she'd waited for this her entire life. Days and nights with Enrico, drowning in his espresso-dark eyes, as he whispered encouraging words.

CHAPTER 12

"Flirting is an Olympic sport in Italy. I spent a semester abroad, I should know."

-Vivian, Guest
Duquan's Downlow on Dating and Love
Podcast episode #104

"Ciao, Bella. A good first day," Enrico said as they walked to the parking lot together. His eyes found hers over the roof of his Porsche. "And by the way, I'm breaking you in easy."

Words that could be interpreted a variety of different ways.

She slid into her MINI, glad she'd driven. No way could she face transit. In spite of the surge of adrenalin she got from Enrico's presence, trying to integrate all the information for her new role had tired her out as much as running a half marathon. There was one more thing she needed to do. She pulled out her phone and called Nate.

"Well, well, well. Nice to know you haven't forgotten us little people," he answered. "How's my favorite local producer?"

"Only your favorite *local* producer? I'm going to have to change that. Are you free right now?"

"What did you have in mind?"

"Fall Fest kicks off tonight. Food trucks, local artist booths, mulled apple cider, largest pumpkin contest. Want to check it out? Confession. I'm luring you there so I can ply you with an apology slice of apple pie."

WAITING FOR NATE, the familiar sounds and smells of the festival gave her a second wind. Roasting hotdogs, popping corn and cotton candy took her back in time.

"Glad I'm on my bike," he said when he joined her. "Parking is impossible."

His hair was mussed from his helmet, and running a hand through it only made it worse. She smiled. Unlike Enrico, whose hair was always perfect.

After winding their way through the booths and food trucks, they settled onto on a bale of hay, balancing hotdogs, cobs of corn, and apple pie. Kids with face paint and balloon animals racing by laughing. They ate, entertained by a juggling street performer riding a unicycle.

As Nate popped the last bite of hotdog in his mouth, she set her paper plate in her lap and gave his forearm a light squeeze.

"Nate, I'm so sorry. I hope the apple pie makes up for the

fact that I didn't tell you the second Merelda approved my show. When I saw you at my party and you already knew, I thought I'd told you. This morning it hit me I hadn't kept my promise. I felt sick about it all day."

He cleared his throat. "I'll admit, it stung to get Enrico's email before I heard it from you. But Adam told me not to be a jerk and say anything last night."

"That's more than I deserve."

"I stopped being upset after hearing your version of the pitch, excited hand gestures and all."

"I still feel bad." She toyed with the heel of her bun, suddenly not hungry.

"This pie is delicious." Nate took another bite. "Buy me another slice and apology accepted."

"Are you always this nice?"

"I'm excited for you. And happy I'll be in studio to see what a great job you do."

"If I last that long," she said with a sigh.

"Bad first day?" He balled up their wrappers and paper plates and tossed them in the trash.

"'Specially after such a great day yesterday."

"Why don't you get me that second piece of apology pie and tell me all about it."

"Deal. Be right back." She quickly returned with apple pie for Nate and mulled cider for herself.

"Okay, spill it," he said.

She blew on her drink. Where to start? "You were right. Sonia is already weaseling up to Merelda, angling for my job if I can't hack it."

"No surprise there."

"Enrico and I met with Ren today. Strategy meeting." She stared into the distance. "I felt like the worst contestant on *Jeopardy* in a show rigged against me. Ren was racking up all the big points and I was still trying to figure out what the categories were."

He made a sympathetic noise.

She took a sip of her cider. "Do you know what a three-pronged approach is?"

"Should I?"

"How about plants in the audience?"

"Like for decor?"

She let out a shaky laugh. "So, it's not just me."

"It was your first day. You'll find your footing."

"I hope so. Ren was really helpful, but she's not going to be with me every day."

"Speaking of Ren," he said as he polished off his pie, "who was she locking lips with at your party last night?"

"Ren was kissing someone and I missed it? It must have been Darius. We don't think he'll last long. He's into CrossFit."

"Ah."

She slid off the bale. "Should we go look for big pumpkins?"

"Sure." They strolled past booths of local paintings, pottery and jewelry. "What else happened?"

"Producing my own show is my dream, but I felt like I knew nothing, especially compared to everyone else. Topped off by Merelda asking me if I should maybe step down. On my first day." She tilted her head back and stared into the sky. "What was I even doing there?"

He gave her arm a gentle shake. "Wrong, Lex. You're the person who knows best how to make this show work. You need to channel your inner Rocky."

"I don't think sports analogies work for me."

"Okay, but you surf, right? Who's the best surfer?"

"Kelly Slater," she said, then paused. "Or John John Florence."

He smirked. "I should have known better than to ask you to pick just one. We'll go with Slater."

"Okay. He's got good psychological game, too."

"Excellent. That will help you hold your own against Enrico. He's not a jerk, but he *is* used to calling the shots."

"But he's the one with the experience."

"I have an idea. Are you up for a little B&E?"

"What? You want to break into Enrico's house?"

He laughed. "I said B&E to make it sound bad-ass, but technically it's not breaking in if I have a key."

She cocked her head. "What are you talking about, Nate Douglas?"

"Feel like stopping by the studio? There's a show filming late."

"Kind of like a refresher course? Peek behind the curtain, absorb all the details, so I can crush it when it's my turn." She beamed at him, infused with a fresh burst of energy. "You're a genius."

"That's what I keep telling people."

THE SHOW BEING FILMED WAS a talk show with only a host, his guest, and a handful of crew members working behind the scenes, making it easy to tour Lexy around.

Up in the control room, she stared raptly at the bank of screens that showed various angles of the studio while they shared a spare headset. It was cute to see her eyes widen as she listened to instructions fired at the camera operators by the director, while camera angles changed, zooming in and out. When the show ended, he introduced her to the team as MHP's newest producer. That earned him a huge smile.

"Their show was a different format from yours," he said, as he walked her to her car. "Only two principles and no studio audience, but I thought it would give you an idea of how things run during production. For when it's your turn."

"Things looked very well-coordinated."

"Absolutely. Nothing beats a cohesive team. Starting with the attitudes of the producer and director. The way they treat the crew can make or break the team atmosphere, which impacts production more than you might realize."

She nodded, as if memorizing his words. "Something I want to get right from the start."

"You will."

As long as you keep Enrico in check.

"Thanks for the crime spree." She pulled out her keys. "I learned a lot."

"Thanks for the apology pie. Here's to a better tomorrow for the girl wearing her producer's hat."

"It will be now." She smiled at him, head slightly tilted.

He propped one forearm on the roof of her car. "I've been meaning to ask you, who's in the running for the host? You find your perfect charismatic-secret-weapon-counselor-type yet?"

She pulled a face. "No. And I doubt I'll find her on Enrico's list. They're all attractive, intelligent women with impressive CV's. But they're all so..." she gestured with her hand, as if searching for the right word to describe them.

"Chic, polished professional. Wearing glasses for that smart librarian look?"

"Nailed it. Totally interchangeable."

"Then keep looking," he said. "Unless—" He hesitated.

He could be way off base. But this was Lexy. She needed his help.

"Unless what?"

"You're not sold on any of the women Enrico chose. A hundred more CV's from the same type, and you wouldn't like any of them any better." He paused. "Ever think maybe a male host is what you need?"

"A male host?" she said thoughtfully.

"More specifically, Duquan."

"Duquan," she echoed, as if testing out the idea.

"Not only does the man have presence, he has the best voice I've ever heard. He's qualified. You know you can trust him. He might be unknown to the TV world, but not to you."

"Duquan," she repeated. "I can't believe I didn't think of it myself. Nate, you're a genius."

"For the second time tonight." He laughed. "I should go for a hat trick."

"Thank you, thank you, thank you." She gave him a quick, fierce hug. "I'm going to call Duke right now and see what he says." She slid behind the wheel and rolled down her window. "I forgot to tell you the good thing that happened at work today. Funny enough, I have you and Duke to thank for it."

He leaned in. "What's that?"

"You two goofs actually helped me with a new show title. And Merelda approved."

"Don't keep me in suspense."

"*Cupid Grants a Second Chance.*"

"It's perfect."

"Don't tell anyone else though."

He saluted. "I won't."

"Now let's see if Duke wants to be the host." She held up

one hand. "Listen. It must be a sign." She turned up the radio and mouthed along to Etta James being sampled on a Flo Rida track, about the good feeling she gets sometimes.

He shook his head, smiling as she drove away. If only he could meet someone on Bumble who was as fun and easy to hang out with as Lexy.

CHAPTER 13

"I took my boyfriend for a couple's massage one time.
Romantic, right? Nope. He hated it. Turns out my
boyfriend's idea of 'relaxing' is climbing a mountain. Now I
go to the spa with my mom."

-Elizabeth, Guest
Duquan's Downlow on Dating and Love
Podcast episode #31

Behind her desk Lexy stretched, still relaxed from the spa weekend with her mom, as she considered how to get Duke in for a screen test. He hardly matched Enrico's vision, but once she had Duke on camera Enrico would see he was the right choice. She could always sneak Duke's video in for their focus group, but she shouldn't have to sneak anything.

With Enrico off on some mystery emergency, this was the time to prepare her argument, not plot how to pull one over on him. Call on her inner Kelly Slater. Start by explaining—

"Look at this!" Ren flew into the room and spun her laptop in Lexy's direction. She settled next to her, clearly looking for a reaction.

"How much coffee have you had? And what am I looking at?"

"These, my friend, are the first *Cupid* hopefuls."

Lexy's eyes widened. The screen was packed with thumbnail shots of dozens of men and women. "Really? Already?" She leaned in for a closer look. "I didn't know you'd started recruiting."

"Sometimes I amaze even myself." Ren mimed buffing her fingernails on her blouse front. "My teaser went viral long before I expected it to, and I couldn't hold them off. I wasn't sure what your time was like. You want me to do some preliminary screening or send them to you as they come in?"

"Send them my way. I can't wait to see who applied. If I get snowed under, I'll let you know."

"Sounds good."

Excitement clamored through her as she stared at the screen. *This was really happening!*

Just then Jules walked past. Lexy jumped up and knocked on the window, gesturing her inside.

"What's up?"

"Only a few days in and Lexy's pulling a power play move," Ren said. "She's inviting you into the inner sanctum, to The Round Table."

"Oooh." Jules curtsied before she sat. "I've only got a sec. The real HRH is waiting."

Lexy ignored their teasing. "You know my surfing friend Duquan? He was at my party."

"Sinfully good-looking with a voice to die for?" said Jules.

"That's the one! What do you think about him as the host?"

"I think Enrico will fight you on it," Ren said. "Duquan doesn't match his vision. But it's an inspired idea. He'd be perfect."

"I can't take credit. It was Nate's idea."

Her friends exchanged a look.

"Nate the Great strikes again," said Jules. "And excuse me if I don't feel even a little bit bad Enrico might not get his way this time. I'm guessing he wants the relationship coach version of Elle Woods from *Legally Blonde*. Just more mature and wearing horn-rimmed glasses."

"Bend. Snap!" All three burst out perky imitations of Reese Witherspoon's character, before dissolving into laughter.

"We've seen that movie too many times," said Ren.

"You're bang on though, Jules."

"I'd better run. My vote's Duquan over Love Coach Blonde, one hundred percent. Good luck with Enrico. Tell him I missed him," Jules said with a wink. Then she was gone.

Lexy turned back to Ren. "You really think Duke would be perfect?"

"I think he'd be brilliant. Not to mention he has that charisma you're looking for."

"True. But he's so different from what Enrico's thinking."

Ren pulled a worried frown. "Don't let Enrico intimidate you, Lex. I've seen him work around other producers so subtly that eventually they believe his idea was theirs all along. You're the producer. You have final say."

"I wish someone would tell Enrico that." Lexy laughed

weakly. "And maybe tell Merelda while they're at it? I worry that if we disagree, she'll side with him."

"Or maybe Enrico will agree that Duquan is a great choice, see what a brilliant producer you are for thinking of it, and shower you with gifts and praise. I heard a rumor he's loaded."

"A girl can dream," she said as Ren left. And her dreams weren't far off what Ren had said. To have Enrico recognize her talent, shower her with gifts and a romantic tropical vacation where she teaches him to surf—

"That doesn't look like a work smile, Bella."

If he only knew...

"Ren came by to show me all the video submissions we've received so far. Tons of them."

"You might not be smiling when we have to go through them all," he teased, as he took off his jacket, undid his cuff-links and rolled up his sleeves. She caught her breath as a sprinkling of dark hair emphasized his masculine forearms.

Be still, my beating heart.

Wherever he'd been, it had put him in a good mood. Her eyes narrowed. Was someone making a play for her new crush?

"You all good?" she said casually.

He gave her a puzzled look. "Perfectly fine. Are the audition tapes ready for the test audience?"

"Not quite," she said. "We're waiting on a couple more."

Come on Lexy Slater. You can do this.

"I had an idea." She injected her voice with as much confidence as she could. "I know you envision the host as a woman, someone empathetic and a good listener. But what do you think about a male host, if we find the right one?" Her words spilled out in a rush.

"You have someone in mind?"

"I do. You met Duquan at my birthday."

"I remember. Great voice."

"Yes. And he has a counselling background, plus he's got a huge following on his podcast. I think he'd be great." She held her breath.

"Let's see what the focus group thinks."

All that stress for nothing.

WHILE LEXY WAITED for Enrico to order dinner so they could start screening the submission videos, she texted Nate.

LEXY

How was your date last night?

NATE

How do you know I had a date?

LEXY

No secrets at MHP

NATE

I didn't tell anyone

LEXY

Tom noticed you put on cologne before you left work

NATE

That's how you know? Tom's too nosy

LEXY

So how was it?

NATE

No comment

LEXY

That bad?

NATE

We met for drinks, I thought we were connecting...

LEXY

Then?

NATE

She plays in a band and had a gig after our date

LEXY

You went to her show?

NATE

She invited me

LEXY

Since you're into musicians, I fail to see the horrible part

NATE

She plays in an all-girl goth band

LEXY

SHE DOES NOT!!!!!!!

NATE

At that point we stopped connecting

LEXY

Hahaha. I'm laughing. But I'm sorry

NATE

I guess her band name Nocturnal Nancy should have tipped me off

LEXY

Laughing harder

NATE

You're a peach

LEXY

In other news. Duke is auditioning

NATE

I'm telling you, he's your host

LEXY

Hope E agrees. K gotta run. Working late.
Sorry your date was a bust

NATE

Don't tell Tom anything

"Thai food should be here in an hour." Enrico hung up the phone and turned his chair so he could view the flat screen taking up most of the back wall. "Let's see what we've got."

Her laptop was already set to cast to the TV, so she cued up the first video. Enrico sat back, arms crossed over his chest, one ankle resting on the opposite knee.

"Are those sailboats on your socks?"

"They are."

Her heart purred. That sexy smile was back. "Do you sail? Or just like cute socks?"

"I wouldn't call my socks cute." He wrinkled his nose.

"I don't think there's any other word for them, Enrico."

"Masculine?"

She laughed. "Face it, you've got cute socks."

"This is me graciously changing the topic. Have you ever been sailing?"

She shook her head.

"I'll take you sometime. You'll love it. The wind in your hair. The speed. There's nothing like it."

"That sounds amazing." She pictured a sunny day. Enrico barefoot on the deck, strong, competent hands at the wheel. The breeze ruffling his hair, his eyes unreadable behind dark glasses. Eyes that held a smile just for her. She hit play on the first video before her mind took that fantasy any further.

The girl in the video looked young. Barely old enough to legally order a beer.

"Hi. My name is Summer." She was sweet and obviously nervous, judging by her giggle and the way she twirled her long, curly brown hair around one finger. "I'm really hoping to get on the show, because I don't know how else I might get a second chance with this guy. You see, I don't really know much about him. His name is Parker and he works in construction. We met last year at the Cascades Music Festival at The Gorge."

The girl's speech grew more animated as she described the outdoor concert she had attended with a couple girl-friends, and the cute guy wearing a Bleachers T-shirt who caught her eye during the weekend-long festival.

"I love that band." Summer said with a perky smile. "So I thought it might be, you know, a sign."

Lexy glanced from the screen to Enrico. Did he just roll his eyes? She turned her attention back to Summer, convinced she must have imagined it.

"At first, I was too nervous to talk to him, but by the last day I thought, 'you have to go for it', otherwise you'll never see him again. When he lined up at one of the food trucks I stood behind him and started up a conversation."

Lexy sighed. "Good for you."

With a sigh that echoed Lexy's, Summer recounted how she and Parker listened to the rest of the bands together, then stayed up all night talking.

"When I realized my phone was dead and my friends would be worried, I told him I'd be right back." She'd returned to find an empty campsite. Parker was gone.

Summer's gaze softened, her voice lowered. "I can't stop wondering about him because it seemed like more than chance that we met that weekend." She looked up, directly into the camera. "Maybe if I get on your show, I'll get to see Parker again and find out if there really is something between us."

Enrico made a noise that sounded suspiciously like a snort, although when Lexy looked at him, he appeared nothing but sympathetic.

"I liked her."

"If each of our hopefuls have a story like hers, we'll never get on the air. We'll be too busy trying to track down Parker-with-no-last-name who maybe-maybe-not works in construction."

"But it's an adorable story. The way she worked up her courage to talk to him and they hit it off. The audience will love it. Girls like her; she's our target audience and maybe our target contestant." She smiled, already imagining how it would feel to reunite a ships-who-passed-in-the-night couple like Summer and Parker.

Almost an hour into viewing dozens of submissions, they came across one where the guy ended nearly every sentence with the word 'so', and just kind of trailed off.

"I'm a rock climber, so..."

So, what? Is there something I don't know about rock climbers? Something that's common knowledge?

"One day there was a girl there, so..."

So what did you do?

By the time the video ended, she had counted seventeen times the man had said 'so' and trailed off his sentence.

"Eighteen," Enrico said.

"What?"

"Eighteen times that guy said 'so', in under three minutes."

She burst out laughing. "I only counted seventeen. He must have been nervous, but it was distracting."

Enrico's grin widened. "I work at Manor House Productions, so…"

"I've never produced my own show before, so…"

They both cracked up.

"I don't think he's making the cut, so…"

They went back and forth a few times, each sentence more outrageous than the last.

Thankfully, Enrico answered the door for their food delivery, giving her time to catch her breath.

She jumped up. "We're going to need some plates and cutlery, so…" Who knew Enrico would be so much fun to work with?

She was still chuckling when she returned from the break room. "Smells delicious."

"Ladies first."

She helped herself to a scoop of everything. Enrico did the same, then sat and scootched his chair a little closer to hers. Intentional or not, she refused to be distracted by the heat from his leg brushing hers. Much.

She hit play, and was soon so immersed in the hopefuls' stories, each one different, all so fascinating, she paid little attention to anything else. Not Enrico, sitting so close. Not her millionth cup of coffee. Not her phone, on silent but within reach.

The next hopeful, Ayeesha, was someone she could easily be friends with. The woman had met the love of her life, Dean, working at a summer camp eight years ago. The prestigious camp drew international staff, and Lexy chuckled as Ayeesha said her summer goal had been to kiss a guy from as many different countries as possible.

"Just kiss. And don't judge me. I was twenty-two and boy-crazy."

Sadly, a promising romance was derailed when the couple's plan to reunite the following summer was curtailed by a family tragedy. Maybe now would be their second chance!

Dean and Ayeesha's story stayed with her as she listened to dozens of others, touched by each one. From the pair wearing matching Seahawks T-shirts, who met in a coffee shop but hadn't swapped numbers, to the travelers who met over Jim Morrison's tombstone in a cemetery in Paris. If only she could help every person who'd sent in a video.

She thudded back to reality when Enrico leaned back and smothered a yawn before he spoke. "You anticipate fifteen contestants to start off, correct? Then the audience and viewers help us narrow it down to five."

"That's right. Each of those five gets his or her own episode with Du—" She caught herself. "Our host."

He sent her an indulgent smile. "I know your heart's set on Duquan for the host. We'll see if the test audience agrees."

"After that, we bring the five finalists together for episode seven, building the tension as our host passes out the envelopes. Cue the anticipation. Everyone waits with baited breath to see who gets their 'second chance'."

Enrico chimed in. "And the object of their desire gets brought in from the green room."

She nodded. "The others leave and the host sits the couple down. The audience hears both sides as to why the two didn't stay together."

"Followed by the counsellor's relationship advice, delivered to resonate with audience members as well as the couple. Whatever happens after that is up to them."

"Right." If the people on stage felt half as excited as she did... Even with no one in her past to wonder about, and no one in her present—she snuck a glance at Enrico—yet, she'd happily live vicariously through the contestants. If their viewing audience felt the same, they'd have a hit.

"In the second season, we do follow ups." Her voice rang with enthusiasm. "Did the couple who reconnected stay together? How are their lives now? The only thing people love more than the feel-good of star-crossed lovers reunited, is a happy ever after."

His smile heated her to the core. "Are you sure you can handle the disappointment of not being able to wave your magic wand and bring all the couples together?"

He really did get her. Her heart beat so fast it was difficult to breathe. "I like seeing people happily in love, so..."

His eyes crinkled in amusement. "I'm a little more jaded, so...

"In that case, my magic wand is coming for you, too."

He pretended to duck.

Apparently, he didn't know there was no escaping Cupid. And right now, it seemed her little winged friend knew what he was doing.

CHAPTER 14

"The only thing guaranteed to make your love life worse than it already is? Swiping right."

-Rachel, Guest
Duquan's Downlow on Dating and Love
Podcast episode #78

CONNOR

You never told me how the date with what's her name went

NATE

Gretta? Nothing to tell

CONNOR

You're holding out on me

NATE

She lied

CONNOR

Don't tell me, she's older than the age
she gave

NATE

Ha! Worse. She listed "plays guitar" under
her interests

CONNOR

And she doesn't?

NATE

Not since she was thirteen

CONNOR

So much for dating a musician

NATE

Jerk

CONNOR

That's what you get for using the Nooky app

NATE

That's what everyone is using

CONNOR

Doesn't mean it's good. PS no one hot is
named Gretta

NATE

Not true. And she's British. That accent...

CONNOR

She sounds cute. Sure you won't let the
musician thing slide?

NATE

She lied

CONNOR

No nooky for Nate ;-)

Can I have her number?

Seconds later Nate's phone rang. Expecting further grief from Connor about the Nooky date, he was happy to see it was his old friend Jeremy. Jer's band, The McClanes, had been an inspiration ever since the summer he went on the road with them as sound tech/roadie/general crew dog.

"Jer, my man. How're you doing? It's been a minute."

"It sure has. Things are good. But I need a favor. We're in the middle of a tour and our sound guy is out with appendicitis. I'm looking for someone who can step in for about two weeks. We have a show in Seattle, so can pick you up before we head through Oregon and into Cali."

He smiled into the phone. "How'd you know I've been missing the dingy hotel rooms, the long drives, late nights, and bad food?"

"I know you, bro. Can you help us out?"

"Let me check with my boss and get back to you."

CALL IT EXHAUSTION HYSTERIA. She and Enrico adding 'so…' to their conversations became a type of shorthand for humor which helped keep things light during a brutally tight schedule. The expression even crept into their emails.

From: enrico.rossi@MHproductions.com
To: lexy.smith@MHproductions.com
Subject: Production details coming along
Ian has confirmed the sound crew, and Merelda has booked the studio dates for filming, so…
E

From: lexy.smith@MHproductions.com
To: enrico.rossi@MHproductions.com

Subject: Ep 1 budget
I've got the final budget spreadsheet ready for
episode one, so...
Lexy

From: enrico.rossi@MHproductions.com
To: lexy.smith@MHproductions.com
Subject: HRH wants host
Merelda is getting impatient. She wants to know
where we are at with selecting a host, so...
E

~

"OUR BOY KILLED IT IN THERE!" Jules said as she and Lexy left
the studio.

"He did, didn't he?" Lexy said proudly. Jules had
been the only staff member allowed behind the two-way
mirror with Lexy and Enrico to watch the test audience's reaction to videos of the auditioning hosts. She'd
been surprised when Enrico suggested Jules join them,
but it made sense to have Jules start mining ideas for
styling the successful applicant. She wished she'd
thought of it.

"I may be bone tired from the move on the weekend, but
I wouldn't have missed seeing those auditions."

"I *was* bone tired from helping you move, but now I'm so
excited about how that went." She bounced on the balls of
her feet as they waited to cross the street.

"You want to burn some of that excited energy helping
me unpack?"

"You know I do."

"Grand." Jules pulled out her car keys to drive them

back. "Do you think Enrico's sulking? Is that why he took off alone?"

"I think he legit had an errand to run. As for Duke—"

Jules ginned. "I'm Team Duke. No contest."

"He blew the cheerleader one right out of the water. And the snooty professor-type woman." She'd expected to be wowed, but Duke had surpassed her expectations.

"I assume you included the favorite aunt type to counteract Enrico's Librarian Barbie picks?" Jules said.

"I had to. She was sweet. Just not right for the show. Enrico has to know Duke is the best choice."

"And ooooh I can not wait to dress that man."

Lexy laughed. "That must be a first. Isn't it usually undressing them?"

Jules winked. "Depends on the situation."

"Let's wait until the contracts are signed."

Jules mock pouted. "Does that mean no quick swing past Becky's Bakery for celebratory brownies? It's on the way."

"I never said *that*. Team Duke brownies. My treat."

To his surprise, Nate fell right back into tour life. As he helped with the loading in, everyone still cursed the fact every bar and theater had the narrowest, ricketiest back staircase imaginable for hauling in all their heavy instruments and equipment. He almost missed the old rattletrap tour van, nicknamed The Death Star, which had been upgraded to a real tour bus.

That wasn't the only change. Instead of being the opening act, the McClanes were the headliners, which meant a better rider and less waiting around. They got first soundcheck time, and he didn't have to man the merch table.

Another change? Jer and the drummer, Soren, both recently married, had their wives on the road with them. Jer's wife, Priya, was a freelance writer for several magazines, and able to work anywhere. She had also started a blog called *Band Life, Tales from the Road,* that had gained quite a following.

Set-up complete, Priya dropped a bottle of water off at the booth where Jer was working away. She pressed a quick kiss to the top of his head, then climbed on stage to take some artsy close-up photos of the instruments. With sound check for tonight's show finished, Nate plunked himself on a nearby amp to text Lexy.

NATE

Got another best band story for ya

LEXY

Let's hear it :)

NATE

Two young guys leaving last night's show. One caught Soren's drumstick and got it signed by all The McClanes

LEXY

I bet the guy was pumped

NATE

Direct quote: Best night of my life!

LEXY

Awww. I love that story. Even if ours are still better

NATE

I won't tell Jer you said meeting him wouldn't be as exciting as seeing Daisy or Pearl Jam, haha

LEXY

Don't you dare, I love The McClanes

And now I want my own signed drumstick

NATE

I might be able to hook you up :)

"Hey Nate. Come here a sec?" Jer called.

He hopped off the amp and made his way across the room. The pub, which would look cozy after dark, looked tired and dingy in the bright light of day.

"I want to show you something," Jer said as Nate slid into the booth beside him. "We're working on a music video." Jer angled his laptop so Nate could see. "We filmed some clips already."

Music video. The very words still had the ability to make him break out in a cold sweat. A bead of it rolled down his back as he watched a scene of The McClanes playing at an old drive-in movie theater.

"We're going for a 'you wish you thought of this cool idea' vibe with a hint of retro," Jer said, as the video cut to the four bandmates eating popcorn.

Flashbacks to his own music video disaster had nausea threatening. Nate cleared his throat and tried to sound casual. "That looks pretty cool, man."

"Thanks." Jer pulled up another video frame. This one showed the band playing directly in front of the drive-in screen. Each of them just a silhouette backlit by the film playing behind them. "We lucked out with our director. He's got great vision."

Nate nodded.

"We want to intersperse some live clips from the road, but they all turn out like this." Jer clicked on yet another video, filmed in one of the tour venues, a gorgeous old theater. "We want some ambient sound and audience noise to bring the viewer into the moment, but we're getting too much. And there's some distortion. Any ideas?"

Nate adjusted several levels in the editing program on Jer's laptop. As long as it wasn't his own video, he should be fine. He played the clip again. "That's a little better, but I've got different software at home. It's a new program, pretty good at cleaning things up. It also does a great job of combining the sound recorded off the mixing board with other recordings." He stroked his chin. "I could set up to record off the mixing board tonight."

"Then we could mix the two and get the exact level of audience noise we want."

"Exactly." He wished he was as excited as Jer.

"I knew there was a reason you joined us for this leg of the tour."

"And if you're open to filming a couple more shows while I'm here..." As he outlined several options, tricks he'd picked up from studio work, Nate's tension eased.

See? Totally fine.

"You learn this from making your own music videos?" Jer said. "I haven't seen any from RDA."

The tight ball was back in his stomach. "From my boss actually," he said, hoping Jer would drop it.

When Jer pulled up the tour schedule to check options for recording venues, Nate let out a slow breath. He was in the clear.

"Are you guys planning to make any videos?" Jer said

suddenly. "You'd get a lot more notice that way. RDA deserves it."

"Nah," he said. "No plans."

Jer propped his elbows on the table and looked directly at him. "She's not going to ruin your career twice, you know."

"Who?"

"Don't play dumb. You know I'm talking about Adele."

Nate lowered his gaze. The curse of a friend who knew you too well.

"She did her damage. But you guys came back better and stronger than ever." Jer leaned in. "The Rainy Day Astronauts really have something. I'd hate to see you miss out because of old news."

For a tense moment he and Jer locked eyes. Nate's jaw clenched. His friend meant well, but he hadn't been there. He didn't know the full story.

"Is Nate fixing the sound on your live recordings?" Smiling, Priya slid into the booth across from them.

Jer held Nate's gaze a moment longer, before turning her way with an answering smile, no sign of any tension. "I hope so. The boy's got mad skills."

"If you're not careful," Priya teased Nate, "he'll try to poach you from your day job."

"If he's not careful," Jer countered, "I'll make filming an RDA video my next pet project."

"Isn't one video enough for now?" Priya laughed. "Who's up for sushi?"

Nate relaxed. Sushi on the road was still a staple. It was reassuring some things never changed.

∼

THE NEXT TWO weeks went by at warp speed. If not for Enrico ordering in food, Lexy would have existed on protein bars and coffee. They'd cut off submissions and were now concentrated on those they'd already received.

Any possibles were passed to other staff at MHP, who did the groundwork to find the 'ones', including Parker-with-no-last-name.

"Toss the pilot in the 'No' pile," Enrico said, as he and Lexy went through another batch of videos.

"Why? That was a cute story. For their first date he booked a Cessna and flew her down to Portland for dinner. So romantic."

"The guy put on the *Top Gun* soundtrack as he drove her to the airport." He rolled his eyes. "Besides, a pilot shouldn't have any trouble meeting a woman."

"Who doesn't love *Top Gun*? And anyone can second-guess their relationship decisions, no matter what their profession."

"Fine. Put him into the 'maybe' pile with all the others your soft heart lobbied for," he said with a mock sigh. She slid him a sideways look. That must mean he secretly approved of her soft side.

Which in no way extended to the older man hoping to meet up with his daughter's best friend from high school. Now old enough that the age difference wouldn't matter.

"Are you sure?" Enrico teased. "You keep insisting everyone deserves a chance."

"Not that creep."

The woman looking for the twins she hooked up with on a beach in Mexico last year also joined the 'No' pile.

"Are some of these even serious?" she said. "Or did they make these videos as a joke?"

The guy looking for an ex-boyfriend who 'just didn't know how good he had it', was another easy reject.

"Blech! I feel like we need to track down the ex, just to warn him."

His gaze met hers. "For once we are in complete agreement."

Like he'd said before. *Simpatico.*

He stood. "As we were for our lunch order. I'll go meet the delivery person."

She gave a dreamy sigh, looking forward to discovering all the things they had in common.

When he returned, the scent of melted cheese made her taste buds water. "Splish-Splash Tuna Melt." Enrico placed a wrapped item in front of her. "With house-made kettle chips."

"Splish-Splash?"

"I guess a *Happy Days* reference is before your time."

"Before yours too, no? You're not that old."

"When I was younger, my brothers and I learned English from watching old *Happy Days* re-runs because that was one of the only American programs we got in Italy. We thought The Fonz was the coolest. We'd run around the neighborhood quoting him and banging things with the side of our fist, trying to make them turn on the way they did for him."

"Awww, I can totally picture little Enrico, his hair styled just like The Fonz." Outwardly, Lexy grinned. Inside, her heart melted. Enrico sharing childhood memories.

He chuckled. "You should have seen me the year I got a black leather jacket for my birthday. I was unbearable." He took a bite of his crispy grilled sandwich.

She watched him, enthralled by his Adam's apple when he swallowed. His lips, when he dabbed them with a paper napkin. Seducing her over lunch without even trying. She cleared her throat. "As a strategy for learning another language, it was very successful."

"You might not believe it, but *Happy Days* had a bigger influence on me than that. It's the reason I wanted to become a television director."

"Even as a kid you knew that's what you wanted to be?"

"The ability to transport people to another time and place, give them a window into a different life, and make them laugh; it seemed like magic to me. I wanted to be able to do that. What did you want to be growing up?"

"In my early teens I was obsessed with *Buffy the Vampire Slayer*, and wished I could be like her. Regular high school student on the surface, but secretly saving the world from evil."

"What kind of name is Buffy? Though Lexy the Vampire Slayer does have a certain ring to it."

She smiled. "It does, but I quickly figured out there wasn't much of a lucrative career to be had in saving the world, and far too much danger."

"I think you're braver than you realize. Perhaps you are saving the world one star-crossed couple at a time."

"I like that. We could have called the show *Lexy the Love Resurrector*."

"Bella, I saw the video tape you submitted to Merelda, remember? We are far better off with Duquan as our host."

"Hey!"

"Hey, yourself. You know I'm right." His eye twinkled at her. "And now, we should return to the show at hand. Ready to cue up the next video?"

She consulted her list and pulled up the next submission.

"By the way," he said, "I invited Duquan to sit in with us."

She resisted the urge to get up and do a cartwheel across Merelda's fancy-ass table. "He's in?"

"He said something about jumping at the chance to work with his 'Lexycakes'."

"That was his nickname for me when I was in my teens. It seems to have stuck, so..."

He flashed a smile. "I think it suits you, so..." They were still chuckling when Duke opened the door. "Good timing," Enrico said.

Lexy jumped up and gave Duke a hug. He stepped back and grinned. "Who would have guessed, all those years ago when we met in the surf that we'd wind up working together?"

"That's almost as crazy a story as some of the ones we've been screening."

Duke moved around the table and shook Enrico's hand. "Good to see you again. I appreciate this opportunity."

"Glad to have you. You were a hands-down favorite with our test audience."

Duke took off his jacket. "I can't wait to get started."

Lexy picked up the remote. "Here's one from a guy named Jack."

They turned their attention to the screen where an earnest-looking young man with short, curling brown hair and serious brown eyes behind his glasses started his story.

"Hi, my name is Jack. I'm sending this from San Francisco, but my story goes back to when I lived in Seattle. If I get chosen, I'd come back to Seattle in a heartbeat if it means another chance with Hailey."

The back of her neck tingled. There'd been a submission last week from a woman named Hailey. Wouldn't it be something if it turned out to be the same person?

She sat forward and listened as Jack described being newly out of a relationship and reluctantly dragged to a fundraiser at a local pub.

"Suddenly a co-worker I didn't know well, came up to me and asked if I was single. He said he wanted me to meet his wife's friend. That moment changed my life. His wife's friend, Hailey, looked so pretty in a sundress with blue and green flowers that I was literally speechless."

"I can't believe he remembers what she was wearing," Lexy said to no one in particular.

Jack went on to describe how he and Hailey started dating and everything was going really well. Then, a few months into their relationship, he received a promotion that included moving to San Francisco. He thought it was too soon to ask Hailey to give up her life in Seattle and the job she loved, to move with him to a new city.

"That's where I messed up," Jack said in his video. "I should have been honest and told her how I felt." Their attempt at long-distance dating fizzled out. "I've always wondered if she would have come with me, if she was disappointed when I didn't ask. Questions that still haunt me. If you pick me I can get the answers, and maybe another chance with Hailey."

"I like him," said Duke. "I think the audience will relate to those 'what if' questions he's been asking himself. But I'm the new kid on the block. I don't know how you've been working your selections so far."

"Lexy likes them all."

"Guilty. Including Jack. Add him to the 'Maybe' pile?"

"We've heard many similar stories," said Enrico.

"Nothing about his stands out from the others. I say the 'No' pile."

"Wait!" She searched the video files. "Remember this one?" She hit play.

"I'm a bit nervous, but here goes. My name is Hailey. You know how people in books and movies see someone across a crowded room? And they just know? Well, that actually happened to me."

She went on to describe a familiar-sounding fundraiser at a pub. "I was there with my friend whose husband jokingly asked about my type. I pointed out a guy across the room with short brown hair and glasses."

"That guy works with me," my friend's husband said. "Hang on, I'll be right back." She looked into the camera. "Long story why it didn't work, but I still have regrets and would like a chance to see if he does too."

Lexy stopped the video, eyes wide as she looked at both men. "They both want to see each other again. Isn't that the most exciting thing ever?" Enrico looked underwhelmed. Duke wore a grin as big as her own.

"Duke, you're here to *help* with selection. Not add another romantic who wants to give everyone a chance."

"Guilty," Duke said, echoing Lexy's earlier reply, and not sounding repentant at all.

"It would be anti-climactic to have those two on the show. All they need is for one of them to pick up the phone," Enrico said.

Spoken like a man.

"Human behavior is unpredictable," Duke said. "And fear can be a powerful block.

"I just had the *best* idea for episode one," Lexy said. "Guaranteed to have the audience crying happy tears." She picked up her favorite pen and began scribbling notes.

"I've seen her like this before," said Enrico. "She goes all Sofia Coppola, writing her ideas, forgetting I'm the one who'll be directing the show." He rose. "Let's leave her. I heard Jules say something about a 'signature style' for our host."

"Lead the way."

The two left and Lexy finished outlining her concept. She tapped the end of her pen to her lips in thought. Her own show, her friend as the perfect host, a kick-ass idea for an unforgettable first episode, all while working closely with a director who was starting to look like the man of her dreams.

A mild panic settled over her shoulders, an uncomfortable tingling. Things were sliding into the 'too good to be true' category. Which was when they tended to go sideways. Or was she being paranoid?

CHAPTER 15

"I was told to write a list of what I'm looking for in a boyfriend. So far I haven't met a handsome, wealthy, generous, pilot/chef, who's an active outdoorsy-type, but also enjoys brunches and wine tastings, who's dynamite in bed, can fix anything—including my car— and is good with kids and small animals. You know anyone?"

-Juliet, Guest
Duquan's Downlow on Dating and Love
Podcast episode #99

Finally! Lexy threw up her hands in triumph. 'Choose the fifteen contestants' was at long last crossed off her list. Before she could fully savor the moment, a timid new intern delivered the bad news to her and Enrico in the boardroom. Two of those chosen had to drop out. The girl stood in the doorway literally quaking.

What did they do? Draw straws to give me the news? Do the interns think I'm another Merelda?

The young woman scurried off the second Lexy thanked her. She's lucky she didn't get 'shooed'. Mentally, she kissed goodbye to her plans for a hot bath, a glass of wine, and her bed. Enrico looked the way she felt. "This should be fun."

"You're the one who wanted to produce her own show. Consider this a minor setback." Arms crossed over his chest, he settled back and did that wide leg-cross a lot of men seemed to favor. One ankle on the opposite knee, displaying his masculinity, waiting to see what she did next.

Scrolling through the videos, she clicked on one of the earlier hopefuls who hadn't made the short list. "What about her?" New city, new job, and Liz had met the love of her life on her first weekend in town.

"It sounds cliché," Liz said on screen, "but the minute we started chatting there was a click. It was beautiful." Sadly, their love story ran aground, for it turned out the woman was a co-worker at Liz's new job, a supported living home for young single moms and their babies. The other woman had a personal rule about not dating anyone from work, and felt strongly about keeping her sexual orientation private.

"What came next were the most wonderful and agonizing four years of my life," Liz said. "Working along-side her, but not being able to express how I felt about her." Now, no longer working together, Liz hoped the show would give them another chance.

Lexy glanced at Enrico. Yup. Not hard to relate to the closeness that comes from working side by side every day. You get to know each other's moods. Today he seemed distracted.

"Enrico? What about Liz for the show?"

"Sure, if you want her."

Hmmm. It wasn't like him not to have a strong opinion. Something was definitely up.

"Knock, knock!" Merelda breezed into the boardroom, a bottle of champagne in one hand, three flutes in the other. She looked over at the screen. "Good idea to include the LGTXYZ or whatever they're calling themselves these days. Having one on our show will help boost our ratings."

Lexy winced, even though Merelda's lack of sensitivity shouldn't be a surprise.

Enrico straightened. "What are we celebrating?"

Merelda looked like she was a cat that recently swallowed a canary. Had she beheaded someone? "I just concluded a bidding war for the rights to air the show."

That got Enrico's attention. "Do tell."

With a flourish, Merelda opened the bottle with expert skill and filled the flutes before she raised hers. "To me," she said. "And my brilliant marketing ploy."

Lexy exchanged a look with Enrico. *Classic Merelda!*

"I had a lot of push-back from the big networks. They view November and December as the dead zone in terms of serving up a new show."

"And...?" Enrico was obviously waiting for the good news.

"I told them it's a major misconception to assume the entire world is caught up in the holiday preparation. Some people dread that time of year. *Cupid* offers the perfect distraction. A chance to see other people whose lives are more pathetic than their own."

Lexy bristled, opened her mouth then closed it abruptly. Now was not the time to tell Merelda their romantic hopefuls were not pathetic.

"Several of the bigwigs thought it would be better to air

the show in the new year. Start fresh and all that nonsense." Merelda waved a dismissive hand. "Stupid idea. Advertisers know consumers have no disposable income in January."

Lexy nodded. When Merelda was on a roll there was no stopping her, and no point interjecting, even to agree.

Merelda paused, watching the bubbles in her glass. "Meanwhile, NBC is looking to jostle their way back to number one. I reminded them of the way Netflix cleaned up the year they aired *Bridgerton* over the holidays." She smiled at Lexy and Enrico in turn. "They're giving us the 9 pm time slot on Thursday between their number one long-running reality show and a fan favorite detective drama. It didn't hurt to showcase Duquan as host. He has quite a following, and the suits feel he will appeal to a wide audience."

Across the table, Enrico met Lexy's gaze, his glass tipped in a silent toast. "Am I right to assume everything is on track?"

"Yes," Lexy said. "Filming starts in two weeks. We're lining up the studio audience, and should have a full house every episode."

"Good." Merelda drained her glass and stood. "To build suspense on the night the winner is announced, the finale will air at the same time across the country. I'm tired of those superior Easterners finding out everything before we do on the west coast."

"I have a question," Lexy blurted, before her boss could exit. "About the show." Not the smoothest segue, but she'd been looking for a way to bring this up since the idea had occurred to her last week.

Merelda raised an eyebrow. No smile of encouragement. Just silence.

Lexy's stomach twisted into a knot worse than her tangled yarn the one and only time she'd tried to knit. She cleared her throat. "I think it would really heighten the show's prestige if we could offer a prize to the winning couple. Perhaps a romantic weekend getaway. I took a look at the numbers, and there's budget for it if we—"

"Oh, you had a look at the numbers, did you? You're privy to the entire budget of Manor House Productions?" Merelda's frosty tone had Lexy drawing her cardigan tighter.

"No," she said slowly. Her shoulders sagged. She glanced at Enrico for support and saw a frown marring his handsome features. He tilted his head slightly, and she had the distinct impression he was annoyed she hadn't talked to him about this first. Resolutely, she pressed her case. "But consider the benefits. The positive publicity a prize like this would bring to the company, through social media posts and—"

"There is no budget, and that's final. Take the win, or should I say *my* win, of our ideal air time for the show and be happy with that." Merelda swept out of the room, taking her glass and the rest of the bottle with her.

"It was a good idea," Enrico said, turning back to the screen to watch the next video. "But you know Merelda. She's all about the bottom line, and *CGSC* hasn't proven itself yet."

She slid her half-empty flute away as she cued up the next submission. The bubbles no longer held the sparkle they had. Enrico was always telling her they were a team. If her idea was so good, why hadn't he spoken up?

∼

"STILL REMEMBER HOW TO USE THAT?" Cam teased, as Nate set the gain on the soundboard for the correct input volume.

"I was on the road *two weeks*," Nate said. Since he'd been back, he'd been buried in pre-production, with Lexy even busier. They'd barely had time for a passing hello. Seeing Enrico glued to her side, he was proud to see she looked to be holding her own.

He checked that everything in his own little sound empire was where it was supposed to be, and working the way it should. He didn't want anything going wrong on the first episode of Lexy's show.

Amazing how the pieces had come together while he was away. They had a host, contestants, and a theme song. The art department had come up with a striking logo, a cupid over a heart with his bow and arrow at the ready. They'd even had a version of it created in pink fluorescent lights for the back wall of the stage, which looked pretty slick.

As he ran a check on the sound equipment on stage, he spotted Duke in the wings. Jules had outdone herself with his wardrobe. In a style she dubbed 'surf meets studio', the show's host was flashy and sharp, while still looking approachable. Not in this lifetime could Nate pull off a peacock-colored jacket over a blinding white T-shirt, black jeans and multi-colored shoes, but on Duke the threads looked just right. Not only that, Nate could see himself sitting down and enjoying a beer with the guy. He'd bet some viewers would tune in each week just to see what Duke was wearing.

"Nate! Over here a sec?" one of the crew called from the back. He was on his way when he ran smack dab into Lexy.

"Sorry," they both said at the same time.

"Nate. I wasn't looking where I was going." She pushed back a stray tendril of hair that had escaped. "You survived life on the road?"

"Luckily I thrive on no sleep and bad coffee. How'd it go picking the contestants? You get everyone you want?"

"You know me. Pure *torture*." Lexy emphasized the last word. "I wished almost everyone could be on the show, but I'm happy with our Legends. Duke's idea to call them that instead of contestants," she added.

"I like it. Did the pilot make the cut? I had the *Top Gun* song stuck in my head for days after you sent me that text about him."

"Sorry, not sorry," she said with a grin. She started to sing "Highway to—"

"Don't." He covered his ears. "It was hard enough to get it out of my head the first time."

"Sadly," she said, when he lowered his hands, "the pilot is now flying an overseas route and can't be here for filming."

"Too bad. But I'm sure the others are great. Break a leg. No, that's what you say to actors. Can I say have a great show, without jinxing you?"

"I guess we'll find out." She blew out a breath. "But save your congratulations for when it's over. I had no idea how many things could go awry at the last minute. Speaking of," she looked over her shoulder to the control room. "I'd better go. I'm sure there's a fire somewhere that needs putting out."

"Nate, you coming?"

Right, the co-worker. "Yeah, me too. No rest for the wicked."

"Hey, did you remember?" she asked, walking backwards down the hall so she still faced him.

"Your autographed drumstick? As if I would forget."

"You're the best. Glad to have you back." Then she turned and hurried off.

Nate smiled when he caught himself humming "Danger Zone".

~

"HAPPY FIRST DAY OF SHOOTING." Lexy tried to act nonchalant as she passed Enrico a small, brightly-wrapped package. Why was her heart pounding? It was only a friendly gesture. Or so she'd told herself as she wrapped it.

"You got me a gift?" He frowned. "But I didn't get you anything."

Below the control room, a buzz of anticipation filled the air as the studio audience filed in and took their seats. Lexy's own nerves had been buzzing like a swarm of bees in her belly all day.

"No need." She smiled. "This is just a little something to celebrate the fact that we made it to this point."

"Enrico? Can you approve this sequence for me?" One of the crew held out an iPad with the episode outline on it.

He grabbed the tablet, her gift squashed against the underside as he scanned the notes. "No, no, we changed this here. Otherwise this is coming in too late."

As he typed edits onto the screen she tried to read his changes, but she couldn't see from this angle.

He handed the iPad back and turned to her. "Sorry, what were you saying?"

She indicated the now-crumpled package.

"Oh, right." His fingers fumbled with the ribbon and paper. Maybe he was as nervous as she was. Their first gift exchange. "TV socks." He held up a pair of black socks covered in vintage TVs, complete with antennas.

"We talked about your sailboat socks, and I noticed the ones with dancing tacos."

Oh God, I'm babbling.

"I thought the TV ones would bring good luck directing the first episode of the show." She shrugged, trying for casual. No need for him to know how long she had spent looking online to find him the perfect socks.

"That was most thoughtful."

She gazed up at him, waiting—

"Hey, Enrico?" One of the camera operators approached with another question and the two were soon deep in consultation. She might as well have been invisible.

The sour taste of panic swilled in her mouth as she took a seat and tried to project a confidence she was far from feeling. What if the show was a flop? What if the audience wasn't engaged? What if the critics panned it?

"Oh, Lexy?"

She jumped up, delighted to be needed for something. "Yes?"

Enrico passed her the socks. "Will you put these somewhere for me?" He glanced around the control room. "Someone get Nate on my headset," he called loudly. "I want to confirm our opening credits cue."

More crushed than the paper from his socks, Lexy sat back down and picked up a headset just as her phone vibrated with an incoming message.

JULES

So proud of you! And don't worry, it's going to be Amazing. Big hugs

REN

Seconding that. People are going to love it. I predict a social media storm when you hit the air

Her friends were the best!

When the opening song came on, her heart started keeping time. The bank of screens held the control room crew's attention, displaying the studio from every angle. She caught her breath as the audience straightened in anticipation. A flash of movement on a different screen showed Duke bounce onto the stage amidst a chorus of cheers and clapping, in an outfit that hit just the right tone. A man you could listen to. A man you could trust. A man you hoped would take you shopping.

Here we go. She leaned forward and forced herself to breathe. Like paddling for a perfect wave; hoping you make the take off and have an incredible ride, not bail and swallow a gallon of seawater.

"The people you'll meet tonight are looking for a second chance with someone from their past," Duke said to the excited crowd. "Sometimes Cupid grants that second chance. Other times he needs a little help. And that's where we come in."

Her attack of nerves abated as Duke continued his opening monologue. Pride lumped in her throat as she watched her show, her idea, her dream, come to life in front of her.

"Each one of our guests tonight is extremely courageous, putting it all on the line for love. Are you ready to meet these Legends?" Duke's voice rose in energy and volume on that last line. The audience's resounding cheer showed he knew exactly how to work the crowd.

Over the headset Enrico's smoothly accented voice cued the various camera operators to catch audience response as Duke worked them into a frenzy of anticipation. The fifteen Legends were escorted out on stage where Duke invited them to sit in the semi-circle of seats facing the audience. Some looked excited by the attention. Others fidgeted nervously, obviously overwhelmed by being here amidst the lights, the cameras, the spectators.

Duke addressed the Legends. "So *they* all," he indicated the audience, "get to hear *your* stories tonight. You're in the hot seat, so to speak." That got chuckles and nods of agreement from those on stage.

"But no need to worry. I feel a lot of love in the room tonight. Can you feel the love?" he asked the room at large. Claps, cheers and whistles issued from every corner.

"I think if they could," Duke continued, "our audience would vote for each and every one of you. I know I would." His smile included all fifteen. Lexy saw several appear to visibly relax.

"But only five of you will move on as finalists, so let's get down to it." The audience and at home viewers were introduced to each participant by name before seeing their video.

So far, so good. Lexy lightly rapped her knuckles on the desk top, though she wasn't sure it was actually made of wood. Watching Enrico in his element, with some sort of sixth sense for where to have the cameras focus to catch just the right emotional reaction, it was hard letting go. Up to this point she and Enrico had collaborated on everything. Tonight's sudden shift was unsettling. But the roles were clear. He was the director, not her. So that left her to... watch?

As the audience and Legends viewed the clips, she had to give the editing team props. Somehow, they had trimmed each video to no more than a minute and a half. All without losing the essence of the stories. The clips captured each Legend's hopeful heart, with enough detail to intrigue the audience and make viewers wish each one a happy ending. Their stories tugged on her heart strings all over.

"From your votes," Duke said, "five of tonight's Legends will get their own personal episode."

Lexy started and sat up straighter. They were already this close to the end?

"Look, Madame Producer." She'd been so immersed in the people on stage, she hadn't heard Enrico join her. "The votes are already starting to come in." He pointed to a band of scrolling numbers in the far corner of a different screen. "Lots of them."

"Before it's even over?"

"What this means, *Miss Sentimental*," he bumped his shoulder playfully to hers, "is that people are watching our show."

Our show. Those two little words gave her a fuzzy glow.

On stage Duke continued to work his magic. "Their stories are all compelling, and tonight was just a taste. You'll want to tune back in as the five finalists share the ups and downs they've experienced on their quest for love."

She could taste the tension building. The audience bent over the handheld voting devices they had been given on entry, sending in their votes. She hoped viewers from home were on their phones doing the same.

"And one of those five Legends, again determined by your votes, will get the second chance they are hoping for. Seeing that individual on stage, reunited with their one that got away, will be a moment you don't want to miss!"

Her anticipation mounted. Her insides buzzed. It was coming. The surprise ending. Which, if it went over like she prayed it would, should really put *CGSC* on the map.

The camera panned a final close up on each Legend as Duke thanked them for coming, offering a smile, a handshake, a hug before he ushered the group off stage. Then he turned to the audience. "Thank you everyone for tackling that difficult task of voting. I'm glad I was exempt. To thank you properly, we have a special surprise for you, coming right up."

Lexy sucked in her breath. She was beyond excited. Because she knew what was coming next.

While the commercials played, stage hands whisked away the empty seats, leaving only two near Duke. The second they went live, the camera zoomed in on Duke's wide smile. The audience stirred in anticipation.

"Creating a show like this is bound to bring surprises. Tonight is no exception." Pride rippled through her. What happened next was all on her. "Tonight, it's my pleasure to introduce you to one more Legend. Come on out Hailey."

A young woman in a sunshine yellow dress stepped onstage and smiled shyly as she took the seat he indicated. Duke sat next to her. "When we saw Hailey's video and heard her story, we knew we had to bring her on the show."

Hailey clasped her hands in her lap and smiled uncertainly at Duke as the overhead screen lit up with the video version of her story. The man had been exactly her type, and an introduction through friends led to a blissful time of dating before he moved several states away for work. Video Hailey told the audience she always wondered 'what if', regretting they didn't try harder to make things work despite the distance.

"You picked him out across a crowded room. That's the stuff of movies," Duke said as the video ended.

"I know," she said wistfully.

"You told me backstage your relationship had still been new. You weren't sure enough of your feelings, or Jack's, to commit to leaving behind your family and friends, your job, for the unknown waiting for you in California. *If* he had asked you to join him. But he didn't."

Hailey nodded.

"Do you know why you're here?"

She shook her head.

"It was a little cruel of us to leave you backstage wondering, when we brought out all the other Legends," Duke said with a smile. "But, you see, we had another video come in with a story similar to yours."

Hailey's jaw dropped as the screen revealed Jack telling the audience, "She picked me out across a crowded room." Jack went on to verbalize his regrets about not asking Hailey to move with him, of being too unsure of himself, afraid of being rejected.

As the video ended, Duke turned to her. "Guess who's waiting backstage?"

Her eyes widened in disbelief when Jack stepped on stage. At Duke's nod and widening grin, Hailey jumped to her feet, took a few steps toward Jack, then halted.

He opened his arms. As Hailey ran to him, he stepped forward and caught her in a hug. The audience leapt to their feet with claps and cheers and a few loud whistles.

"What are you—? How did—." Hailey shook her head as words escaped her.

He smoothed her hair with a shaky hand. "I can't believe you're here." Holding her close, he smiled down into her eyes. "That you made a video about me, too."

Duke approached the reunited couple, his smile almost as big as theirs. "Jack, you told me backstage your life didn't feel right without Hailey in it."

"It didn't. So, I thought I'd better take a dramatic step to get her back." Jack clasped Hailey's free hand.

Like many of the audience members, Lexy dabbed a tear.

"Where are the friends?" Enrico spoke into his headset.

"Pan over to them." The camera picked up a couple in the crowd. From the stage, Duke directed Jack and Hailey to where the pair stood grinning and waving. Hailey and Jack waved back then, still holding hands, took the seats Duke indicated.

Duke gave the audience a triumphant smile, as if they were all co-conspirators. He had such a gift for reading people. "Neither Jack nor Hailey knew the other one was in the green room next door. They both thought they were being brought on here as one of the semi-finalists." He turned to smile at each of them in turn.

"It feels like a dream," Hailey said, her eyes shining on Jack. "One I don't want to wake up from."

"It's clear neither of you forgot about the other, and wished things had turned out different. Now that the second chance you both hoped for is in front of you, I want to help you make things last this time." Duke leaned forward, elbows on his knees, face earnest. "Jack, you worried Hailey wasn't ready to leave her home, her job and friends to be with you. What if she rejected you?" Jack nodded.

"Hailey." Duke shifted in his seat to face her. "Moving cities when a relationship is so new is a big risk. But you didn't tell Jack how much you cared about him. You were afraid his feelings weren't as strong as yours, and finding that out would be hurtful."

"One of my regrets," she said to Jack, who kissed the top of her hand.

For Lexy, the audience ceased to exist; as if Duke was talking directly to her. Was fear holding her back? Was it too soon to tell Enrico she was starting to have feelings for him? She didn't want to miss out on the possibility of her own happy ending.

"I get it," Duke said. "Being vulnerable is hard. But it's

also how we fully connect with other people. By letting them in. Letting them truly see us."

Hailey drew a shaky breath. "Being vulnerable is scary, but not as scary if it's Jack. I trust him."

"I know what it's like to live without Hailey. And that is far worse than any fear I have of being rejected."

"Are you ready to tell her how you feel?"

Jack turned to Hailey and took both her hands in his. "Hailey, I love you."

"You love me?"

"I never stopped, and I—" Jack hesitated. "I didn't want to assume anything, but I put in for a transfer back to Seattle."

"I love you too, Jack." She gave him a tremulous smile. "I've been looking at jobs in San Francisco,"

"To Cupid!" Jack lifted their joined hands and kissed her knuckles. The audience let out a collective, "Awwww."

The closing music started a light fade-in. Duke rose and the couple rose with him. "Well now that everyone needs a tissue, we hope you will keep in touch and let us know how things work out. Where you end up living together, and all the rest."

"We will," Hailey and Jack said in unison.

"All of us here at *CGSC* wish you the very best." Duke turned to the audience "As for *you*, tune in next week to find out which five of our Legends made the finals."

The second Lexy heard, "And we're clear," she took off her headset. When she turned to Enrico, the admiration in his eyes caught her breath.

He leaned in close and her heart skipped in delight. "Your surprise ending was inspired." Her entire body tingled at his nearness, his praise. "If not for you, I would not have realized they were looking for a second chance with each other."

"You mean good things *can* come from being sentimental?"

"Good things like ratings, anyway."

Her smile faded. Maybe they were just co-workers.

He moved closer, one hand on her arm. "I'm teasing. You just might turn me into a romantic after all."

CHAPTER 16

"If my sister hadn't invited this woman on our rec league softball team out for drinks with us after the game one night, then suddenly had a 'friend with an emergency', leaving the two of us alone, I wouldn't be engaged today."

-Noah, Guest
Duquan's Downlow on Dating and Love
Podcast episode #42

Nate pulled his truck into the studio parking lot and turned down his stereo before anyone caught him singing along with "Bitch Better Have My Money" by Rhianna. He'd laughed when the song had come on. Marcie was always sneaking tracks onto his playlists as a joke. This song's attitude behind the lyrics made it punchy and fun. If last night's episode of *Cupid* was any indication, Lexy might be pulling her own attitude, bargaining with Merelda for a pay raise. As he searched for a Rihanna GIF to send Marcie, his phone vibrated with a text from Jer.

JER

See what you're missing at the diner this morning???

He chuckled at a photo of the saddest stack of pancakes with bacon he'd ever seen, swimming in a pool of grease.

NATE

Was that supposed to lure me back on the road? Because that is tragic.

JER

Whoops. Meant to send this one

The next photo was an adorable selfie of Jer and Priya, coffee mugs raised.

JER

Priya says to tell you we miss you and to come back

NATE

Marginally better. You kinda ruin the photo though ;-)

Is she ready to leave you for me yet?

JER

No. But there was a Cora looking for you at last night's show

NATE

What? The one I had a beer with after the Portland gig?

JER

How many Cora's have you dated lately?

NATE

It was ONE BEER

JER

Must have been some beer

NATE

You didn't give her my # did you?

JER

I was tempted, haha

Lucky for you, I was real happy with the edited video clips from the tour you sent me. They're perfect for the music video. Thanks bro!

NATE

Welcome. Glad they worked out

JER

Cora won't be calling. Catch ya later

Nate hurried through the maze of hallways in the studio. With any luck, Ian wouldn't notice he was a few minutes late.

"Got your tux ready?" Tom, one of the other sound techs slapped him good-naturedly on the back. "Lucky you, getting picked to work on that new show."

"What?" he asked, still distracted by Cora trying to track him down. One night of listening to her talk non-stop about all her Tik-Tok followers was enough.

"Chicks dig guys in a tux, man. Certifiable fact." Tom grinned. "Just pick up any issue of Cosmo or one of those other girly magazines."

"Dude, I have no idea what you're talking about. And since when do you read Cosmo?"

"Haven't you heard? *CGSC* smashed the old debut record for any production out of MHP."

"Really?" Lexy must be ecstatic. He'd suspected she was onto something that day when he showed up with pizza, but he'd never imagined this type of success.

"The conversation on social is all about the show. Check it out." Tom started scrolling on his phone. "Clips with Duquan have gone viral on every platform." He turned his screen to show Nate Duke spreading his arms wide saying, "Can you feel the love?" on a loop. "One episode in and the guy's already got a catch phrase."

Just then Jules headed toward them. "Hey Jules! Tom was just showing me the social media icon you created."

"Isn't it awesome? All I did was dress the guy to suit his personality. The rest was all him. But I will take a *little* credit for how fabulous he looks." She grinned. "Ren predicted this social frenzy. The poor girl is working like a mad woman trying to keep on top of everything."

"Duquan's podcast was already popular," Tom said, "but his follower numbers are now in the stratosphere. Plus, I heard from Katie in makeup, that Sarah from payroll over-heard Merelda in her office rehearsing her acceptance speech."

The MHP rumor-mill might actually explode with the speed at which today's gossip was traveling.

"You've got even better sources than me," Jules said. "She was actually rehearsing a speech already?"

"I trust what Katie says."

Nate nodded. It was no secret that Merelda's pride and joy was her collection of awards won over the years by her shows.

"Awards season baby. That's what I'm talking about," said Tom. "If The Queen wins another shiny trophy, she will be very happy and that may trickle down to us. She might even give out bonuses."

Nate doubted there'd be bonuses, but it would be something if Lexy's show picked up a Golden Globe, or a People's Choice. Hey, why not an Emmy?

Jules nodded enthusiastically. "Between preliminary numbers, and the buzz on social which, let's be honest, is the real indicator these days, if this keeps up, the show's a shoe-in to be nominated."

"See, Nate? You lucky dog. The Queen always has her top worker bees at these events. I hear the after-parties are off the hook."

"It's true, Merelda always takes an entourage with her. And you, Handsome." Jules lightly patted his cheek. "Let me know if you need a plus one." Her phone chirped. "Gotta run, gents."

"You know Miles, the intern?" Tom said. "He's got an uncle who owns a casino and the Vegas bookies are running a pool on who makes it to the finals."

Nate chuckled. "Miles is new. You sure he isn't saying that for the attention?"

Tom shrugged. "I'm just telling you the word on the street."

"Right. You never add any details of your own."

"Can't help it if I have a flare for storytelling," Tom said with a grin.

"I don't know if it's you, or my new lucky socks that get the credit," Enrico said as he entered the conference room, all smiles, "but yesterday's filming was my smoothest first episode ever."

His new lucky socks that were back in her bag where they'd been on her way to work yesterday? Barely unwrapped?

She swallowed her disappointment, letting Enrico's enthusiasm override the fact that he hadn't asked for them back. He'd had a lot on his mind.

"I hope you found a suitable way to celebrate a successful first shoot." His eyes sparkled. Eyes that matched the color of his tie.

"If by celebrate, you mean fell asleep as soon as my head hit the pillow?" she said. "Then yes, I definitely did."

Any hope that they might have celebrated together had been dashed by his hasty exit yesterday. Instead, her commute home, full of vivid memories of their interactions over the last month, was her only consolation. His smiles, his teasing, his laughter. The times he boosted her confidence with compliments, or referred to the two of them as a team. Her skin had flushed when she recalled every one of the many light touches and special smiles he sent her way each day. Her growing feelings couldn't be all one-sided? Could they?

"According to Merelda, the first nationals look good." He took a sip of coffee. "We'll know more when the final numbers come out this afternoon, but I'd say we really kicked it from the park, so..."

She pulled her gaze from the small spot on his jaw that looked like he'd missed it when shaving "We what?"

He raised a brow. "That's the expression, right?"

"I think you mean 'knocked it out of the park'?"

"Right. Knocked. I forget. You Americans love your baseball, while we Italians are passionate about football, which you like to call soccer."

Passionate. Enrico was definitely a man of strong passions. One of which she hoped would—

"I spoke to the team tabulating results to see which contestants will make up the final five. Since there were many more votes than we anticipated, it could take a while."

Wasn't that her responsibility as producer to speak with the team? "Should we help?"

"That's not our job. Could you please cue up episode one's footage? Knocked from the park or not, we need to look for ways to improve episode two."

They were dissecting the video frame by frame when Lola and Brian arrived. Lola was one of the staff tallying the avalanche of votes but why was Brian from IT with her? Please don't let there be a problem.

"You have numbers for us?" Enrico said.

"Yes." Lola licked her lips nervously. "As you know, we received more votes than we anticipated. Far more than our system was set up to handle. We were trouble-shooting the problem this morning; even began a manual tabulation."

"But that was going to take too long," Brian interjected. "So I went ahead and experimented with writing a code that when applied to the existing program, I felt certain would be able to—"

"Skip to the important part, please," Enrico said. "Do we know our final five contestants?"

"We do." Ignoring Lexy's outstretched hand, Lola passed Enrico a file. Shouldn't it have come to her as producer, rather than the director? Or was she being petty?

"We had headshots taken of all the Legends last night, so I printed out your top five. I added their bios, and what we know about their lost love."

"Wonderful." Lexy resisted the urge to snatch the file away and see their final five for herself.

Enrico continued flipping pages. "May we have the room please," he said, without looking up. No doubt his director's mind was already plotting future episodes based on what he was reading. Before she had a chance to even look. "And I don't think I need to remind you that these results are confidential."

Lola nodded and left. Lexy craned her neck trying to see the photos over Enrico's well-defined shoulder, just as someone cleared their throat. She looked back. Brian stood there, waiting.

"Brian," she said. "Was there anything else?"

Brian glanced down and shuffled his feet. He cleared his throat again. "The code I wrote is quite advanced and allowed for a much faster calculation rate. Especially as the existing program had previously been overwhelmed by the sheer volume of numbers and the speed they were received."

She and Enrico exchanged a look as they waited for Brian to make his point.

"I have ideas to refine the code for tabulating votes for our future episodes, anticipating a potential growth in viewers, and I thought I could join you in here while I work on it, in case you needed to consult with me."

Poor guy was probably looking for any excuse to get out of his basement dungeon. But it wouldn't be here with her and Enrico.

"Hey gang, I hear the nationals are in and they're great." Duke shouldered his way in. "Plus, Ren told me everyone and their grandmother is calling, trying to wrangle audience tickets." His grin widened.

"Duquan," Enrico said. "Perfect timing. I have the names of the five who will be moving forward into the solo episode phase with you." He held up the file. "Brian, if you wouldn't mind closing the door on your way out."

After one last glance around the room, Brian left. Lexy

winced as he closed the door with more force than necessary.

"Okay, here's who we've got." Enrico began sticking the headshots up on the whiteboard. "Emma."

"I'm glad she made it," Lexy said. "She's the one who got married in Vegas, but didn't tell anyone."

"Liz."

"Liz made it too? The woman of her dreams worked for the same non-profit, but they never dated at the time."

"Ayeesha."

"Yay! They met at a posh summer camp but he was Australian."

Enrico sent her an unreadable look. "Ryland."

"Awwww. He had the instant connect with a woman on the ferry, but never asked for her number. How cool if he gets the chance to see her again."

"Summer."

"You mean and 'Parker-with-no-last-name'?" she said teasingly to Enrico. "From the outdoor concert? Just imagine reuniting those two."

"Do you remember everyone's story?"

She smiled, brows raised. "I might."

"Right." As he spoke, his eyes stayed on her and turned her insides into a gooey puddle. "Next up is figuring the order of the finalists' solo episodes." He took off his suit jacket and rolled up the sleeves of his shirt. And it wasn't even Forearm Friday. She might need a fan.

"We need to keep tension and viewer interest high to ensure the audience keeps coming back."

"Ideas?"

She sat forward. "We could go in order, lowest to highest since we have the advantage of knowing who got the most votes. That ought to keep people tuning in to see if their top choice made it."

"That's one possibility." After consulting the file, Enrico re-ordered the photos. "This is in order of popularity." His brow furrowed as he studied the row of smiling faces. "Or," he said, stroking his chin, "we reverse it and start with the highest."

"I have a question." Duke leaned forward, elbows on the table, fingers steepled. "Why do the numbers matter? My podcast listeners tune in for the stories. So let the stories determine the order. Who gets their second chance is less important than the how and why."

Duke was right. "It's not the destination, it's the journey." She remembered teasing Nate about using that old cliché, as he laughed at her over pizza on her deck.

"We say the journey *is* the destination in Italy, so I follow that much," said Enrico. "But how does that help with our show order?"

"*To All the Boys I've Loved Before*," Duke said.

"*Definitely, Maybe*," Lexy said.

"Now you've lost me. I'm clueless," said Enrico.

"*Clueless*. Perfect." While she and Duke both laughed, Enrico looked more confused than ever.

Duke's deep, booming laugh trailed off. "Sorry. Old habit. Lexy and I sometimes see how long we can hold a conversation using only movie titles. You're the first person to successfully join in without even knowing the game."

"*Clueless*." Enrico said. "The movie about the girl who wears yellow plaid, and tries to set up her teachers?"

Enrico knows the movie Clueless?

"Yes," Duke said. "Like Cher Horowitz in the movie, there are lessons our Legends have to learn. Lessons that will resonate with our viewers."

She forced her attention from Enrico's chick-flick insights. "Duke's right. What will capture the audience's attention, and their hearts, is hearing how our Legends got to where they are now in their quest for love. And where they go from here."

"And they'll be willing to share this on National television?" Enrico said.

Duke grinned. "Leave it to me."

"This guy can get you to share things you never thought you would." She should get him to work on Enrico.

"I'll schedule a preliminary meeting with each of them," Duke said. "Get their story, then work out the right order to introduce them to our audience."

"Great," said Enrico. "The sooner the better."

"Let's go through the tapes again. Help me prepare for the meetings," Duke said. "This time we'll focus less on what they're saying, but more on how they're saying it."

"And what they're not saying," she added.

"Don't forget the part where we ruthlessly examine their hopes and fears and past decisions under a microscope on live TV," Enrico said dryly.

"Better not let Enrico talk to the Legends, he'll scare them off." Duke pulled his notepad closer. "Start with Summer. She met Parker at the music festival years ago. Yet something is keeping her stuck in the past, caught on the idea of him, of them together. I want to know why."

"Isn't it possible they truly shared a special connection and are meant to be together?" She deliberately didn't look at Enrico as she spoke.

"It's possible. I believe in love and destiny and fate. But I also know from experience that fear is a powerful motivator that can cause us to act in ways to protect ourselves."

"What would Summer be afraid of?" Lexy asked.

"Fear of failure, of dependency on another person, or not being good enough, are some of the more common ones."

"Fear of losing yourself in a relationship," Enrico said. "Having to make too many compromises for the other person."

She flashed him a surprised look. Enrico's life seemed charmed, a man to whom everything came easy. Was his old-world elegance and easy flirtation a cover for heartbreak in his past?

"Sounds like you're speaking from experience," Duke said.

"Not my own experience," Enrico said. "I've been listening to your podcast."

"You're a quick study." Duke sat back in his chair, eyes twinkling. "And I'm flattered."

Lexy watched the exchange between the two men. With any luck Enrico would make her his next subject. She'd be happy to have him give her a long, leisurely study.

CHAPTER 17

"Years ago, my wife thought she was winning in the birthday gift department, giving me tickets to see my favorite band. She thought she was surprising me with tickets to see the Beastie Boys. It was actually the *Backstreet* Boys who came to town."

-Reed, Guest
Duquan's Downlow on Dating and Love
Podcast episode #56

"**H**ey Marce," Nate said into his phone. "The show's about to go on air. What's up?"

"Looking for clues to what my big brother, who got me the best birthday gift, would like for his own birthday."

"You always get me something great. Whatever you pick I'll love it."

"Seriously? That's all I get?"

"Nate, you good to go?" Ian said.

"Gotta run." Nate hung up on her threats to get him scented candles, and slipped on his headphones. "Copy."

There was an electric excitement in the air. Not just among the audience, but the crew too. Often, working in the studio became routine, but no one was phoning it in these days. Everyone was pushing themselves to be at the top of their game, stoked to be a part of this overnight smash success.

"Can you feel the love?" Duke asked the audience, receiving thunderous applause in response.

Not after a bunch of useless Nooky dates.

Duke was onstage with a guy named Ryland who'd met a woman on the ferry, only to regret not asking for her number. It turned out the woman, Siobhan, had the same regret. Except she went as far as taking out an "I Saw You" ad in the free arts and entertainment paper.

As the show switched from opening credits, to Duke's introduction, to Ryland's submission video, Nate adjusted the sound between videos and live mics, sliding the levers up and down on his soundboard with practiced ease.

"My favorite part of your story," Duke said to Ryland, "is that you only found out about the "I Saw You" post because your friend's Spanish girlfriend reads it regularly to learn English. She recognized the ad was about you." A murmur ran through the studio audience.

Nate was with them. What were the chances? And what did the guy do? Not much or he wouldn't be here.

"But you never contacted her. What happened, man?" Duke asked gently.

"I don't know. I guess I choked."

Duke's earnest gaze stayed on Ryland, encouraging him to elaborate. Nate was glad he wasn't in the hot seat. Duke had a gift for getting people to open up without prodding.

"We had such a connection," Ryland said finally. "Maybe the idea that we were fated to meet on the ferry that day freaked me out? I'd been burned badly by my ex. I didn't want to set myself up for that again."

Yup, I get that.

"So, you felt something for this girl, but you got spooked. Yet she felt something too, since she went to the trouble to try and find you."

"I guess," Ryland said. "I didn't think about that."

"I'm wondering. How do you see yourself? Do you see the amazing person you are, and all you have to offer in a relationship?"

People watching shifted in their seats, but not out of boredom. They were leaning closer, so as not to miss a thing. Were they relating to Ryland? Or relating to the things Duke was saying?

"Ummmmm," Ryland stared intently at the floor.

Duke straightened in his seat, addressing the audience. "I'm going to bring someone in on the video monitor here." He turned to Ryland. "Someone who I think knows you pretty well, and has a message for you."

Duke and Ryland angled in their seats to see the screen behind them where a woman appeared. She shared the same chestnut hair color as Ryland.

Ryland turned pale. "My sister?"

Nate felt for the guy. He could totally see Marcie doing the same thing. He only hoped this girl had nice things to say about her brother.

"Thanks for joining us, Rebecca," Duke said solemnly.

"Hi Duke. Hi Ryland," she said. "Ry, you are absolutely the best brother in the world. You have a wicked sense of humor, even when you use it to poke fun at me."

Sounds like me and Marcie.

She smiled. "When I was in hospital after that car accident, you came to see me *every* day. Even the nurses were in a better mood when you were there."

Ryland chuckled. "They couldn't resist my charm."

"That's what I'm talking about. You make people feel good, and it's effortless for you. It broke my heart to see the way your opinion of yourself changed after Carrie broke up with you."

Duke gave Ryland an encouraging nod. "You two seem to have a great sibling relationship. Those amazing qualities that your sister sees, and that I see in you; you have to see them too. And that only comes from loving yourself."

"Yeah," said Ryland. "I stopped feeling good about myself after all the terrible things Carrie said when we broke up. I worried Siobhan would think I was terrible too, once she got to know me."

"Now that you know how it happened, does that help to change the way you see yourself?"

"Maybe."

"That change, finding a way to love yourself again, is going to set you up with confidence that will ultimately make you stronger in your next relationship."

"I'm rooting for you, Ry," Rebecca said from the screen.

Judging by the audience's reaction, they were rooting for Ryland, too. Nate blew out a breath as they cut to a commercial. Thank goodness Marcie was focused on his birthday and not his love life.

The show was achieving exactly what Lexy had hoped. Touching people's lives. Maybe even making them look in the mirror and recognize similar traits in themselves. He'd worked a lot of shows but none had made him the least bit squirmy. Until this one. When it came to relationships, he was as guilty as the next guy of self-sabotage.

~

"Who, at work, would you fuck, marry, and kill?" Ren asked Jules and Lexy as the three lingered over a cozy Sunday brunch. Outside, a fierce Seattle rain lashed at the restaurant's windows.

"Excuse me?" Lexy almost spat mimosa all over her Benny.

Ren poked at her Sunrise Skillet Hash. "You know. Like the game where you're given the name of three celebrities, and you have to choose which of them you'd kill, which one you'd sleep with, and who you'd marry. But I thought we'd play the work version."

"Renata," said Jules. "Did someone at work mess with your social media algorithm again? Because if one of them turns up missing, you're already looking suspicious."

"What kind of game *is* this?" Lexy asked.

"Just play. It's funny."

"All right, this'll be easy." Jules ticked them off on her fingers. "Bentley, the new junior in makeup thinks he can have my job one day. Kill. I'd sleep with Enrico." Lexy's jaw dropped. She smothered a gasp. *Her* Enrico?

Jules shrugged. "Who wouldn't? I bet he knows how to show a woman a good time, but he is way too much of a flirt to bring home to meet the family."

"I think it's a European thing," Lexy said, feeling the need to defend him. "Making women feel special."

"Enrico's welcome to make me feel special in bed. Or, you know," Jules snickered. "On the kitchen table."

"You are incorrigible," Ren said.

Lexy was used to Jules's outrageous comments. But it was different when the subject of her friend's saucy remarks was the man she had growing feelings for.

"Now who would I marry?" Jules tapped a finger to her lip in thought. "You know who's fun? And cute? Tom, in sound. If I had to pick someone, I'd marry him."

"Good list. I think I'd kill Brian in IT," Ren said. "The guy is so awkward I just want to put him out of his misery."

"Ah, a mercy killing," said Lexy. "How kind of you, Ren."

"I know." She tossed her glossy black hair. "And I'm with Jules. Enrico to sleep with for sure."

Lexy's voice came out in a squeak. "You'd both pick Enrico to have sex with?"

"Wouldn't you?" Jules said.

I was thinking I'd pick him to marry.

"I guess," she said quietly. This supposedly funny game wasn't so amusing all of a sudden. She knew women liked Enrico. And he liked women. That much was obvious. But lately she'd been thinking about him in a different capacity. Someone she'd proudly take home to meet her parents.

"I like the guy," Ren said, as if reading her thoughts. "He oozes charm and is handsome as sin. If needing the attention of every female in the room is covering up an insecurity, I'm happy to have him compensate by being extra attentive in bed."

"Or the table?"

"I'm more conservative. I'll leave the table to you, Jules."

"And who would you marry?" Lexy nabbed a roasted potato off Ren's plate, hoping they'd both forget it was her turn next.

"I'll say Jake. He's a freelance photographer MHP has been using for social media photos, especially your show, Lex."

"Does he count?" said Jules. "If he's just a contract photographer?"

"My game, my rules. He counts."

Jules nodded. "Wait. Is this your way of telling us you're interested in him?"

Ren waved her hand dismissively. "Nah, I'm just enjoying working with him. He's got a keen eye for photography, and a sharp business sense."

"Uh-huh. But you're not interested," Jules said with feigned disbelief.

Ren neatly deflected. "Your turn, Lex."

"I really don't know." She couldn't tell her friends *now* that she would choose Enrico to marry. "Do I have to kill someone?"

"You do."

"What if I kill Merelda and take over MHP in a coup?"

Ren and Jules both doubled over laughing.

"It's perfect." Jules dabbed her eyes with her napkin. "And we definitely need another round of mimosas."

"You were supposed to pick a guy," Ren said. "But your answer is too funny to reject. What about the other two?"

"Honestly, I don't know. I can't think of anyone for either."

"We'll help you," Jules said. "Enrico to fuck. He wins that category across the board."

Lexy started to shake her head, to deny she found him attractive, but gave a weak smile instead. It was just a silly game.

"And for you to marry—"

"Nate!" Jules and Ren said in unison, smiles giving way to laughter over their shared answer.

"What?" said Lexy. "Nate? No. We're just friends."

"A solid basis for any marriage," said Jules.

"You know after Tyler, I—"

"We know, we know," interrupted Jules. "You won't date anyone you're friends with. Which we should discuss another time, because I think there's a flaw in your logic, but for now, don't spoil Ren's game."

"I'll give you a choice." There was a wicked gleam in Ren's eye. "Either you marry Nate," she paused dramatically. "Or Brian."

"Ugh. Didn't Ren kill Brian? Okay, fine. I'll marry Nate. Happy?" She drained what was left of her drink. Just in time for their server to bring another round. She couldn't believe her friends would both jump Enrico if given the chance.

"Great game, Ren," said Jules, popping a strawberry in her mouth. "Lex, now that our future marriages are sorted, and we know who we need to help each other bury, how's everything with the show? From the outside, it looks like things are fan-frigging-tastic. But how is it really?"

"A lot harder, and way more work than I ever imagined when we filmed those video clips in Connor's garage. Back then my biggest concern was if Merelda liked it."

"And now?"

She hesitated. How to explain she wasn't on top of the world the way she'd expected? "It's no longer just my boss I'm trying to impress. The whole country is watching, and the show's doing so much better than I dreamed that it's actually freaking me out."

"You're freaking out because your show is a success?" Ren said.

"I know. It makes no sense. But what if next season flops? What if the sponsors dump it? What if the network doesn't renew it?"

"As my granda' always said," the Irish was turned up in Jules's voice again. "Any man can lose his hat in a fairy wind."

Lexy laughed. "I can always count on your Irish wisdom.

But what exactly is the knowledge I'm supposed to get from it this time?"

"Some things are out of our control."

"Obviously," Ren said sarcastically.

Jules pointed a finger at Lexy "So there's no use worrying about those things you listed off. Don't borrow trouble."

"Thanks, Granda' O'Shay."

"He was also famous for saying marriages are all happy—it's having breakfast together that causes all the trouble." Jules laughed. "I still haven't figured out that one."

"So we avoid having breakfast with Tom, Jake, and Nate, once we're married to them," said Ren. "Problem solved."

"Sláinte," said Jules, holding out her champagne flute. Lexy clinked glasses with her friends, not caring when their boisterous laughter drew curious looks from nearby diners.

Granda' O'Shay may be right about some things, but nothing would stop Lexy from eating breakfast with Enrico if she got the chance.

CHAPTER 18

"My husband and I met on Thanksgiving when we both showed up to the emergency room with cuts on our hands from electric carving knives. To this day, neither of our families will let us near one of those things."

-Maggie, Guest
Duquan's Downlow on Dating and Love
Podcast episode #119

Lexy giggled as she read her mom's text about missing her at Thanksgiving dinner. Going by one of the emojis, she'd tried a new eggplant recipe. If her mom only knew what the eggplant emoji really meant.

She'd had no choice but to stay in town. Rather than follow the lead of other networks and air a repeat on Thanksgiving, the production house had rolled the dice and aired a new episode, a risky ploy that could have blown up in their faces, but had paid off big. Going by the numbers, the most popular 'after family Thanksgiving dinner activity' had been to watch *Cupid Grants a Second Chance.*

The show's bubbly contestant, Emma, had wound up alone in Vegas, due to friends canceling at the last minute. Felix had been there alone for the same reason, and when they met and shared similar stories, it added to their feelings of kismet. Their whirlwind romance had included a spontaneous wedding, followed by a quickie divorce. But Emma was having second thoughts.

"Excellent job with the Thanksgiving episode, Lexy," Merelda said as she passed Lexy's desk, leaving Lexy in a state of shock as her boss glided up the steps to her office.

She'd heard the hive murmurs earlier about Merelda being in an uncharacteristically good mood following last night's episode, but a compliment was totally out of character. This was clearly the moment she'd been waiting for. The best chance she was going to get.

Hoping this move didn't get her fired, Lexy breezed past Joey with a vague statement about being summoned, knocked on her boss's door and hurried inside before the sharp, "Enter" was issued.

With a sigh, Merelda put down the file she was reading. "Yes?"

"I have a proposal regarding the *CGSC* prize for the winning Legend."

"There is no prize. We've already settled this issue." Merelda picked up the papers she'd been reading.

"I've organized one." Lexy took a determined step forward. "I grew up in Cannon Beach, Oregon. It is nationally recognized as a top travel destination in the Pacific Northwest. People back home are eager to support the show's success, and several local businesses jumped at the chance to donate experiences and services that showcase the area. Including accommodations for our winning couple at a B&B."

Merelda slid her glasses down the bridge of her nose, pinning Lexy with a stare over the rim of her designer frames. Lexy's stomach quivered slightly. Still, The Queen hadn't cut her off yet, or dismissed her.

"Several restaurants and cafes are contributing meals," she forged on, "including a beach picnic lunch, and a romantic dinner for two. Beach bike rentals, a craft brewery tour, and a couple's massage will complete the package." Now for the hard part. "All that's left is for MHP to cover travel expenses," she finished in a rush.

Merelda continued to regard her coolly. Lexy worried her bottom lip, waiting for the guillotine to fall. At last, her boss spoke. "You went behind my back."

Lexy gulped. Nodded meekly.

"When I expressly told you there was no budget."

"I did it *because* you said there was no budget. Not awarding a prize doesn't reflect well on the show. This way we are able to offer—"

"Clearly, you leave me no choice," Merelda interrupted. "Manor House Productions will cover travel expenses. Congratulations. You have your prize package." Sliding her glasses back in position, The Queen returned her attention to the file on her desk, dismissing Lexy with a shooing motion of her hand.

As she closed the door, she thought she heard her boss say, "I must admit, I'm impressed. That's something I would have done." She shook her head. Low blood sugar must be making her imagine things.

Munching a granola bar at her desk to prevent any further auditory hallucinations, she scrolled through her work emails for the most urgent ones. She almost skipped past one from a Marcie Douglas, until she remembered Douglas was Nate's last name. Why would his sister be emailing her?

From: Marcie.Douglas44@gmail.com
To: lexy.smith@MHproductions.com
Subject: Top Secret!
Hey Lexy,
It's Nate's sister Marcie. I got your contact info from the MHP website. I love the raincoat you picked out for my birthday. Nate's birthday is coming up and I wanted to invite you to a party we're throwing him on Sunday. I think he'd really like it if you were there.
Marcie

Great sleuthing by Nate's sister. She checked her phone's calendar. Good, she was free. She emailed her acceptance and a short time later the time and location popped into her inbox.

She hadn't been to the MoPOP, the Museum of Pop Culture, for years, not since before they changed the name from the Experience Music Project. What a perfect venue for Nate's party. Now to top the birthday card he had given her.

 today was Nate's birthday. It was too busy living up to its reputation as 'Rain City'. Dodging the puddle outside the cab, Lexy raced across the street. A streetlight illuminated the unmistakable combination of colored and textured metals that was her destination.

Love or hate the architecture of MoPOP, it certainly made a statement.

Inside, she smoothed her slightly-damp hair, glad she'd indulged in a last-minute shopping spree with Jules that only caused her credit card to weep a little. Jules had assured her the emerald cut velvet dress was a stunner, perfect for all her holiday parties. If she got time off to attend any.

Ahead on her right, the sounds of music, talking, laughter, and the clinking of glasses spilled out of the event room. It felt weird not having Jules and Ren at her side.

"There you are!" A girl with Nate's green eyes and dimpled smile all but pounced on her when she entered the room. "I'm Marcie. I stalked you on Insta, so I'd know what you look like. Nate talks about you a lot, but you know, leaves out the important details."

She instantly relaxed. "Hi. I told Nate if I ever got to meet you, we'd have a lot to talk about."

"Oooooh, you've got dish on my bro. I like you already. And you know the guys, right?" Marcie guided her to Nate's band mates from the Rainy Day Astronauts. "Connor helped me put this together."

"Hi guys." She noticed Adam, the keyboard player, had his arm around a familiar-looking brunette, who turned at the sound of her voice. "Danielle, I didn't know you'd be here."

"Adam invited me. We've sort of been seeing each other since your birthday party." Danielle snuggled in closer to his side.

"Hey, Lexy," Connor said. "You were dressed different last time, but I like this look, too." Connor casually draped an arm over Marcie's shoulders. "Can you believe Lexy turned me down when I asked her out?"

"I can. She's way too smart to go out with the likes of you."

Connor bent his head closer to Marcie's and Lexy thought she heard him murmur, "Then what does that say about you?"

Hmmmmm, so that's the way the wind blows...

"I hear congrats are in order," Adam said. His fair, closely-shaven hair matched the short scruff on his chin, and he'd traded his typical T-shirt for a black button-down dress shirt. "It sounds like your show is a huge success." His winning smile had sent more than one female fan into a frenzy. "Probably thanks to using Connor's garage."

"Totally true." she smiled back. "Definitely the garage setting sealed the deal."

"Glad we could help." Griffin, a striking African-American man, wore his hair knotted into tight spikes sticking up from his head. On stage, the drummer came across as shy, but maybe he just took time to warm up to people.

With a parting wave, Marcie steered her a hard right. "Mom's dying to meet you."

An attractive woman around the same age as Lexy's mom was fussing with a 'Happy Birthday' banner strung between two pillars. A tall man near the second pillar was trying to follow her directions, but appeared to be all thumbs and the banner hung crooked.

"Looks great mom," Marcie gave her mother a kiss on the cheek.

"You're just humoring me because you wouldn't let me put up any baby photos."

Marcie exchanged a look with Lexy. "Nate owes me." She gestured with one hand. "Mom, this is Lexy. You know. From Nate's work. My mom, Linda. And this is Walter."

Linda shook her hand. "It's nice to meet you, Lexy–

from–Nate's–work. Nate was thrilled for you when the show got approved."

Walter nodded. "Great show. Everyone's talking about *Cupid Grants a Second Chance,* which deserves a toast. Decorations are not my forte," he said, "but I'm very good at bringing wine to beautiful women, so let me put that skill to use." With a squeeze of Linda's hand, he headed for the bar.

Lexy glanced around. "Perfect venue for a musician's party," she said, hoping she'd get a chance to look at some of the artifacts housed in glass display cases throughout the room.

"It was Marcie's idea," Linda said.

"Actually, Connor gets the credit." Marcie smirked. "Nate thinks he's meeting Connor here for a documentary on the history of the guitar pick. As if anyone would want to watch that. Other than Nate. He's such a music nerd." Her attention swung to the doorway. "And here's the nerd now!"

With a hop and a skip, Marcie made a beeline for the door and a puzzled-looking Nate, who was greeted by hugs and handshakes and hearty back slaps. He looked different than at work or when playing on stage, a difference she couldn't quite put her finger on.

"Here you are, ladies." Walter returned and handed her and Linda each a glass of wine, raising his own glass in a toast. "To Lexy's continued success."

"Thank you. I'm not sure the show would exist without Nate's help."

Linda beamed. "What a nice thing to say."

"Talking about me again?" Nate leaned down and kissed his mom's cheek, then shook Walter's hand before he turned to her.

"Happy birthday!" She gave him a hug. "You aren't disappointed this isn't a documentary on the guitar pick?"

"I knew it was too good to be true," he said with a rueful grin. "But I'll try to enjoy myself anyway. Don't want Marcie to feel bad."

"Better not tell her I only came for the cake," she joked.

"Our secret." When he smiled down at her, butterflies started bashing around inside her, followed by a slow, tingling warmth that spread through her limbs. She moistened her lips, remembering their kiss in the garage.

"It's been lovely to meet so many of your friends, especially Lexy," his mom said.

"Isn't she great?" His hand brushed her arm while his eyes remained locked on hers. She pulled her gaze away first.

"I'm so proud of you, sweetheart." His mom beamed as she spoke.

He slung an arm around his mom's shoulders. "Not half as proud as I am of you."

His mom lit up even brighter. "Flatterer." She patted his arm before she took Walter's hand. "We'll let you young people mingle."

"Your mom's great," Lexy said as the older couple walked away hand in hand.

"I'm lucky," he said. "Drew the short straw when it came to dads, but hit the jackpot in the mother department."

"I can see you did." She wondered what the story was with Nate and his dad, then pushed the thought away. Not the time to ask. Just then Nate was hailed from across the room. He took a step, then hesitated.

"Go," she said. "As birthday boy, you are extremely popular tonight." She gave him a playful push toward the friend who had called his name.

"I'll find you later," he called, walking away.

She set down her empty wine glass and wandered over

to a glass display case on the far side of the room. One of Biggie Smalls's suits was on display. She'd known the notorious rapper had been a big man, but she was dwarfed standing next to his suit.

"You a fan of Biggie?" She turned to see Connor behind her.

"He loves it when I call him Big Poppa."

"A woman who can quote 90's hip-hop? No wonder Nate was so keen to help you."

"Don't tell him I said this, but I suspect he's hiding a romantic soul beneath his motorcycle jacket, layers of flannel, and that aura of rockstar."

"Right down to the Chuck Taylors he always wears." Connor laughed. "The number of times he's let something slip about a romcom he's watched..."

"I caught that, too," she said. "He blames growing up in a house full of women, but I don't buy it."

They grinned at each other.

Connor sobered. "It was good to see him so happy filming the videos with you. To finally see that dark cloud blow away."

"Are we talking about the same Nate?"

"Most people didn't see it, but the guys and I knew it was there."

She remembered the look that flashed in Nate's eyes in the garage when she'd brought up RDA filming a music video. The night they kissed.

Connor took a sip of his beer. "Ever since the Adele Fiasco."

"Adele?"

"Nate's ex. I thought he might've told you about her."

She was sure the shock showed on her face. "Nate dated Adele? As in 'Rolling-In-The-Deep-Adele'?"

Connor threw back his head and let out a roar of laughter. "No, not she of British music royalty fame. Nate's relationship was with non-famous, small town Ohio Adele, who moved out west to go to college."

She laughed too. "Right. Of course. I don't know why I thought—" She shook her head. "Are you talking about the ex who made a big scene at one of your shows and a video of the whole thing was put on YouTube?"

"Yeah, it was a very public breakup. I used to wish bad things would happen to her after what she did to him."

As Connor stared at a glass case displaying one of Elton John's costumes, she knew he wasn't seeing the yellow embroidered pants and jacket, but something from the past.

He sighed. "I guess I'll let karma sort her out."

She placed a gentle hand on his arm. "You're a good friend."

"A good friend who couldn't stop that train wreck." He planted a hand over hers briefly. "I'd be over it by now, except I can tell Nate hasn't let it go. He still feels guilty."

"Why would Nate feel guilty?"

He tilted his head her way. "How much has he told you?"

She fidgeted with her necklace. "Just that his girlfriend 'lost her shit' at your show and it ended up on the Internet."

"Not my place to say more." He paused. "Except this. After what went down with Adele, Nate got this screwy idea about only dating a fellow musician. Someone who will understand his commitment to our band."

"You think he's wrong?"

"Of course he's wrong." He grinned. "Look at what an unstable bunch we musicians are. Adam, Griffin, and I take great delight in pointing out all the failed musician couples out there. On that note," he pointed to another display case. "See those boots worn by one of the guys from KISS? I better find the birthday boy and remind him that Gene Simmons's relationships didn't work out with either Cher *or* Diana Ross."

"Like I said, a good friend," she teased.

As he strolled away, she wandered through the other displays, her mind more on what he had said about Nate than on Janis Joplin's feather boa, or the Run DMC Kangol hat.

"Are you having a good time?" She was jolted out of her thoughts by Marcie, who linked arms with her. "I think Nate's having a great birthday. I'm so glad Connor and I planned to have it here." Marcie cast a glance her way. "And I'm extra glad you could make it."

As they headed back to the others, Marcie kept up a steady stream of chatter, during which she learned that Marcie had followed in her mom's footsteps to become a nurse and loved her job, that she hadn't seen her dad since he walked out on the family when she was two, and that she was happy her mom met Walter but it was strange to have a parent who was dating.

"I think it kind of threw Nate when mom started dating Walter this year. When dad left, Nate really stepped in, always watching out for Mom and I, taking care of us, like he had to be the man of the house even at seven years old. Then suddenly he's ousted from that role, and he's not sure what his new role is. But he's the best big brother, and that's all I need him to be."

She filed that information about Nate away for future reference. She was learning a lot about the guy tonight. What might he have learned about her at her birthday party?

"You throw a great party, girl!" A handsome bearded

man with a stunning woman on his arm, stepped up to give Marcie a hug.

"Jer! Priya! Nate must have been so surprised to see you."

"We wouldn't have missed it," Jer said.

"Jer, Priya, this is Lexy," Marcie said by way of introduction. "The genius behind the show Nate's working on now."

"Oh my gosh," Priya gushed. "We are such huge fans of *Cupid Grants a Second Chance*. I cry at every episode. In a good way."

"She does," Jer confirmed.

"As if you don't, you big softie," Priya retorted with a poke to his ribs.

"Thank you. That means so much," Lexy said. "Now it's my turn to fan-girl. I'm a massive McClanes fan. Thanks for signing the drumstick Nate gave me," she said to Jer, then turned to Priya. "I started following your blog when Nate was on the road with you. You're a talented and entertaining writer."

"Thanks." Priya beamed. "Learning I've got a new reader never gets old."

"We'd better go say hi to the rest of RDA," Jer said, looking to where Connor, Adam and Griffin stood together laughing. "Catch up more later, Marcie. Nice meeting you, Lexy."

"Bye, Marcie! Great to meet you, Lexy. Thanks for making a show that warms my big soft heart." Priya and Jer strolled off hand in hand.

"They're adorable," Marcie said with a sigh.

"Speaking of adorable," said Lexy. "Did I notice Connor looking your way an awful lot tonight?"

Marcie flushed and leaned closer. "If I tell you something, you have to promise not to tell Nate."

She drew an X across her heart.

"Connor is totally hot, and kind of a flirt. I didn't think he'd ever see me as anyone other than Nate's little sister, and then one day—" She beamed. "It's like he finally noticed I grew up."

She nodded, encouraging Marcie's tale.

"When Nate was away with The McClanes, I ran into Connor at a show. We hung out, one thing led to another and he kissed me at the end of the night. And wow, what a kiss."

She recalled having a similar reaction when she kissed Nate. But she wasn't about to share that with Marcie. Nothing had come of it, and nothing was going to. They'd both agreed on that. "Then what happened?"

"We went on a couple of dates. I thought things were going really well. Then he got all noble on me. Said we couldn't take things any further. Nate was his best friend, and that made me off limits."

She sighed and rolled her eyes. "Men!"

"I know, right?" Marcie said. "Though Nate would probably pound Connor if he found out."

"I repeat, 'Men!' So, what are you going to do?"

"I'm not giving up, that's for sure. I've got a plan to help Connor see past the whole 'best-friend's-sister' thing."

"Good for you. If I can do anything to help, let me know, I make a good wing-chick."

"Thanks. And if you need help with my brother, I've got your back." Marcie winked.

Oops. Somehow Marcie had gotten the wrong idea. "Nate and I are just friends," she said quickly.

"Mmm hmmm," Marcie said with a smirk. "Just let me know, sistah."

After Marcie left to hatch phase one of 'Operation

Connor', Lexy swapped stories with Priya about the joys and fears of bringing a creative project to life. She lost her new friend in the crowd as the guests jostled them to where Marcie and Nate's mom were wheeling out a tower of cupcakes decorated with flashing sparklers. She joined the others in an off-key rendition of "Happy Birthday". As she stood, debating which flavor to choose, someone grabbed her hand.

"Quick. This way. While no one's looking."

Startled, she followed Nate through a doorway and up a roped-off staircase with a 'closed' sign.

"I suppose, since it's your birthday, you won't get in trouble for this?"

"It's in the official birthday rulebook."

He led her upstairs, the crowd below in full party mode, singing along with Bryan Adams's "Summer of '69". Caught up in the moment, she started singing along quietly. "Spent nightmares down at the drive-in. And that's when I met you."

Nate whirled, an amused grin on his face.

"What?" she said, suddenly self-conscious. "Just because I don't have your voice—"

His grin stretched even wider. "What lyrics did you sing?"

"You know the lyrics."

"Oh, I know the lyrics. But I don't think you do."

She said nothing as he inched even closer. "Did you sing 'spent nightmares down at the drive-in'?"

"Those are the words."

"No, they aren't. But it just made my night that you think they are. Come on." He grabbed her hand, leading her forward. "We're almost there."

"Where are we going?" She'd never been aware of his

calluses before, but she could feel them tonight. Guitar-playing calluses.

"Back to where it all started."

The sign said 'Guitar Gallery'. The room was in shadow, lit by glass display cases where individual spotlights shone on a treasure trove of instruments dating back to the early days of Rock.

She stopped next to him, drinking it in for a second before going inside.

His green eyes met hers with an easy familiarity. "The first time I saw this, it was like I was struck by a jolt of electricity. The hair on my arms stood up, my heart started racing, I could hardly breathe." He stopped in front of Jimi Hendrix's guitar. "Seeing all these guitars, the impact these musicians have had, I knew I wanted to be a part of it. Playing music, connecting with people."

"You do. I see it every time I watch you play. The way the crowd responds."

"My favorite, my Fender Telecaster, I saw in the music shop one day. I wasn't even looking to buy a guitar, but I saw it on the wall and thought, 'there she is.' I took it down and something in me settled, just clicked in place the first time I held her."

A tingle chased down her spine. "That's how I felt in the surf shop when I first saw my newest board. It was love at first sight. I knew before I checked the dimensions that she was the perfect size. And she was coming home with me."

"To love at first sight," he echoed softly, his eyes on hers. "And not just guitars."

Her breath caught. A flush of heat poured through her as he took a step closer.

CHAPTER 19

"Music is my first love. And she always will be. Just don't tell my fiancée. Wait, no one's going to hear this podcast are they?"

-Declan, Guest
Duquan's Downlow on Dating and Love
Podcast episode #27

Tension rippled the air as palpably as that of an approaching storm where you can feel it coming and are poised for it to hit, but it's not here yet. Nate sucked in a long breath, relieved and disappointed when Lexy spoke, breaking the spell.

"I think we just discovered the crossover between surfing and music. Certain gear is magic."

Her voice echoed the reverence he felt and a heated glow spread through his chest from sharing this special moment. "Like everything in here."

Being in the Guitar Gallery always heightened the feelings he'd just shared with Lexy. The awe. Wanting to be a part of something bigger than himself. The desire to reach people through his music.

Then there were the other memories. "I brought Adele here once. My ex. The nightmare in my past. I tried to share this with her." He indicated the guitars. "She didn't get it at all."

"I know what you mean." Lexy nodded sympathetically. "When you're sharing something so personal, and you don't feel understood."

"Adele was from a small town in Ohio. Grunge wasn't in her blood the way it is mine, I guess."

"Grunge in *your* blood, salt water in *mine*."

He smiled. "It's nice you know what I'm talking about."

"Even if I wouldn't want to sit through a documentary on the history of the guitar pic?" Her voice gentled. "What happened with her?"

"You didn't look for the video?" In her shoes, he wouldn't have been able to resist.

"I did a search," she admitted, "but I didn't find it." Her eyes were soft on his. "I'm sorry I looked."

"Don't be. I would've done the same."

"Maybe it's not there anymore?"

"Oh, *it's there*. Did I mention things were so bad we had to change our name? Probably why you couldn't find it."

She shook her head. "That's awful."

"The demise of Underground Anthem." His gut still tightened when he said the name.

She cocked her head, a thoughtful expression on her face. "I like Rainy Day Astronauts better."

"Lucky for us."

"I'll say." She gave his shoulder a playful poke.

"We were doing well; booking lots of local gigs. Getting good reviews. Not bad for a group of kids just out of college. We decided to film a music video."

"Ahhh..."

"Yeah. Now you know why I reacted the way I did when you brought it up." He moved on to the next guitar. A beautiful 1965 Epiphone Casino owned by Howlin' Wolf.

"You don't have to tell me."

He stared at Wolf's guitar, blew out a breath. "Maybe it'll help exorcise those demons."

"In the place that reminds you why you wanted to be a musician."

"Exactly." He shoved his fists in his pockets. As they strolled through the gallery, he recounted that fateful evening. It was easier when he could look at these historic instruments instead of at her. "We were transitioning from a hobby to making a name for ourselves." Somehow, looking into the display case was like viewing his own past. "The better the band did, the more insecure Adele got; jealous of every girl who came to our shows." He shook his head. "I couldn't convince her she had nothing to worry about."

"Sounds tough, "she said. "When something important in your life is going well, while another part of your life is coming apart."

"Totally." He rubbed the back of his neck. "Adele grew increasingly moody, needing a lot of attention. But the guys and I were caught up in planning the video for our song "Chasing Dreams". The premise was the story of a group of friends trying to make it from their small town to the city to catch our show. But they keep running into all these problems. Flat tire, missed their exit and got lost, traffic jam, stuff like that. Determined not to miss it, they had to problem solve."

"Fun idea. Creative."

"Thanks. Plus, you see clips of us prepping in between their mad adventure. The pressure mounts when we start playing and they're still scrambling to get to the venue. High stakes and a satisfying ending. I thought she'd be excited for me. I guess I didn't want to see how much she wasn't."

"You said she lost her shit."

"Yeah. Everything was going great. We had a super crowd. They knew we were filming. This was for the scenes in the video when the show starts and the friends aren't there yet, and for when they finally make it. The energy in the bar was off the charts. I was chatting with the crowd between takes, keeping the stoke going. Suddenly, Adele pushed to the front yelling my name. Angry."

"No one stopped her?"

"They thought it was staged. Part of the video. People stepped back so she was front and center. Everyone's eyes were on her."

"What did she say?"

"She said if I loved her, I'd quit Underground Anthem. Said it was ruining our relationship." A quick glance at Lexy saw no judgement, only sympathy.

"Then she got mean. Saying things like I'd never leave because I needed the attention of all my groupies, though she called them something worse. She accused me of cheating, then approached women around her, demanding to know if they'd slept with her boyfriend."

Lexy gave his arm an understanding squeeze.

"I still remember the moment people realized it wasn't part of the video and started to record what was happening. You know those nightmares where you watch something bad unfolding, and it feels like time has slowed down, but you're powerless to stop it?"

Eyes wide, she nodded.

"It was like that. Adele kept yelling at me. Yelling at girls in the crowd."

"What did you do?"

"What *could* I do?" He paced in front of the guitars, reliving that agitation and sense of powerlessness. "I tried to defuse the situation, but the calmer I stayed, the angrier Adele got. She grabbed a pint of beer off some guy's table and threw it at my head. Luckily, I've got quick reflexes," he said with a mirthless laugh.

"At least you're making a joke about it."

"I haven't been able to before now." It was true. The shame was always so huge, making light of it had never been an option. "Where was I?"

"The beer glass."

"Right. Security stepped in. But the damage was done."

"The video on YouTube."

"Yup. More than one. Even that wasn't enough for Adele. She was all over social media, accusing me of cheating. Had her friends claim I slept with them."

"Why would anyone believe her?"

"People get off on the misery of others. She even wrote things on the Facebook page I keep for family. My *grand-mother* was reading her lies."

She made a sound of empathy.

"After a break, we re-branded, and started over." He ran a hand through his hair. "The worst part is it didn't just impact me, but Connor, Adam, Griffin; it derailed their music careers, too. Anyway, now you know the whole sordid tale."

She gave him a side hug. "If it's confession time, my sordid tale involves breaking the heart of my best friend, my first boyfriend, when I ran off to follow my dreams. He's a

Cannon Beach boy at heart who'd never be happy in the city. I thought I was doing him a favor by not making him choose." It was her turn to pace. "I'm pretty sure I broke my parents' hearts, too. Giving them the impression the small town they loved wasn't good enough for me. I felt so selfish, hurting everyone I loved."

"That doesn't sound selfish to me. It sounds brave." He placed his hands on her shoulders to emphasize his point. "It takes guts to go against what everyone tells you is best. Especially the people you love. To be true to yourself and follow your dreams."

Her shoulders lifted with her sigh. "Maybe..."

"No 'maybe' about it."

"I don't ever want to hurt anyone I love like that again."

"Of course not. But look how *CGSC* is changing peoples' lives."

She brightened. "And someday, when your guitar is on display here at MoPOP and they write about lead singer Nate Douglas, the fact that your earlier band, Underground Anthem, had such a juicy past will be a plus. It will make people more eager to see the guitar that used to belong to you."

"Yeah, right."

"I'm serious. I can see a whole display here about the history of the local band, Rainy Day Astronauts." She spread her hands, as if envisioning the future. "Chronicling their influence on the Seattle music scene."

"Cut it out." But he chuckled, touched by her belief in him, in RDA.

"I even have proof." She snapped open her little purse and handed him an envelope. "*Rolling Stone's* latest." Her smile lit up her entire face.

"The music magazine doesn't print anything this small."

"Just hurry up and open it."

He pulled out a photoshopped card, threw back his head and laughed. The card showed him on the cover of the November issue of Rolling Stone, and a caption that read, "Happy Birthday to Local Music Legend." Inside were quotes about him, credited to famous musicians.

"They say legends are born, not made. Well, Nate was born and bred in the heart of Seattle's music scene, and it shows." — Dave Grohl

"If I could pick one musician to jam with for eternity, it would be Nate Douglas of the Rainy Day Astronauts." — Eddie Vedder

"Shit that boy can play!" — Jimi Hendrix

The quotes were followed by Lexy's message:

Happy Birthday to an incredible musician, and an even more amazing friend. I know I've said this already, but my show would not exist without you. There's no way I can ever pay you back, but that won't stop me from trying. What's the name for Apology Pie, when there's no apology required? Whatever it is, you've got a slice coming your way. XO Lexy

A warmth washed over him. His throat thickened. "Thanks, Lex. I love it." He flipped back to the picture on the front. "Maybe I'll get you to print me a large copy. Put it up in the jam space to make the other guys jealous."

"Glad you like it." She moved closer and gave him a hug. "Happy Birthday, Nate."

He smiled down at her. "You've got some skill with Photoshop. Music Legend, huh?" he said, his arms still wrapped around her.

She pulled back enough to look into his eyes, rested a palm against the front of his shirt. "Undeniably." She gave his chest two gentle pats with her finger tips. "And you know what else? While RDA will likely be immortalized in the MoPOP someday, no one is going to put my surfboard on display. People won't gawk at it, wondering about the woman who rode it."

"Guess you'll never be as famous as me."

"Notorious, you mean."

He laughed and slung an arm around her shoulders. Maybe, with her help, he'd succeeded in exorcising those demons at long last. "About those song lyrics you were singing earlier."

"I have no idea what you're talking about."

She elbowed him in the ribs and he laughed again, suddenly having a serious rethink about his decision to only date a musician. As the sounds of the party grew louder, he pulled her to one side before they went in.

"Nate?" Her lips were parted. Irresistible. "Did you forget something?"

Maybe.

Before he could say a word, they were spotted.

"There you two are," Priya said. "Can I snag Lexy? I've got an idea for a social media crossover between her show and my blog."

He slid his arm from Lexy's shoulder. "Of course."

"Good. Because I'm stealing *you* for a minute." It was his mom. Had everyone been watching for their return? His mom walked him over to a relatively quiet corner. "Are you having a good birthday?"

"The best. All my favorite people. Bonus, for the music memorabilia."

She gave him a look he remembered from when he was a kid. Love, concern, and a mother's innate ability to see below the surface. "I was relieved when you and the boys started playing together again. I hope you never stop going after the things that are important to you."

He gave her a tight hug. "I love you mom. You don't have to worry about me. I'm happy."

"That's all I ask." She took his arm. "Except what's this I hear about you only dating musicians? Is it smart to limit your options like that?"

What was she? Reading his mind? Not the time to tell her he was having his own second thoughts. "I'm going to kill Connor."

CHAPTER 20

"I married my high school sweetheart. That man is lucky social media didn't exist back then. I don't even want to *think* about all the embarrassing videos of him that would be out there still."

-Evelyn, Guest
Duquan's Downlow on Dating and Love
Podcast episode #45

Back at home, without taking the time to change out of her dress from the party, Lexy sat down to search Underground Anthem on YouTube. Earlier this evening, as she got ready, she had wondered what it would be like walking into tonight's party on Enrico's arm. The quiet thrill of knowing she was his choice, and he was hers.

But, as Enrico's date, she would have missed out on that magical conversation with Nate in the guitar gallery. There had been something so special as they each revealed an intimate memory from their past. Not to mention connecting over the unexpected parallel between surfing and music. She wouldn't have wanted to miss that.

On-screen, she saw what looked like the video. She clicked on it. "Let's see what a horror show you are, Adele."

And there it was. Filmed on someone's cell phone. Exactly as Nate had described. Except he'd left out some of the more colorful language Adele had used.

Her hands curled into fists. Nate deserved a prize for keeping his cool as Adele shrieked at him, accusing him of cheating with multiple "groupie sluts" in the crowd.

Where was Buffy with a handy stake through the heart when you needed her? Adele was certainly sucking the life out of Nate. When he pleaded with her to go backstage with him and talk about it, she screeched, "Backstage! That's where you take *them* isn't it? They love fucking a rockstar backstage." The crowd let out a collective gasp. Just as it looked like sympathy might swing in Nate's direction, a woman yelled, "You give it to him, sister! You don't take that from *no* man."

She winced as Adele hurled the glass at him, yelling that she hated him and it was over between them. Her heart was pounding by the time security arrived and led Adele away.

"Never trust a woman wearing super shredded jeans," she said aloud. "Not even when they were trendy." She felt bad as she watched Nate return to the mic and apologize to the crowd before walking offstage, the guys flanking him protectively.

She watched the video again before scrolling through some of the comments. Brutal! Strangers had been quick to jump on board trashing Nate and the band. Yet, look at the way they'd recovered and rebranded. You couldn't keep a good band down. The way Seattleites love RDA, the time was certainly right for the band to put out a killer video.

Maybe there was something she could do. She smiled to herself, imagining how it would feel to help the guys and pay Nate back for everything he'd done for her.

~

MARCIE LEANED back against her kitchen counter. "Aren't you going to thank me?" She looked at Nate expectantly.

"I already thanked you for the amazing party you threw me last week," he said. "You need more? You're my favorite sister. The best thing since sliced bread and the invention of the hoverboard."

"Nice try. I'm your only sister. And that's not what I meant."

His eyes narrowed. What was she up to?

"I have something else to thank you for? You should be thanking me for racing over to fix your oven. Which seems perfectly fine, by the way."

"I'm talking about a certain someone I invited to the party."

Just as it dawned on him that Marcie's SOS text about her oven being 'on the fritz' was a lure to get him over here, she pounced.

"What are you going to do about Lexy?"

He straightened and wiped his hands. "In what way?"

"I know you like her. Like really *like* her. Is it wrong to want to see my big brother happy?"

He flashed to how he'd felt with Lexy in the Guitar Gallery. Vehement denial on his part would be a dead give-away. "Lexy and I are friends. Who said I like her?" *If,* since his birthday, he'd been rethinking his 'musicians only' dating rule, his sister did not need to know.

"No one had to. One look at your face when I say her name...bro, you're easier to read than *The Hunger Games*." She Marcie-laughed at her own humor.

"You're totally misreading this situation." A statement he would defend with his dying breath.

"Lexy not being a musician is a stupid reason not to at least ask her on a real date."

He groaned. "Connor got to you, too?"

"I also happen to know your coffee date yesterday sucked."

"Tell my former-best-friend he's dead to me. And yes, my date with the girl who travels around singing at children's festivals in a group with her five siblings—*in matching outfits*—was awful. Not that it's any of your business."

She gave him a smug smile. "Back to Lexy. Have you told her you're interested?"

He pulled at the nonexistent collar of his T-shirt.

"How's she supposed to know if you don't tell her?" She held out her hand, palm up. "Female mind-reading only goes so far." She took a bite of a chocolate chip cookie.

"Where'd you get that? Did Mom bake cookies for you and not me?"

"We both know I'm mom's favorite," she teased. "I'll give you a cookie if you promise to ask Lexy out."

"You are the worst sister. I knew it when I tried to trade you for Joey Armstrong's 'Fruit by the Foot' at recess in grade three. Joey was too smart to want a sister."

"You know you love me."

He held out his hand for a cookie. She just gave him the eye.

"If I promise, can we drop the subject?"

She slid the cookie container his way. "I know you crossed your fingers behind your back. Don't force me to take matters into my own hands."

She would too. Time to go on the offensive, same as on the basketball court. Lexy was going home to her parents for Christmas, but maybe—

"By the way, I heard Daisy Jordan is playing a show in town on New Year's Eve. Wasn't it her video Lexy was in, that you took a screen grab for her birthday card?" She took another bite, all wide-eyed innocence.

He wasn't fooled for a second. But he had to admit, the show was a perfect excuse to ask Lexy out.

"I'M REALLY NERVOUS." Ayeesha, today's Legend, smoothed her skirt and adjusted her blouse in the dressing room mirror backstage.

"Take a deep breath," Lexy said. "You'll be great."

"How do you know?"

"If you can manage a large group of rambunctious kids for the summer, you can definitely handle this crowd."

"Camp was years ago. I was a different person."

"You've got a great story, and Duke to help you tell it. He's got you."

"Okay." Ayeesha took a deep breath then blew it out. "Thanks, Lexy. Whether I get a second chance with Dean or not." Her lips trembled. "This whole experience has meant so much to me."

Lexy's heart swelled. This was what it was all about. Realizing her dream to make a difference in the lives of others. Setting the stage for Duke to work his magic with the Legends and everyone involved, including those watching.

An emotional rollercoaster captured by Enrico's skill and shared with the world. Team work. Nothing she could have ever accomplished on her own.

"On in five," one of the crew announced.

"They're gonna love you." She gave Ayeesha a quick hug, then hurried to the control room.

After the unprecedented success of episode one, it was hard to believe things only got better. Ratings were through the roof. Today they were filming the last hopeful Legend before the final episode.

"Ayeesha was one of my favorites to dress," Jules said, as Lexy passed by. "Wait till you see what I've got lined up for her next week."

She blew a kiss, grateful to have Jules for those details. She had enough on her list for their finale, the moment where she got to reunite the winner with his or her 'one' for a second chance.

She waved to Nate on her way past the sound booth, hugging her secret to herself. Just the other day, details for the Artist's Trust Grant had popped up in her emails. Since scrounging for money was no longer part of her job, she almost hit delete before something caught her eye. As she read it again, an idea blossomed. What if she went after the unrestricted project-based award on behalf of Nate and the band? Seed money to fund a music video. One she could produce for them.

Applications were due December 31st. If she succeeded, her efforts could help increase the band's visibility, a thank you to Nate for his help in the early planning stages of *CGSC*. It was a win-win-win.

Cutting it close, she stepped into the control room and put on her headset just as Gabe, one of the cameramen, gave the 3-2-1 countdown to filming. Her heart fluttered when Enrico grinned and gave her a thumbs up. The man or the moment? Likely both.

They started rolling, leaving no room for thoughts about anything except the show. Other than the little giddy one about how excited Nate would be when she presented him with the grant.

THIS WAS EXCITING! Crammed elbow to shoulder around a pub table, the fake evergreen garlands and colored lights adding a festive glow, Lexy smiled at Enrico seated next to her. He had invited the whole *CGSC* team out to celebrate the successful wrap of Season One. She prayed there would be a Season Two.

"A toast." Enrico raised his highball glass and looked around the long table of exuberant MHP employees. He stood to get everyone's attention, nearly banging his head on an inflated snowman hanging from the ceiling.

Watching him, warmth spread through her chest and sent bubbles of delight up into her throat. He had come to mean so much to her in such a short time. His acknowledgement of the team endeared him to her even more.

"Thanks to everyone's hard work and commitment, the show is an even bigger success than we could have imagined. Tonight's finale is going to thrill our audience beyond belief."

Due to the popularity of *Cupid Grants a Second Chance*, local pubs had started playing the show on TVs usually reserved for sports. Tonight, the place down the street from the studio lot was packed with patrons waiting for the show to start.

"And the one person we truly could not have done this without—"

"Me!" Gabe shouted in jest.

"To Gabe," several other camera operators cried, clinking glasses as beer sloshed over the sides.

Enrico chuckled good-naturedly. "In addition to Gabe's skill with pans and zooms," he placed his warm, solid hand on her shoulder, "the woman who started it all." When he smiled at her that way it felt like they were the only two in the room. Her body couldn't decide whether to dissolve into a molten puddle at his feet, or explode like fireworks on the Fourth of July.

"As skilled, dedicated, and passionate a producer as I have ever had the pleasure to work with." His hand remained comfortably on her shoulder.

"To Lexy." Nate started the cheer, which was echoed by everyone at the long table.

"Thank you," she said quietly to Enrico when he sat back down. His praise of her capabilities as a producer sank into her very bones. Supplanting old doubts and criticisms from Mr. Snyder.

How do you like them apples, professor? You miserable old fart.

Gradually she became aware that the cheers had died down and her coworkers were all looking at her. "Thanks everyone." She bobbed her head, a flush heating her face. "To all of you." She raised her pint glass. "And to Cupid."

"To Cupid."

She sent Enrico a sideways look. Was Cupid paying attention? Did he know where she'd like him to aim his next arrow?

No one in the pub batted an eye as the cheers from their table grew more raucous. Fans were here to watch the *CGSC* finale, with no clue that the people responsible were seated in their midst.

How exciting to anonymously watch the final show with the viewers and witness their reaction. She'd wondered if some of the customers might recognize Duke, incognito in a Seahawks hat, but pubgoers were far more interested in their drinks than the MHP table.

Enrico leaned in. "We did it, Bella. I have no doubt we hit the Big Three tonight."

Entertainment, Emotion, and Engagement were the top goals in television broadcasting. The running joke was that it's actually the Big Four, because on the list, 'profit' starts with a silent E.

She clinked her glass to his. How about her own fourth E? *Enrico*. He'd been as attentive and flirtatious as ever, but things between them hadn't progressed beyond that. She got more texts from Nate, for heaven's sake.

She slanted Enrico a covert glance. Shouldn't he have made a move by now? Or was his toast setting the scene for later? Could she expect more than compliments and special attention after tonight's show aired?

When the opening bars of the theme song filled the air, everyone's focus shifted to the multiple screens around the venue where the final five Legends sat in a semi-circle facing the audience, and Duke bounded on stage. Jules had given his elegant maroon suit a touch of casual by pairing it with a T-shirt that read 'Give Love a Chance'.

"People!" His voice boomed from the TV speakers. "Can you feel the love?" His familiar catch-phrase elicited cheers from the studio audience echoed by those around them.

"It's our final episode. At last, the answer to the question on all of our minds. Who will be reunited with a love from their past on this very stage later tonight? To which of our final five Legends will Cupid grant a second chance? I'm as anxious as the rest of you to find out."

Even though she'd been in studio for the filming, Lexy felt as if she was watching for the first time as Duke approached Emma, the one who got married in Vegas, to share a few words with her.

Lexy tore her gaze from the screen long enough to see the effect the show was having on the patrons around her. There wouldn't be a dry eye in the house when Duke was finished.

"Shall we order nachos for the table?" asked someone seated near Lexy.

"Shhhh!" Loud whispers from all around.

On screen, Duke was talking to Ryland, reminding him of the importance of loving himself for who he is.

"Hey, Ryland!" called someone in the studio. "Is your sister single?"

Duke gave the audience a moment to laugh. It helped release the mounting tension generated by the final episode. "You're welcome to submit a video for Season Two of *Cupid Grants A Second Chance*, man. See if she's interested. But for now, let's return to our current Legends."

Ayeesha gave Duke a tremulous smile and nodded as he reinforced her inner strength and newfound courage, her confidence to now take a chance on love.

Lexy looked around the table, her gaze settling on Enrico. If the success of *CGSC* hadn't boosted her confidence to take a chance on love, what would? When the show broke for a commercial, she headed to the restroom.

"That Ryland sure is cute," said a young twenty-something, as she meticulously touched up her lipstick. "If Siobhan doesn't want a second chance, I'd go out with him"

Her friend giggled as she looked in the mirror and

flicked her fingers through her bangs. "I know, I already posted that comment on the show's Instagram page."

The first woman playfully hit her friend's shoulder. "OMG, you didn't!" She shook her head. "I hate you for thinking of it first."

Lexy took extra time drying her hands and smoothing her hair, hoping her eavesdropping wasn't obvious.

"If a guy I had dated sent in a video about me." The woman waved her lipstick like a magic wand. "That'd be it. I'd be won over in a heartbeat."

"You could submit your own video next season."

"I would if there was anyone I wanted a do-over with." Lipstick dropped the tube back in her purse. "I wonder how many other eligible guys sent in videos to *Cupid Grants* and didn't even make it in the top fifteen?"

Cupid Grants? That's kind of better than CGSC.

"So true," said Bangs. "If guys are submitting videos to that show, you know they're serious about wanting a relationship. Imagine *that* dating pool!"

"We'd have a way better chance with some of those guys than the ones on Tinder or Nooky," said Lipstick, pursing her lips at her reflection.

"I know. Tinder Guys are, like, so...Ugh." Bangs pulled open the door.

Lexy knew from Ren that people were enjoying *CGSC* and relating to the Legends, but this was the first time she'd overheard strangers discussing it. And they wanted a second season! She resisted the urge to skip back to the table.

As she went to slide into her chair, the server was on Enrico's other side delivering his drink. "Thank you, Bella," she thought she heard Enrico say.

Her hand froze on the back of her chair. Must have been her imagination. She sat and turned her attention to the closest screen, as Duke moved on to Liz. Lexy could relate to having feelings for someone you worked closely with, yet having to keep things professional.

Okay, not quite the same situation as hers, but still...

Suddenly the chorus from the song "I Believe in a Thing Called Love" by The Darkness played in the studio. The lead singer wailed in falsetto. Duke mimed an air guitar. With the show generating so much emotion, he and Nate had planned this to help lighten the mood. Duke grinned charmingly as Liz took her seat. "I couldn't resist."

In the pub, Nate gave Duke a high-five across the table. "Worked like a charm."

On screen, Duke had words of wisdom for the last Legend, Summer. She looked innocent and fragile, eyes never leaving Duke's as he encouraged her to continue on her newly-discovered pathway. One that didn't rely solely on fantasy.

"Legends, I hope each of you takes away at least one useful lesson to enhance your life and relationships now and in the future. That goes for everyone in the audience too, and all of you watching from home. At last, the moment you've all been waiting for is here."

A drumroll sounded. All five Legends formed a line on either side of Duke, who held out five large envelopes in a fan shape. Each one bore the name of a Legend.

"We've grown to know and love you all over the past weeks," he said as he handed out the envelopes. "But tonight, Cupid is only granting a second chance to one of you." Duquan held center stage. "Thanks to all of our loyal viewers who voted at the end of last week's episode. Now," he paused dramatically and addressed the audience. "Are you ready?"

Clapping, whistling, and stomping of feet backgrounded an enthusiastic "Yes!"

"Please face the audience," Duke instructed.

All five held their envelope as if it might burn their fingers.

Lexy joined the entire pub as they collectively held their breath, every eye in the place glued to the TV screens.

"It's gotta be that babe Summer," a guy in the back called out, breaking the silence.

"I'm Team Liz," cried someone else.

Suddenly the pub erupted in noise as people shouted out their top pick.

"Ayeesha all the way."

"Rooting for Ryland."

"Emma for the win."

"Remember, only one of you will have the gold logo on your card," Duke said from the TV. "The rest will be red. Are you ready?" He signaled the audience to count with him. "Five...Four..."

The pub patrons joined in. "Three...Two...One!"

Lexy felt Nate nudge her shoulder with his. She turned to look at him. 'You did it,' he mouthed.

She smiled back and mouthed 'We did'.

"And the winner is, Ayeesha," Duke's voice boomed. "Congratulations!"

A deafening cheer drew her eyes back to the TV to see a stunned Ayeesha holding the golden Cupid.

Lexy sighed in delight watching the finalists gather close, hugging, laughing, crying. Bubbles floated down from the ceiling onto the audience and the people on stage, creating a magical atmosphere.

The jubilance on TV was contagious. Enrico wrapped an arm around her. "Look what we created." He smiled, looking so deeply into her eyes she swore he could see her soul. "You should be very proud."

"So that means Ryland is still available?" Lipstick from the restroom stood near one of the TVs, her voice carrying over the din.

"Quiet everyone," called Bangs loudly. "Here comes the best part. The reunion."

Enrico shifted his arm to rest across the back of her chair as everyone focused back on the TV. Duke was on stage with Ayeesha, who was smiling and wiping tears from her cheeks.

"Our voters got to play Cupid," Duke said, "and they chose you. I think it's time. Don't you?" He turned to the audience, who roared in agreement. "Dean, would you please join us on stage?"

She knew what was coming, yet Lexy's heart swelled with happiness again as a handsome man, looking slightly self-conscious, stepped onto the stage. After the two exchanged an uncertain look, Ayeesha ran across the stage and threw herself into his arms for a kiss. It didn't matter that Dean's bouquet of forget-me-nots was getting crushed. This reunion was the stuff of fairytales and movies. Every woman in the pub let out a satisfied sigh at the same time.

"Congratulations, Ayeesha. Dean." Duke gave Ayeesha a hug and shook Dean's hand. "You two have quite the story. And I suspect, it's only going to get better."

Dean took Ayeesha's hand in his and smiled at her. "I think so too."

"So, Dean," Duke said. "We've heard a lot from this wonderful woman here, but I have to ask. What was it like for you to learn that Ayeesha wanted a second chance with you?"

"I was contacted by someone from the show, so I already

knew, but when I saw her submission video and watched her solo episode, I was floored. I'd been hoping to see her at the camp reunion next year and beg her to give us another try." He turned to Ayeesha. "Seeing you tonight, I don't know how I thought I could have waited another whole year."

"We know you two have a lot to catch up on. To help with that, *Cupid Grants a Second Chance* is sending you on an all-expenses paid trip to picturesque Cannon Beach."

Picturesque Cannon Beach. Lexy laughed at the way Duke described her hometown as if he'd never been there.

Duquan turned to face the audience, leaving Ayeesha and Dean looking at each other as if they were the only two people in the room. "All you devoted fans can follow our happy couple on their trip through photos that will be posted on our social media accounts."

The show's closing music began to play. "We wish you both the very best." Duke raised his voice to be heard over the music.

More bubbles fell on the couple as Dean picked Ayeesha up in a hug and twirled her in a circle.

All around Lexy, the pub was abuzz with excitement as people relived their favorite moments of the episode, and speculated on the other Legends and the possibility of a second season. Boisterous MHP staff congratulated themselves on having a part in making this hit show.

Next to her, Enrico took his phone from his pocket, stood and stepped away from the table. Out of the corner of her eye, she saw his expression turn from smiling to grim. He returned and spoke into her ear. "Check your phone. Merelda needs to see us immediately."

"Now?" She unlocked her phone screen to see a text from Merelda.

MERELDA

Get here now. As in five minutes ago.

Still on the phone, Enrico pulled her chair back so she could stand and gather her things. "Yes, yes. I'm on my way," he said into his phone.

"And bring your producer with you." Merelda yelled so loudly, Lexy heard it over the noise in the pub. She gulped.

Across from them, Ren jumped up. "You got a text, too? Merelda wants to see me and she sounds pissed."

"Come with us," said Enrico. "I'll drive."

"Hey." Nate held out his phone. "Merelda is calling an all-company meeting first thing tomorrow. You know what it's about?"

She shook her head.

"I got that email too," Jules said, scrolling through her phone. A murmur ran around the tables as others saw the summons.

"We're getting bonuses," Tom said loudly. The other 'noise boys' at his table cheered and thumped their beer glasses.

A giant pit of ice formed in Lexy's stomach. This wasn't about bonuses. Something was very wrong.

CHAPTER 21

"You know when I realized it was love? When I found out her guilty pleasure movies were the *Fast and the Furious* films too. Except Tokyo Drift. No one likes that one."

-Sam, Guest
Duquan's Downlow on Dating and Love
Podcast episode #86

"This feels like that part in *Mad Max*," Ren said, squished against Lexy in the passenger seat of Enrico's sports car. "Where Furiosa and the women she rescued are being chased across the desert by the War Boys."

"Judging from Merelda's voice, this is worse." The car jerked as he punched the gas.

"There's something worse than being chased by psychotic post-apocalyptic warriors in souped-up tankers and vehicles that shoot flames, whose only goal is to kill you?"

"Are we being sued?" Lexy asked.

"I don't know," Enrico said, tight-lipped, as he accelerated through an amber light.

When the Porsche screeched to a halt in front of the building, they scrambled out and hurried inside. Lexy's anxiety ramped up as they practically ran to Merelda's office, where The Queen was pacing the length of her Kvadarat rug.

Eying Merelda warily and looking as if they would rather be anywhere else, were Brian from IT and one of the MHP lawyers. A glance at her boss's face and Lexy's fears reached epic proportions. Even Enrico's hand on the small of her back provided scant reassurance.

She heard Ren say quietly under her breath "Oh, shit. I think I know what's wrong."

"Finally." Merelda stopped pacing and crossed her arms over her chest. "Have you heard? We've been hacked."

Hacked?

"Renata?" Merelda arched one brow as Ren frantically scrolled through her phone. "Have you discovered the problem?"

Ren swallowed audibly.

"Could you please fill in our esteemed producer and director?"

"It appears—" Ren nervously cleared her throat. "Looking back through our various platforms, it appears the winner's name began appearing in posts everywhere around 7:30 pm. Our time."

Lexy glanced around the room, still unclear what the problem was.

"Before the commercial break," Ren said.

Lexy exchanged a look with Enrico, then shifted her gaze to the others. "The winner was leaked to the media before the contestants opened their envelopes on stage? How is that possible? Someone from the studio audience?"

"They wouldn't dare!" Merelda spat out venomously. "The NDA they all signed made it very clear they'd wind up in court if anyone breathed a word. Yet somehow, the winner was leaked before it was announced on air."

"You bargained hard to have the finale air simultaneously across the country, so East and West Coast viewers all found out the winner at the same time. After all that, the surprise was still ruined?" Lexy said.

"Precisely." Merelda resumed her pacing. "Someone is out to destroy Manor House Productions."

"Are they trying to sabotage the company? Or the show?" Enrico asked.

"The show. The company." Her elegant hand gave a furious flip of the wrist. "It amounts to the same thing. A personal attack on *me*." Merelda slammed both hands down on her desk and glared around the room. "And when I find out which one of my contemptible, underhanded, thieving competitors is behind this," her hands curled into fists, "I will wipe them off the map. They'll never get near TV production again. They won't even be able to get a job as a *janitor* in a TV studio when I'm through."

"Damage control first," said Enrico. "What's the fallout?"

"I just got off the phone with the network," Merelda said. "They'll take a beating from the sponsors once word gets out."

"I wonder why the hacker waited till the last minute to leak it," Lexy said.

Merelda continued as if she hadn't spoken aloud. "The fact that the damage was minimal—this time—means nothing. Someone has access to our database, and there is no telling what havoc they'll wreak next time. They could ruin us."

"We won't let that happen," Enrico said.

Merelda's expression hardened further. "If I find out they had inside help, an accomplice from within, so help me..." Lexy could practically hear the whoosh of a guillotine blade descending.

Enrico's voice was remarkably calm. "Where do we start?"

"Renata, I want you to hire someone to find out where the hack originated."

"Right away."

"Brian, you go over our online security system with a fine-tooth comb to discover if the hack came from within these four walls."

"You're looking internally?" Lexy stared wide-eyed at the others. Out for dinner and drinks with everyone to watch tonight's airing had felt like family. Could one of them be trying to sabotage the company?

"If there is a rat in our midst, I want them caught and I want them punished."

"If it was someone at MHP, I'd be leaving town in a hurry and changing my name," Ren murmured in her ear.

"I have already called for a meeting tomorrow," The Queen continued. "I want every single person who works here in attendance, where I will make myself very clear on this matter." Merelda reached for a decanter on her sideboard. "Now get out there and find me some answers."

JULES PROPPED herself on one corner of Lexy's desk, "We're

on for the annual tree decorating at your place this weekend, right?"

"Of course." Lexy brightened. She could invite Enrico. Let him see her place. Maybe he'd stick around after the others left. Maybe—

"What's a good time for your trusty Christmas Decorating Angel to arrive?"

"Wish I'd known about the Christmas Decorating Angel last weekend, Jules." Nate must have overheard the tail end of their conversation. "I really could have used one. I put up the lights at my mom's house and Walter insisted on helping." Nate bridged a hand over closed eyes, shook his head at the memory.

"Bet that went well. I heard the guy can't even hang a birthday banner." Jules laughed.

"If I'd known, I would have called your sister," Lexy said. "We could have sat in lawn chairs drinking hot apple cider and entertained ourselves watching you and Walter."

"You would have, wouldn't you? And here I was ready to offer you an orphaned Christmas tree in need of a home. I got it for my mom, like I do every year, but Walter beat me to it."

"What a terrible boyfriend your mom has," Jules said. "Someone let Santa know to put that man on the naughty list."

"Do we call him a 'boyfriend' at his age?" Nate shuddered. "Please no."

"I'd be happy to give your spare tree a good home this holiday," Lexy said.

"Sounds like serendipity to me." Jules hopped off Lexy's desk. "You should stick around for the decorating, Nate. Lexy makes a mean mulled wine."

"You up for an extra Decorating Angel?" His green eyes flirted with hers.

"No one would mistake you for an angel," she teased, "but it's always great to have an extra set of hands." She liked hanging out with Nate and all, but his weren't the hands she'd been hoping for.

After her friends left, she glanced at Enrico's unoccupied desk, and rose. Best track him down before she lost her nerve. She found him on his phone in the boardroom, and knocked lightly on the glass. He beckoned her in.

"I can't wait either." He ended the call, the look of joy on his face sending her pulse racing. She smiled back, anticipating a cozy evening at her place after the others left.

"Ah, that expression. Do I sense visions of sugar plums dancing through your head?"

More like visions of him and her together. She pulled out a chair across from him. "What are your plans this weekend? Want to come help decorate my tree? I bribe my helpers with festive drinks and treats." She drew out the word 'treats' in a sing-song, coaxing tone. "Jules and Ren will be there too," she added quickly. It shouldn't take much to encourage him to linger after the others left.

"I won't be here this weekend. I'm going home for Christmas."

"To Italy?" She masked her disappointment as the image of her and Enrico cuddled on the couch in front of the fireplace with Christmas lights twinkling in the background melted faster than a snowball in a bonfire.

"Knowing the show would be wrapped, I bargained with Merelda for extra days off. I leave tomorrow morning."

"So soon?" Not even time for any sort of intimate pre-Christmas get together.

"It's nice to know you'll miss me. The timing isn't ideal, with the leak still unsolved, but I have to go. It will be the first time in several years the entire family is together. All forty-two of us."

Her jaw dropped. "Forty-two?"

"We Rossis have a reputation as lovers, not fighters." He winked. "My dad took that to heart. I have two older sisters and eight younger brothers."

"And you all get together in one place?"

"My Nonna has a large home, some might call it a castle, that fits us all."

"A little different from Christmas at the Smith's. How did they take it when you moved to a different continent? My parents had a hard enough time when I moved one state away."

He rose. "They understood my reasons. I know you can handle things in my absence. Or will I come back to learn you've allowed every single applicant on the Valentine's Special?"

She stood as well. "Without you to keep me in line, I make no promises."

He gave her that heart-fluttering smile. "I'll have to take my chances." He reached for her hand and raised it to his lips. "Have a wonderful holiday, Bella. I look forward to more successful episodes of our show in the new year."

"Me too. Happy Holidays." As he left, she smoothed her hand, still feeling the imprint of where his lips had been. For the first time in her life, she could see herself one day missing her family Christmas traditions to take part in someone else's.

❧

DID a Christmas tree have the same impact on a female as showing up with a bouquet of flowers? Probably not. Nate set down the tree and rang the doorbell on Lexy's houseboat. He'd arrived early on purpose, before the others got there. Marcie's words echoed in his head. 'How will Lexy know how you feel if you don't tell her'?

How hard could it be? He could get up on stage in front of hundreds of people. But telling Lexy he had feelings for her, and asking her on a date was a whole other matter. Even though he had the perfect way for them to see in the new year. What could go wrong?

So many things. She could already have a date. She could tell him she didn't share his feelings and give him the dreaded, 'but I still want to be friends'. She could even—

"Nate." She sounded breathless as she pulled open the door. "And my tree. It looks perfect."

She looked perfect. Jeans and a white sweater that looked incredibly soft, topped by a red Christmas apron with a gingerbread man on the front. "How can you tell when it is still all tied up?"

"Elf intuition." She opened the door wide, gesturing him in. The air was tinged with the pleasant scent of mulling spices.

"Let's prove me right. Over there if you please, sir. I've got the stand set up by the window."

Together they wrestled the tree into place, twisting the pegs so it stood straight and tall.

"So much easier with two." She took a step back. "I'm right. It's perfect. Let me get some water for it."

"Here." He handed her a small plastic bottle of some elixir the tree guy had sold him to add to the water. "Supposed to make it keep its needles longer and smell even better."

"A friend who delivers a tree, puts it up, stays to help decorate, *and* brings tree elixir? I'm putting you in my calendar for next Christmas."

Heat flared in his chest at her words. Time for her to stop thinking of him as a friend, though. He followed her into the kitchen and leaned a hand on the counter beside her. Close enough he could smell her shampoo. Was that vanilla? A scent that would surely haunt his dreams. Made him want to lean in just a little closer. The air between them felt charged.

"Lexy, there's something I've been wanting to—"

Just then the doorbell chimed. She turned, brushing against him as she squeezed past. "Seems everyone's excited to get here and start decorating."

His shoulders sagged. A heartbeat from telling her how he felt, now the moment was gone. "Seems like it." He shoved his hands in his pockets and leaned against the counter, watching as Jules and Ren spilled inside, their arms laden with who knows what. Jules looked even taller with an antler headband tucked into her curly red hair.

The girls chattered away while shrugging out of their coats and unloading their packages. Lexy got busy ladling out cups of mulled wine. As she handed him a mug, their fingers touched briefly. She looked up into his eyes. "Sorry, we were interrupted. What were you going to say before these two showed up?"

"I, uh—" Not how he saw this moment going, but he could adapt with the best of them. Make it work.

"I wondered what you and your ponytail were doing for New Year's Eve. I heard our pal Daisy Jordan is coming to town. I've got connections and I managed to get two floor tickets to the concert. Do you want to go to with me?" Maybe this was for the best. Telling her how he felt on New Year's would be more romantic, wouldn't it? Women liked that kind of thing.

"That's so fun. The girls and I planned to do something together. Maybe we can all go." She looked at Jules and Ren, who nodded.

"Lucky guy," Jules said. "Instead of one cute chick on your arm, you can have all three of us."

Also not part of his plan. Was he wrong to pray the show was sold out?

Lexy turned back to him. "You say you've got connections. Can you get two more tickets?"

"Yeah, I've got a guy," he joked, "We go way back. His name is Ticketmaster."

"Already on it," Ren said, phone in hand.

"Floor is general admission, right? Jules said. "No seats, so we'll be able to stay together."

"Shoot." Ren frowned. "The floor is sold out."

"Buy us whatever tickets you can," Jules said. "We'll find you inside, Lex. If I can't charm my way past the usher and get us onto the floor, I'll wear beige for a month." She shuddered in mock-horror.

"I got tickets," Ren confirmed. "It's official, we're all going to see Daisy."

"Great." Nate feigned enthusiasm. Was there a possibility the girls wouldn't be able to join them on the floor? Yeah right. This was Jules. She could convince the usher she *was* Daisy Jordan if she set her mind to it.

"Now that we have plans for New Year's, it's tree time." Lexy beamed. "Once I put on *Love Actually*."

He pretended to groan. "Not every chick's favorite sappy Christmas movie."

"How can you resist?" Jules teased. "An aging rock star

making a desperately embarrassing comeback with a corny Christmas song."

He caught a sudden glimpse of what lay head. The regrets he'd feel if RDA didn't take their music and their name to the next level. "Why do I feel like I'm being visited by the Ghost of Christmas Future?"

The girls erupted into a fit of giggles.

Watching humor dance across Lexy's face, a hum of anticipation rippled through him. She was going to the concert with him. He would be with her at midnight. He didn't need the Ghost of New Year's Future to warn him if he wasn't careful, Jules and Ren could interrupt his moment with Lexy then, too.

CHAPTER 22

"Trying to be sexy one Christmas, I picked my boyfriend up from the airport wrapped in saran wrap with a big red bow. I waited in my car in the arrivals lane, excited for him to 'unwrap' his gift when we got home. How could I know he'd offer a ride to his mom's friend who was on the same flight?"

-Annie, Guest
Duquan's Downlow on Dating and Love
Podcast episode #100

Lexy yawned on her way to meet with the girls at The Coffee Pod for their annual post-Christmas-debrief. She'd gotten back from Oregon late last night. Please let Ren's source have learned something about the leak.

"Any news?" she asked.

"Is no news better than bad news?"

She sagged. She'd known that if Ren had anything to share, she wouldn't have waited to tell her.

"Time for the headline game, holiday version." Jules said, in a blatant attempt to cheer her up as the barista handed over Jules's Americano.

Ren jumped on it as she leaned against the iconic whale mural and waited for her drink. "One headline to sum up our holiday. Lao Lao causes holiday havoc. Woman knocks over entire dessert table trying to nudge her granddaughter under the mistletoe with 'nice young man'."

Lexy giggled, trying not to choke on her latte.

"It's like she thinks if he kissed me, he'd have to marry me. My grandma is obsessed with all things Jane Austen." Ren rolled her eyes as she picked up her cappuccino and the three headed out the door.

"I've got mine," Jules said. "Crowd in uproar! Lentil Loaf is *not* turkey. Jules unknowingly accepts invitation to a vegan 'orphans Christmas' with neighbors." Her dramatic shudder conveyed her thoughts on lentil loaf.

"You poor thing," Ren said, in mock-sympathy. "Even Tiny Tim got a proper turkey dinner on Christmas."

"Ha-ha."

"My turn. You'll believe mine, because you know my mom," Lexy said. "Producer nearly dies of embarrassment watching for whales at Ecola State Park. Her mother mistakes man beside her on the viewpoint platform for Matthew McConaughey, and proceeds to gush what a big fan she is, and how much she loved him in *Magic Mike*."

"Oh, Jill." Ren was still chuckling as they reached the office and she held the door open for the others.

"You know how many people are up there with binoculars looking for whales this time of year? Everyone around us overheard her. I'm lucky there's not a video of it on TikTok." She trooped upstairs, Jules and Ren on her heels.

"I wish there was," Jules said.

"A video on TikTok of what?" Nate was coming down the stairs as they went up.

"Nothing," said Lexy. "You're here early."

"Grabbing something on my way to the studio." He stopped on the landing. "What video?"

"I'll fill you in later," Jules stage-whispered, then raised her voice back to normal tones. "We're getting caught up on the holiday season in two lines or less. How would you sum up your Christmas?"

"Me? Uh, still no Batmobile under the tree from Santa despite my repeated requests, and I trounced my sister in our annual family Farkle tournament for the twelfth year running."

"Not bad," Ren said.

"Gotta jet." Nate continued down the stairs. "I'll expect to hear all yours. You can tell me on our way to the concert in a few days." He gave a backward wave on his way out the door.

THANK God she'd had the coffee shop transition. One disadvantage of living on the West Coast was the rest of the country started their work day hours before her. So, it appeared did Merelda. For lurking among her many emails, flagged as important, was a signature Merelda Power Play, demanding her budget for the Valentine's special 'yesterday'. Christmas. She replied to anything urgent then resumed work on the budget, the hack at the end of Season One niggling in the back of her mind.

"Shame the way the season ended, Lexy." As if reading

her mind, Smug Sonia stood at her desk wearing new glasses that looked like a cheap knock-off of a pair of Merelda's designer frames. Her thin lips pulled down in a look that Lexy guessed was supposed to portray sympathy, but more closely resembled Pennywise, the evil clown from *It*.

"We'll get to the bottom of things," Lexy said.

"Someone better," Sonia flung over her shoulder. "Or Season Two will die before it's even hatched." Through narrowed eyes, Lexy watched her leave, grateful Sonia's desk was on the far side of the hive and out of her field of vision. Or should she be wanting to keep an eye on the enemy?

Their saboteur had only spilled the winner's identity moments ahead of the show's reveal, not early enough to wreak any lasting damage, but enough of a threat to seriously shake up MHP's reputation within the industry. Which is why she wasn't surprised to be summoned to the Throne Room, where she missed Enrico's confident presence. He wasn't due back till the new year, and she'd heard nothing from him. Work-related or otherwise.

One look at Merelda and her stomach clenched, prepared for the worst. Her boss always held court sitting behind her desk, yet today she stood rigidly beside it. Oh, God. And waving Lexy to sit. Another power play. Tower over the intended victim. Warily, Lexy perched on the edge of the indicated chair.

"How was your Christmas, Lexy?" A warning bulb lit up in the back of her brain. Was The Queen sharpening her stinger?

"Umm..." No way for Merelda to know she'd been working on a grant for someone other than MHP. Was there? "It was nice, thanks."

"Do you want to know how mine was?"

"Yes....?" The back of her neck prickled. If only this was her and Merelda bonding.

Merelda stalked around her desk and leaned toward Lexy, palms flat, arms rigid. "My Christmas was not 'nice'. Mine was terrible. I couldn't enjoy anything. I didn't sleep. I was plagued with thoughts of who would dare attempt to sabotage my company."

There it is! I am a horrible employee for daring to enjoy my holiday after what happened during the finale.

"Brian hasn't come up with anything?"

"No." Heaving a dissatisfied sigh, Merelda sat, steepled her fingers and gazed past her, out the window.

Lexy swallowed her panic. She had never seen The Queen less than one hundred percent in control of a situation.

Merelda shifted her attention to Lexy. "Do you know *how* I've made it as far as I have in this industry?"

She put on her most interested, hanging-on-every-word face.

"Gut instinct," Merelda stated flatly. "It's never let me down. And right now, it is sending up warning flares."

Lexy leaned forward.

"Someone wants me to bleed. And they have no problem making *you* bleed along with me."

She preferred to keep her blood inside her body, thank you very much, including metaphorically. "You think this is more than just a random hack? That it's part of a bigger plan against you and Manor House?"

"I do." Merelda sat back in her chair and closed her eyes as if she was channeling her inner goddess. "This cannot— must not—happen on Season Two."

Lexy nodded vigorously. A second strike would be disastrous. "Once we find out how we were hacked, we'll be able to stop anything like this from happening again."

"I don't want platitudes. I want action!" The commanding tone of Merelda's voice could give drill sergeants a run for their money.

"What can I do?" Did she really say that out loud?

"You can get to the bottom of this catastrophe ASAP. We need to get things contained before word gets out to the other studios. That would be beyond disastrous."

She stood. Best to look like she was primed for action. "On it. I'll go talk to Brian and check in with Ren." As she started for the door, the truth hit her. She'd just been cleverly outmaneuvered on the croquet court. Gut instinct? Laughable. More like Merelda's uncanny ability to manipulate people into doing exactly what she wanted that had got her where she was.

"And Lexy?"

Hand on the doorknob, she turned. Maybe she'd get a few words of trust or encouragement after all.

"As the first show you've produced on your own, you don't want this to be the reputation that follows you around."

Her hand slipped on the doorknob. Wouldn't that make Professor Snyder's day.

Lexy's next few days were no better. Brian had taken the rest of the week off, so she couldn't make any progress there. Meanwhile it was nearly impossible to go anywhere in the office without catching Smug Sonia's calculating gaze.

Almost as if she knows something I don't.

~

"NATE, I knew you'd be the object of envy showing up with three gorgeous women," Jules said once they made it through the entrance and onto the concourse. "You're getting jealous looks from every guy that walks past us."

"They must not have seen you cozying up to the security guard on your way in."

"Practicing for later," she said with a mischievous grin. "We'll come find you when we can. Don't have too much fun without us."

Lexy waved her fingers. "Head for the front, close to the stage. We'll keep an eye out for you."

As Nate hustled her along to their gate, throngs of people rushed past them in all directions, and he grabbed her hand. "Hang on, pony tail. I don't want to lose you."

"I didn't know Daisy had so many fans."

"Anniversary of the release of her most popular album. Shrewd marketing."

She nodded, tempted to tell him about the grant she'd applied for on his behalf to help with RDA marketing. But why get his hopes up? She'd wait till she knew for sure one way or the other.

On the floor, Nate continued to hold her hand as they wound their way through the crowd to a spot near the front. His grip had a solid, easy warmth. But what was causing the faint hum beneath her skin? Anticipation of tonight's performance?

They didn't have long to wait before the opening act, a group Lexy hadn't heard of, lit up the stage with their infectious grooves and undeniable charisma. Their set was an electric mix of funky rhythms, powerful horns, and high-octane energy that ignited the crowd. At one point she gripped Nate's arm and leaned in to say, "They're really good. Where are they from?"

He placed his mouth so close to her ear the heat of his breath tickled her earlobe. "New Orleans, like Daisy. Great, huh?"

She nodded, happily rocking from side to side with the beat. When the set ended, she clapped and whistled with everyone else. She looked around her. "Any sign of the girls?"

He shook his head.

"What if they don't make it to the floor, or they can't find us?" She scanned the stands for a glimpse of a tall redhead next to a petite Asian.

"If Jules can sweet talk her way past that usher on the gate, and I'm betting she can, then a measly few thousand Daisy fans won't stop her from finding you."

The second opening act took the stage. Completely different sound, but equally fun and full of energy. Like if Florence and the Machine did a collab with Rage Against the Machine, was Nate's description. The singer was a master at hyping up the crowd, and by the time she walked off stage with her bandmates, Lexy was super-charged by the crowd's collective energy as they waited for Daisy. She turned around, on the lookout for Jules and Ren.

"Daisy'll be out soon," Nate said. "Should I brace myself for any of her lyrics you've misheard and sing out loud?"

"A girl gets one little Bryan Adams line wrong," she laughed. "You'll never let me live that down, will you?"

"Not any time soon."

The crowd's roar interrupted them. She spun around, threw her arms in the air and let out a cheer as Daisy and her band bounded onto the stage.

"Hello, Seattle. Thank you for choosing to spend your New Year's Eve with us." Daisy sounded exactly the same as that day on the beach.

The crowd went wild.

"We've visited your city many times. If there are two things Seattle is known for," Daisy said, "it's coffee." She paused as the audience chuckled. "And Nirvana."

The cheers grew deafening. The bassist leaned into his mic and got the crowd chanting, "Coffee and Nirvana. Coffee and Nirvana."

"So, who better to appreciate our humble beginnings," Daisy said loudly, capturing their attention again. "Fifteen years ago, we put out a little album called *Coffee, Chords, and Confessions*."

The screams grew even louder.

"Back then we actually played *in* coffee shops. We never imagined how far we would come. And it's all thanks to you, our amazing fans."

Nate playfully bumped Lexy's shoulder. "She's talking about you."

"If you've been with us from the beginning, you'll recognize this track." Daisy adjusted her guitar.

At the opening chords, Lexy nodded. She'd played this one on repeat in high school. She loved Daisy's older songs as well as the newer ones, for different reasons. Daisy's talent had been evident at an early age, but the journey the singer had taken since, refining her style as she matured, was the stuff of great artists.

"I can see you up there one day," she told Nate, as Daisy launched into the first single off her debut album. "You and the band deserve a bigger audience. If that's what you're after," she added. Didn't all musicians aspire to make it big? Funny. She didn't know Nate's long-term dreams, even though he knew hers.

Hours later, Lexy was blown away by the stamina of all the performers. The band had been giving it their absolute all, nonstop. Daisy told stories, swapped out her guitar with regularity, and made her way from one side of the stage to the other in order to connect with the audience in every corner of the venue. At one point, they all left the stage except the drummer, who performed a solo, drumming so fast Lexy thought his arms were going to fly off.

At the final cymbal crash, the rest of the band appeared on a small stage at the back of the arena. They performed an acoustic set that was hauntingly beautiful.

"Do you ever do that?" she asked Nate. "With RDA?"

"We'll do an acoustic song now and again. Tone the energy down. Get a little more intimate. But no," he said with a smile, "I've never changed stages."

"You may already know this," Daisy said, as the band filed back to the main stage, "but my favorite music video of ours was filmed right down the street from here."

"Forgive Daisy," the bassist said. "She's not from around here. By 'right down the street' she means waaaaay down the I-5, across a state line, all the way to Cannon Beach." They continued to joke back-and-forth as they took up position on the main stage again.

Nate gave Lexy's ponytail a playful tug. "It's your song next."

Her chest tightened. Her skin tingled.

When the song *Beach Dreams* started, she sang her heart out along with Daisy Jordan and most of the audience, confident she got every word right.

As the clock's hands inched toward midnight, the band kept going without a break. The faint smell of cannabis wafting through the crowd didn't diminish her awareness of Nate next to her. His intriguing fragrance of spicy cologne mixed with well-worn leather teased her nostrils and made her insides quiver.

He said something. His eyes smiled at her but his words were swallowed up by the music.

She smiled back, shook her head. "I can't hear you."

He put his lips next to her ear. Tried again.

This time she caught part of what he said, and guessed the rest. As Daisy led the countdown, she leaned toward him, tried to project her voice over the noise in the arena. "I love her too, she's so great live."

He gave her a puzzled look. Then his expression shifted. His eyes darkened, locked on hers.

Her breath hitched.

The crowd grew louder as the seconds passed, even though it felt like time stood still. "Three. Two. One. Happy New Year!"

Nate pulled her close. Lowered his head. She dampened her lips—

"There you two are!" Jules and Ren jostled into them, effectively breaking the invisible spell. Nate looked away. But not before she caught a glimpse of what looked like disappointment. He'd wanted to kiss her.

Caught up in the emotion of the music, the electricity in the air, and the fact that it was midnight on New Year's Eve, she'd wanted to kiss him, too.

No gym membership on her list of New Year resolutions. Top billing went to getting to the bottom of things at work. Starting with Brian's den in the lower bowels of the house, aka 'The Dungeon'. On her way to the back stairs, she ran into Sarah, from payroll.

"Hey, Lexy. You going down?"

Lexy wrinkled her nose. "Unfortunately."

"Take something to Brian for me?" Sarah handed over a file folder.

"Sure."

Sarah gave her a grateful look. "Just take care Brian doesn't get the wrong idea. You don't want him asking you out again."

"Don't remind me." On her first day, Brian had set her up with a work email and access to the company files and resources. A few days later he'd appeared behind her as she unlocked her car after work and stammered his way through asking her out.

She'd declined gently, using the old 'Sorry, but I don't date people I work with' line. Hopefully today wouldn't result in a repeat. She gave her most professional-sounding knock, a 'work colleague with a question' tap tap, before she pushed his door open. "Hey, Brian. Happy New Year."

"Lexy." He jumped and stammered out something that might have been 'happy new year'. Most of the floor and the one other chair in the dimly-lit room, were piled high with boxes of spare computer monitors, loose cords, extra keyboards, and other technological whatnots.

"Do you keep your office cluttered like this to deter visitors?" she joked as she attempted to step into the room without toppling any of the piles.

"You shall not pass the threshold."

She froze.

He gave a nervous chuckle and wiped at his sweaty forehead. "Just kidding, you're nothing like a Balrog. You can come in."

"A Bal-what?" She leaned against the door jamb, judging it the safest spot.

"A Balrog. You know, the iconic scene where Gandalf

saves Frodo and the others by stopping the Balrog from crossing the bridge after them?"

"Ah, yes. A *Lord of the Rings* joke." That she didn't get. But she forced a small laugh. She needed him on her side.

"Listen, I'm not here to tell you how to do your job or anything. It's just that, as producer, Merelda is holding me accountable to get to the bottom of the hack. So, I'm under pressure."

His eyes darted nervously around, not making contact with hers. "I'm working on something." His fingers raced across the keyboard as he made a loud humming noise. Time to make her escape. Before she could, Brian sat back, took off his glasses and rubbed his eyes.

"I wanted to confirm my suspicions first, and I just did. The initial post originated from this office."

Her heart sank. "Are you sure?" This made it personal, as Merelda's gut insisted. But who and why?

"I'm positive."

"So we haven't been hacked. It's a leak. Can you tell who?"

"Whoever it was knows what they're doing. They used a whole bunch of different portals." While Brian went on about firewalls, encrypted connections, and remote authorized users, she fidgeted. No wonder TV show detectives were always impatiently cutting off their tech wizards' long-winded explanations which no one else understood.

When he drew a breath to elaborate on IP addresses routed through relay proxies, she jumped in. "Does this mean you'll be able to figure out who was responsible?"

"It'll take a while." His chubby fingers returned to his keyboard. "This is complex work," he said, reminding her of the way he'd boasted to her and Enrico about his new code for tabulating votes. "Once I cross-reference our system logins with some digital data files, I'll have the answer."

"That's great. Please let me know as soon as you find out. Come straight to me, no one else."

Brian nodded. Was he blushing?

Afraid she was veering dangerously close to being-asked-out-again territory, she made a break for it as fast as she could without actually running.

Panting after her jog up the stairs, she ran into Ren in the break room waiting for the coffee machine to spit out its elixir.

"Where's the fire?"

"Basement. Brian," she said, catching her breath. "Bad *LOTR* jokes and a deathly fear of being asked out again."

"Why were you talking to Brian?"

"The Queen put me in charge of figuring out what happened. I went to find out if he had made any progress."

"Oooh, you got Merelda-ed." Ren poured her a coffee.

"I got Merelda-ed bad. And whoever first started using our boss's name as a verb is a genius."

Ren patted her arm sympathetically. "Did Brian find anything?"

"He claims to have traced the original post through a bunch of portals, whatever that means, and discovered it originated from our office."

"Hmmmmm," Ren said absently, tapping her fingers against her coffee mug. "You know Brian's the nephew of some friend of someone Merelda knows, right? He's fine with emails and basic in-house IT, but I think he's in over his head with this."

"I didn't know he was a favor hire, but I think so too. Anything from your source?"

"Still digging. It's a complex web of multiple posts on a

variety of platforms. She's trying to follow the strands and find the connection between them all. That should lead you to whoever was set on sabotaging the show. But it's going to take some time."

"I know, I know, it's not like on TV," she said with a sigh. "I appreciate your tech person helping us out."

Just then Brian burst into the room, panting as if he'd run up the stairs. "It was him! Enrico Rossi."

CHAPTER 23

"Dating is hard these days. All the single, attractive, funny, kind men I meet already have boyfriends."

-Giselle, Guest
Duquan's Downlow on Dating and Love
Podcast episode #22

Hours later, Lexy still couldn't believe Brian's accusation. Her gut clenched every time she replayed his words. Her heart outright denied the possibility of Enrico being involved, despite what Brian had said. The second she spotted Duke outside the art gallery, the pressure in her chest started to ease. She threw herself into his arms.

"Lexycakes." His large frame enveloped her as he hugged her back. "You're a peach for coming with me." Letting her go, he took a closer look. Concern darkened his eyes. "What's happened?"

She sucked in an uneven breath.

He tucked her arm through his and led her inside. "First things first. Let's get you some champagne."

The huge open space gallery held a tastefully displayed collection of oversize photos depicting candid snapshots of couples. From a close-up of a pair of hands clasped with fingers linked, to an adorable elderly couple on a park bench, feeding ducks.

She took advantage of the moment to compose herself. "*Love in Focus*. Cute title."

"The photographer is a friend and asked me to say a few words."

"Given the subject matter, I can see why having the host of both a relationship podcast and the hottest reality TV show on love would be a huge benefit to their opening night."

"I'm glad you could come with me since Paul can't make it until later."

"You get a date, and I get the listening ear I need."

He took a sip of champagne. "Whenever you're ready."

In front of an image of a laughing couple wading in the ocean, she poured out the day's events. It helped that Duke worked on the show. "I swore Ren and Brian to secrecy for now. I haven't even told Merelda. But I'm worried word will get out." She fidgeted with the tip of her ponytail. "I've got to let Enrico know what he's facing."

She'd been ignoring the unhelpful inner voice, which had been very opinionated lately regarding radio silence from Enrico. "The thing is, I *know* Enrico. I know he wouldn't have done this."

"Are you sure? You said you saw him on his phone before the winner was revealed. Which means he had opportunity."

"I'm positive. With every fiber of my being." The next photo they passed captured a couple attaching a lock with their initials to a love lock bridge. After admiring the picture, Lexy turned to face Duke. "You don't think he did it, do you? I mean, you've seen firsthand how dedicated he is to the show. He's got nothing to gain by leaking the winner."

"It doesn't matter what I think." He rested one hand on her shoulder, his dark brown eyes serious on hers. "But for the record, no. I don't think Enrico's responsible."

She let out a breath she hadn't realized she'd been holding, as the rest of the tension drained out of her body. "Where's the photo of you and Paul? Surely your friend snapped a pic of the most devilishly handsome couple around."

"He's saving it for the next show." They stopped in front of a striking photo of a middle-aged couple smiling into each other's eyes from the bucket seat of a Ferris wheel. "Hey," he said. "Don't these two remind you of—"

"My parents, yes." The corner of her mouth quirked up fondly. "Except my mom is afraid of heights." She studied the couple depicted as she thought of her parents and the bond of love between them even a stranger could see. No resemblance to her own tattered relationship past, never mind the confusing present.

She turned to Duke. "Will I ever find what they have?"

He ran a comforting hand over her hair. "They set a high bar for relationship goals. And it's not wrong to want that for yourself."

"I just don't know if it's even possible."

"Tell me. If you found 'the one'. The fairytale romance your parents have, and some photographer captured the two of you in a moment of joy, what would it look like?"

Immediately, an oft-conjured image came to mind.

Enrico and her on stage together, accepting an industry award for the show. Thunderous applause, their clasped hands raised high, as they exchanged a special look.

"I know you see something," he prompted.

She frowned. Was the image as strong as it was a few weeks ago? Before Enrico left for the holidays? Before the almost-kiss at midnight on New Year's Eve?

"We're onstage together, receiving an award," she said with conviction. "Eyes for no one but each other." She concentrated on creating that powerful visual. Feeling it.

He nodded, his expression full of understanding. "Just remember," he tipped her chin so she was looking him in the eye. "It's not being *in* the relationship that makes you a success. It's *who you are* in that relationship."

She put on a playful tone. "Have you ever considered becoming a relationship coach? You'd be really good at it."

He laughed.

"Hello, Handsome." Paul joined them, and he and Duke exchanged a kiss. "Hi Lexy." Paul smiled, his eyes still on Duke. "Thanks for being my stand-in."

"Any time."

"Your conversation looked far too serious for an art opening."

"Lexy's having drama at work," Duke explained.

Silently she thanked him for keeping the rest to himself. He was good that way.

"Is it the hunky sound guy who's in a band, and helped you out?"

"No." Duke answered for her. "It's the director."

"The sexy Italian? I really thought you were going to end up with the musician."

"Sorry to disappoint you. There's no boy drama. It's

actual *work* drama. A problem with the company. I can't say more than that."

"Bor-ing." Paul took a sip of champagne. "Wait, is the sexy director in trouble?"

She hesitated. "Yes."

"No longer boring. You've got to save him."

"Ha! Right. I've got to save him." She looked at the photograph and thought back to what Duke said before Paul arrived. What type of person did she want to be in this relationship with Enrico? The type of person who went to bat for her man, for starters.

"Babe, can we go here one day?" Paul said.

She followed them to the photograph Paul was talking about. It showed a couple in their wedding finery kissing in front of the Roman Colosseum. A couple in Italy. Where Enrico was right now. It had to be a sign.

"Paul, you were absolutely right." She hugged him.

"I always am. Just ask Duke," he said with a wink.

"Hold on, *I* do all the listening and *you're* the one getting credit?" Duke said teasingly.

"Thanks to you too, Duke." She hugged him even harder. "I'm going to do it. I'm going to save the guy...the company...the world."

And create my happily ever after.

SAVING any of those things was harder than she'd thought, starting with the guy. She didn't want to leave a paper trail by sending a work email to Enrico, even asking him to call her. If he was smart, he wasn't even checking his work email, and the nine-hour time difference made things tricky.

Since another day passed without Brian miraculously

realizing he'd made an error, and she couldn't put off talking to Merelda much longer, she had to do something. She stared down at her phone and the text she had yet to send.

LEXY

Enrico. There's something you should know.
Call me when you can

Good idea? Bad idea? Her finger hovered above the send button just as her phone chimed with an incoming text. Startled, she unintentionally hit send. Her heart sped up.

Imagine if Enrico was texting her at the exact same minute? Surely that would mean—

Nope. A text from Nate's sister appeared.

MARCIE

Remember when you said you make a good wing chick? How about tonight? The guys are playing at The Ship

LEXY

Of course I'll be your wing chick. What time?

MARCIE

On stage at 8. Let's go early and get a table. Meet there at 7:30?

LEXY

See you then

The Ship and Anchor was filling up fast as she and Marcie grabbed a table with a good view of the stage and enough seats for the guys to join them between sets.

"Thanks for inviting me." She pulled off her gloves and heavy coat which she laid over the back of her chair. She hadn't seen RDA play in ages; the perfect distraction.

"I'm glad you could make it." Marcie unwound her long

scarf. "Especially when the weather makes you want to curl up inside by a fire in your PJs."

"What kind of friend would I be if I couldn't brave sleet and sideways gusting wind to keep you company while you ogle your man on stage? How's it going with Connor, anyway?"

"Baby steps. Tonight is phase three of making myself irresistible. I can tell I'm getting to him," Marcie said with a satisfied smile. "And any groupie who thinks about hitting on him had better watch out."

"Hey, Marcie." Their server approached. "We're excited to have your brother and the band back for another show. What can I get you?"

"Hi, Cammi. It's so cold out, I'll start with an Irish Coffee."

Lexy nodded. "Make that two, thanks."

"And can you send the guys a pitcher of beer at the end of their set?" After Cammie walked away, Marcie grinned. "Phase three includes sending Connor beer so he owes me a drink in return."

"That boy is toast." She returned the grin before subtly checking her phone. Still nothing from Enrico. She placed it on the table, face up, so she could see any incoming calls.

"Have you seen my brother lately? He says the show he's been on since *CGSC* wrapped is not nearly as fun."

"Since New Year's, only in passing." *New Year's*. Her heart stuttered a moment before resuming its normal beat. She covered it with a cough. "For the record, I don't see how any show could be as fun to work on as mine." She looked around the pub. "Where *are* they?"

"Oh," Marcie waved a hand vaguely at the stage. "They're in the back doing whatever secret ritual they do to psych themselves up before going on stage." She laughed. "I've learned it's best not to be around for that."

Whatever their secret ritual, it worked. The four walked out all charm and charisma, exuding a confidence that musicians around the world seem to generate. When Nate spotted her beside his sister and smiled, her stomach fluttered.

What was *that* about?

She and Nate may have shared a moment at the concert —an almost-moment, she corrected herself—unless she'd imagined it. He hadn't said anything, acting his usual Nate-self ever since.

Marcie let out a dreamy sigh. "What is it about musicians that makes them so sexy?" She had raised her voice over the music as they started their opening song. "Brother excluded."

"There's something," Lexy agreed. "The hot firefighter, the heartthrob musician, they're stereotypes for a reason."

The other stereotype, the scantily clad female groupies were there en masse in their crop tops and high heels, all arms in the air and swirling hair and squeals, so obvious it was amusing. Until it wasn't. Why wasn't Nate ignoring them? Instead of flashing his dimple and gesturing for more when they started singing along to the chorus.

"What's with Prima Donna up front?" A black-haired woman was gyrating her hips directly in front of Nate. Skinny low-cut jeans looked like they'd been painted on.

Marcie rolled her eyes. "The one aiming her glittery belly button ring at my brother, trying to hypnotize him into putting a matching ring on her finger? She hasn't missed a show in months. I'm surprised she hasn't thrown her panties at him yet."

She pressed her lips together. She'd watched Nate play

before, and never felt this twisting in her gut. She couldn't be jealous. Could she? She tried to sound nonchalant. "Why is Nate encouraging her? She doesn't seem his type."

Marcie gave a half-laugh, half-snort. "A girl like that thinks she's everyone's type and sets out to prove it."

"Has she tried to prove she's Connor's type?"

"Connor likes the attention because—duh, he's male—but he's smart enough to see the danger sign around her neck. Besides, I think she's hoping to snag herself a lead singer."

Does Nate recognize the danger sign?

Not judging by the way he reached down to touch Prima Donna's outstretched fingers while Griffin played a drum solo.

She squared her jaw. Why should she care? She had no claim on Nate. He could date, or 'encourage' anyone he chose.

"Connor told me once that groupies are like vampires—never invite them in."

She laughed. "Good advice."

"Ooh, I love this one," Marcie said, as the next song started. "Connor sings on it." She grabbed Lexy's hand. "Let's go dance. We can show those girls a thing or two."

Several songs later, Lexy was still laughing as she half-fell into her chair. "You're a fun dance partner."

"Back atcha."

"Prima Donna didn't like it when you elbowed her out of the way and we took over front and center." Impressive the way Marcie had smiled and wormed her way through the crowd to the front, towing Lexy behind her.

"No, she didn't. She tried giving me the death glare." Marcie shrugged. "I'm immune."

Just as the guys took a break, the beer was delivered on

stage and Adam started pouring pints for everyone. Connor lifted one in their direction. "You're the best, Marcie."

Which earned her and Marcie another glare from Prima Donna, who crossed her arms and chattered indignantly to her friends.

Marcie giggled. "Did she just stomp her foot?"

Suddenly, Prima Donna broke from the pack, aimed a superior smile in their direction, and walked purposely across the pub as the band left the stage. She ran straight into Nate. Beer drenched the front of her shirt.

Was he apologizing?

Prima Donna was the one who'd instigated her own personal wet T-shirt contest.

"Oh no," Marcie muttered as Nate unbuttoned the denim shirt he wore over a plain white T. "He's literally giving her the shirt off his back."

"No."

"My big bro is wired to help anyone in need, but he hates dishonesty and manipulation. Wait until I tell him she did it on purpose."

Lexy couldn't rip her eyes from the scene unfolding in front of her, or explain the hollow feeling as Nate smiled at his one-woman fan club. It's not like it was Enrico, with some stranger throwing herself at him.

"Hey Lex, your phone is ringing." Marcie passed it over. "Someone named Enrico. Doesn't he work on the show?"

"Enrico?" She looked at Marcie blankly, then at her phone screen. "I've got to take this." She stood quickly, and grabbed her coat. "Enrico? Sorry, it's loud in here. Let me get outside where I can hear you."

CHAPTER 24

"I know it happened in *Notting Hill,* but unless you're Hugh Grant, spilling a drink on a woman never works."

-Natalie, Guest
Duquan's Downlow on Dating and Love
Podcast episode #47

Nate cursed his clumsiness in his rush to reach Lexy. He hadn't stopped thinking about her since New Year's, when they'd been interrupted yet again. Tonight, when he'd stepped on stage and looked over—there she was. He could hardly wait for the first break.

"I'm sure it will dry," the girl in front of him said, shaking droplets from her fingers. Luckily, she was smiling.

"I'm sorry," he said. "Here." He started to unbutton the long-sleeved jean shirt he wore over his T-shirt.

"Oh, you don't have to..." Her words trailed off. She stood waiting expectantly. "I guess I am a little cold." She looked up at him from beneath eyelashes too thick to be real. "Body heat will help."

He did a double take. His movements slowed. Suddenly he felt an arm slung around his shoulders.

"Sorry to interrupt," Connor said. "But I need to borrow this guy."

The girl frowned.

"Band stuff. Can't wait." Connor passed her an RDA shirt he must have snagged off their merch table. It looked like an XL. "On behalf of the band, let me apologize for this klutz. He's still being house-broken." Connor sent her his most disarming smile. "And please accept this shirt from all of us." Without waiting for a response, Connor steered him away from her.

The first thing he noticed as they approached Marcie's table was Lexy's absence. The second was the matching smirks from Adam and Griffin.

"How do you get yourself into these situations?" Adam said. "I could see her coming a mile away. And man, you do not want any part of that Hot-With-a-Side-of-Crazy."

"I saw her coming." A blatant lie. His whole focus had been on Lexy.

"And walked into her anyway?" said Griffin.

"Then decided to give her your shirt?" added Connor.

"What else could I do? I spilled beer all over that poor girl."

Adam snorted. "Poor girl my ass. You know she made a beeline for you, right?"

He lowered himself into a chair. "She did it on purpose?"

Marcie poked his arm. "You're lucky Connor has a kind heart and stepped in." She beamed at Connor.

"I did it to save all of us the headache of that woman

hanging around. We don't want magnets like her sticking to our Sir Galahad's armor." Connor patted his shoulder.

"Where's Lexy?"

"I saw her leave," Adam said.

His stomach dropped. "What? She left already?" When he'd seen her earlier, he'd hoped she was here to pick things up where they'd left off the night of the concert.

"She stepped out to take a phone call from Enrico," Marcie said. "It sounded important."

First Jules and Ren and now Enrico. He stared at the door, willing her to come back before their next set started.

"Who was the one Nate rescued on the lake when she dropped her kayak paddle and couldn't get back to shore?" said Connor.

"What are you guys talking about?" said Nate.

"Oh, just our favorite of Nate's Infamous Clingers," said Adam.

"When your protective big brother persona spilled over beyond your own sister, you amassed quite a list of women who took your nice guy actions the wrong way." Connor raised his eyebrows at Nate as he took a swig of beer.

"And they say chivalry is dead," Adam said.

"Nate's Clingers don't say that." Griffin guffawed. "That's why he can't get rid of them."

"Is the girl covered in beer your new Vi?" Lexy stood at his elbow in her coat, nodding in Prima Donna's direction.

She came back! His heart gave a happy bump as he pulled out the chair next to him.

"Vi." A chorus of groaning voices ran around the table.

"Lexy, you fit right in." Connor raised his glass.

She did. Why hadn't he seen it sooner? Looking closer, he saw worry shadowing her eyes. The show? Or something else? He wished they were alone so he could ask her. Seeing her empty glass, he called a server over. "Can I get you another cider?"

Her smile brightened his night.

"Lexy, you met Vi?" Marcie chirped.

Lexy wrinkled her nose in an endearing way. "She called him 'Natey'."

"That does it. She just got moved to the top of the list," said Adam.

Nate sent his friend a look of disbelief. "You have a list?"

"Being written as we speak."

"There are so many to choose from, it's hard to narrow it down," Marcie said with false sweetness.

"Who knew being a nice guy could get you into so much trouble?" Nate sipped his beer. "Besides, I'm not the only one who's had a woman get too attached. What about Griffin and Jasmine?"

"She's Connor's family's friend," Griffin protested. "I didn't want to be rude to her. And where was the warning?"

"Connor was too busy chasing after Jenny Gillespie at his family's Fourth of July party that year," said Adam.

"Can you blame me?" Connor gave a wolfish grin. "I'm a sucker for a red bikini."

"What about Adam?" Griffin turned to their keyboard player. "You made us walk out of a Taco Bell one time because a girl you knew from high school was working there."

"Told us she followed you around all senior year," Connor said.

Nate laughed. "Because you wrote a song for her. Wasn't it called 'Your Love Knocked Me Over Like Hurricane Katrina'?"

"Hey. Like you never wrote a sappy song for a girl in high school."

"High school?" said Connor. "Nate's *still* writing sappy songs for women, then wonders why they get the wrong idea."

"I get all the best dirt on them when they get like this," Marcie stage-whispered to Lexy.

"On that note," Nate said. "Isn't it time for our next set?"

"Sure is," Adam slapped him on the back. "Let's go, Natey. This time try to keep your beer in your glass and your clothes on."

REN

Meet me at the Coffee Pod before work tomorrow? I've got news on the leak and you're never going to believe it.

LEXY RACED up the stairs of Manor House two at a time, heart still pounding from Ren's disclosure. Typically, Merelda was here long before anyone else. She had to see her right away. And talk to Enrico. He was back today, but hadn't answered her frantic texts.

"I'm in early because I have to leave to take my kid to the orthodontist today," Stan said from behind his desk. "What's your excuse?"

"I need to see Merelda. It's urgent," she gasped, trying to catch her breath.

"Get in line. She hauled Enrico into her office as soon as he walked through the door."

"Enrico's already here?"

"Yup. Him and Brian are in there with her."

Oh no!

"And let me tell you, The Queen did not look pleased. Whatever the emergency, I'd hold off if I were you."

"Thanks Stan, but this can't wait." As she approached Merelda's office she tensed, hearing Enrico's raised voice through the closed door.

"I can't explain why it leads to me, but I am not the source of the leak, Merelda. We've worked together long enough I thought you would trust my word."

She reached to knock, then pulled back.

"Brian, are you positive?" Merelda's clipped tone was unmistakable.

She strained to hear Brian's response. "Absolutely. As I explained, once I ruled out any RATS—that's Remote Access Trojans, I combed through the metadata on our own network. Using an RMM system, I ran an analysis of our InfoSec—Information Security. I could cross-reference Media Access Control and MAC addresses, plus compare remote logins with their authentications. Computers don't lie, and the evidence leaves no doubt Enrico is the culprit."

"RMMs and metadata? You're not even speaking English." Enrico sounded frustrated and angry. "How am I supposed to defend myself?"

Her cue. After knocking, she opened the door and entered in one move.

Merelda spun. Icy eyes narrowed. The three stared at her, rigid and tense.

She jumped in before Merelda could order her to leave. "Are you sure you want to stick with your story, Brian?"

"Lexy!" Merelda interjected. "I expect an answer from you as to why I was kept in the dark. Brian says he informed you of his findings days ago."

Ren's intel gave her confidence. "You put me in charge. I didn't come to you before vetting all the information." She turned to Brian. "About that story."

"There's no story. It was Enrico. I'm the only one capable

of tracing the data and tracking the information through the various portals used."

"Computers might not lie, but people do. It must be easy to 'trace' the data when it's all made up," she said.

Brian's face whitened. "You don't know what you're talking about."

Merelda remained uncharacteristically silent, her gaze traveling between the three of them.

"You thought you covered your tracks and could lie about the rest. Did you forget we used Ren's contacts and hired someone outside the company to look into this," she said. "Someone more qualified."

"*I* am the most qualified."

Lexy turned to Enrico and placed her hand lightly on his arm. "I knew you couldn't have done this," she said gently. "No matter what Brian said." She felt some of his tension abate. "Tasked with getting to the bottom of things, I had Ren's cyber sleuth call in reinforcements. She'd been making progress, but there were too many posts across too many media platforms for one person to track back to the original source."

Merelda's toes began to tap in impatience. "I assume there's a point to this."

"It turns out Brian," she gestured in his direction, "created multiple cloned social media accounts with the intent to leak the winner early." Contempt tinged her words.

Brian glared at her. "Why would I do that?"

"I have no idea. But you never expected we'd have someone other than you looking into it."

"You spineless *figlio di puttana,*" Enrico said. "Why point the finger at me?"

Brian's face flushed an angry red. "Because you get

everything," he shouted. "The looks, the shows, the money, the attention, Lexy—"

Merelda made a sound of disgust.

"You were so dismissive of me when I made that slick program to tabulate the votes for your show."

"I wasn't dismissive. I was doing my job, and trusted you to do yours."

Brian looked around the room. "You all think you're so smart. You couldn't run this place without me."

Merelda sucked in a sharp breath. "We'll see about that. You're fired, effective immediately."

Please say 'Off with his head!'

"It will be up to Enrico whether or not he presses charges."

Merelda picked up her phone. "..... please escort Brian from the premises."

"But my office. My—"

"Anything personal will be returned," Merelda said, as Brian was led away.

Lexy swallowed as she faced Merelda. "You should know Ren's friend is here going through Brian's computer."

Merelda gave her a hard look. Had she overstepped?

"And why is that?"

"*My* gut instinct," she said. "I have my doubts about Brian being smart enough to dream this up by himself." She steeled herself for Merelda's chastising comment.

Instead, there was silence. Was that an almost-smile tugging at the corners of her boss's mouth? A slight nod of her head?

"I had the same thought," Merelda said. "Brian strikes me as unlikely to act alone doing something so rash."

"Thank you for believing in me," Enrico said to Lexy.

Still absorbing her boss's almost-approval, she'd forgotten he was there.

Merelda interrupted before she could answer. "We both did. Now shoo you two. The special won't plan itself." She flapped one hand in the direction of her door.

"I'd say this calls for a celebration," Enrico said.

"I love a celebration." Especially with Enrico.

"I'll order a special lunch while we work on the Valentine's episode." He headed for the stairs. "And do invite Renata. I wish to thank her as well."

Not quite what she had in mind.

She'd almost reached her desk when Smug Sonia stepped in front of her, blocking the way.

"I saw them take Brian away."

She sighed. Word would be out soon enough. "Brian breached the trust of MHP and no longer works here." She tried to move past, but Sonia stood her ground.

"Did he say why he did it?"

"It's still under investigation."

Sonia feigned sympathy. "Bites for you to have so much controversy around your first show. What if the sponsors don't renew for next season?"

She was sick and tired of Sonia butting in and interfering, doing her best to make her feel inferior. "Sonia, mind your own business for a change."

Sonia recoiled as if she'd been slapped. "Well—" She huffed before she marched off, no doubt trying to stir up a different hornet's nest.

"Hey Lexy, where's Enrico?" Joey, Merelda's personal assistant walked briskly toward her waving a fistful of paper.

"Right here." Enrico looked grim. "I need to see Merelda. Lexy, you come too."

Her mind raced as she followed Enrico and Joey back to Merelda's office.

"Merelda," Enrico said, "I just—"

"Me first," Joey interrupted in his high-handed way.

Merelda looked almost amused as she looked from one to the other. "This is turning out to be quite the day. Joey?"

"Nominations just came out for Excellence in Nighttime Television," he trilled. Merelda snatched the printed papers out of Joey's hand. "Made you a copy," Joey said with an imperious look, as he handed Lexy a second set of papers.

Enrico shifted to stand behind her so he could read over her shoulder. Her heart clamored, aware of his breath on the back of her neck as they scanned the list together. She had to read it twice to make sure her eyes weren't playing tricks. Then Enrico rubbed her shoulder. It wasn't wishful thinking.

"Best new show in the Television Entertainment category." She half-turned his way. "Best director in the Television Entertainment category. Best host in Television Entertainment. We got nominations in three categories?!"

She let out a startled laugh when Enrico picked her up in a hug. As she stared down at him, his strong hands around her waist and his eyes smiling up at her, she wished this moment would never end.

"I took the liberty of chilling champagne just in case," said Joey. "Shall I bring in the bottle?"

Enrico set her down, but didn't step away. Having him at her side was exactly what she and Duke had talked about.

"My news first," Enrico said, one arm loosely draped over her hip. "What Lexy said about Brian not working alone got me thinking. I caught up with him in the parking lot."

It looked like Merelda tried to raise a brow, but too much Botox prevented the movement. "And?"

Enrico gave Lexy a squeeze before he pulled his arm away. "I wasn't familiar with the term gut instinct, but I am now. Brian was goaded on by someone on staff. Someone who took advantage of his insecurities and led him on to believe she had feelings for him. That by sabotaging our show, it would prove he returned those feelings."

Two pinched white lines became visible near Merelda's nostrils. "I assume he disclosed this other person's name?"

"He did. But I think it would be best to find solid proof before you deal with this person. There's bound to be something incriminating on Brian's computer. Right now, it's a case of he-said, she-said."

She admired his integrity. Having just been falsely accused himself, he didn't want to do that to someone else.

On the way back to her desk, Jules bounced across the room and gave her a quick, fierce hug. "Congratulations. I knew you'd come up with a brilliant show idea. And now the rest of the world thinks so, too."

"Thanks." She beamed. "I don't know what was better; getting my show approved by The Queen, or having it nominated."

"Just wait till you clean up at the awards show. That'll top everything."

"Ssshh. No jinxing."

Jules studied her closely. "Your eyes are sparkling. From more than just the news." She gave a knowing look. "You had a cheeky nip in the middle of the work day."

"Is it considered cheeky if the boss pours it for you?"

Jules laughed. "I guess not. See you later, my brilliant friend."

She all but floated back to her desk. Even her computer

was in a good mood, her inbox overflowing with congratulatory messages. As she skimmed through them, her breath caught. Nestled among the congrats and kudos was an email from the Artist's Trust. She closed her eyes and said a silent prayer. Her fingers trembled as she clicked on it and began to read.

Dear Ms. Smith,
We are pleased to inform you that your application to the Artist's Trust Grant has been selected as one of the winning...

"Yes." A grin stretched across her face. Even more good news. She couldn't wait to tell Nate.

She pulled out her phone, then paused. The music video was still a sensitive issue for him. She needed to find the right time to tell him in person. She tapped a finger to her lips in thought, then smiled. The awards show! They could celebrate their mutual success. Jules was right, she *was* brilliant.

Not mentioning the grant, she sent Nate a quick text about the nominations. She might not be first with the news, but at least he'd hear it from her, too.

Gran always said bad things came in threes, but weren't good things supposed to come in threes, too? She glanced up as Enrico walked back to his desk. He paused to loosen his tie and roll up his sleeves before sitting down. Lexy sent up a prayer to the *Goddess of Good Things* that this handsome, appealing man be her third.

CHAPTER 25

"If anyone deserves a little payback from karma, it's my ex-girlfriend from high school. When we were dating, I saw her at her locker between classes and went to give her a kiss. She stepped back saying, 'I broke up with you. Haven't you checked your email?'"

-Tristan, Guest
Duquan's Downlow on Dating and Love
Podcast episode #111

The second she reached the hive, Lexy knew something was different. The usual hum from the worker bees was missing. Everyone sat quietly at their desks, heads down. No one looked up as she passed. Not even Enrico.

She dragged her chair to his desk. "What's up?" she whispered. "Did someone die?"

"Not exactly." He kept his voice low. No chance of anyone overhearing.

"Then what—"

"Sonia was fired last night. By email."

She fell silent. She hadn't been a fan, it was true, but—

"By email." In their industry, there was no bigger insult. Studying his somber features, realization dawned. "It was her."

He nodded. "Not only was Sonia working with Brian, she orchestrated the entire scheme. She preyed on his vulnerabilities by pretending to be interested in him."

"I can't believe she'd stoop so low to further her own career."

"She intended for the winner to be revealed earlier in the broadcast, but Brian felt guilty about his involvement, and waited till the last minute."

"You knew it was her, but you were too much of a gentleman to say anything until you had proof."

"No need for more false accusations."

"Does everyone know?"

"Just that she's gone. No other details. Merelda wants it left that way." He made a wry face. "She doesn't want anyone on staff to know she was betrayed by *two* members of her team."

"I won't say anything."

He gave a brief nod. "I trust you." When his eyes fastened on hers, she almost melted, sensing there was a lot more he wanted to say. Only now was not the moment.

~

MARCIE

Is it amazing???

NATE SNAPPED a quick picture of the shimmering ballroom at the Hyatt Regency Hotel and texted it to her, a glitterati event of who's who in the Seattle Film and Television Industry. Hard to say what sparkled more, the jewelry and gowns worn by the women, or the giant overhead chandeliers. Large, exotic bouquets graced the room, and servers in white jackets wandered between guests offering trays of hors d'oeuvres. Round tables for twelve dressed with white cloths were set up for the formal part of the evening. Even the chairs had elegant cloth coverings.

NATE

I thought it would be fancier…

MARCIE

Haha, bro. You know you're at a classy event when even the chairs are wearing tuxedos. Wish I was there. Send more pics

He ran a finger around the inside of his collar, then tugged at his bowtie. The chairs were probably more comfortable than he was. His mom and sister had insisted a tux was required when attending an awards show. Looking around, he was glad he'd listened.

Clearly not everyone got the black-tie memo. Beyond the man in an obnoxious yellow suit, he spotted Lexy, surrounded by producers and other film personnel, Enrico at her side. He hoped the director didn't spend all night glued to her, or he'd never get any time with her.

She'd been away over Christmas. Jules and Ren had unknowingly interrupted things on New Year's in a case of terrible timing. Then came the drama of the social media leak with Enrico being falsely accused. Not exactly the ideal time for a soul-baring confession. Neither was immediately after he had spilled beer all over some other woman.

But tonight was the night. It felt right. Their friendship had really developed over the planning of the show. After the gala seemed like the perfect time to tell her he was falling for her.

Ugh. He had to come up with a better way to say it than that.

"How's my favorite 'sound hound'?" Duke held out a fist for the ritual greeting the two had adopted.

"I'm good." He bumped the bottom of his fist to the top of Duke's and Duke returned the gesture. "How's the Host with the Most?"

"Glad to hear you're back with us for the Special and Season Two."

"Me too. Just got the news today. Ian said there's no way Merelda will change up the dream team, especially if she wins."

"Duquan." A woman, clearly a reporter with her photographer in tow, interrupted. "You've been nominated tonight as Best Host in Television Entertainment. What do you think about your chances?"

In his typical modest fashion, Duke told the reporter he was fortunate to be the face of the show, but it was a team effort, and that everyone he worked with was at the top of their game. "Including Nate." Duke clapped Nate on the back. "He's in charge of sound, and always makes sure I sound good."

"A tough job, I can assure you," Nate said.

The reporter picked up on the joke. "I'll bet. Can we get a quick picture of the two of you?" He and Duke posed for the shot before the reporter moved on to find other prey.

"She's probably thinking we look like twins in our tuxes."

Duke let out a booming laugh. "Twins separated at birth."

Duke's distinctive laughter must have caught Lexy's attention, because she looked over and waved.

"Doesn't our girl look radiant?" Duke nodded in her direction.

"She does." Lexy could have been a shimmering mermaid, wearing a gown that shifted color every time she moved. It reminded him of the ocean with different depths revealing ever-changing shades of turquoise. Plus, no missing the way it clung to her curves. "I'm so happy she got this nomination. She worked really hard and deserves the recognition."

There'd been a lot of hype since the nominations were announced, with the odds in Lexy's favor. Make that MHP's favor.

"I've known her since she was just a grom," Duke said. "Hauling a longboard that must have weighed more than she did down to the beach. She was very determined, even then."

Nate followed Duke's gaze. Enrico, hand on Lexy's waist, leaned in and said something that made her laugh. The back of his neck prickled. "I guess Enrico gets some of the credit." Whenever he'd seen them lately, Enrico had been extra attentive and considerate of Lexy. Must be the guy's way of showing his appreciation. After all, she'd saved his hide, and his career.

Duke shook his head. "For the show's success? No way, man. He's good at what he does. But this show is all Lexy." Duke looked at him knowingly. "Lexy and the person who helped her formulate her ideas from the very beginning. Who supported her and believed in her."

Nate didn't know what to say. "She earned this night."

"She did." Duke nodded. "And I couldn't be prouder." He studied Lexy thoughtfully a moment more. "You ever been surfing?"

"I tried once in Hawaii." Nate forced a laugh. "I spent more time swallowing sea water than riding waves."

"Sometimes you can be sitting on your board in exactly the right spot in the water, and the perfect wave comes to you. But that's rare. Most of the time you have to paddle like hell to get yourself in position for the wave you want. Then paddle even harder to get yourself into the wave."

"Okay..." Where was this going?

"But when you catch that wave, pop up, and ride along the face..." Duke sighed with satisfaction. "It's the best feeling in the whole world. And totally worth all the hard work."

"You're not telling me this so I'll try surfing again, are you."

"No. I'm telling you this because I'm wondering why you're still sitting there waiting for the wave to come to you. It might be time to start paddling, buddy."

"Any chance you have a music analogy for me?" Though he thought he knew what Duke was getting at. And by that analogy, he'd already started to paddle toward Lexy.

Duke chuckled. "I'll let you think about it. But speaking of music, Lexy said you guys sounded really great at the pub the other night. I'll have to come and hear you play sometime."

"Anytime," he said. "Let me know and I'll put you on the guest list."

"Maybe I can interview your band on my podcast."

"Isn't it a relationship podcast?"

"It is." Duke smiled. "But my guests include anyone I think would be interesting to have on the show. I'd be curious to explore the dynamics between members of a successful Seattle band. You must have your share of highs and lows, of joy, frustration, compromise and love, just like any romantic relationship. And you make it work."

"Huh," Nate said. "Interesting. I've never thought about it like that before, but you're right."

"Let me know if the others are willing."

"They sure like to talk. Especially Connor and Adam. They'll say yes in a heartbeat."

"Great." Duke clapped a hand on his shoulder. "We'll set it up."

"Ladies and gentlemen, if you could please be seated." A woman spoke into a microphone on the stage at the front of the room. "The award presentations are about to begin."

"Here we go." Duke started toward MHP's table.

Nate followed, still mulling Duke's words. Where Lexy was concerned, it seemed he'd just been given her big brother's blessing. Now if he could only get her alone.

"Why am *I* so nervous?" he said. "I'm not the one nominated." Granted, if the show won, he'd be up on stage with the rest of the team, but win or lose, it wasn't all on him. Then he spotted Lexy at the table, and knew exactly why he was nervous.

"PINCH me so I know I'm not dreaming," Lexy said to Enrico. "No wait. Don't. If this is a dream, I don't want to wake up."

"I assure you it is very real." Enrico's voice so close to her ear gave her goosebumps. "Bella, you deserve all this and so much more."

She tilted slightly and leaned against him. Since the incident in Merelda's office with Brian, Enrico had been constantly at her side. Like tonight. And even though they'd been putting in the same crazy long hours of pre-production they did last season, things were different. He was more solicitous, making sure she was all right, and had everything she needed. He hadn't even challenged a single one of her contestant choices for Season Two.

"Your lips to the judges' ears," she joked.

"You don't need any extra help." The way Enrico looked straight into her eyes made Lexy's insides turn delightfully gooey. "I've got a very good feeling about you tonight."

"Am I perchance drinking champagne with this year's Best Director in Television?"

"It's possible," he said with a saucy wink.

"Well, you look like a winner in that tux."

"Me? I look like your average man in a tuxedo. An Italian tuxedo, but still."

She snorted. "Average man." Who was he trying to kid?

"You on the other hand—" Enrico held her fingertips and took a step back, his gaze running slowly over her body from head to toe like a lover's touch.

She shivered. If he could do that with simply a look—

"You are a vision. Every bit as enchanting as those mythical sea creatures Homer writes about who lure sailors to their death."

"Thank you, I think." If she had a siren's powers, she would definitely lure Enrico home with her. He could help her out of this shimmery confection for starters. "Once again, Jules was my secret weapon."

"Come, my siren." Still holding her hand, Enrico led her to the table reserved for Manor House Productions.

Nerves that had calmed while talking with Enrico began fluttering in her belly again. "Now I know how our Legends felt. Wondering which envelope holds the winner's name."

"Lexy, you sit here." Merelda patted the seat on her right. "Enrico, I'd like you on my good side, please."

"You're the boss," Enrico said. "Though you know you don't have a bad side." Merelda preened.

Lexy resisted a sneak peek at her phone. Her mom had messaged earlier. She knew her parents and a group of their closest friends would be gathered around the TV, drinks in hand and a table full of snacks, rooting for Lexy and *Cupid Grants a Second Chance.*

"I heard there's going to be a special guest performer tonight," Lexy overheard a guest gushing at the next table. "Someone big."

"Do you think it's Lady Gaga? Or maybe Billie Eilish?" her companion asked excitedly.

"As long as there are no meat dresses," Merelda murmured dryly at their own table.

"Is this seat taken?" Nate slid into the chair on Lexy's other side.

"Saving it for you," she said with a smile. She couldn't wait to tell Nate about the grant. But first things first. "I'm so happy that if we win Best New Show tonight, you'll be one of the people on stage with me." She gave his leg an excited squeeze.

"If we win, no one will notice anyone else up on stage. Not with you in that dress." He rested one arm across the back of his chair, angling himself toward her. "You look incredible."

"Thank you." She eyed his glass, then gave him a teasing smile. "Is my dress safe? You're not planning on spilling your drink, again?"

He laughed, the music started, and the host ran onto the stage amidst a flurry of applause. She knew who he was, but for the life of her, couldn't remember his name.

"I thought it was going to be Neil Patrick Harris," said the same woman hoping for a Lady Gaga performance, who seemed poised for an evening of disappointments.

But not me...I hope.

On the other side of Merelda, she caught Enrico's gaze on her, and from that moment on barely heard a word of the ceremony. The evening led off with awards for excellence in technical accomplishments. She clapped for the presenters, nominees and winners, nodding and smiling on cue, but the closer they got to awards *CGSC* had been nominated for, the harder it was to concentrate. By the time nominees for best host were read, her heart was pounding so loud, everything else faded into the background.

The envelope was opened in what seemed like slow motion. She held her breath as the presenter leaned closer to the mic. An eternity passed before she heard Duke's name. A cheer rose, especially from the MHP table, and Lexy jumped to her feet cheering loudest of all.

Across the table Duke rose leisurely, flashed his trademark smile and made his way to the stage. As comfortable on his surfboard in the ocean, as at a black-tie event, he had the crowd completely captivated before his first words.

"Can you feel the love in the room, people?" More cheers. "Because standing up here, I'm telling you, I can feel the love!" His smile encompassed the entire room. "Amazing things can happen when you follow your heart. I moved to Seattle for love, which brought me the incredible opportunity to host *Cupid Grants a Second Chance.*"

Her heart swelled with pride as she listened to her friend thank all the right people, including the contestants for having the courage to tell their stories, everyone at the gala for supporting the show, as well as the at-home viewers.

"I want you to keep your tissues handy, because we'll be

back, bringing you all the feels and more on our Valentine's Day Special."

Merelda smiled in smug satisfaction at the way Duke seamlessly promoted their next episode. If anyone here wasn't already watching the show, they would be now.

The award for excellence in directing a show of noteworthy entertainment value was next. This time it was Enrico who rose and made his way on stage, charming the crowd with his acceptance speech.

He was two parts confidence, one part European elegance, and one part humor; shaken not stirred, and garnished with sex appeal. When he stared directly into her eyes as he thanked the MHP team, tingles raced from the top of her head to the tips of her toes.

A few awards later, only her category remained. As the presenter listed the shows nominated for Best New Show in Television Entertainment, she fought a sudden wave of nausea and light-headedness. Now was not the time to lower her head between her knees. Not as one of the cameras near the stage panned their table, zooming in for a close-up. She managed a modest smile before the camera moved on.

CGSC had already won twice. Was it greedy to hope for this one as well? To be known as the person who produced the best new show on TV this year? Time slowed to a trickle. The wait was agonizing. She held her breath, hands clenched in her lap until Nate reached over and took her hand in his. He gave a gentle squeeze, forcing her to look at him.

When she did, he mouthed, 'Move over ponytail'. The words he'd written in her birthday card. She smiled gratefully. His words calmed her racing heart, unknotted her stomach, and allowed her to breathe. Passing out right now, with the camera focused on their table would be as embarrassing as Jenifer Lawrence tripping up the stairs on her way to accept the Oscar.

"And the winner is—*Cupid Grants a Second Chance.* Manor House Productions. Lexy Smith, Producer."

She froze. The world moved in slow motion as Nate reached to hug her at the same time Merelda rose, pulling her to her feet. Then everyone at their table was standing; clapping, cheering. Enrico reached for her hand and guided her up the steps behind Merelda while the rest of the crew brought up the rear. Of course Merelda led the way. Lexy didn't mind. This was her show. Her baby. Her win. Her moment.

Move over ponytail is right!

As she stood onstage, about to step up to the microphone to make a speech on behalf of her team, she caught Duke's eye. This moment onstage, ready to accept her award, Enrico so close she could feel his body heat, was exactly the vision of success she had described to him. If it didn't seem as fulfilling as she expected, she chalked it up to nerves. Surely, tonight she and Enrico would move toward making her other dream a reality.

Duke smiled and blew her a kiss as she took a deep breath and stepped up to the microphone.

"Thank you—" Her voice sounded shaky. The mic let out a dreadful screech. Nate stepped forward, adjusted the mic, then stepped back.

This time her voice sounded strong and confident as she thanked Merelda, Enrico, Duke, and the entire cast and crew of Manor House Productions for being one hundred percent behind the show from its earliest inception. In a rush, she thanked the jurors for their vote, and the Legends, as well as the audience. She hefted her award in the air in victory.

Sounds of applause and the cheers of her team rang out before they were ushered backstage where a team of onsite engravers etched their names onto their trophies. From there, they were left to make their own way back to the table.

During the closing speech, Lexy discreetly checked her phone and saw messages from both her parents. Her heart swelled even bigger. She looked down at the statuette in front of her. Could this night get any better? She cast a demure glance at Enrico from under her eyelashes. Absolutely. After celebratory drinks with the others, she and Enrico could slip off to do some private celebrating of their own.

As Enrico helped Lexy to her feet, a female voice called his name from across the room. Beside her, Enrico tensed. She turned, but didn't recognize the woman.

"Enrico! I'm here." Two security guards were making half-hearted attempts to keep the woman out of the ballroom, but she continued forward, making her determined way toward them. She wore a dramatic red gown, pouting full lips painted to match. Her long dark hair fell in glossy waves. She was drop-dead gorgeous.

"Enrico, who is that?"

Enrico didn't reply. He stared at the woman as if seeing a ghost.

The security guards gave up trying to stop the stunning newcomer, turning instead to hold back the hoard of paparazzi who had followed her into the hotel. Her dramatic entrance drew the attention of everyone in the ballroom. Cameras and phones were aimed her way amid loud whispers and awed murmurs. "...Isabella Ricci.... Italian film star...."

"I tried to get here in time for the ceremony," the woman said as she drew near, "but my flight was delayed." Her voice as exotic as she was, her English was delightfully accented.

Just like Enrico's.

Ice crawled down Lexy's spine. Dread settled in the pit of her stomach. "Enric—"

She didn't get a chance to finish before the tall beauty threw herself into his arms and kissed him. Lexy froze in shock. Enrico did not push the woman away. In fact, he kissed her back. *Really* kissed her back. When the embrace finally ended, the newcomer continued to cling to his arm. The only person who didn't look shocked was Merelda.

Enrico's voice was low and urgent. "Isabella. What are you doing here?"

Isabella, who looked like she had stepped out of the pages of a fashion magazine, gave him a radiant smile. "Darling, did you think I wouldn't want to be here to support my talented husband as he received this prestigious award?" She tossed back her hair and let out a husky, seductive laugh. "There's nowhere else I'd rather be. I'm just sorry I missed it." She aimed a practiced pout at the cameras.

Enrico has a *wife*???

Lexy felt as if she'd been simultaneously punched in the gut and drop-kicked off the Seattle Great Wheel. She barely noticed her award slip from her fingers and hit the carpet with a dull thud. How could this man she'd been building dreams around have a wife she knew nothing about?

CHAPTER 26

"Stars—they're just like us! Yeah, right. You think Margot Robbie ever went on a date where the guy lied about his height, showed up wearing a holey T-shirt, trash-talked his ex the whole time, ordered twice as many drinks as her, then insisted they split the bill?"

-Sasha, Guest
Duquan's Downlow on Dating and Love
Podcast episode #4

Conversation swirled around Lexy as she stood outside with the team while everyone slowly climbed into the limos Merelda had rented for the event.

"Can you believe it? Enrico's married to Isabella Ricci!"

"Why didn't he ever talk about her? If I was married to the hottest Italian movie star, I'd be bragging all the time."

What started out as a fairytale evening complete with a handsome prince, had disintegrated. Midnight had passed and she was Cinderella, back in her rags, having watched someone else kiss her prince.

"Yeah. I loved her awesome fight scene in the fountain to get the briefcase full of detonators and stop the attack. All those bad ass moves she pulled off in her soaking wet dress."

"I know. She's such an empowering role model for women."

"I haven't seen him on the red carpet for any of her movie premiers. But he must have been there, right?"

Lexy wanted to cover her ears. All around her, people were raving about Isabella Ricci. At the party, instead of basking in the aftermath of the show's win, the conversation would be all about Enrico's secret wife. The last thing she wanted was to listen to her excited co-workers speculate on the circumstances of Enrico and Isabella's relationship, while she tried to block out the image of the couple's kiss.

"I saw them get into a cab," Duke said quietly beside her. "I don't think they'll be coming to the afterparty."

At least she would be spared some of her humiliation.

"But what do you say we blow this popsicle stand anyway, Lexycakes?" Duke said. "Go have our own celebration."

She nodded numbly. Her brain recognized that going with Duke would get her away from here. Away from this.

"You coming Nate?" Duke asked.

Belatedly, she realized Nate had been standing on her other side, buffering her as much as possible from the enthusiastic MHP gossip mill and its latest fodder.

"Sounds good." He took one arm and Duke took the other, walking her away from the limos. "It will be a while before they realize we're not there, by which time they'll be too drunk to care."

"There's a great tiki bar down the block that Paul loves,"

Duke said. "I'll text him our change of plans." She didn't care where they went. As long as it was dark. And she could hide.

"This place is great," Nate said, as the host led them back to one of the booths along the wall.

The bar's dim interior suited her perfectly. She needed to escape. Thereby avoiding the tidal wave of emotions that she knew would hit her at some point.

"I think we'd better get this girl a Fish Bowl," Duke said as they sat down.

She nodded. She could use a double.

"Fish Bowls all around, and one for Paul who's on his way," Duke told their server.

"I'm not sure I'm a Fish Bowl kind of guy," Nate said hesitantly.

"That's fine, I'll have yours." Earlier, she'd told Enrico not to wake her up if she was dreaming. Now the idea of waking up to find tonight had all been a dream was immensely appealing.

I should be so lucky.

"Did someone say Fish Bowls?" Paul sat down and kissed Duke. "It seems like the right choice under the circumstances." He leaned across the table. "Did I hear things right? Your sexy director has a secret movie star wife? Are we in a telenovela?"

She saw Duke's subtle shake of his head.

Paul turned to Nate. "You must be Nate. I've heard a lot about you. Nice to finally meet you."

"You too." They shook hands.

"Did either of you know Enrico was married?" She couldn't stop the words from popping out of her mouth.

Duke and Nate both shook their heads.

"Do you think anyone else knew?"

"Doubtful," Nate said. "Knowing the MHP gossip mill, word would have gotten around."

"But why would he keep her a secret?"

"He must have had his reasons," Duke said. "No one in love wants to keep it to themselves." He shared a smile with Paul. "Maybe for her career?"

"I guess," she said. "But I can't think of a good enough reason to hide something like that."

Duke looked at her sympathetically. "I know the two of you became close working together. I'm sure it was hard on him keeping such a secret from you."

"Oh, thank God," she said under her breath as their server approached with a tray full of the oversize cocktails. She reached for the first one to land on the table, grasping it in both hands before taking a huge sip of the boozy fruit mix.

Nate asked the server for a beer.

"Spoilsport," she said, without heat.

"Here's to the table full of winners I'm sitting with. I'm so proud of all of you, and the success of your show." Paul lifted his Fish Bowl high over the middle of the table and everyone clinked glasses. "Now let me see those golden awards."

She and Duke placed their statuettes on the table, which Paul took as a photo op. "Awards and Fish Bowls with a tiki bar backdrop. So many good hashtags for this," he said, arranging the items on the table to the best advantage.

"While David Loftus here is busy taking photos—" Duke said.

"It's true I follow several food and drink photographers on Instagram, which Duke likes to tease me about," Paul said.

"While he's busy," continued Duke, "I'd like to take this opportunity to thank you Lexy. For inviting me to audition."

"As soon as Nate suggested you, I knew you would be a perfect fit," she said. "The show would not have been the same, nor as successful, without your thoughtful and insightful conversations with our Legends."

"And Nate," Duke said, "thanks for suggesting me, man. Working on *CGSC* has allowed me to spread my messages of love to an even wider audience than my podcast."

She placed a hand on Nate's arm. "Between your help at the beginning, then filming my pitch and suggesting Duke, you were instrumental." She lifted her glass. "To Nate."

Nate shook his head. "To Cupid."

"To love!" said Duke.

An order of Tiki Nachos which Paul promised were 'fit for the Gods' arrived, along with another round of drinks for everyone except Lexy, who had already started on Nate's rejected Fish Bowl. Duke and Paul engaged in a lively debate over their new Roomba. Paul was ecstatic that having the robo-cleaner meant he no longer had to vacuum their condo, one of the items on his weekly chore list. Duke insisted it was to help keep things clean between vacuuming, which Paul still had to do. Each was trying to get Nate to side with them, which he deftly avoided.

Lexy's mind returned to Isabella's arrival, playing it on repeat. Each time, she felt more and more stupid for not having seen it coming. For having fallen for Enrico's charm, seeing what she wanted to, spinning out her dreams about the two of them.

The debate ended in a draw and Duke stood, reaching for his coat and scarf. "We're off, kids," he said. "Stay and finish your drinks. See you tomorrow."

She and Nate stood for hugs and handshakes.

"Congratulations again everyone," Paul said.

"By the way," Duke said, "my wonderful man here picked up the tab as a congrats on our big win."

Paul waved away their thanks. "You all earned it. Good night!" He took Duke's hand and the two of them strolled out of the bar.

"They're the best, aren't they?" she said as she sat back down.

"Good guys," Nate agreed. "Lucky you met Duke in the water all those years ago."

"Must have been fate," she said with a contented smile. She sipped her drink and looked at him. "Do you think we were destined to meet, too? Some reason I picked up your latte that morning on my way to my interview? So you could share your intel about Merelda?"

He chuckled. "How many Fish Bowls *was* that for you?" He sobered. "You would have nailed the job anyway. Merelda only hires the best." He reached for one of the curls Jules had pulled loose from her up-do. It slid slowly through his fingers, then slipped free and sprang back into shape.

Her pulse rate kicked up a notch. She was still too wired on adrenalin from the evening to feel anything from the alcohol. Her reaction to Nate was different. Like that first kiss in the garage, only amplified.

"You were so cute that morning on your way to the interview, equal parts nerves and determination."

"You saw all that?"

"Somehow, I knew you'd get the job. Which meant it wasn't the last I'd be seeing of you."

She laughed. "Little did you know."

His look softened on her and did funny things to her insides. "Little did I know." He glanced around the near-empty bar. "I think we shut the place down. Let's get you home."

"I don't want to go home." She wanted to forget what happened earlier tonight with Enrico's wife. As if she could. Devastated. Hurt. Foolish. Feelings surged through her, overwhelming her.

"Well, it looks like we need to get out of here."

He was right. Staff loitered near the bar, waiting for the last few customers to leave so they could cash out and go home.

He pulled out his phone. "I'll order an Uber."

As she started to put on the long, fuzzy, fake fur coat Jules had loaned her, he helped her into it. Its weight made her feel cozy and safe. So did his arm around her waist, guiding her to the door.

"Don't forget to take a tiki fortune." The host pointed to a tall wooden tiki statue holding a large seashell filled with folded slips of paper.

"After you."

"If you insist." She stepped forward, reached into the shell and swirled her hand around for the 'right' one, which she pulled out with a flourish and unfolded. She read aloud, "Lono, the God of peace and luck advises you to say yes to an unexpected invitation. It will yield delightful results." She pocketed it. "Your turn."

He took the first one his hand touched. "Kanaloa, God of the sea—wait. This one must be yours, ocean girl."

"You picked it, it's yours. Keep reading."

"Kanaloa, God of the sea, says if you step up to help a friend in need, you will be rewarded." He grinned. "A reward from a god sounds good to me."

"The Tiki gods seem to know you well. A friend in need," she mused teasingly. "Got any of those?"

"Must be you." He held the door open for her. "You don't want to go home, and I happen to have a cool place to hang out with a great view and an impressive record collection. Wanna come back to my place?"

"Wait." She stopped abruptly and cocked her head at him. "Was that an unexpected invitation, Nate Douglas?"

"I guess so."

"That settles it. The Tiki gods decreed it, and I wouldn't want to risk angering any of them."

"Nope, don't want to upset the gods." Their ride slid up to the curb and Nate opened the door.

"Besides," she flashed him a grin before she got in. "You had me at 'record collection'."

TAKING Lexy back to his apartment was not how he'd imagined the night ending. Historic music institutions like The Rendezvous and The Showbox whizzed past in a blur outside the car window. He'd always believed he was destined to live in this neighborhood, Belltown being 'Ground Zero' for the grunge era. That was the kind of destiny he believed in. Not some corny fortune from a bar. And yet...

He fingered the folded slip of paper in his pocket. *Rewarded*. Dating Lexy would be more than a reward. It would be the ultimate.

She shifted to follow his gaze. "I love living on the lake, but this area is really great. So much history, lots going on, and totally walkable. That's one downside to living on a houseboat."

"I like it." The car glided to a stop and Nate helped Lexy out. "Thanks man," he said to the driver.

He unlocked his apartment door, doing a mental scan of what might greet them on the other side. He'd put his laundry away, thankfully. And having grown up sharing a bathroom with two women, he knew to leave the toilet seat down. He'd made his bed, not that— Still, it never hurt to be prepared.

"What a fantastic apartment," she said as she stepped inside.

His place was on the top floor with over-height ceilings, the far wall original brick. Loft-style living quarters were one open big space. A doorway at the back led to a small bedroom and bathroom. He didn't have a lot of furniture, but every piece had been chosen carefully.

He walked around the island and opened the fridge "Water or soda?"

"Water thanks. I had enough sugar in those rum drinks." She dropped her coat on the couch as she crossed the room to his records. "Wow, you weren't kidding about your collection."

"Surpassed only by Adam's." He handed her a bottle of water, then took a sip from his before placing it on the windowsill.

"No Rainy Day Astronauts album?" Her voice was joking as she flipped through the records.

"We'd love to have one," he said, "but we'd need to be making a lot more money to justify having a vinyl version pressed. For now, it's all digital, and some CDs to sell at our shows."

"I like that you have a mix of vintage albums and newer stuff."

"Yeah. Vinyl just sounds better. Don't get me wrong, Spotify is great for putting together a mixed playlist, or exploring new music. But when you find something you like, it's worth investing." Like her. He'd never met a woman as enamored with his music collection as he was.

She pulled a record off the shelf. "You have the Black Pumas? I love their song "Colors". His voice gives me goosebumps."

"The whole album is incredible. Reverential retro-soul paired with buckets of passion. Every track is great." He took the record from her, slid it out of the sleeve, and placed it on the player. "Wait till you hear it like this."

She closed her eyes and began to sway as the opening drum roll gave way to a slower, more sultry beat. "It does sound better, though I'm sure your system helps."

"I couldn't have subpar equipment at home." So much for baring his soul to her tonight. Once again, the timing was off. Her reaction to Enrico's wife showing up clued him in that she'd had more than just a work crush on the direc-tor. Tonight's roller coaster ride of highs and lows had left her vulnerable. She needed 'friend' Nate.

She opened her eyes and looked directly at him. "Thanks for being there for me. It means a lot."

What was she, reading his mind?

More like torturing him, her eyes never leaving his as she continued to sway.

It was sexy as hell. And totally unfair, with him trying to keep his hands off her. Give her time to recover, before he told her how he felt. His throat grew dry. He coughed discreetly to clear it. Moonlight shone through the window making her dress shimmer as she moved. "I can't remember if I told you earlier, but you look incredible." Damn, his words came out lower than he intended, intimately husky. Her eyes darkened with some unnamed emotion, while a faint blush crept over her cheeks.

"You're looking pretty good yourself," she said. "There's

something about a man in a tux that's so..." She let out a dreamy sigh.

"I'm glad you approve."

A few graceful sways brought her in front of him. "Since you were there for me," she smoothed her hands over his jacket, "it's time for your reward."

He placed his hands atop hers, stilling her movements. A sudden bolt of panic shot down his spine. "Lexy what are you doing?" Sure, he wanted her. Had since the Guitar Gallery on his birthday. But the timing— To tell her how he felt about her—

"Making us both feel good." She loosened his tie, then pulled it out from his collar and let it fall to the floor.

He licked his lips. "Lex, this is a bad idea."

"And if I don't agree?" She started on the buttons of his jacket. "What if I think it's a really good idea?"

He placed gentle hands on her shoulders, making an attempt to cool things before they got out of control. "You're shell-shocked right now. You'll think on things differently in the morning."

"I won't. I promise. Just make me forget everything for now. Everything except you and me." She clung to his lapels and pulled his face down to hers.

Any remaining shred of resolve flew out the window the second her lips found his. Her kiss started off sweet and tentative. An instant later it ramped up to full octane lust. She tugged his shirt free, sliding her warm hands across his back. He caught her head in his palms and slanted her face, deepening the kiss before he ploughed his hands through her hair, loosening the curls.

Her body molded to his, the clingy fabric of her gown more an enticement than a deterrent. She felt alive, fluid and responsive in his arms, as he nibbled the sweet spot between her bare neck and shoulder. She shuddered. The heat of her womanhood against his thigh sent a surge to his cock that felt almost painful. Had he ever needed a woman the way he needed her?

His hands cupped the undersides of her breasts before inching higher, fitting her perfectly to his palms. Her nipples felt taut and crested as she moaned and swayed against him, plucking ineffectually at his buttons so she could slip her hands inside the front of his shirt.

He sucked in a breath as her fingers ruffled the hair on his chest, fitted against his pecs before sliding lower, past his navel to his waistband. She let out a huge sigh of frustration before her hands roamed lower to find his hardness. He steeled himself to keep control. He'd imagined this scenario more than a few times, him and her together, but nothing had prepared him for the reality as she stroked him through his trousers, her lids half closed and dreamy, inviting his kiss.

Once he could finally breathe, he scooped her into his arms. She looped one arm around his neck, while her free hand splayed his chest, impatient fingers burrowing beneath his half-open shirt. She leaned in and took a deep breath.

"You smell so good."

So did she. A sweet scent he couldn't identify, but knew he would never forget. This scent. This night. This moment. This woman.

She weighed nothing in his arms. As he carried her to his bed, he caught the faint words of Eric Burton as he sang about wanting to know someone better. A totally fitting sign from the gods he didn't believe in. Exactly the way he felt about Lexy.

The short walk to his room took forever. The way she

kept kissing him he could barely see straight. Once there, he set her down slowly and carefully, keeping her glued to his side. Moonlight spilled through the window over the bed. Enough light that he could read her expression as he tilted her face up to his.

"Are you sure about this?"

"Absolutely."

He still had no clue how to tell her the way he felt. This way, he could show her instead. No chance he'd fumble that. He trailed a slow, gentle stroke down her arm, rewarded when those sky-blue eyes of hers darkened and grew heavy.

"I know I said I love a guy in a tux, but let's get you out of it." She reached for his last few buttons while he unzipped the back of her dress.

She slipped her arms free. In one smooth movement the dress slithered from her shoulders to her hips and legs, before it puddled on the floor like a shimmer of sea water.

His eyes followed the movement of the dress, all the way to the high-heeled sandals on her feet. "I love a woman in heels," he said. "Let's keep you in them."

"The gods said you'd be rewarded. The shoes stay on."

Her bra and thong panties were so translucent they left little to the imagination as he struggled out of his tux, a suddenly far more complicated process than taking off a pair of jeans. But she came to his rescue, helping him out of the last of his clothes. He repaid the favor, laying her on the bed and peeling off her delectable lingerie, sampling her skin as he did so. Finally, he was naked and lying next to her.

But not for long. One slick move and she was on top of him, straddling his midsection and reaching for his cock. He pulled her forward and filled his mouth with her breasts, lashing them with his tongue, rewarded by a rush of damp heat that spilled from her to him.

Sanity prevailed long enough to grab a condom from his nightstand and hand it to her. He was sheathed in record time as she shared her dampness, then slowly eased him inside.

It was a night for honoring Lexy, and now it was his turn. She was hot and tight and he let her take the lead, move at her own pace as she adjusted the fit and the angle and slowly started to move. He nearly came apart hearing her throaty purr of pleasure. The sexiest moment of his life.

CHAPTER 27

"I never believed in tarot cards and all that woo-woo stuff.
Until a tea leaf reader accurately described the next man I
would date. I met him a week later. Now I give even my
fortune cookie fortunes a second read, in case there's something I need to know."

-Grace, Guest
Duquan's Downlow on Dating and Love
Podcast episode #62

L exy woke to early morning light filtering through the
window, and the cozy length of Nate's body spooning
hers. A glance at the bedside clock told her they still had
time before work. She snuggled closer. Being wrapped in
Nate's arms felt glorious. Maybe, deep down, she'd known
since the night they'd kissed in Connor's garage that they
would end up here at some point. And here felt so right.

Delightful results, her fortune had predicted. She couldn't

agree more. Last night started off being about making herself feel better, giving in to the mutual attraction between her and Nate. And maybe the dress had turned her into some sort of siren, different from the way she normally acted, but somewhere between then and now things had shifted. She gave a contented stretch. The anguish of the awards show drama took a distant back seat to waking up next to Nate. He stirred as she rolled over to face him.

With a secret, satisfied smile, she idly traced designs on his chest with one fingertip. As he clasped her free hand and raised it to his lips, her inner voice ruined the moment, reminding her she had broken her rule about not dating a friend.

Quiet! Technically this wasn't dating, this was sex. Perfectly healthy, mind-blowingly hot sex.

He levered himself on one elbow and kissed the top of her head. "I'll get us some water. Maybe rustle up a snack. We sure used up a lot of energy." She heard smug satisfaction in his voice as he sank back down. "Just as soon as I'm able to move."

Her inner voice clamored louder. What if she hurt Nate?

Especially now that they'd slept together. She cared about him. She wanted to help him. She sat bolt upright. The grant!

"I can't believe I forgot to tell you." She beamed down at him. Given everything that had happened in the last twelve hours, the grant approval had slipped her mind. What better time than now? When they were closer than ever.

"What?"

"Just a sec." She leaned over the edge of the bed, fingers grasping until they caught hold of his tuxedo shirt. She slipped it on and fastened a couple of middle buttons.

"I never thought I'd say this." He stacked his arms under

his head and gave her a lazy, sexy smile. "But that looks way better on you."

"Not true. You looked very handsome in this last night." She studied him from under half-lowered lashes. "Though I preferred the way you looked as I took it off you."

He lunged for the shirt, starting to slide it down her shoulder. "I bet I'll feel the same."

"Wait!" Laughing, she placed a firm hand on his chest and eased him back. "I have news." Her eyes sparkled. "Exciting news that can't wait."

"First you clean up at the awards show, then we spend an incredible night together. I don't know how much more good news I can take."

"I've been waiting for the right time to tell you."

He half-sat. "I've been waiting for the right time to tell you something too." He looked so cute and sincere, but it couldn't be nearly as life-changing as what she'd been keeping to herself.

"Me first." She savored the anticipation of his reaction. He'd be surprised initially. Pleased that she cared enough to apply on his behalf. Elated at the outcome. No longer was it only her dream and career making huge strides, but his music dreams could take off, too.

"Hurry up then." He started playfully poking her. "Tell me."

"I applied for a grant from Artist Trust for an unrestricted project. To produce a music video for an up-and-coming local band." She pressed her fingertips together. "And I got it." She held her breath, waiting for his reaction. "We got it!"

Clearly, he was overwhelmed, too surprised to speak.

She explained how the application had come across her

desk. The extra care she took filling it out. The words rushed out of her with such enthusiasm it took several moments to realize his expression wasn't one of joy, the way she'd expected.

"Don't you see? This means I can produce a Rainy Day Astronauts video for you, and we..." She trailed off as the shuttered look on his face finally sank in.

He gently brushed her aside then swung his legs over to sit on the edge of the bed, his back to her.

She put one hand on his bare back. "What's wrong? I thought you'd be excited. Think what this means. The opportunity for RDA."

He shrugged off her hand. "I think you should go," he said quietly.

"What? Nate, talk to me." She tugged the sheet up, suddenly cold.

"What's wrong?" He turned to face her. "If you have to ask, I don't know you as well as I thought. And you don't know me at all."

"I *do* know you," she said urgently. "I know Adele hurt you, but that's so far in your past. I wanted to help—"

"Help?" He barked out a laugh. "Taking the darkest moment from my past, the damaging experience I told you in confidence, and doing the worst possible thing with that information, is helping?" He stood and grabbed a pair of jeans, hastily pulling them on. "Next time you think about helping me, don't."

She reached out a hand. "Can you sit back down and talk to me, please?"

"There's nothing to talk about." He stood rigid. Crossed his arms. "You know the reason the band has never made a music video. And we're not making one now. Give the grant back. Or find some other local group to produce a video for.

We're not taking it." He pulled an old Sonics hoodie over his head.

"But Nate," she said, desperate to turn things around. "What if Connor and—"

"Leave the guys out of it." He stared off into the distance. She could see the muscles of his jaw working.

"You all deserve this chance. Who knows where it could lead? I truly thought this experience would be good for RDA. For you."

"I know you did," he said softly, his gaze meeting hers. "That's what makes it worse."

The bleak expression in his eyes cracked her heart wide open.

He ran a hand through his hair. "Let me order you an Uber so you can go home and change before work." He turned and left the room.

She sat frozen, stunned by the abrupt turn of events. How had the mood shifted from joyful intimacy to painful distance so quickly? She hugged his pillow, gutted by the knowledge that she had put that wounded look in his eye.

The whirring of the coffee grinder from the other room, sudden in the silence, jolted her to action. She slid out of bed and began gathering her clothes, moving in slow motion. As if one wrong move might cause her to shatter. The beautiful blues and greens of her mermaid gown turned blurry with unshed tears as she slid it on. Rapidly, she blinked them back, managing to get the zipper halfway up on her own. Holding her shoes, she padded into the other room.

"Um, Nate," she said hesitantly. "Can you—" she cleared her throat. "I need help with my zipper."

He turned toward her, gently moved her hair aside. She

felt the backs of his fingers brush against her skin as he finished zipping up her dress.

His hands paused at the top. "Congratulations again on your win last night Lex," he said, still so close behind her that his warm breath whispered across the nape of her neck. "No one deserves it more than you."

Her chest tightened. A lump formed in her throat. So many possibilities for what she wanted to say tumbled through her mind, but she couldn't give voice to a single one. All she could manage was a nod.

Abruptly he dropped his arms and stepped back as if he had been burned. "Your Uber will be here any minute." He grabbed his coffee mug off the counter. "I need a shower. See you at work."

She watched him retreat, hoping he would turn and look at her. Hoping he would change direction and walk back to her so they could talk this all out. She wanted his dimpled smile back, his green eyes laughing at her the way they'd been a short time earlier.

The bathroom door clicked shut. For a wild moment she considered following him in, forcing him to hear her out, convince him that making this video would be an important move for him and the band.

Remembering the look of raw anguish on his face stopped her. His earlier words, when she tried to explain she thought the grant was a good thing, echoed in her mind. *I know you did. That's what makes it worse.* The quiet resignation in his voice, as if her hurting him had been an inevitable outcome.

Blinking back more tears, she let herself out of his apartment before she added to the pain she'd already caused.

CHAPTER 28

"My boyfriend is really sweet about celebrating the little things. He once brought me home a cupcake because for the first time, I finished reading my Book Club book *before* the night of Book Club."

-Hannah, Guest
Duquan's Downlow on Dating and Love
Podcast episode #125

MOM

Hi honey. All our friends and neighbors want me to host a party after your big win. We're all so proud of you. You must be busy celebrating in the city, but can you let me know when you can make it home so we can congratulate you Cannon Beach style? xx

LEXY

You're right. Celebrating. Call you later this weekend. XO

Ugh! She tossed her phone on the couch cushion beside her. Not celebrating. Beating herself up. Her own personal *Fight Club.*

Enrico with a wife? This whole time. How could she not have seen that?

She'd been too busy building castles in the sky. Actual castles. Like her fantasy of celebrating Christmas in Italy with him next year. Her stomach clenched and her skin prickled all over at the memory.

With Enrico out of the office and Nate in studio, she'd had a slight reprieve. She'd even managed to escape work before Jules or Ren caught her—they'd been bombarding her with texts about the gala all day. Luckily everyone was busy. Merelda had buzzed through the hive more frequently than usual, cracking the whip and making sure idle speculation about Isabella Ricci didn't impact productivity.

Thank God it was Friday. Blaming too much champagne and too little sleep, she'd begged off drinks with the girls, promising to fill them in soon. Back home, this morning's conversation with Nate played over and over in her mind. A break from the alternating hurt and embarrassment over Enrico, this memory was even worse.

The expression on Nate's face. The hurt in his eyes. Him thinking she had stabbed him in the back. It all brought back memories of similar hard conversations with Tyler, making her feel like an absolute slug of a human.

Instead of handing Nate what she thought was a shiny wrapped present, she'd lobbed a grenade into the middle of their friendship. Or whatever fledgling romance had started after the gala. She had no idea how to make things right. A simple apology wasn't going to cut it.

She held one of her cute, tropical print pillows over her face and screamed into it. Then she padded to the kitchen for her tub of salted caramel ice cream.

Back on the couch she turned on the TV, planning to binge all the Bourne movies in the hopes that Matt Damon could take her mind off things. Before she could click on Netflix and search the first film, she was hit with today's news story. The biggest scoop at home and abroad, Hollywood's newest power couple: actress/model Isabella Ricci and her award-winning director husband, Enrico Rossi.

"Their secret romance feels ripped straight from the plot of one of Isabella's romantic comedy films," gushed the reporter. "It makes you wonder if their relationship was actually the inspiration for Enrico's hit TV show *Cupid Grants a Second Chance.*"

"The hit TV show was *my* idea!" she yelled at the screen. But the damage was done. The self-berating started again. The pathetic way she played up anything that fit her narrative, and ignored all the other signs. Like the fact that Enrico hadn't once kissed her in all of those months. If anyone knew the disgrace of her own love life, they'd never let her produce *CGSC*. She would be an absolute joke!

Thinking about her love life led her back to thoughts of Nate. Unfortunately, even ripped, brilliant, and endearingly amnesiac Jason Bourne was not enough. He couldn't stop her from replaying her last conversation with Nate. The sinking feeling in the pit of her stomach, wishing she had done things differently.

Bourne was racing around the streets of Paris in a car like hers when she heard her phone chime with another incoming message. She grabbed for it, then swallowed her disappointment. Not Nate. Still, Duke's psychic radar for when she needed support had her almost smiling.

DUKE

Pour yourself a bubble bath. That's an order. Dinner is being delivered in an hour. Just enough time to soak and put on comfy clothes. Love you Lexycakes

PS Be ready at 5 AM tomorrow. There's a swell coming in, and the tide will be good in the morning. I'm picking you up for a Dawn Patrol. No excuses

NATE TOOK A SWIG OF BEER, set the bottle on his coffee table, leaned back against his couch cushions, and continued absently strumming his Fender Telecaster. Usually playing settled his mind. Not this time. He'd been so angry at Lexy that morning. Applying for the grant without his knowledge, telling him as if she had done him the greatest fucking favor. Thinking he would be delighted to make a music video, when she damn well knew why he wouldn't.

His chest constricted. This thing with the grant brought everything back, including his guilt. Not just over Adele, but what had happened to the band because of her. Who knows where they'd be now if that whole mess hadn't gone down? Starting over had set them back. His fear of making a music video, not willing to risk the potential social media backlash if someone made the connection between Underground Anthem and Rainy Day Astronauts, kept them there.

He was right to be angry with Lexy. And yet...

If I'm so right, then why do I feel so horrible?

His fingers stilled. The hurt look on Lexy's face, that's

why. The bewildered confusion when he shut her down and told her to leave. The tremor in her voice when she asked for his help doing up her dress. When she'd told him about the grant, he'd been sucker punched so bad he'd needed her gone. No explaining his reaction or asking why she'd done it. He'd crushed her spirit. He was an asshole. He reached for his beer. Sipped contemplatively.

His mom had insisted on family dinner that night to celebrate. Entertaining her and Marcie—and Walter—with stories from the awards show had been a temporary distraction. His mom and sister were two women who knew him, loved him, wanted the best for him. They never brought up the idea of him making another music video. That was how people who cared about him behaved. They didn't go sneaking around behind his back.

But he couldn't let go of the wounded expression on Lexy's face as she left his apartment. So stiff she looked brittle. Fragile. That wasn't the look of someone who had deliberately set out to hurt him. Intentionally opened up an old wound and poured a gallon of salt in it. Guilt gnawed at his gut. He knew Lexy. She had a good heart. A ginormous heart, actually.

Was it possible they were both wrong? She should've asked him, but he reacted badly? Hmmm. He played the chorus of R.E.M.'s "Everybody Hurts". Michael Stipe was a wise man.

So he had some making up to do, once the salt had stopped burning in his wound. He'd let things settle, then reach out to her later this weekend. See if they could meet up and talk things out.

His phone rang. He snatched it off the table. Lexy? No. Adam.

He set aside his Tele. Cleared his throat before answering. "Hey man, what's up?"

"Tell me you don't have plans this weekend. If you do, you've got to cancel them. I landed us a gig at the Commodore Ballroom."

"Isn't that in Canada?"

"Yup. Pack your passport. We're going to Vancouver to play an iconic venue listed as one of the top ten most influential clubs in North America."

"The acoustics are supposed to be phenomenal. So many big names have played there. How did you get us in?"

"Worked my connections. The opening act had to cancel. Singer has laryngitis. We're the new openers."

"Adam, you're my hero."

"I know. How soon can you get over to Connor's? We've got to sort and pack our gear. Hitting the road early."

"Give me ten minutes to chuck some stuff in a bag. I'll crash at Connor's. That'll make morning logistics easier."

"See ya soon, bro."

WILLING THE DOUBLE dose of caffeine to hurry up and do its job, Lexy was waiting with her surf gear and travel mug when Duke pulled up just shy of 5 a.m., as promised.

"Morning," he said with a chipper smile. "Pass me your board."

"I hate the getting up part," she said as he strapped her board on the roof with his. She slid her Rubbermaid tote with her wetsuit beside his in the back of his Ford Explorer. "But what a good feeling to be up early and heading for a surf."

They had done hundreds of Dawn Patrols back in the

day. Get up before the birds and drive through the darkness to be at the beach as the sun is coming up. If you are really lucky, you might have the waves to yourself for a while before all the other surfers start rolling in.

"A mini adventure, while most people are still asleep."

"And breakfast burritos on the way back, right?"

"Of course. It's tradition."

Traffic was light and she settled in for the two-and-a-half-hour drive to Westport, enjoying Duke's mellow morning playlist; from Otis Redding to Alabama Shakes.

"You're putting up a good front, girl," he said when they were about halfway. Up till now they'd been talking about past surf exploits, how things were between him and Paul, and which Seattle landmark was more iconic: The Space Needle, Pike Place Market, or the Pink Elephant car wash sign. "But I know you."

No avoiding his searching look.

"Something's on your mind. Feel free to unload on wise old Duke."

She laughed. "You're hardly old."

"But wise."

"Yes, wise." She hesitated. "I don't want you to feel like this is a work session, when we're just a couple of friends going surfing."

"Listening to a friend is not work."

She blew out a breath. "Where do I start?"

"At the beginning."

She mock-rolled her eyes, but after a few halting words, the story poured out of her. With his usual intuition, Duke had been aware of her feelings for Enrico. He listened patiently as she told him about her recent self-recriminations, then admitted everything that happened between her and Nate after the tiki bar.

He blew out a breath. "That's a lot to be hit with at once Lexycakes. Enrico's secret wife showing up after your big win, you and Nate together, his reaction to the grant."

"Like falling off a wave in big surf and getting held under, coming up for a breath, glimpsing sunshine, then taking another wave on the head."

"Good analogy."

"I didn't even have my bearings after the Enrico reveal. Never mind my powerful feelings for Nate, followed immediately by his rejection. Why is this happening?"

He glanced at her sympathetically. "Don't shoot the messenger. But you know what they say. We have lessons to learn in life, and if we don't learn what we need to, life keeps hitting us with more of the same until we do."

"I must have *really* not learned my lesson yet, to get so bombarded."

"It's also an opportunity."

"So, what *is* my lesson?"

He laughed, that same melodious laugh she'd first heard out on the ocean all those years ago. "Uh-uh. You have to figure it out for yourself for it to have any real impact. Remember our contestants?"

"The Legends?" What was with the sudden shift in topics?

"Think back to their stories. Each one had a lesson to learn. It took courage to face what they needed to realize or change in their lives. Those universal lessons can apply to any one of us."

She chewed the inside of her bottom lip, running the list through her mind. Feeling worthy, being vulnerable, not getting caught up in the fantasy...

What is my lesson? Why can't I see it?

"Do you remember when you broke up with Tyler and came to me, crying inconsolably?"

"Not my finest moment, but yes. You let me cry all over your hoodie, then got a carton of Cookie Dough ice cream out of the freezer that you kept for just such emergencies."

"You told me you felt really guilty about that break up, hurting Tyler. When did you finally forgive yourself?"

Her eyes widened. "I... I don't think I have," she said slowly. "It was easier to hang onto the guilt than forgive myself."

He nodded. "What else?"

"I didn't feel worthy of being with someone else after hurting a good guy like Tyler; selfishly choosing my dreams over our relationship." Was that a lightbulb moment? "Could my guilt have impacted my romantic relationships since?"

"See? You don't need me to tell you what your lesson is. Forgiveness. Feeling worthy. Loving yourself." He reached over and patted her knee. "When we don't feel worthy but we still crave love, a common coping tool is to build fantasies in our mind, where we feel that love from someone. Enrico was that fantasy for you."

"You're right. I created a total fantasy about 'us'. His attention made me feel good." She'd built Enrico up in her mind as some sort of demi-god, dreaming about how perfect he would make her life. Perfect because she didn't have to do any of the hard work herself. She could just twirl into her castle with her prince.

"Don't beat yourself up too hard. Enrico was getting something out of it, too."

"He was?"

"Think about it. You're married to one of the most beautiful, lusted-after women in the world, but no one can know.

Because the love of your life convinced you that having a partner would be bad for her image."

"Ouch. You're right. That would hurt. And make you feel unworthy. Marriage is supposed to be a partnership."

"Your coping strategy was to nurture a fantasy. Enrico's was flirting, to get the attention and approval from other women that he didn't get from his wife."

"I hope things will be better for him. Maybe he can learn to love himself again and feel worthy." Her fantasy may have imploded, but it wasn't Enrico's fault she'd let her imagination run away with her, reading more into every casual touch, misreading his attention.

"The thing about fantasies. They're easier to face than reality. We don't get hurt in our fantasies. And we don't hurt other people."

She nodded. Made sense.

"So my question for you. What reality were you avoiding by building this fantasy around Enrico?"

Hit by a blast of frigid air, she gasped as she wrestled into her wetsuit, trying to distract herself with the morning vista, the sky awash in streaks of pink and gold. Its reflection was mirrored on the water's surface as wave after wave peeled toward the shore. After adding another layer of wax to her pretty turquoise board, she walked to the water's edge where she and Duke paddled out past the break at the Jetty.

"I love a good Dawn Patrol," he said as they sat on their boards, waiting.

"When are you going to get Paul on a board?"

"Ha! That will only happen someplace warmer like Hawaii or Mexico. I love the guy, but he's a wimp."

Just then a set came in and he paddled for a wave. She cheered aloud as he popped up and slid down the face, the move looking as effortless as everything he did.

Eyes on the horizon for the next set, Duke's earlier question rolled over in her mind. *Was* she avoiding something? His comment about not getting hurt in a fantasy teased the edges of her brain. She drew a lungful of the salt-tinged air, then almost fell off her board as the truth slammed into her.

All these months, I've been falling in love with Nate. And I've made a complete and utter mess of it.

The ease and camaraderie when they went shopping. His understanding and help as she developed the show. The flash of heat when they kissed in the garage. Their time alone together at his birthday. Watching him on stage at The Ship. Falling-in-love feelings that she denied because she hadn't experienced them since Tyler, and it scared her. What she felt with Nate was so much stronger, bringing up her fear of hurting someone. Of being hurt.

Her handy 'I don't date friends' rule had been a perfect shield, a way to protect herself. Same with building her fantasy world around Enrico. Duke had told their contestants that allowing oneself to be vulnerable with another person was a strength not a weakness. Yet she'd been afraid to be vulnerable.

As the telltale bump of an approaching set materialized in the distance, she maneuvered her board to face the shore. Maybe it wasn't too late. Maybe she could convince Nate to give her a second chance. Make him see she'd wanted to surprise him with the grant, not go behind his back. Convince him that she'd applied for the grant motivated by something more than helping out a friend. Motivated by her feelings for him.

Eyeing the wave, she lay down on her board and started

paddling closer to where it would break. She needed to convince Nate it didn't matter if RDA made a music video. He was enough for her just the way he was.

As the wave got closer, she adjusted her position at the peak then dug her arms in deep, paddling hard to get into the wave. She popped up. Felt the speed as she dropped in, her board angled across the face. The instant elation of a great ride sang through her veins.

"Yeeeeew!" She heard Duke cheer as he paddled past her on his way back out. "Atta girl."

She cut back, then turned her board into the wave, picking up speed with the move and extending her ride, grinning like a fool.

Taking that first incredible wave as an omen of good things to come, she texted Nate while Duke drove them to get breakfast burritos. Before she chickened out.

LEXY

Nate, I'm so sorry. I'd like to talk. Are you free to meet up this weekend?

CHAPTER 29

"Living in Bellingham, your dating app will send you profiles from Canada. It's closer than Seattle. So I tried it, I dated a Canadian girl. At first it felt romantic, crossing the border for the possibility of love. It quickly became a royal pain."

-Zack, Guest
Duquan's Downlow on Dating and Love
Podcast episode #96

"Why is the border lineup so long this early in the morning?" Adam whined from his coveted shotgun seat in their rented van.

"Why don't the rest of you have NEXUS cards?" Connor grumbled from the driver's seat.

"While we have some time to kill," Griffin said, "seems like a good opportunity to grill Nate."

Nate grunted. "Grill me about what?"

"The awards ceremony. Lexy. Whatever's eating you," said Connor. "Take your pick."

"Nothing's eating me."

"Bullshit." Adam covered the word with a cough.

"Your show won multiple awards and you hardly told us anything about the snazzy evening or the afterparty," said Adam.

"You weren't yourself last night, organizing the gear," said Griffin.

"And something's still off today," Connor said.

"We're about to stand on the same stage where Sammy Davis Jr., KISS, David Bowie, the Ramones, Snoop Dogg and the Beastie Boys have all stood. You have to get your shit together." Adam tapped one of Griffin's stray drumsticks on Nate's knee. "Spill."

He was trapped. In a van inching toward the border painfully slow. By his stubborn friends who wouldn't give up until they knew what was wrong. In fairness, he'd do the same if roles were reversed.

"The gala was very snazzy. Everyone who worked on *CGSC* really poured their heart and soul into it, but no one more than Lexy. It was exciting to be there with the team, getting recognized for our efforts."

"Especially Lexy," the guys chorused.

"I heard the win was upstaged when the director's secret-actress-wife made an unexpected appearance," Adam said.

"I heard she's a bombshell." Connor smirked.

"Correct on both counts." He lifted the lid on the stocked cooler sitting on the floor of the van. Took out a soda, offered one to the others, cracked the lid and took a sip. Delay tactics.

Griffin rolled his hand in a 'get on with it' gesture.

He swallowed. "Don't hate me when I tell you I skipped the party afterward."

Groans echoed off the van walls.

"You were our inside man, and you weren't even inside?" said Adam.

"Lexy, Duke, and I opted for a smaller crowd. We met Paul at a tiki bar down the street."

Connor raised a knowing eyebrow.

He acknowledged the look. "My momma raised me not to kiss and tell. Let's just say the night brought Lexy and I closer."

Simultaneously, each of his friends offered some version of "It's about time."

"But..." Connor again.

"In the morning, she told me she had applied for an Artist Trust grant, and got it."

"For the show?" Griffin asked.

"For us. To make a music video."

"Really? That's amazing...." Griffin's words trailed off. "Isn't it? That was really nice of her."

"It sure was," said Connor. "Which is what you said to Lexy, right, buddy?" His tone implied he knew otherwise.

Nate hung his head. "It pushed some buttons. I told her RDA would not be making a music video, and to find another band."

"Lexy knows about Adele?" Adam said.

"I told her a while back."

Since starting back up as RDA, he'd worked even harder on anything to do with the band. Trying to make it up to his friends. Trying to alleviate the guilt for his part in their downfall. Bringing that woman into their lives.

"The video's not as bad as you think." Adam turned around more fully in the passenger seat. "You've built it up in your mind as this giant thing." He pointed at Nate. "Was it horrible in the moment? Yeah, absolutely. But it happened years ago."

Griffin toyed with a rip in his jeans. "Even if anyone connected it back to RDA, all you'd get would be props for the way you handled a difficult situation."

"That thing that happened with Adele is an albatross around your neck man, weighing you down," Connor said. "And you're the one who put it there. Let it go. Forgive yourself. Move on. We all have."

"I'm not charitable enough to thank Adele," Adam said thoughtfully. "But I think Rainy Day Astronauts is a better name for us."

Lexy said the same thing.

He absorbed their words. His friends didn't view the situation the same way he did. They weren't angry at him. They didn't blame him, and never had.

"How'd Lexy take your shutdown?" Connor said quietly.

He ran a hand through his hair. "I'm not sure. I, uh...told her to leave."

Three pairs of eyes shot his way.

"I know. Asshole move. But she caught me off guard. We'd had this incredible time together and then she—" he looked down at his shoes, shoulders hunched.

"Dude," Adam said in a hushed tone. "You've got to fix this. Pronto."

"I know. I already figured that out on my own last night. Then you called. Then there was a flurry of packing and instrument checks and gear loading."

"Excuses, excuses."

He nodded. Reached toward his back pocket for his phone.

Where was his phone?

He leaned behind his seat to check the side pocket on his duffle bag. "Shit."

"What?" Connor asked.

"I must have left my phone in your garage. I plugged it in to charge last night. Shit," he repeated.

"You want to borrow my phone?" Connor offered.

"Not for this, thanks. I'll have to connect with her when we get back. But can you text my mom and sister for me, so they don't worry?"

"Sure thing."

Adam turned to face the front as they continued to inch forward. "Gawd! I thought we'd be closer than this by now."

"You're worse than a kid," said Connor.

"Which means I have time to regale you with more Commodore Ballroom facts," he said cheerfully, not at all bothered by Connor's playful insult. "For example, did you know that in 1979, the Clash made their North American debut at the Commodore. And in 1981, for under five dollars, you could have seen the relatively unknown Irish band U2."

"Hey Nate," Griffin said, "when you patch things up with Lexy, make sure to tell her we *do* want to make a music video."

"Yeah, don't forget that the way you forgot your phone."

"As long as you don't try to make me wear Bono glasses in the video," he joked. But seriously, he owed it to the guys *and* to Lexy to fix things. Which might take more than a simple conversation.

~

WHEN NATE HADN'T ANSWERED her text, she tried again, sending him a funny meme about getting a new guitar. The photo showed two men laughing uproariously, with the caption: I bought a new guitar and then she asks, "Are you gonna sell the old one?"

She had added, 'it works for surfboards too'. Still no reply. The butterflies that took flight in her stomach after she sent the first message had now traded places with an electric mixer. Churning in her gut. Was he *that* upset?

Still worried, she sipped her vanilla latte as she strolled through Pike Place Market with Ren and Jules, the other two people she owed an explanation.

"It never would have worked out with you and Enrico anyway." Jules punctuated her point with a swing of her coffee cup.

Lexy gave her a questioning look.

"Imagine taking him surfing on your romantic vacation to Hawaii, and he strips down to a budgie smuggler." Jules snickered.

Lexy sputtered out a laugh. "You assume Enrico wears a speedo?"

"Honey, he's European."

"#saynotonuthuggers was trending last summer," Ren said, causing Jules to laugh harder.

"Lucky for me then, he's already married," Lexy said. "I narrowly avoided a catastrophe."

"I'll say." Jules swung an arm around her in a quick, supportive hug.

"I guess you could have lent him a pair of your board shorts," Ren said. Her deadpan delivery held for only a split second before the vision of Enrico stuffed into Lexy's pastel board shorts had them doubled over.

"My stomach hurts." She straightened, wiping tears of laughter. "I definitely should have confided in you both sooner."

"I can't believe you didn't tell us you had a thing for

Enrico, but I will forgive you," Jules said, taking a sip of her Americano. "Eventually."

"That's the kicker. My feelings for him weren't real. Like Duke said, I was creating a fantasy as a way to cope. Telling the two of you would have made it more real."

They stopped to watch the fishmongers entertain tourists by tossing a fish back and forth before wrapping up the purchase. Lexy was as much a sucker for the performance as the visitors.

"Are you worried it's going to be awkward at work now?" Ren said.

"Promise me you'll keep what I'm about to tell you in the vault."

Jules and Ren solemnly made 'cross my heart' gestures.

"Merelda told me he's trying to break contract. No one else knows, so you can't say anything."

"And if he comes back?"

She shrugged. "I should be spared from dying of embarrassment, because he had no idea the things I was imagining about him. Us."

"Maybe he won't come back," said Jules.

Ren chimed in. "I think Ariana Grande said it best, "thank u, next"!"

"Speaking of next—"

"Oh my God, there's more?" Jules said.

She explained about applying for the grant, and how upset Nate was.

"I remember that video with his ex; she's a real piece of work. No wonder he was gun shy about making a new video." Jules paused at a sale rack outside a second-hand shop. She studied a vintage jean jacket with colorful birds embroidered on the back before they moved on.

"You saw the video?"

"Smug Sonia showed it to me when I started. Tried to turn me against Nate. Not happening."

"Not a way to make friends." As they passed the Giant Shoe Museum she snuck a peek at her phone. Still nothing from Nate.

"So with your big ol' Lexy heart, you unintentionally touched a nerve. Don't worry, Nate the Great will come around. He'll probably even want to make the video."

Ren narrowed her eyes. "Wait, when did you tell him about the grant?"

"After the gala."

"Oooh." Ren winced. "Between Enrico, Isabella, and Nate, no wonder you avoided us the next day.

"Hang on," Jules said. "Clarify 'after the gala'."

Heat flooded her cheeks. "We went back to his place."

"I knew it!" cried Jules, throwing a fist in the air.

"Shhhh." She looked around to see if they were drawing attention.

"Finally," Ren said, drawing out the word. "We've been waiting for the two of you to catch on to what was so obvious to the rest of us. I'm so happy you two are together now."

"Slow your roll. We're not together. I messed up bad with Nate, and now he's not answering my texts."

"How was it before you messed it up with your little surprise?" Jules asked.

"So good." Her eyes softened.

"Awwww."

"But girls, something must be seriously wrong with me. To go from thinking Enrico was 'the one', then finding out about his wife, to believing it had been Nate all along only I'd been too blinded by Enrico's charm to see it."

"Honey," Jules said, "you're being too hard on yourself.

Enrico's megawatt smile was enough to blind anyone. Throw in close proximity working together, late night dinners, and the European flirting gene. In your shoes I probably would've proposed months ago." Jules grinned and rubbed Lexy's shoulder.

"I hate admitting this. I feel like a terrible person. To find out about Enrico's wife that way— In hindsight, my ego was more hurt than my heart. And Nate was there to make me feel better. Except it was so much more. And I ruined it."

"You'll make it right," Ren said.

"I'm planning to call him tonight. But what if he is still so upset he won't even talk to me?" She couldn't bear the way things were between them. If she couldn't repair the damage, how could she ask him to give her a second chance?

She let out a pent-up sigh. "You know how in the movies, when the main character has to overcome a break up, or some other life setback, and there's a movie montage? They show snippets as she works out and gets a makeover and whatever else. Then the story picks up again later on, when she's not so upset anymore? I want that. Can I fast-forward a few months in my life with a cute series of vignettes? Bypass all the turbulent emotions to where everything with Enrico and Nate doesn't feel so dreadful anymore?"

"Cute vignette number one: Lexy buys herself a gorgeous bouquet of market flowers." Jules pointed.

"Three for twenty dollars," she said, reading the sign. "Bouquets for all of us, on me."

READY FOR HER time-lapse montage to a suitable soundtrack à la Bridget Jones, flowers in hand, Lexy walked up the hill from Pike Place. Jules had dragged Ren back for another look at the jean jacket while she left to run a few errands. She hummed Chaka Khan's "I'm Every Woman" under her breath, as if it could bring on the empowering, sped-up version of the next few weeks of her life.

What a relief to share everything with her friends. As for Nate, maybe she could—

"Lexy?"

She looked up and almost dropped her flowers. "Tyler?" Her voice rose to a shrill pitch on the last syllable.

He reached out to prevent the bouquet from slipping, and smiled. "Sorry. Didn't mean to give you a jolt. You looked deep in thought."

"Thank you. Yeah. No. I was just—" She glanced between the market and Tyler, then gave a nervous laugh. "Sorry, let's start over. This is a surprise. It's nice to see you."

"Same. You remember my brother Carter?"

Belatedly, she noticed the young man standing beside Tyler. "Cartsters. You're all grown up."

What was the protocol? Did she hug the two men? Shake hands? She settled for shifting the flowers to a more secure position and offering a welcoming smile. Fake it till you make it. "What brings you to Seattle?"

"Tyler brought me to help him pick out a ring," Carter blurted proudly.

She blinked. "A ring? As in a *ring* ring?"

"Yup, that kind. For Mary Beth. You met her on the beach that time." Tyler rubbed the back of his neck. "Carter, why don't you go check out the Gum Wall at the Market and I'll meet you there."

"Gum Wall? Cool! See ya, Lexy." Carter gave a wave and strode away.

"Nice seeing you, Carter," she called after him. "You sent him to the Gum Wall? So gross."

"Yeah, but he'll love it."

"So... Congratulations."

"Thanks. Assuming she says yes." He rubbed his neck again. "Congratulations to you, too. Your show is the talk of the town."

"Thanks. My mom keeps asking when I'm coming home, so she can throw a big party. So far, I've been putting her off. You know how she can be."

"My mom mentioned something about a party. When those two put their heads together, resistance is futile." He grinned and shook his head.

Silence stretched between them. Now what? They'd covered the basic pleasantries, congratulated each other. If he asked her opinion on a ring, she might step into traffic. Slow moving traffic, of course. Just enough of a bump to get her out of it.

He studied her, as if coming to a decision, then blew out a breath. "There's something I've been wanting to say to you. I've been looking for the right opportunity." He paused as if collecting his thoughts. "I wanted to thank you. For breaking up with me when you did. That took guts."

Sorry, what?

"Thank me? But I hurt you," she said. "You called me selfish."

"Yeah, stung like hell at the time. No one likes to get dumped. You hurt me, so I tried to hurt you back. But you did the right thing. For both of us. I just couldn't see it at the time."

"The right thing?"

"Sure. We were on the fast track to taking the easy road. Making our folks happy, settling there. You working in the gallery and me in my dad's hardware store. We probably could have made a go of it for a while, but eventually I think it would have stifled both of us."

"Stifled?" Why couldn't she manage more than repeating Tyler's words?

"You had a vision. Saw a big world out there you wanted to conquer, and the courage to go for it. Look at you. Producer for a prestigious production company with an award-winning show. I'm so proud of you."

Wasn't this what she wanted? To be a success and have Tyler know she didn't regret her decision. So why didn't she feel the elation she'd expected?

"But I left you behind," she said quietly. Her old friend 'guilt' wasn't done with her yet.

"It was the kick in the ass I needed at the time. To re-evaluate my life. Now I'm about to propose to the love of my life. I'm up for a promotion in a career I love. I never would have chosen this path if not for you. So yeah, I've been wanting to thank you."

"I don't know what to say." Tyler, planning a proposal while her love life continued to be a shit sandwich inside a dumpster fire on board the Titanic.

"Say you're as happy as I am." With one hand gently holding her upper arm, Tyler leaned over and kissed her cheek. "Take care, Lexy."

She was still mulling over the day when she got home and dumped her purchases on the counter. Her ex was getting married. He was glad she broke up with him. He'd *thanked* her.

He wanted her to be as happy as he was.

Taking the first step toward that, she picked up her phone, took a breath and called Nate. Voicemail. Deflated, she left a message, barely registering what she said.

Phone beside her in case he called back, Lexy re-read Gran's letter, searching for wisdom between the lines. In a movie, that would have been cute vignette number two. Gran's letter would have contained the magic solution. In reality, Gran apparently had thought she was smart enough to find her own answers.

They've got it so much better in the movies!

CHAPTER 30

"I was in a new relationship and texted my boyfriend a question. A few hours later I was convinced he had been in a car accident and was in a coma. What other *possible* explanation could there be for him not texting me back?"

-Nora, Guest
Duquan's Downlow on Dating and Love
Podcast episode #1

Nate put away the last amp in the garage, stretched his complaining muscles, and retrieved his phone. Right where he left it, plugged in by the beer fridge. Shit. Several texts and a missed call from Lexy. She must think he hated her. Truth be told, he was feeling better about things than ever. The straight talk from the guys during the border wait had released the large albatross named Adele he'd been carrying too long. They had spent much of the drive home debating which song to make a video for, and what that video should look like.

"Yo," Adam called from the door. "Can I grab a ride home?"

"Yup. Just let me..."

It was too late to call Lexy. Adam had insisted they make the most of being in Vancouver. Following a satisfying hang-over brunch in Gastown, he dragged them to every record shop they could find. Not that anyone complained. Each of them had brought some vinyl treasures back across the border.

NATE

Hey Lex. Not ghosting you, I promise. Long story. Adam got us a show in Vancouver. Left my phone charging at Connor's. Too late to call now. Can you meet tomorrow after work?

After a weekend of thinking he'd been angry and ignoring her, he'd be lucky if she agreed to meet up at all. If she did, he'd take her for dessert. His turn to buy apology pie. It might take a whole pie to patch things up and convince her to produce a music video for the Rainy Day Astronauts.

From: merelda.stirling@MHproductions.com
To: MHproductions.com
Subject: *CGSC* Director update

To all Manor House Productions staff,
I expect your utmost discretion with the following information. This is to inform you that Enrico Rossi

is stepping down as Director of CGSC effective immediately. He has been called away due to a family emergency. I remind you that Enrico is still part of the MHP family. You will speak of him accordingly, in all conversations inside and outside the workplace. Failure to do so will result in severe consequences.

I am in the process of reviewing potential candidates and selecting a new director. Meanwhile, I leave the show details to Lexy Smith, as producer. She will work with Duquan to determine the initial selection of our next potential Legends. Ian Campbell will designate one of his team to liaise with Lexy from the studio end. Please refrain from replying to this email. Any additional information will be delivered to those working directly on the show, as I see fit.

Merelda

LEXY RE-READ the email a third time, relieved Enrico would not be returning, worried about who Merelda would choose to replace him. Not to mention offended that Meralda had not shared the news personally before sending this out to the entire staff. Of everyone, she was the one most affected.

A shadow fell across her desk. Speak of the devil.

"I assume you got my email."

"Yes, Merelda."

"I don't want anyone saying the success of Season One was a fluke. Or that Enrico was the sole reason. I expect the Special to be a smashing triumph, and even higher ratings for Season Two. Understood?" Merelda's jewelry rattled with the force of her words. She must be supremely ticked off that Enrico wasn't returning.

"Understood. I expect nothing less myself." It was true, and she felt confident she could deliver.

"Hmpf." Merelda nodded once, then marched off to find her next victim.

She would almost rather stay and endure more of her boss's lecture, but it was time to face the music. Or, more accurately, the musician. She closed the doc called Valentine's Special before she messed it up even more.

She and Nate were meeting after work. She hoped he would accept her apology and they could resume their friendship. When she'd finally heard from him, it felt like someone had lifted a weight the size of Cannon Beach's famed Haystack Rock off her chest. To get a second chance at a relationship with him, she needed to undo the damage first. Earn back his trust.

A bell tinkled as Lexy entered the desert café, Sweet Revenge. Nate was already at a table. Her heart squeezed. When would she stop hurting the people she cared about?

She pulled out the chair across from him and perched on the edge, trying to gauge his mood. Braced for what he might say. Her shoulders lowered and her spine relaxed when she saw a faint smile cross his face.

"Hi."

"Hi." She let out a slow breath.

"Crazy news about Enrico. It's all anyone at the studio talked about this afternoon."

"Same at the Manor."

"Did you already know?"

"I found out in the same email as everyone else."

"Really? She should have talked to you about it first." He shook his head. "That's Merelda for you."

"Tell me about it."

They lapsed into silence. She spun the sugar bowl at the side of the table, avoiding his gaze.

"Thanks for meeting me," he said finally, handing her a menu.

She looked at the logo embossed on the cover. "Sweet Revenge? Should I be worried?"

A corner of his mouth quirked up. "It's a dessert place. I heard they have good pie."

Normally she'd have trouble deciding from such an extensive menu, but she picked the first one she saw. They ordered from a friendly server sporting a pin on his collared shirt that read 'Sugar Daddy'.

"Nate, I cannot tell you enough how sorry I am," she said, as soon as their server stepped away. This was harder than she'd thought. "I should have talked to you about the grant first. Not presented it as a done deal. I should have talked to you more about the idea of RDA making a music video."

"You don't have to—"

"Please. Let me get this out. I knew the video was still a touchy subject for you, a lingering shadow, and I wanted to help. It seemed obvious to me that facing your fear, getting back on the horse—now I'm the one talking in clichés—however you want to say it, I thought it could be incredibly beneficial. For both you and the band. But that wasn't respectful. I'm not in your shoes. I don't know what's best for you. I was afraid if I told you in advance, you'd shut it down."

"You're right. I would have."

Lexy twisted her pendant. "My other fear was that you *were* ready to move on, and would get excited about making a video. If my application was rejected, and I'd gotten your hopes up for nothing."

He shook his head.

She reached across the table for his hand. "You've done so much to help me with my show. I saw this as an opportunity to repay the favor. And I did the exact opposite. Instead of thanking you, I hurt you."

"Coffee." The server dropped off two brimming mugs and a jug of cream. "Pies'll be out shortly."

She released him. Busied herself pouring cream.

He blew on his coffee. Let out a breath. "You didn't hurt me, Lex. If I was hurting, it was all on me. Shit I hadn't let go of yet. And because it stung, I lashed out at you. Pushed you away."

"A natural reaction." She wrapped her hands around her mug. "I understand I stepped way out of bounds. You said to find another band, but I'll just return the grant money for someone else to use. I hope you know how sorry I am."

"I'm the one buying the pie. This was supposed to be my apology." He offered a rueful smile. "And I am. Sorry. I was such a jerk. I'm grateful you agreed to meet with me, after the way I treated you that morning."

"Of course I would."

"I was caught off guard, and my knee-jerk reaction was to feel betrayed. But there's no excuse for shutting you down and kicking you out."

"It was a difficult moment. For both of us."

"Cherry pie for the lady," their server deftly slid a plate in front of Lexy. "My favorite," he said with a wink. "And for you, sir." A plate landed in front of Nate. "Our famous house-made apple pie. À la mode."

With his fork, Nate tapped at the ball of ice cream melting on top of his pie. He looked up at her. "No question applying for the grant came from a kind place. I know you wouldn't deliberately hurt me. If I could have seen through my Adele-haze, I would've realized that right away. It didn't take long, but by then I had behaved terribly."

"It's all right."

"It's really not. I tried to call you on the way to Vancouver. And realized I forgot my phone." He forked a bite of pie. Then reached across and helped himself to a chunk of hers. "We're sharing, right?"

She swallowed her smile. "I don't recall agreeing to that."

He pushed his plate her way. "I thought it's what we do."

She took a big chunk of his pie, making sure to scoop up some of the ice cream with it. "Your call would've saved me a lot of misery last weekend."

"Again, sorry. If it makes you feel better, we had a long wait crossing into Canada, and the guys spent the time chewing me out about you. By the way, they are all stoked to have you produce an RDA music video."

"They are?"

"The comments went something like Connor saying, 'Lexy is brilliant, she's a friend, not to mention an award-winning producer who has already dug up some cash to put toward this.'"

"Aww, that's sweet."

"It was followed by Griffin saying, 'We'd be idiots not to take the opportunity'. And Adam stating, 'Which we are not. With one possible exception.'"

"Meaning you."

"Guilty. I'm going to really catch hell if you already gave the grant money back."

"It's yours. But no pressure. Seriously. This was supposed to be a gift and a thank you. If you're not ready to make a video, or never will be, that's fine. As long as we're still friends. That's the only thing I care about." She put down her fork. Looked him in the eye. "Are we?"

"BFFs. Pinky swear." He held out his finger and the knot in her stomach unraveled the rest of the way as she linked her pinkie with his.

"More coffee?" Sugar Daddy stood there, pot in hand. They both nodded.

"So, you had a gig in Vancouver?"

"Yeah. The Commodore Ballroom."

"Rainy Day Astronauts are international stars now."

"I don't know about stars, but the crowd was fired up. Really engaged. We sold a lot of merch after our set." He stirred cream into his refill. Leaned forward. "The venue is incredible. Been around since the '30s. They've got this sprung dance floor that was originally built—wait, sorry, I sound like Adam. But the dude was hitting us with facts about this place all weekend."

She laughed. "Sounds like Adam."

"Promise me you'll put it on your bucket list to see a band there someday. It's worth it."

"Maybe we can road trip together to see someone there." She fiddled with the handle on her coffee mug. "Now that we're friends again."

He glanced out the window. Looked back at her. Gave a brief nod. "Yeah. Cool. Friends' road trip. I'll keep my eye on their calendar."

"Just not before the Valentine's Special. My life is going to be insane until then."

CHAPTER 31

"My husband thought proposing on a Jumbotron Kiss Cam at a basketball game would be romantic. It was not. But I said 'yes' anyway because, you know...love."

-Sophie, Guest
Duquan's Downlow on Dating and Love
Podcast episode #20

"I've seen scarier defense in a game of musical chairs," a player from the other team said to Nate, who snorted out a laugh as he checked the other dude. It was surprisingly mild for late January. Even more surprising for Seattle, the rain was holding off into their third pickup game of the day.

His team got possession of the ball. He faked a back door, made a hard cut to the three-point line to catch a perfectly timed pass from Conner. Wide open, he hoisted up a shot for their first win of the afternoon, only to see the ball clang off the front rim for yet another miss.

"Shit," he muttered.

"What the hell, Nate?" Adam said. "You're shooting so many bricks, you could build a house."

The ball bounced directly to the other team's forward, who let loose his own three-pointer...splash! Their third straight win.

Nate's teammates groaned.

"Hey-Oh!" the other forward cheered. "That's a clean sweep, boys."

"Thanks to Nate's broken-ass jumpshot. Hey Conner, get some Febreeze on the kid. He stinks."

"Febreeze this." With a cheeky grin Nate waved his middle finger. The other guy feigned a tackle.

"See you guys next week?"

"Make sure to bring tissues," Adam called. "You'll be crying tears of defeat."

"Not if Nate keeps playing like he's half dead."

"Believe me when I say, next time I'll be your worst nightmare," Nate said.

"Okay, Steph Curry." Their opponents walked away whistling.

"You were really off your game today," Connor said as they guzzled sports drinks. "Is it because we're heading to the garage to plan our video? I thought we cured you of your albatross."

"Nah, I'm good there." He zipped up his hoodie, cooling off now that they'd stopped running. "I'm just as amped as the rest of you to finalize our vision so we can get going on the actual shoot."

"If it's not Adele, then what?" Connor put on his coat. "Is

it because Lexy'll be there? I thought you two hugged it out and are all buddy-buddy again."

"We are. Can't a guy just have an off day?" He didn't want to admit the buddy-buddy part was the problem. After spending the night with her, he didn't want to be just friends. But that's what she put on the table over pie and coffee. He'd already screwed things up once with her. He didn't know how to tell her that he loved her, without risking screwing things up again.

Griffin shouldered his bag. "It's awesome that Jer volunteered to help with the vid. You said he'll Zoom with us for our planning meeting?"

"Yeah, he'll be a real asset." Anticipating seeing Lexy at the RDA round table later today, he knew it would be agonizing just staying friends. Not when he wanted more. He knew enough about the movies his mom and sister loved, to know he needed a plan. It had to be big, and it had to matter to Lexy. Figuring that out sounded about as easy as Curry hitting a no-look, off-balance three at the buzzer.

VALENTINE'S DAY and everything was almost perfect. Work on the RDA video was going great. They'd started filming scenes. Working on the project, the band took their game to a whole other level. Lexy liked the new director on *CGSC*, and they had an outstanding Special about to go live. From Ren, she knew anticipation on social media was through the roof. They were getting so much love across all their feeds.

Her parents were in the audience tonight, more excited than kids in a candy shop. The only thing preventing her life from being perfect was Nate. Despite her surfing epiphany last month, she was no closer to knowing how to tell him she was in love with him.

Producing the video for him and the guys, prepping for the Special, everything had been easy and fun between them. Like old times. Problem was, she didn't want old times. Setting a February fourteenth deadline to talk to him hadn't worked as well as her deadline to pitch her show.

"I still can't believe I missed the chance to meet your infamous ex," Jules said, when Lexy ran into her and Ren in the hallway of the studio.

"What guy *thanks* you for breaking up with him?" Ren said. "And means it?"

"Ladies. It was weeks ago now. It's time to let it go."

"Okay, I'm off. Last-minute wardrobe check on the Legends."

"I'm going with her, to where the action is." Ren tapped her iPad. "I'll manage our media accounts from there."

"See you both after the show."

"Getting tipsy from chocolate and bubbles with your besties while perusing art will be better than last year," Ren said.

"When some idiot gave you an ugly fern in an even uglier pot," Jules added.

She laughed. "Just don't let my mom call our evening out 'Galentine's Day' when you see her back stage. Gak!" She made a mock gagging motion. The ten-minute warning sounded, and she hurried to the control room.

With half her concentration focused on her checklist, making sure everything was set for the episode, the other half returned to Nate. Their friendship and trust felt tenuous. She was terrified if she told him how she felt and asked for another chance at a relationship, she might lose him for good. She'd almost lost his friendship once. She couldn't go through that again.

She had to do something. Friendship-only with the guy she loved was its own kind of purgatory. She twisted her gran's ring on her pinky finger. She'd worn it for luck with the show, but...

Can you send me some love luck Gran? Maybe you made friends with Cupid up there and can put in a good word?

Time to focus. They were live. She smiled as the opening bars of "Best of My Love" by The Emotions came on and Duke danced out on stage. The guy had moves! And it was the perfect feel-good opening for the Valentine's Special.

Chris, her new director, sent her a thumbs-up. Merelda had hired him on a trial basis, and if the Special worked out, he'd direct Season Two. He was married with two kids—she'd seen the family photo—had a quick sense of humor, was a team player, and seemed to be coping well under pressure. She hoped Merelda gave him the job.

"It's not fair Duke looks better in his T-shirt than I do," Chris joked.

She'd splurged and ordered custom T-shirts for the entire crew, to get them in the festive spirit for the Special. The shirts were red with a mischievous, winking Cupid, captioned with, 'Cupid Grants a Second Chance—Especially on Valentine's Day'.

"Pan the audience." Chris spoke through his headset to one of the camera operators.

She caught sight of her mom and dad in their seats grinning like mad and waving at Duke.

"Your parents look like they're having a blast," Chris said.

"They are, and they've got a romantic date in the city planned afterward."

The lights and music changed on cue. She bounced on the balls of her feet. They were coming up on the first surprise of the show. An update from Ayeesha and Dean on their honeymoon in Australia.

The on-screen clips started playing, showing Ayeesha and Dean in front of the Sydney Opera House, cuddling koalas, and waving from Crescent Head Beach, surfboards under their arms as they ran into the ocean and paddled out.

She sighed at the romance of it all. A surfing honeymoon. She wondered if Nate would consider giving surfing a try. If they ever got past being friends.

"What about you? Got any big plans tonight after the show?" Chris asked her while they were on a commercial break.

"I know the owner of an art gallery who puts on a Valentine's event every year."

"Wild night at the art gallery?"

She chuckled. "Complete with erotic works of art and live nude models wearing only body paint, so it could be. But Ren, Jules and I are really going for the chocolates and champagne."

"Have fun for me," Chris said. "The most romantic thing I can do for my wife these days is pour her a bath and put the kiddos to bed on my own."

Still chuckling, she turned back to her monitor, excited for the next big surprise of the episode. Emma and Felix, the couple who met in Vegas, were getting re-married on the show in a few minutes. The Officiant was with them in the Green Room. Following the ceremony, gallons of rose petals would be dropped among the audience.

But first, several teaser videos from new Legend hopefuls for Season Two. She was reading a message from Ren that their socials were inundated with positive comments on the honeymoon update, when she heard a familiar voice. Her eyes flew to the screen.

"Hi, my name is Nate. The woman I'm looking for a second chance with knows I've got a bad history when it comes to videos. She'll understand the significance of me making this for her."

"Hey!" called out someone in the audience. "That's the lead singer from The Rainy Day Astronauts."

As if from a distance, Lexy heard cheers going up around the studio from locals who were obviously fans of the band. She felt light-headed. Her ears were ringing. Nate had made a video for *her*?

"Chris, what is this?" She'd never seen this video. Hadn't approved it.

"Surprise." The director winked.

"We were friends for years," on-screen Nate was saying. "Recently, our friendship shifted to... well, more than that. Unfortunately, when she did something thoughtful and generous, I let my past get in the way. I messed things up badly, so I figured I needed to do something big if I had any chance of winning her back."

She stared at the screen, her heart pounding. Was this real?

"She's funny and smart, compassionate and courageous. Since the idea for this show was all hers, I know she believes in love and second chances. I'm hoping Lexy Smith, our show's producer, will give me one."

She needed to get to Nate! But her feet wouldn't move. She remained riveted to the screen and Nate's story. On television. In front of everyone they worked with.

And he said I'm *courageous?!*

"She accepted my apology, and we've built our friendship back up. But it turns out that's not enough for me. I know how great we can be together, Lexy. Will you let me prove it?"

Her skin tingled as if she was being showered with the sparks from a sparkler. She hugged herself to contain the joy threatening to burst out of her.

"I hope you'll let me be the person you keep adding to your list of Best Band Stories with. Who gets to make life decisions with you based on tiki fortunes. I'll happily be the guy to share my restaurant meal with you for the rest of your life, so you don't have to pick just one. If they ever make a documentary on the history of the guitar pick you don't have to watch it with me, but I'd love it if you did. And I pinky swear I'll never jinx anything by telling your secrets. What do you say, Lexy? Will Cupid grant me a second chance with you?"

At last, her feet came unglued. She raced down the hall and into the sound booth. Her heart was so full of love it had stretched to fill every available inch of her chest, making it hard to breathe. She had a split second to register the uncertainty on Nate's face before she threw herself into his arms. Arms that closed around her as he picked her up and spun her in a circle.

Behind her, she heard Ian. "We're on commercial. Get outta here you two, before you screw something up. I got this."

Nate kept hold of her as he hustled them into the corridor. "That video was my version of John Cusack holding up a boom box outside your house. I couldn't figure out how to work a Black Pumas song into it, though."

She smiled up at him. "Your version was perfect."

"Marcie may have had some input."

"I love your sister."

"And Duke helped me with the video."

"That man is scary good at his job."

"I hoped that if I was way off base, he wouldn't let me go through the embarrassment of putting my video on the show."

"You weren't off base at all. I've been trying to work up the nerve to tell you I want more than friendship, too." She reached for his hand. "In your video you said I was courageous, but you're the brave one. And thanks to you, Cupid is giving both of us a second chance."

He gently smoothed his hands over her hair and looked into her eyes. "I love you, Lexy."

She pulled his head down for a kiss. A kiss that spun out longer and longer.

Yup. Wow! When I kiss him, just wow!

"I love you too, Nate. I realized it when I was surfing—I do some of my best thinking in the water—and I've been trying to find a way to tell you ever since."

"This works," he said with a grin, then kissed her again, a kiss that said more than words ever could.

Eventually, the sounds of the show intruded. "I should get back."

"The show will be okay without you for another few minutes." His hold tightened. "I'm not sure about me." He pulled her close, resting his chin on the top of her head. "I like the way you think in the water. It might be time for you to get me out on a board with you."

"You'll go surfing with me?"

"Absolutely."

Maybe she would get her Australian surfing honeymoon after all. Just then the familiar strains of the wedding march swirled around them.

"If I didn't know this was part of the show, I'd think this music right now is my sister's handiwork."

She laughed. "Emma and Felix are getting married. Come on." She took his hand and led him to the control room so they could watch the happy couple exchange their vows a second time. As the pair kissed to seal their vows, and the audience was showered in rose petals, she had a feeling this time it would last. Just as she had a feeling about her and Nate.

"That's a wrap!" The misty-eyed audience smiled and chatted enthusiastically as they exited the studio with their gifts from Manor House. A long-stemmed red rose and a trio of chocolates. The Valentine's Day Special had gone off without a hitch.

"What are you doing tonight?" Nate said as the show credits rolled across the screen. "Want to come watch us play at The Soundbox?"

"*I'd* love to. But that would mean convincing Jules and Ren, to give up champagne, chocolate, nude models, and erotic art for the four of you."

"I know firsthand you can be very persuasive when you want."

She flushed at his heated look, remembering that night in his apartment.

"See you there at nine? I promise you all champagne."

"I'll be there. The girls can't have wanted to go to the art show *that* badly." Today was turning out better than she could have hoped.

Valentine's with Nate. It was like a warm hug around her heart.

"Told you. Persuasive." He tugged her ponytail. "As an added bonus, it'll make Connor jealous when I show up with you."

"I think Connor's got his eye on someone else."

"Who?"

"Can't say."

"Who? And how do you know?" Since they were the only two in the control room Nate backed her up against the wall, his body pressed to hers.

She shook her head.

"Are you ticklish?" he said, going for her ribs. "No? I'll find your weakness."

"Nate. You are my weakness." And she pulled him into another kiss.

"Don't think I won't exploit that," he murmured against her lips.

"I'm counting on it."

"One more thing," she said as they walked out to find her parents. "Did you really mean it about sharing restaurant meals with me for the rest of our lives?"

"The ace up my sleeve." He grinned. "If you were wavering, I knew that was the clincher that would get me my second chance."

EPILOGUE

Cupid Grants a Second Chance, Season Two, episode one.

"Are you sure about this?" Lexy asked, twisting the pendant on her necklace; a gold disc from Nate with the words 'Party Wave' etched on it. She stood facing the wall of monitors in the studio's control room.

"Absolutely," said Chris, officially her new director.

On stage, Duke was introducing the next Legend. A nervous-looking older man hoping to make it to the final five. He smoothed a hand over his salt-and-pepper hair.

"Your show is too big of a success," Chris grinned at her. "The Queen knows that. You're her golden goose. If she axes you, she can kiss all her shiny new trophies goodbye. She wouldn't dare."

"I hope you're right."

"Cue Camera C," Chris said into his headset.

"Here goes nothing," she murmured as the man's video submission began to play. One they had purposefully kept secret from their boss.

"Hi, my name is Howard. The woman I am hoping for a

second chance with is incredibly successful," the man onscreen began. "She is beautiful, confident, and influential. I understand people can find her intimidating," he gave a nervous chuckle, "but I know another side of her. A softer, vulnerable side."

Lexy raised both eyebrows at Chris. "It doesn't matter how many times I have watched his video, I still don't believe it."

"I guess I should start by telling you how I met Merelda," Howard continued in his video.

He'd been at a drive-in movie. He'd completely missed the film, unable to take his eyes off the woman two cars away. As the story unfolded and he described waiting for his opportunity to approach her, Lexy felt the familiar fluttering in her chest. "I'm rooting for him."

"Of course you are," Chris chuckled.

"I can't help it. He's so *likable*. Even if I can't reconcile the kindhearted woman he describes to our terrifying boss who crushes dreams beneath her red-soled Louboutins."

"Hey, Lex." Nate poked his head in the door, grabbed her hand and pulled her out of earshot of Chris. "I couldn't wait to tell you. Merelda was at the studio today and I overheard her talking on her phone."

Her gut clenched. Her skin slicked with ice. They'd been so careful. There was no way she could have found out about Howard's video.

"It seems Season One of *Cupid Grants a Second Chance* was so popular," Nate continued, "she's been approached to do a UK version."

"Really? That's amazing." A rush of relief flooded through her, followed by fizzing excitement. Her show was going international?

"And guess who's angling to direct it."

"Someone I should know?"

"Enrico."

"No way. I wonder if she'll let him?"

"Probably."

"You overhear all the best stuff." She gave him a quick kiss. "How clever of me to start dating one of the noise boys."

AFTERWORD

Happy Birthday Lexy, dear.

You are a bright and shining star and you are blazing your own trail. I am so proud of you for that. You remind me of myself in that way. I was a bit of a rebel in my day, you know, marrying your grandfather and moving out West with him. I love your father very much, and I'm proud of him and Jill for the job they did raising you. Cannon Beach was a wonderful place for you to grow up. You had the safety and security of a close-knit community, the creativity that town fostered, and wild beauty to explore in those forests and beaches in your own back yard. I was thrilled for you when you discovered surfing. I could see what it meant to you, and the confidence you gained from being a part of the surf community.

But as much as Cannon Beach was a great place to grow up, and the perfect place for your dad and mom to settle, it wasn't your place to settle down. There was always a glimmer in your eye that told me you had a desire to explore further afield, to see bigger places, and to do bigger things with your life. I saw the courage it took for you to tell your parents, and Tyler - who was your first love - that you were moving to Seattle. But you did it, you followed your dreams, and I can't emphasize enough how important it is that you did that, and that you keep doing that.

I saw how conflicted you were about not staying to take over the gallery, and I know the guilt you felt about moving so far away. But honey, your parents both want what is best for you and this is it. I see you thriving in Seattle, at your job, and with your friends. The joy just comes off you in waves. If you had stayed, your parents eventually would have felt disappointed for you, and guilty that they held you back from your dreams. So by doing what was right for you, you actually did everyone a favor. One day, I think even Tyler will see that.

Our first loves are very special, but they are not always our true loves. I can see you have been starting to wonder if you are ever going to meet the man you are meant to. The doctor tells me I don't have much time, but I am going to have your dad keep this letter and give it to you on your 30th birthday. I know what a significant birthday that is and I want you to remember on this special day that I am always with you in your heart.

Maybe by the time you read this letter you will have already met your man. If you haven't, my love, don't worry. You are such a bright light, generous and loving, compassionate, enthusiastic, and beautiful on the inside as well as out. And I know that an equally beautiful soul will take up residence in your heart very soon. Trust your Gran on this. Having spent over fifty happy years with your grandfather, I can tell you it is the most incredible and magical feeling to be with the love of your life. I wish for you to experience that too, and I will be watching down over you to make sure that you do. And if you are ever missing me extra, my love, you can bake the chocolate zucchini loaf I used to make, that you loved as a child. I know you have the recipe. Smell is powerful for evoking memories. You bake that loaf and you will remember all the times we did that together and we will feel closer again.

Love always,
Your Gran

AFTER AFTERWORD

Read on to get to know *The Boys in the Band* a little better. Just four talented guys with a tight local following. And when it comes to love? Oh, they're about to fall *hard*.

Stay tuned to see who falls next. We'll be posting updates on @Carissaharperauthor and CarissaHarper.com

Duquan's Downlow on Dating and Love
"We Love to Love our Seattle Bands"
Podcast Episode # 150, with The Rainy Day Astronauts

Duke: Welcome to another episode of Duquan's Downlow on Dating and Love. I am your host Duquan, but friends call me Duke. Joining me today, I'm excited to have members of popular local band The Rainy Day Astronauts. Thanks for being here today guys.

Nate: It's a pleasure. Thanks for having us.

Duke: As many of my listeners know, in addition to hosting this podcast, I also host the new hit TV show *Cupid Grants a Second Chance*. Nate is the head sound tech for the show and that's how we met. When I found out he also plays in a band, I knew I wanted to have the group on as guests. So, let's do a quick go around with your names and what instruments you play.

Nate: My name's Nate. I play guitar and lead vocals.

Connor: I'm Connor. I play bass and I'm backup vocals.

Griffin: Griffin, drums.

Adam: Adam, keyboard. They try to make me sing sometimes, too.

Duke: You know this is a relationship podcast. So I may be

asking you about your love lives, but I'll start you off easy. How many years have you guys been doing this together?

Nate: Connor and I started playing together in high school and we met these two in college. That's when RDA was born.

Adam: Notice he's not saying how old we are?

All: (laughter)

Duke: Seattle is known for its music scene. How does that influence you as a band?

Adam: There's such a rich musical history in this city, we've obviously been influenced by the greats like Pearl Jam, Nirvana and Sound Garden.

Connor: There's something about grunge that really speaks to you when you're in the rebellious teen stage, which is when Nate and I were first playing together. (laughs) I think it kept him out of reform school.

Nate: And Jimi Hendrix influences everyone.

Duke: Even me! So what would you say you each bring to the table? What's your role in the group dynamics, outside of the instruments you each play?

Griffin: Well, Connor brings his parents' garage. That's our jam space. Without that we might have kicked him out of the band ages ago.

All: (laughter)

Connor: Hey! I've been in the group longer than you, wise-guy. You think this dude with his spiky baby dreadlocks is all shy and sweet, but then he gets warmed up and he slays you!

Adam: Griff's got a point. At least Connor brings a rehearsal space to the team. The only reason we keep Nate around is because his mom bakes for us. She makes the best cookies!

Connor: And don't forget his smoldering good looks on stage.

Nate: Shut up! (laughs) Duke, why'd you ask me to bring these guys again?

Duke: Smoldering good looks, eh? Is it true what they say about musicians, that you get a lot of interest from the females in the audience?

Griffin: It's true what they say about drummers, anyways.

Adam: What? That they have good rhythm?

Griffin: You know it.

All: (laughter)

Griffin: Wait, I didn't mean that the way it sounded. I meant that women... Not that... Guys!

All: (more laughter)

Connor: And he's single, ladies.

Adam: Plus, check out those arms from all that drumming. Swoon.

Duke: Griffin, you're single? He's nodding. What about the rest of you? Are any of you in a relationship?

All: (murmurs of no)

Connor: Although, I don't know that Nate is technically available. Are we allowed to talk about a certain hard-working, intelligent, funny blonde, Duke?

Nate: Connor!

Connor: A blonde who will remain anonymous. We'll call her Blue Crush.

Adam: Oh… I see what you did there. She's a surfer and Nate has a crush on her…Blue Crush.

Nate: I thought we were friends. Honestly Duke, just throw them out. We don't need them for the interview.

Duke: (laughs) I think this interview is going great. But I'll help you out Nate. You four handsome, available dudes all have a distinct role within the band dynamics. Different strengths you bring to the group.

Nate: We do. And excuse my friends, whose minds are clearly in the gutter, but in all seriousness, Griffin does have exceptional rhythm, even for a drummer. We'd be lost without him. And he's got a good ear for it. He always has creative ways for us to play around with the tempo. And when we're working on new material, he'll make interesting suggestions for how the other instruments can mesh with what he's doing on the drums. It's a gift.

Griffin: Thanks, bro.

Connor: That's true. And as you can see by Nate being the first one to give a compliment, it's not just for his mom's killer brownies that we keep him around. I don't know if any of us have ever really acknowledged this before, but Nate is kind of the glue that holds us all together. He and I had been messing around in the garage since we were kids, but when we met these two later on, it was Nate who put the invitation out there for them to come and jam with us and see what we could do together. He's the one who really thought we could be something. And here we are.

Nate: Aww, thanks man.

Connor: How's that for some love on your podcast Duke?

Duke: It's great. I can see the love and camaraderie between you all that comes from years of friendship.

Griffin: I'll throw some love out there. I was teasing Connor about using him for his garage—

Nate: By the way, it *was* his parents' garage when we started jamming there. Connor and his brothers bought the house off his folks when they moved to Florida. So it's kind of cool that it's the same space. Lots of history there. But just to be clear, it's *Connor's* garage now. We don't still go to his parents' house to jam.

Griffin: Right, yeah. And because we spend so much time there, it's a second home for all of us, and Connor makes sure it feels that way.

Adam: Guess that makes you 'Dad', Connor. (laughs)

Griffin: Kind of. Because we all hang out there, as a group and individually, we end up going to Connor for advice, or to vent.

Nate: Plus, he's got a wicked sense of humor. When we're all frustrated with the creative process, something isn't working right, Connor is the one who cracks a joke and breaks the tension. Which keeps us from killing each other.

Duke: You guys *are* like family. I like that.

Griffin: If we're family, I'm definitely the younger brother.

Connor: Yeah. Spoiled.

All: (laughter)

Duke: And what about you Adam? How do you fit in?

Nate: Adam's got the most tattoos. He gives our band street cred.

Adam: I think it's pretty clear I'm the brains of the operation.

Connor: I'd like to disagree just to keep his ego in check, but it's true. He's got an encyclopedic knowledge of bands, and music history.

Nate: Yeah, Adam is our secret weapon at music trivia night. I'm good at recognizing songs, but this guy can tell you song title, artist, album, release date, interesting facts about the band. It's wild.

Connor: His knowledge makes him good at the business side of things for us, which is convenient.

Griffin: The way his brain works, he's good at problem-solving, and puzzles, which makes him good at writing lyrics – fitting what we want to say into a few words or lines. Like fitting together pieces of a puzzle.

Duke: Like the way you all fit together to create The Rainy Day Astronauts, and the incredible music you make. And speaking of music, with Valentine's Day coming up I thought you could help our listeners out with their playlists. What do you consider the best love songs? What's on your list? I'll take one song from each of you.

Connor: That we'd actually listen to?

Adam: "Closer" by Nine Inch Nails.

All: (laughter)

Connor: Great song, but I'm not sure those explicit lyrics qualify it as a love song, man.

Adam: Def Leppard, "Love Bites"?

Duke: I've listened to your music, you sing about relationships. I know you all have big hearts.

Nate: With his voice and style, anything Otis Redding sings sounds like a love song to me. "These Arms of Mine" make the list.

Connor: Good one. For me it's Maroon 5, "Sugar".

Nate: What? Really?

Connor: Just kidding. There was a time when every girl I knew was obsessed with that song. (laughs) For real now, I'm going with the incredible Etta James, "At Last".

Griffin: I'll take another talented female vocalist, Lauryn Hill. "Killing Me Softly With His Song" by the Fugees. Wait, is that actually a love song? Now that I think about the lyrics...

Duke: As judge, I accept that song.

Adam: I thought about picking "Romeo and Juliet" by Dire Straits, but I feel like we need something a little newer on the list or the kids will think we're a bunch of geezers.

Connor: Can't have that.

Nate: It's not our fault they really knew how to write a good love song back in the day.

Adam: "Love on the Brain". And as much as I like RiRi, I dig the cover version by Cold War Kids and Bishop Briggs. That keyboard intro? So good.

Connor: Thanks for bringing us into the 21st century at least.

Nate: What about you Duke?

Duke: There are so many good ones that I have a hard time choosing. But right now, in this moment? I'm feelin' Leon Bridges's "Coming Home".

Nate: Nice choice. A modern song that sounds and feels vintage.

Duke: Exactly. And that wraps up today's episode. Thanks once again to Nate, Connor, Adam and Griffin from The Rainy Day Astronauts for joining me. They don't know it yet, but I'm going to get the guys to toss out a few more song titles, and I'll put together a Valentine's Day playlist that you'll be able to access in the link below. Our Love Day gift to you!

ACKNOWLEDGMENTS

As a very first collaborative writing project, we had help and encouragement from so many people. We appreciate you more than we can say. But we'll try. Huge thanks go out to:

Jocelyn, for helping us determine Nate's favorite guitar, and for her insight into band life. You are a total rockstar.

John, thanks for helping us write an authentic guys pickup game. (One of the funniest things anyone has ever said to us is "You kind of wrote a 'sexy' basketball scene. Is that what you wanted?")

Sammy, for their sensitivity reading of our queer characters and appreciating the Roomba joke.

Margo, at Up&Up Designs for creating our lovely and ever-changing website.

Kelly, for listening to how we hoped our cover would look and turning our wish-list into reality.

Anna, for sharing her social media knowledge (we confess, this is not our area of expertise).

Kim and Rashmi for always brainstorming the right song for the scene, current slang, and anything else we had a question about.

Amanda for being there through all the high points and the challenges. Get ready for more rambling texts about the storytelling process as we start the next one.

Mary, the younger cousin Lexy's age we could fact check things with like: did movie rental stores still exist when you were growing up? And: what songs do you consider 'nostalgic'?

Josh, a fellow writer and something of a music expert, we appreciate you sharing your knowledge of both.

Lance, for being such a great sounding board and a

source of calm in the chaos of collaborating, and helping with our logo.

Whitney for patiently editing our early effort and kindly pointing out the many flaws, along with ways to make the story better and stronger.

Gina, for taking the photos for our logo.

Shelley, Janet, and Erin, for the detail-oriented and nit-picky job of copy editing.

To our friends who shall remain nameless. but let us borrow their great "how we met" stories for our Legends (and take creative license with them as needed).

All the other family and friends who have supported us and cheered us on throughout this project.

Kathleen and Reyna

ABOUT THE AUTHORS

Carissa Harper is the pen name for mother-daughter writing team, USA Today Bestselling Author Kathleen Lawless, and her daughter Reyna. They live on Vancouver Island where Reyna spends as much time as possible on her surfboard, while Kathleen prefers to sit on the beach and watch. They love to hear from their readers.

CarissaHarper.com is where you can find out more about us and what's up next for *The Boys in the Band*.

We hang out here @carissaharperauthor Please join us.

We hope you enjoyed our first collaboration; *Cupid Grants a Second Chance*. You might not know how important reviews are, but they mean a lot. Just a few words saying you enjoyed the book would bring us much happiness. Leave a review wherever you purchased *Cupid Grants a Second Chance* or on Goodreads or BookBub.

BB bookbub.com/authors/carissa-harper

instagram.com/carissaharperauthor

9 781989 873700